How the Light Gets In

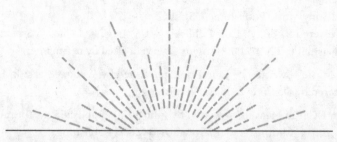

How the Light Gets In

A Novel

Joyce Maynard

WILLIAM MORROW
An Imprint of HarperCollins*Publishers*

FIRST EDITION

Designed by Leah Carlson-Stanisic
Art by Morphart Creation/Shutterstock, Inc and Vitvider/Shutterstock, Inc

Library of Congress Cataloging-in-Publication Data has been applied for.

ISBN 978-0-06-239830-7

24 25 26 27 28 LBC 5 4 3 2 1

For Graf Mouen. Friend for life.

There is a crack, a crack in everything.
That's how the light gets in.

—Leonard Cohen, "Anthem"

Prologue

O f all the pictures that still haunt her twenty-five years later, of that day they brought Toby to the hospital, Eleanor has no idea why this would be the one that has lodged in her brain.

It concerns her husband, Cam. A moment in the waiting room, somewhere in the middle of that awful stretch of hours the two of them waited to find out whether their son would live or die or end up somewhere in between.

It isn't what you'd think a person would retain of that night—not the image of Toby lying blank-eyed and motionless on the stretcher. (Toby, motionless? In four and a half years—the sum total of his life so far—Toby's body had never stopped moving. Neither had his brain.)

The ambulance hadn't even come to a full stop before they were throwing open the doors, lifting the stretcher out—four large men in EMT gear holding aloft the terrifyingly still form of a very small boy, barefoot, the tail he'd attached that morning, made from a sock stuffed with Kleenex, still safety-pinned to his shorts. He'd told them he wanted to know what it felt like to be a stegosaurus.

A path had cleared before them, of people in white jackets who must have understood that every second mattered here. None of them knew how long Toby had been there when Alison found him face down in the pond.

Eleanor had watched it all unfold: the doctors racing past, following alongside the stretcher with their white jackets flapping behind them, calling out orders. The feet of the nurses—all those white shoes, racing to keep up, their rubber soles making a soft squeaking sound on the linoleum. And more doctors converging from all directions, more machines, more nurses—a man with an IV pole dodging to get out of the way, a candy striper pressed against the wall, somebody's stethoscope hanging out of her pocket, slapping against her hip—and a woman's voice howling, over and over, a single syllable. No.

This was Eleanor's voice, Eleanor who howled. Eleanor, running behind the doctors, calling out "Don't let him die."

No doubt Ursula was running alongside, too—Ursula, the one who long ago appointed herself the person in their family who would keep her sights fixed on the sun, no matter what, never mind that she was only seven years old. Now she would have been telling her mother, "You'll see. Toby's going to be okay."

Somewhere a little way off, Alison—the realist—would have leaned against a door offering nothing in the way of encouragement or good cheer. Until this day, the connection between Alison and Toby had been the closest of any in the family. Ali and her brother took violin lessons together, and though not generally given to effusive displays, it was always Ali who had clapped louder than anyone when Toby performed one of his wild made-up songs, as he so often did for them. "You wait and see, Mom," she used to tell Eleanor. "Toby's going to be a rock star someday."

Observing the scene at the hospital as she did that night—and knowing what it meant when a person stopped breathing for as long as Toby probably had—Al had conveyed an attitude of total resignation concealing despair. Yeah, right. The boy she had adored was gone. She had no intention of accepting a substitute.

Everything had happened so fast that there was only a blur of voices, faces, wailing. At first, all Eleanor had known was that with every passing second Toby's brain cells might be dying, if they weren't dead already. Hurry hurry hurry. Faster faster. Go. The metal cart had flown past, with the limp form of her son stretched out on it—still wearing the pink pajama top with a picture on the front of Pee Wee Herman that Ursula had handed down to him, that he never wanted to take off, and that crazy tail of his.

Just for a second an image came to Eleanor—who knew why?—of a television game show from her youth, Supermarket Sweep, where contestants raced through the aisles of a store—tearing around the supermarket corners as if it were the Indy 500, throwing groceries in their carts in the hopes of ringing up the highest total at the checkout to win the big prize.

Then dead stillness. Toby had been taken to a room somewhere on a bed, hooked up to so many tubes and wires that there would be no way of recognizing a child lay hidden in there.

Eleanor could only imagine the doctors working on him—this boy who, hours before, had filled his pockets with rocks, same as he always did, and wandered down to their pond (singing one of his made-up songs, most likely, or telling himself one of his wild stories). This was her amazing boy who talked to Mr. T and celebrated the webs between the toes of his left foot. "I'm part boy and part frog," he'd told them. "I'm looking for my brothers."

Sometimes he was a frog. Sometimes a dinosaur. Sometimes a Teenage Mutant Ninja Turtle, Michelangelo.

Inside the room Eleanor was not allowed to enter, a screen would have been monitoring the activity of her son's brain cells. Not quite a flat line, but close.

No doubt all of these things happened that night, but now—close to a quarter century later—Eleanor can summon only the vaguest memory of these parts of the story, or of the endless twelve-minute drive to the hospital that came before it, following behind the ambulance, or the doctor coming out of the examining room, holding his clipboard, arranging his face before he spoke to them.

We did everything we could.

We'll just have to wait and see. Assess the damage.

When she thinks about that night—as she still does, after all these years—the memory Eleanor keeps returning to is of her husband, Cam, and their two older children, Ali and Ursula, in the waiting room after they took Toby away to work on him. Eleanor's brain stays stuck on this one image of Cam, standing in front of a vending machine in a corner of the visitors' area, trying to buy a pack of peanut M&M's for Ursula. The machine had taken his money but the M&M's never dropped into the slot.

Unlike Eleanor—who, in those days, had regularly visited a place she'd named Crazyland—Cam was never one to display large or troubling measures of anger. He'd hit the side of the machine a couple of times, the way a person might when on the floor, playing with a young child whose toy—something battery operated—has temporarily gotten hung up on a piece of carpet or a table leg. No big deal. Tap tap. Off you go.

Cam had remained patient. Calm. Seemingly unfazed. The issue of the money lost to the candy machine was a problem he could solve, unlike the problem of what was going on with Toby.

To look at Cam as he was in that moment, a person would have had no clue.

He had approached the nurses' station—still laid-back, with that easy, graceful ambling gait of his. He'd smiled at the nurse on duty—an unusually pretty young woman wearing a ponytail that seemed to shoot out from the top of her head like an erupting volcano and (God knows why Eleanor remembers this) an I HEART Boston Terriers button. This nurse had appeared to be charmed by Cam, as women always were—as everyone was—and even more so by the fact that here he was, this handsome red-headed dad who'd somehow ended up at the hospital on a beautiful summer day—evening now—which had to mean there was some kind of problem going on, but you'd never know this to look at him. The man who'd presented himself at the nurses' station (flip-flops, shorts, just at that point in the day when an unshaven face appears its most sexy) looked like nothing more or less than a concerned father, just wanting to get a pack of peanut M&M's for his daughters, and needing change.

"I was wondering if you could help us," he'd told the nurse. "My girls haven't had a thing to eat since lunch. The machine just took my last two quarters."

A minute later there she was, the pretty nurse, with a couple of boxes of chocolate milk and three slices of cake, one with a candle in it. "What do you know?" she'd said. "It was my birthday today and the girls on the floor got me this. Perfect timing, huh?"

This is the part Eleanor remembers perfectly. The look on her husband's face as the nurse handed him the plate.

From where she stood in the waiting room watching this scene play out (she stood, because to sit at this moment was impossible; she couldn't stop pacing), Eleanor wanted to scream.

Our son might be dying. Our son might be dead. Or brain dead. What are you doing thinking about M&M's? How can you eat cake?

She might have thought this, too—or maybe it was later when the next thought hit her. And it's your fault.

PART I

The Death of Cam

1.

Somewhere Over the Rainbow

]H[er boy is almost thirty years old now. His father newly dead. It's 2010 and Eleanor's fifty-seven.

Of their children, only Toby has chosen to accompany Eleanor to the crematorium. Slow, gentle Toby, who can't drive, but when not riding his bike, as he does every season of the year regardless of weather, occupies the passenger seat as Eleanor's constant companion. Because he loves old TV shows on Nickelodeon, he's familiar with *The Lone Ranger*. Sometimes he calls himself Tonto. Now here they are, side by side, heading off to the cremation of his father, Eleanor's former husband, Cam.

Ursula, who gave birth to her second child a few months earlier, left a message on Eleanor's voice mail. "Orson's got an ear infection again and Lulu's come down with another cold. Jake's off at some basketball game. What else is new?"

Hearing the words, Eleanor registers a familiar stab of pain. Her daughter's communication with her in recent years—infrequent as it has become—always carries a tone of quiet disapproval or irritation. Ursula appears to have adopted the view that everything that has gone wrong in her life might in some way be attributed to Eleanor's failures as a parent. About her father, their middle child seems only to hold on to the lovable parts.

"I'd rather remember my dad when he was alive than watch his body get put into an oven," she'd said in her phone message.

So Ursula will not be present for Cam's cremation. Neither will Al. Unlike Ursula, Al appears to bear no resentment toward Eleanor. He is not a person who chooses to revisit the past as Ursula does. To Eleanor and Cam's firstborn child it's simple: Al had loved his father, loves his mother, and accepts that his parents did the best they could. No point dwelling on what might have gone differently or better. Al is dealing with a different kind of struggle from anything Ursula or Toby have faced.

Al is thirty-three years old, married to Teresa, running their start-up, making more money than they have time to spend. The event that might have been excruciating and traumatic—his choice of making the transition from daughter to son—seems to have set him free. The person he'd been once—the child Eleanor once called her older daughter—had lived in a state of nearly constant uneasiness in her own skin for her first twenty years of life, the unending discomfort that comes when a person feels that the body they inhabit is not their own.

In their family they avoid Al's deadname now. He's simply Al, the older of Eleanor and Cam's sons, and his life would appear to be going well, with one large and painful exception.

Earlier this year, Al and Teresa invested months—also thousands of dollars—in a potential adoption, only to learn as the final papers were about to be drawn up that the birth mother had changed her mind about letting them raise her baby.

"Everything was great until the agency raised the topic of my transition," Al told Eleanor after the adoption fell through. "She told the social worker she wanted her child to grow up in a 'normal family.' What are we supposed to say to that? Who's to say what normal is anyway? Particularly as it relates to a family."

"I'm so sorry," Eleanor told him. "You and Teresa will be the best parents a child could have." *Will be,* not *would be.* She needed to offer Al as much optimism as she could muster. No qualifiers.

As is always the case for Eleanor, when witnessing her children's sorrows, she wishes she could fix this. Or simply help. Eleanor is trying to accept the lesson—a long time in coming—that some forms of grief children experience are for them, alone, to address.

Elijah—Cam's son with his second wife, Coco—would have made the trip home for the cremation of his father if he could, but his band, Dog Blue, is on tour in Ireland. In her old dream of how things would go in her family, the children would have been together to mark the death of their father. But so little of her old dream has ended up matching the way things have turned out.

So it's just the two of them, Eleanor and Toby, who make the drive to the crematorium. "Dad always liked bonfires," Toby observes, looking out the window at a row of mini storage units, a boarded-up liquor store. "He just probably never thought what we'd be burning up was him."

They pull into the parking lot behind a Jiffy Lube. Whatever she might have imagined a cremation was like, the scene at Heavenly Rest bears no resemblance.

At first Eleanor thinks she must have gotten the address wrong. The building looks like a car wash or an airplane hangar, but then she spots the plastic sign with an image, partly chipped, of a lily resting on a hillside. They've come to the right place.

Once inside, the two of them are greeted by a man who introduces himself as Jerry. He's wearing a Hawaiian shirt. "You probably expected a suit," he tells Eleanor. "But the way I see it, people who've recently experienced the loss of a loved one have enough sadness on their hands. I try to remind my clients of the happy things in life. No long face!"

Eleanor looks at Toby. It often seems to her that the way her son's brain works now—the way his brain has worked for almost twenty-five years—reveals a clarity that escapes other people, the ones with a higher IQ. Hearing Jerry's remark, Toby just shakes his head, his bafflement revealing not so much a failure of comprehension, in Eleanor's view, as it does understanding. He and Eleanor are in the presence of a fool.

The walls are cinder block but someone—Jerry? No evidence of other employees—has laid a piece of carpet on the vast expanse of bare concrete floor, probably from one of those remnant stores. Near the back of the building something along the lines of an altar has been set up (though what it resembles most is a bar) with a pair of mismatched candlesticks and a vase of carnations and an American flag.

"Do you have it?" Jerry asks. Eleanor has no idea what he's talking about, but Toby remembers. "The picture of Dad," he reminds her. "They told us we could bring one."

"That's okay," Eleanor says. "We know what he looked like."

What Cam looked like when he was young and healthy, she means. Not at the end. One good thing that seems to happen when a person dies after a long illness is that finally the image of how he appeared for most of his life can supplant the pale, gaunt specter he'd become.

"You expecting anyone else?" Jerry asks. Eleanor shakes her head.

"My dad had a bunch of friends," Toby tells him. Never mind that he and Eleanor will never see this man again. Toby wants Jerry to know Cam was a well-liked person. More than that. Well-loved.

"He played softball for the Yellow Jackets. First base." Toby announces this as a person might if their father had played for the Red Sox.

"Also, he made wooden bowls. Out of burls."

"Burls?"

"From a tree. Those big knobby things that stick out from the trunk sometimes. My dad turned them into bowls."

Toby has brought one to the crematorium. With a lid. They'll use it to transport Cam's ashes back to the farm.

"Well, then," Jerry says, clapping his palms together. "If we aren't waiting for any other guests, let's get this show on the road." The gesture he makes reminds Eleanor of a TV weatherman, launching into his report on conditions for a holiday weekend.

He disappears behind a small door at the back of the space. When he returns, he's pushing a cart with a box on top shaped like a coffin but made of cardboard. Inside: the body of the man Eleanor loved before she loved any other man.

"You wanted the economy model, right?" Jerry says. "Most of our clients opt for plywood at least."

"Cam was never one to care about those kinds of things," Eleanor tells him. If it wasn't hardwood, it didn't matter. And anyway, the whole thing was about to go up in smoke.

"We had to use an extender," Jerry says, with a faint tone of apology. "Your guy was on the tall side."

"Six foot three," Toby tells him proudly.

Jerry pushes the cart across the floor. The wheels squeak. Eleanor remembers that night in the hospital—Toby on the stretcher, surrounded by doctors trying to save his life, flying down the corridor on a wheeled cart not discernibly different from the one now transporting his father's body.

Nobody is in a rush this time.

Up until now Eleanor hasn't noticed, but at one end of the vast, cavernous space presided over by this odd person in his pineapple-bedecked shirt stands a piece of equipment resembling a propane tank or an oil drum. Only it has a door on the front. Jerry opens this. Inside, flames.

"That's where you're putting my dad?" Toby says.

"Ashes to ashes," Jerry says. "It's hella environmental."

"It looks like our woodstove back home," Toby offers. "Only bigger."

"Anybody care to say a few final words?" Jerry again.

"That's okay," Eleanor says. "How about you, Toby?"

Surprisingly often at moments like this—not that there had ever been a moment just like this one—it will be Toby, of all the members in their family, who finds the right thing to say. Something simple no doubt, but weirdly fitting. Now, when Eleanor looks over to her son, she sees that he is weeping. In the four days since Cam took his last breath this is the first time she's seen Toby cry. Eleanor has not wept, either, and still doesn't. If she didn't know this before, she does now: There is no single way for a person to express grief.

Toby shakes his head. Sometimes there's so much to say that the only thing for it is to remain quiet.

"We're ready," Eleanor tells Jerry. He pushes a button on the side of the altar. From a pair of not particularly good speakers comes a familiar song, a familiar voice. It's Israel Kamakawiwoʻole, the Hawaiian singer whose album she often plays while at work at her drawing table, *Somewhere Over the Rainbow: The Best of Israel Kamakawiwoʻole.*

The first time Eleanor heard this particular rendition—with its spare, simple ukulele accompaniment—she had been driving back to Brookline from one of her bowling nights in Akersville with Toby. She'd had to pull over alongside the highway to listen.

"I guess now I'll always associate this song with Cam's body going up in flames," she says to no one in particular.

It's happening. Tongues of flame encircle the cardboard box.

The whole thing is over in minutes. Jerry disappears briefly again. They can hear the sound of scraping and clattering, as if someone were cleaning a chimney flue or the grate in a fireplace.

When Jerry returns he's holding what looks like a shoebox. He places it in Eleanor's hands.

"Peace be with you," he says. "Enjoy."

2.

He might as well have suggested they go skydiving

It takes a little over an hour, driving back to the farm. In the seat next to Eleanor, her younger son is studying a piece of granite he found in the parking lot outside the crematorium. Toby can occupy himself with a rock for an hour. A person could see this as evidence of his limited brain capacity, but to Eleanor, it's more about how Toby sees things others miss. He's not in a rush like so much of the rest of the world. Like herself, for instance.

Ten minutes from leaving the crematorium—the ashes of her former husband still warm in the burl bowl where her son placed them—her mind veers off in a hundred directions.

Just over a year has passed since that day Eleanor returned to their old farm for the wedding of her older son, Al, the day Cam told her he had a tumor in his pancreas. Years had passed since the two of them had seen each other. Eleanor was living in Brookline then, as she had since the divorce. After his marriage to Coco fell apart, Cam had taken out a loan so he could buy out Coco's share of the farm. He had remained there with Toby. When he'd told Eleanor about the diagnosis, she'd made an offer that must have taken him by surprise, as it did their children. Given the years of bitterness between the two of them that preceded this moment, nobody could have been more surprised by the offer than Eleanor herself.

"You're going to need help," she'd told Cam. Three days later she'd moved back to the farm.

People she knew in Boston were baffled. Her friend Jason—the closest Eleanor has to a brother—was incredulous. How could she return after all these years to the place it had broken her heart to leave, to care for the same man who'd abandoned her? Just when she'd finally freed herself of the family responsibilities that had consumed her for so long and she'd finally reclaimed her life.

"I'm doing this for my son," Eleanor told her friend. Though Toby functioned far better than anyone had predicted after the accident—when the neurologist told them he might never speak again—he was not a person to live on his own, and even less so, to manage the care of a dying man. Goats, he could handle, and cheesemaking—thanks to the assistance of their neighbor, Ralph. Hospitals, scans, prescriptions, infusions—those made no sense to Toby. He could deliver twin kids in breech position in the middle of the night in a barn where the temperature hovered below freezing. He could sit all day by the bed of his dying father or hold a crying baby for as long as it took to get her to sleep, or—unable to drive—ride his bicycle in a rainstorm up a mile-long hill for his weekly bowling night. He couldn't fill out insurance forms. He couldn't go online to make an appointment with the oncologist. He couldn't pay the bills.

But supporting Toby was only part of the reason Eleanor had returned to the farm. Cam's illness revealed to her something she could not have recognized twenty-five years earlier: If you loved someone deeply once, if you had children with that person, if there had been a time when the two of you called yourselves a family, the connection could never fully disappear. Cam had been many things to Eleanor in the past: lover of her youth, father of her children, witness—with her—to the worst event of their lives.

He'd also betrayed her.

Who Cam was to Eleanor, at the end of the day, was a man with whom she'd shared the biggest part of her history, including three children. She had loved him once. In a certain way, she always would.

They were standing in the tent at Al's wedding as the festivities were winding down—the DJ's musical selections having shifted from the songs of their youth to bands and artists unknown to either one of them. "Want to take a walk?" Cam had asked her. He might as well have suggested they go skydiving, the invitation was that unexpected. That unlikely.

They had made their way down the dirt road they both knew so well. They stood together at this waterfall when they were young—the place they swam naked together, once, the place where they'd conceived their first child, and where Eleanor had seen Cam kissing another woman—the one for whom he'd left her.

"It looks like I'm going to die," Cam told her.

Eleanor felt her heart turn over. It was as if the bridge they were standing on, that had stood for a few hundred years, had given way.

"I'll take care of you," she had said to him. Simple as that.

"That sounds good," he said. "Thank you."

3.

Trying to save our marriage and perhaps catch a few fish

In the movie version of the year just past—the brutal stretch of months leading up to Cam's death—the two of them would have become lovers again. He would have died in Eleanor's arms.

The two of them were long past that. Even if Cam had been capable of lovemaking, Eleanor could no longer imagine their bodies wrapped around each other, though in those last days she helped him to the toilet, and once peeled off her own clothes to hold him up in the shower. She could do this thing—stand naked, pressed against the naked husk of her former husband—because it was so clear to them both that all sexual feeling between them had drained away, leaving nothing but dry, cracked earth.

They took walks together as long as Cam was able. They played Parcheesi with Toby. They went to the movies one time (a stupid comedy featuring Adam Sandler) and laughed in a way that probably had nothing to do with what was happening in the movie, mostly no doubt because they just needed to laugh. Cam had his eyes on the screen. Eleanor kept her eyes on Cam. *Remember this,* she told herself.

If you could separate what was going on in their lives from what was going on in the country, it was an exciting time. Barack Obama had been elected. The future—for their country if not for Cam—seemed hopeful. They talked a little about their children—Eleanor's worries about Ursula's marriage, her concern over the difficulty Al and Teresa were having in their attempt to adopt a baby. They did not discuss Toby, or the question of what would happen after Cam died. Who would look out for him as his father had? Eleanor thinks now that the two of them didn't talk about that because they had no answer.

They did not speak of Cam's prognosis. But Cam lived, those last months, as a man does when preparing to leave the world. One by one, he gave away the vast collection of wooden bowls he'd made in his woodshop over the last thirty years. Burl wood, sanded smooth as a baby's cheek. Eleanor could remember the exact patch of woods where they'd come upon many of these. "My brother and I haven't had much of a connection since we were kids," he told Eleanor, studying a particular bowl she remembers him making, from a piece of wood they'd found together on a camping trip up north one time. He chose two of his best bowls for the grandchildren. "They never got to know me," he said. "These may give them an idea of who I was."

For Eleanor, he chose one of the smallest bowls, the most delicate. She could remember that he'd been working on it the day she went into labor with Toby. When she moved out of their old farmhouse, she'd left the bowl behind. "This time, hold on to it, okay?" Cam said. "To remember me by."

Not much chance she'd forget.

Cam showed Eleanor how to work the clutch on his truck and walked her through his shop, suggesting the prices she should ask on Craigslist—after; they knew what *after* meant—when she put some of his tools up for sale. Eleanor read out loud to him from the new book she'd been working on (the latest in her series featuring the adventures of a ten-year-old girl orphan who explores the world), and when the drugs Cam took made Parcheesi too hard for him to follow, he and Toby played Go Fish and War. From where she sat in the kitchen, drawing, she could hear their voices as her younger son and his father slapped down their cards. It was almost like old times, only it was nothing like old times, really.

They often sat together by the woodstove. Even in warm months, Cam felt cold all the time by this point. That night he was shivering. He reached out to take Eleanor's hand and stroked it with his long, rough fingers. A hand she knew well.

His fingers paused over a scar—barely visible, from a night early in their marriage when she'd been angry that her Christmas present from him had been a knife. Where was the romance in the gift of a knife?

She'd picked up an onion then and sliced into it. Too fast, too hard, unaccustomed to a knife as sharp as the one he'd just given her. The blade had broken the skin. Blood pooled on the cutting board.

"I guess you wanted perfume or jewelry," he told her.

"What did I know?" she said.

By February—seven months since Eleanor had moved back to the farm—Cam's pain had gotten so bad that she sat with him for hours in the night, reading out loud from the Kurt Vonnegut novels he had loved, sitting next to his bed in the same old rocker where she'd once nursed their babies and recited the words from *Goodnight Moon* (no need to consult the pages; Eleanor knew every line) or sang "The Riddle Song" over and over, until whatever child it was who had been fighting sleep finally yielded to it.

How can there be a chicken without a bone, a cherry that has no stone, a ring with no end, a baby with no crying?

Then came the answers. *A cherry when it's blooming, it has no stone. A ring when it's rolling, it has no end. A baby when she's sleeping has no crying.*

"What was that song you used to sing to the kids?" Cam asked her one night. Springtime now. "Can you sing it to me?"

Sometimes Eleanor fell asleep in the chair—so exhausted she'd drift off in the middle of a sentence. Waking in the middle of the night, she'd put her ear to Cam's chest to hear if he was still alive.

She could still remember the sound of his breath coming fast and hard, times they'd made love. Now each inhalation sounded like a question. *Will this be the last?*

In May they signed up for hospice, which meant that every day a woman came to the house to deliver three small vials of morphine. That day's supply. This Eleanor administered as a person might feed a baby bird that had fallen out of the nest. One drop at a time.

For all the years of their marriage, Cam's flaming-red hair had made it easy for Eleanor to spot him in any crowd. As the drugs ate away at him—the drugs and the cancer, both—all that remained of that glorious halo of his were a few tufts, soft as milkweed, and as white. In those last few weeks, his body had wasted away as if something were consuming it from the inside out. Cancer could do that to a person, she now understood.

By midsummer—nearly a full year since the day she'd learned about Cam's diagnosis and moved back to the farm—he no longer ate and took in little water. He seemed barely conscious of the things going on around him—visits from his old softball teammates, his brother from Texas. Ursula had been coming down from Vermont to see her father throughout the year. Now came Elijah. He missed his band's Montreal show to say goodbye. No sign of his mother, Coco.

One time when the pain was particularly bad—mostly to make it through to the next dose of fentanyl—they'd found a video online of Sinead O'Connor singing a duet with Kris Kristofferson of a song that took on a whole new meaning now. "Help Me Make It Through the Night."

Yesterday was dead and gone, and tomorrow's out of sight. That was the two of them, all right. Just as Kris Kristofferson was singing, Eleanor reached for Cam's hand. She stroked his skin, thin as parchment now. Thinner than that.

Al flew in from Seattle—coming straight from a meeting with his board of directors and taking an early flight from Boston the next day. "You've been a good father," Al told Cam, the morning he left.

"You're a good son," Cam told him. His words, delivered to a man whom he had once called his daughter, carried the message Al needed most to hear.

Times when people came by to see Cam, Eleanor stepped out of the room to give them privacy. But more often than she might have imagined, she'd kept vigil by the bed. Sometimes she put on a CD of an artist or a song Cam had loved—recognizing, as she did so, that all she knew of his musical taste was what he'd listened to a quarter century before. Mostly the two of them had gravitated to alternative artists, but Cam had loved Fleetwood Mac, because he'd had such a crush on Stevie Nicks. Eleanor wondered if he even remembered. A whole chapter of their lives had passed that remained unknown to the other. She had no idea what kind of music he'd listened to with Coco, or if he still cared about the old songs—Townes Van Zandt, Iris DeMent, Greg Brown, and his all-time favorite, John Prine. Whenever he'd performed within driving distance—even times when money was tight—Cam and Eleanor had driven to hear him.

Their favorite had been a song called "Lake Marie"—one of the weirder ones, about a couple who head off to a remote lake together as their relationship is falling apart. There were a couple of lines Eleanor loved in that song: *Many years later, we found ourselves in Canada. Trying to save our marriage and perhaps catch a few fish. Whatever came first.* It had become a saying between them—a code. Eleanor could remember how, times he was on the road at some craft fair, when he'd call home, and she'd ask how things had gone, that's what he'd say to her.

Trying to save our marriage and catch a few fish. For a while there, Eleanor used to think that summed up their relationship.

She was sitting in her spot next to his bed, sometime during those final weeks with Cam, when even the fentanyl wasn't enough for the pain, but they hadn't put him on morphine yet—the middle of the night probably, when neither one of them could sleep.

Maybe it was the altered state a person enters into, caring for a dying person, that led her to say what she did to him that night. She didn't expect he'd take in her words.

"So I guess we didn't manage to do either one," she told him. He'd seemed barely conscious at the time. Maybe she was just talking to herself at that point.

For the first time in a couple of days, he'd opened his eyes and looked into hers.

"What do you mean?" He spoke to her as if from someplace far away. The bottom of a well. A whole other galaxy.

"Save our marriage. Or catch any fish."

"*Oh that,*" he said. Even with all those drugs in him, Cam knew what she was talking about. A chapter from a book he'd read a long time ago. A piece of clothing he'd loved once, devoured by moths.

"Do you think we could have done it?" she asked him. Could they have saved their marriage, was what she meant. She was wondering if they might have worked things out, gotten through the trouble with Coco and all the rest of it. Stayed together. For that one moment, she imagined an alternative universe in which she might still be married to the dying man in the bed. What if none of it had happened—no Coco, no Brookline condo, no angry Ursula, no Timmy Pouliot. No Elijah. She said their old lines from "Lake Marie" to him one more time. About the marriage. The fish.

"There was that brook trout I reeled in down at the falls that time with Toby," he told her.

"Catch and release doesn't count."

"I guess I was never very good at fishing," he told her. "Or marriage."

4.

Nothing left but you and me and the wind

End of summer. Cam was drifting in and out of the world now. Mostly out of it. He asked Eleanor to put on a record for him

of Warren Zevon, called *The Wind*, made in the final months of
the singer's life, when he was dying of lung cancer. On some of the
cuts, you could actually hear Warren Zevon having a hard time finding the breath to complete a line of a song. There was a duet with
Emmylou Harris on the album called "Please Stay," where Warren
Zevon seemed to be talking straight into the ear of whoever the
woman was that he loved. *Will you stay with me to the end?* it went.
When there's nothing left but you and me and the wind.

Just when she thought no other song on the album could cut
deeper than that one, along came another called "Keep Me in Your
Heart."

*"Sometimes when you're doing simple things around the house, maybe
you'll think of me and smile,"* sang the dying Warren Zevon.

"I'll think of you every time I see a burl. Or when I'm sitting in
some movie theater and a person sits in front of me who blocks my
view."

Tall as he was, by the end Cam weighed probably a hundred
pounds, not that there was any point for him to get on the scale.
His skin, nearly translucent, seemed already to reveal every bone, a
perfect anatomy lesson. As a person who had spent a portion of her
days at a drawing table for most of her life—the human figure, her
specialty—Eleanor found a certain comfort in taking out her sketch-
book and drawing him. Once it had been difficult getting Cam to sit
still for her. Hours went by in which he barely moved.

Summer was ending, though they barely noticed the seasons.
One night as she sat there drawing, Cam—on morphine now, three
days since the last time he'd spoken—had opened his eyes. He raised
himself a little off the bed. He looked at Eleanor with a gaze she
remembered from times, giving birth, when she was the one lying
down, and he was holding her shoulders or stroking her legs, coaching her through those last hard moments before their baby burst into
the world.

There was an urgency in the way he looked at her. As if he'd run
out of words, and this was his last, his only way of letting her know
something of vital importance.

"I didn't deserve this," he said. Eleanor understood Cam wasn't talking about the cancer or registering a complaint about the un-fairness of life. He was expressing humble gratitude of a kind she had not known from him before, for the fact that she was here with him, taking care.

"You're a good woman, Ellie," he whispered. "I'm sorry I let you down."

Here was what she knew now, that she hadn't admitted to herself all those years back. The failure of their marriage had been a two-way street. Each of them had let the other down—Cam with his inability to pay attention; for Eleanor, her inability to forgive. The surprising thing was that here they were—the two of them together again. All the old passion had burned away, but also the anger.

Later that night, Eleanor woke for no discernible reason. Some-thing compelled her to climb the stairs to Cam's hospital bed and to lean in close, listen for his heartbeat.

Nothing.

There was no point waking Toby or calling the children. That could wait for morning.

She did, then, something she had not thought to do for the entire time she had been taking care of him. The man on the bed had been many things to her—but he was the father of her children, the hus-band of her youth. Slowly, she lowered herself onto the bed beside him and lay there, one hand on his chest. She couldn't say if she stayed there five minutes or two hours. Out the window, the light from a full moon she hadn't noted until now illuminated a strip of the back field like a gash.

It was over. What now?

5.

The feel of bare feet on carpet

Eleanor had loved the farm more than anywhere else she ever lived or ever will. She and Cam were married in the field in back of the old house. Their babies were born on their bed.

She'd planted a garden every May and swam in the pond they'd built here, canned tomatoes in September, tromped through the snow in the woods out back in search of that year's Christmas tree, supported whichever child was learning to skate that winter—Cam holding one hand, Eleanor the other.

Every March when the children were very small and the snow first melted, they constructed little boats with the cork people they'd made placed inside and brought them down to the waterfall. They'd stand at the water's edge for a moment, first, just taking it all in—the boats, the passengers, the brook, the world beyond. After Eleanor had helped the children launch their little boats, they all ran alongside following their vessels, cheering them on, suffering the loss of one boat or another, and their cork people passengers, much as Eleanor followed the three people she loved best in the world as they made their way out into the world.

After Cam told her he didn't want to be married to her anymore, it had been Eleanor who packed up and left their house. Inexplicably—to her lawyer, who urged her to reconsider, and to her friend Jason—she signed over the farm to Cam.

Jason was a therapist, and the one friend with whom she'd maintained connection from her days growing up in Newton. "If I wasn't gay, I'd have married you in a hot minute," he used to say. At Eleanor's wedding, it had been Jason who walked her down the aisle—which hadn't been an aisle, in fact. It was the field in back of their farmhouse. Hearing the news of Eleanor's decision to give Cam the farm, which had been hers in the first place, he had practically thrown the telephone against the wall.

"It makes me nuts, seeing you let the guy who never came up with the money for a single mortgage payment and cheated on you with your babysitter end up with the place you bought and paid for all those years."

"Cam doesn't have enough money to buy me out of my share," Eleanor said. "I just want our children to have that place someday. It's their home. And anyway, I don't have the strength for a fight."

"You're the strongest person I know," Jason said.

Maybe one form of strength, she told him, was walking away.

"This place means way too much for me to stay there now," she said. "That farm was all about our family."

"You still have a family," Jason told her. "Just because your husband left, that doesn't change."

6.

A Herkimer diamond and a selenite wand

][t was the spring of 1986—the year she turned thirty-three—when Eleanor left the farm. She found a condo in Brookline not far from where Jason lived with his partner, Hank, in a location chosen in large part for its superior schools. Al, who had already revealed a passion and talent for everything to do with computers and programming, won a scholarship to a science academy for gifted and talented students. Even at age nine, Al talked about creating a software company. His body may have betrayed him but his laptop never did.

None of the children warmed to their new home but it was hardest for Toby. The sound of cars out the window unnerved him. He missed climbing trees. He didn't understand why he didn't hear frogs out the window at night anymore, or see stars. Most of all, though, he missed his father. Since the accident, Cam had become Toby's principal caregiver, and the one who seemed best able to help repair his damaged brain.

One night a week, after the separation, and then the divorce, Cam had driven down to Brookline to spend the afternoon and evening with his son. Those nights Toby spent with Cam—attending yoga class, going out for pizza together in the North End after—were the highlight of Toby's week. Seven years old when he'd moved to the city, Toby remained baffled at what they were doing living in this strange new place. Sometimes, when Eleanor tucked him in at night, he'd ask when they were going home.

"This is our home now," Eleanor told him.

"I don't like it here."

Whatever grievances Eleanor held on to, concerning the man she married, she knows this: Cam had been a good father. Eleanor can say this now, as she could not once. All those years, she'd stayed angry at Cam for the one moment in his life as a father when he made a terrible mistake. What Toby remembers—what all three of their children remember—are all the times he built snow forts with them and played soccer in their back field. Saturdays out in the studio whittling animals out of wood scraps. Cam making a big pot of chili on a snow day and setting a blanket on the floor in front of the fireplace.

"Let's pretend we're pioneers, out on the trail," he'd say, ladling the chili into their bowls. He taught them cowboy songs. "Let's go camping by the brook and look for crawdads."

After Toby's accident, it was Cam who worked with Toby all those hours, making up exercises to reprogram his damaged brain, taking him to Sunset Yoga at the senior center, carrying him in on his shoulders, driving four hours to bring him to a mineral show, and the Gilsum Rock Swap, with his bucket of rocks to trade.

Every year Toby saved up his money for the day of the rock swap. Cam never failed to bring him there. Every year he brought home a bucket of treasures and the one prize specimen Cam always let him pick out. Larimar from the Dominican Republic one year. A giant amethyst geode. A Herkimer diamond, set into a piece of granite. His favorite of all: a long, narrow wand made of selenite. When you placed a flashlight under it, the wand took on the most magical glow—transforming the crystal into something they could imagine a superhero whipping out in the climactic scene of a showdown with the forces of evil. The night Cam and Toby came home from Rochester with the selenite crystal wand, Toby insisted they all walk out into the darkened field with him—Toby, carrying the selenite—to watch as it illuminated the darkness from within.

It had crushed but not surprised Eleanor when, less than two years into their time in Brookline, Toby asked if he could move back to the farm and live with his father full time. "Don't feel bad, Mom," he told Eleanor, the day Cam drove up to bring him back. "You can come see me any time you want."

After Toby returned to the farm, Eleanor could feel the pull, for Ursula and Al, to do the same. More and more as time passed, they wanted to spend their weekends in Akersville. By the time Al reached eighth grade—seventh, for Ursula—both of them had rejoined their father and Toby, full time.

Eleanor had found herself on her own in the city then—driving to Akersville to visit her children on weekends. (*Visiting* one's own children—there was a baffling concept for a mother who until then had known only the constancy of daily life with them.) Times she drove up to the farm she took the three of them out for dinner or the movies. She asked about school, friends—Al's new computer, Ursula's science fair project—but she saw what was happening, too: Eleanor knew less and less about the rhythms of her children's days, which now included Coco and then a baby brother. They had all fallen in love with Elijah, naturally.

Eleanor could hardly believe this, but a whole new family had formed that seemed to replace the one she'd known in her old days on the farm.

On their visits with Eleanor, Al and Ursula were careful to say little if anything about Coco and Cam, let alone Elijah, but when she saw Toby, his stories were all about the treehouse he was building with his dad and Coco, a camping trip they had taken together, the great blueberry pancakes Coco had made for them over the fire. As a baby and toddler—but even when he got older, and started being able to do things that Toby could not—Elijah was always happy to sit on the floor with Toby, playing the simple games he loved, over and over. For Al, and even Ursula, there was always the memory of who Toby had been, before, and the sense of what had been lost haunted them. But Elijah had never known Toby any other way, and cheerfully accepted his slow, unconventional brain.

Elijah was a gift in Toby's life. The most important person of them all, in certain ways. But it was strange, and lonely, for Eleanor, that the person with whom Toby had the closest connection now was a boy she had never met.

7.

No one to care for

The children's departure from Brookline left a vast open space in Eleanor's life. For all the years of her marriage—just ten of them—Eleanor had remained so focused on being a mother that she had never allowed herself to make her career a priority. The work she did—writing books, drawing her comic strip, and, when she gave that up after Toby's accident, designing greeting cards— had represented a way of supporting her family more than anything else. Though she sometimes allowed herself to imagine what it might feel like to spend an entire day at her desk or her drawing ta-ble, uninterrupted, she never made that kind of space for her work. She used to say her artwork was raising her children.

As hard as it had been when she spent her days taking care of her children, and as much as she'd longed for freedom to pursue her own work, now that she had it, the absence of her children felt as real as a physical ache. Long after she left the farm, Eleanor still had this experience sometimes. She'd wake in the night and forget she wasn't still in their old farmhouse. It would take her a moment, re-membering where the door was, the bathroom, the window. At their old place the floors were made from wide oak boards milled a couple of hundred years before. Swinging her legs over the edge of the bed in her dark Brookline condo, her bare feet touched down on carpet.

"Where am I?" she once whispered to herself.

She had not forgotten how it used to feel, back in the old days, when she had longed for even fifteen minutes to sit quietly with a book or to soak in the tub without one of the children calling out to her. But with days on end now in which she had no one to care for—no one but herself—Eleanor barely knew who she was any-more.

8.

A man who liberates lobsters

In years past—starting when Toby first returned to the farm, and for all the years after, while Cam was healthy, Eleanor would drive up from Brookline every week to meet her son at the diner in town. (They met up in town mostly because of how hard it was—how hard it continued to be, for a long time, for Eleanor to turn down the long driveway that used to be hers, too. See their old house. The garden where she'd grown her tomatoes. The diner was less complicated.)

On those diner nights, back when he was younger, she'd give Toby a stack of quarters and let him put them in the jukebox. More often than not the song he chose was "Dead Skunk." Though Toby hardly ever sang anymore, when Loudon Wainwright got to the line *"stinkin' to high heaven,"* he belted it so loud everyone in the whole restaurant could hear.

"Maybe we should keep our voices down," Eleanor would say to him.

"But it's a great song, Mom," he told her. "I thought people might like to sing along."

So many things that come easily to other people are confusing for Toby. Or maybe it's this: Toby sees the world differently from other people. Things that matter to some people don't matter to Toby. Things other people don't care about matter a lot to him.

One time, outside the grocery store with Eleanor, on a particularly cold day—seeing a woman outside the store wearing nothing more than a jean jacket—Toby took off his brand-new parka and gave it to her. Once, on a day trip to the ocean—in the space of time it had taken her to park the car at a lobster pound—Toby spent fifty dollars he'd saved up to buy an amethyst geode he'd been talking about all year to purchase five jumbo lobsters, and before Eleanor could stop him, deposited them back in the ocean. "I didn't want those guys to get boiled in a pot," he explained to her.

Her younger son possesses surprising talents. He can't follow a recipe, but he invents his own. He can't play an instrument as he had once, but if he hears a song once, he can whistle it, with vibrato even, and he hums all the time—haunting tunes he makes up himself. He's fearless and dogged: he rides his bicycle in all kinds of weather—even during a snowstorm. (Eleanor has given up trying to persuade him to wear a helmet. "My brain got messed up already," he points out. "Why worry now?")

Years after meeting a person, Toby can remember their name. He gives surprising attention to his wardrobe, though his choices are unconventional. (He wears overalls every day for his work in the barn. But when an event calls for a different kind of apparel, he's likely to come up with some combination of attire that might include an old cape and a top hat from the costume box or a vest that probably last fit him when he was ten years old. Two different shoes. Two mismatched socks. A tie, strangely knotted.)

The year Toby turned nineteen, he told his father he wanted to get a job. Recognizing that it was unlikely his younger son could get a regular job doing anything more than bagging groceries, the two of them had taken a weeklong course in making cheese in Western Massachusetts. When it was over, Cam had outfitted his old woodshop with equipment for a cheese-making operation.

Over the years the two of them—Toby and Cam—continued to master the art of creating goat cheese. They'd brought on a manager, Ralph—a retired dairy farmer from down the road who'd missed working with livestock and—more so, probably—liked Toby. With Ralph's help and Cam's instruction, Toby had managed to start packaging wheels of cheese, with a flower—a Johnny-jump-up— pressed into the top of every wheel. At first this had been no more than a hobby to occupy Toby, but a couple of years before he died, Cam had gone through the mountains of paperwork required for certifying cheese and the two of them had started bringing Toby's cheese to farmers' markets.

Now Toby actually makes a little money with the business— enough to pay Ralph and build a small savings account. But it's not the money that matters to Toby. It's his goats.

Eleanor remembers thinking, the day of Toby's accident, that his life was over—and she wasn't wrong that his life, as they had known it before, had ended that day.

The life Toby has made, in the aftermath, is—in the balance—not a bad one. He doesn't look at what happened to him that day in the pond as a tragedy. It would be tragic only if he were miserable, and he's not.

Toby as he is now occupies a world in which stress barely exists. He loves his family. He knows every inch of their farm. He never wants to be anywhere else. All Toby lacks in life, he says, is a girlfriend. In the absence of a real one, he keeps a picture of Scarlett Johansson next to his bed. "I'm going to meet her someday," he tells Eleanor. "I think she'll like me."

Hearing him say this now, Eleanor's at a loss. How can she tell her son he'll never marry the woman he idolizes—or anyone else, more than likely? How can a person as innocent and hopeful as Toby get by in the world of people who operate so differently from himself?

Eleanor knows the answer to this: Toby will tend to the goats. Eleanor will tend to Toby.

9.

A certain number of chromosomes

][n the kitchen of the farmhouse now—the new farmhouse, the place Cam lived with Coco—Eleanor sets down the bag of groceries she's picked up on their way home from the crematorium to make dinner for herself and her son. While she's chopping vegetables for salad the phone rings. It's Elijah calling from the West Coast—a bluegrass festival somewhere in Oregon.

"I'm sorry I couldn't be there with you two today," he tells Eleanor. "You doing okay?"

After all these years, Eleanor still registers gratitude at the surprising gift of this young man in her life—a person her children speak of as their brother, though unrelated to her by blood. After speaking briefly with Eleanor, he asks her to put Toby on.

Eleanor steps away from the kitchen to give her son privacy. Still, she catches a phrase now and then of what Toby is telling the man whom he still speaks of as his little brother.

"Do you think Pops is going to talk to me in my dreams some-times, Lije?" Toby is asking his brother. "He might come back as one of my goats."

There's a long silence then. Sometimes, when Elijah's on the road with his band, he plays Toby a new tune over the phone. He must be doing that now, because Eleanor can hear Toby softly humming along and tapping his foot.

It doesn't surprise Eleanor that the first one to call is Elijah. Al—who had another interview with an adoption agency today—will probably check in later to hear how things went at the crematorium. Ursula won't.

After he hangs up, Eleanor comes back into the kitchen with the salad and their grilled cheese sandwiches. Toby sits across from her at the table, staring at his plate. He gets up without touching the food.

"If it's okay with you I'll pass on dinner, Mom," Toby tells Elea-nor. "It was a hard day. I need to spend some time with the girls." He means his goats. It's not milking time, but Eleanor knows that sometimes Toby just likes to sit with his animals out in the barn, talking to them or humming.

As she makes her way down the hall to the room where she's been sleeping all these months, Eleanor stops to look out the window. She watches her younger son trudging slowly out to the barn with that odd, loping gait of his. All she wants at this moment is for Toby to be safe. But somewhere, too, a small voice whispers to her. "When will it be my time?" Just when she'd finally carved out a life for herself in the city—after all those years of tending to her children and her husband—here she is back to the beginning again.

Never mind the chill in the air: Eleanor sits on the porch, a CD of Sinead O'Connor on the stereo. She's put the song "This Is to Mother You" on an endless loop and poured herself a glass of wine. A little before midnight the phone rings again. It's Al, calling from the West Coast.

"Oh jeez," he says, no doubt recognizing from his mother's voice that she must have been asleep. "I dialed before remembering what time it was there. It's been a rough day."

A rough day, definitely. *His father newly dead. The cremation.* But it turns out—and here comes another reminder, in case Eleanor needed one, that there comes a time in the lives of one's adult children when whatever it is that's going on with their parents no longer features as the most important aspect of their lives—that her son is talking about his and Teresa's most recent attempt, that afternoon, at convincing an adoption agency to let them become parents.

Anyone meeting Al now—anyone spending time with the man he has become—would have no reason to recognize he'd started out his life identified as female. But ten years before—not long after his surgery, in response to a brutal attack on a transgender woman at a club in Seattle—Al published an op-ed piece in the *Seattle Times* in which he'd identified himself as a man who'd undergone transition. All anyone has to do if they're checking up on him—as every adoption agency he and Teresa have contacted has surely done—is to Google his name to learn this part of his story.

"I was never ashamed of my choice," Al told Eleanor, after the first agency turned them down. "I thought it was my responsibility to speak up for others who'd gone through what I did. But if I had to do it over again, I'd probably keep quiet. I didn't set out to be some poster boy. And I wasn't bargaining on all the judgment."

"Today it happened again," he says. "First the social worker gave this speech about how important it was for parents to embrace their true identity and convey a sense of openness and acceptance around issues of gender to their children. And blah blah blah. Then she told us that they didn't feel comfortable placing a baby with us."

From where she sits—upstairs in Cam's old bedroom, the middle of the night—Eleanor feels her heart sink. She knows how badly her son wants this. His disappointment is hers now.

"'Given the climate of volatility around issues of gender at the moment,' she said—or something like that—'we feel it's best to place the infants whose birth mothers have enlisted our services in a more traditional home environment.'

"As if the only thing that could affect a child's emotional well-being is how many chromosomes his father was born with," Al says. He's not a man prone to bitterness or sarcasm, but she hears it in his voice now. "Like there aren't a million other issues that could be challenging in a child's life. Their parents might get drunk every night or stop talking to each other, but at least they've got the right body parts.

"Like having your parents get a divorce and children having to leave their home and see their parents hating each other isn't up there in the scale of traumatic events for a kid," Al says. "Like *that* never happens."

10.

An empty hammock. A girl who liked Popsicles.

The day after Eleanor and Toby attended Cam's cremation, Eleanor moves into the upstairs bedroom. She hangs her clothes in the closet and folds her sweaters and T-shirts to put in a drawer. To make space, she has to clean out Cam's things first, but this is not a difficult task. With the exception of a couple of old favorites—his faded Yellow Jackets shirt, a vest he used to wear back in his days of selling at farmers' markets, and a sweater Ursula gave him one year with a reindeer on the front whose nose used to light up but no longer did that he put on every Christmas—Cam was not a man who gave much thought, if any, to his wardrobe.

It takes Eleanor less than half an hour to clean out the drawers. She considers, for a moment, holding on to a bow tie she remembers Cam wearing the day they got married. But what's the point? This, too, goes in the bag for Goodwill.

They met at a craft fair in Vermont where Cam was selling his hand-turned burl bowls, with a goat named Opal tied to his stand and a hat with a single turkey feather on the band. He may have been the most handsome man Eleanor ever met, but that wasn't the thing that struck her. It was as if nuclear particles emanated from his body, or maybe light—a kind of life force unlike anything she'd observed in anyone else, ever—and a capacity for playfulness she loved, an ease and comfort about himself. When he invited her to follow his old truck back to the cabin he lived in it seemed to her that she'd found the home she'd been looking for all her life.

"I think we should make a family together," Cam told her. Al— Alison, then—was born within the year.

They weren't the first two people who ever fell in love, had babies, and then lost sight of each other. Gradually, their lives became consumed by the daily business of caring for their children—packing school lunches and hanging laundry on the line, paying bills, preparing meals, arguing about whose turn it was to wash the dishes, where the money was coming from. Eleanor didn't have a studio to do her work, back in those days, and it was hard finding a quiet space when she needed to place a call to her editor in New York. She'd purchased an extra-long telephone cord to reach into the closet to block out the sound of children in the background. Sometimes, during these conversations, she'd hear Toby banging on the closet door for her. Or Ursula, announcing that somebody had just spilled tomato juice all over the floor. Somebody was hungry. Somebody lost the sword to his Playmobil pirate.

Then Eleanor and Cam didn't make love much anymore. But she never questioned the choice she'd made, to raise her children or to love this man. It was the accident that changed everything.

She and Cam stayed together another few seasons after that, but what Eleanor understands now is that it wasn't just a part of her son's brain that died that day. So did her marriage. At random moments in her day the image would come to her of her husband asleep in the hammock, when he should have been keeping an eye on Toby.

A hot summer day. A four-and-a-half-year-old boy wandering down to the water's edge, his pockets filled with rocks. Cam, stretched out on the hammock. Alison running to the pond. The two of them—Al and Ursula—screaming. *It's Toby. He isn't breathing.*

Eleanor shooting up from her desk, so fast she spilled a whole bottle of india ink. Pushing on Toby's chest. Dialing 911.

Cam, making his way to the water, looking dazed, like a person who's just woken up from a nap. Which he had. He was such a person.

She saw that empty hammock, still swinging after he'd heard Eleanor calling out to him and he'd leapt up and taken off running to find their boy—too late. Eleanor and the girls had reached him already and lifted him out of the water.

She can still hear the sound of her own voice screaming the question: *Where were you?*

Their family fell apart. Al retreated behind a closed bedroom door to the reassuringly controllable universe of the computer. Ursula spun in circles, trying everything a seven-year-old could think up to get her parents to fall in love with each other again. Cam spent his days with Toby, doing those endless physical therapy exercises and yoga postures in the hopes of rewiring their son's brain. His silent penance. No matter what he did, never enough.

Eleanor disappeared into her studio, designing greeting cards. Someone had to pay the bills.

If you had asked Eleanor at the time what caused her marriage to end she would have said, "My husband fell in love with our babysitter," and no doubt this was part of the story. It wouldn't have been hard to fall in love with Coco as she was in those days—with that long, lithe body of hers, that habit she had of biting her lip with a look of intense concentration on her face as she applied toenail polish, a different color for every nail. When Eleanor pictures her now, she still sees a sixteen-year-old girl spinning cartwheels across the grass on the softball field, hopping up after to stick a piece of gum in her mouth and blow a perfect bubble, laughing and tossing her hair when it popped. Hitching up her shorts but not so much as to conceal her perfect midriff, unscathed by stretch marks.

Eleanor knows now—as she could not have admitted to herself, once—that Coco's flat stomach and boundless appetite for pleasure weren't really what had destroyed her marriage to Cam. By the time Coco cartwheeled off with her husband, he and Eleanor were already in trouble. Coco didn't break their marriage. She just picked up the pieces.

Eleanor knows this now: It was hardly ever only one partner who wrecked a marriage. Eleanor had played a big role in the divorce, too, though it was only in those last months she and Cam spent together as he was dying that she was able at last to acknowledge her part in the story.

Over all those years, Eleanor could never forgive Cam for letting Toby fall into the pond, and as surely as the salt on winter roads corroded the underbelly of their old truck, her bitterness ate away at all the good feeling, until all she could see in her husband were his failures. Eleanor had not stopped loving Cam but a feeling equally insidious—possibly more so—had seeped into her heart. She'd lost respect for him.

Ten years into his marriage to a woman who could not look at him without remembering the picture of that empty swinging hammock and the ambulance tearing down the driveway carrying their son, what man would not feel stirred by the vision of a teenage girl, sucking on a grape Popsicle with the juice trickling down her neck as she gazed at him with a look of unconcealed adoration? Eleanor hadn't watched so intently anymore, as her husband rounded the bases on softball nights, graceful as an antelope—but Coco did. Eleanor no longer looked Cam's way when he got up from the dirt and brushed himself off after sliding into home, then strode over to where Coco was giving the children a lesson in performing cartwheels, and lifting one of them to the heavens, like a trophy, grinning as he took off his cap to reveal that amazing red hair.

Coco had been able to provide for Cam what Eleanor no longer could, which was adoration. After what happened to Toby, Eleanor could never again look at Cam without seeing the man who'd failed to take care of their son and allowed him to incur terrible injury.

Coco could still see Cam as a hero—a loving and endlessly playful father, a brilliant artist who could turn misshapen outcroppings from trees into strange and beautiful vessels. How could you not fall in love with such a man?

So had Eleanor, once. But to Eleanor, by that point, there was something almost sickening about witnessing Cam's capacity for happiness and simple joy, in the face of their family disaster. To

Eleanor, Cam was a fraud, a failure at the most important job he'd ever had, taking care of their children. To Coco, Cam must have looked like a god. Coco would have restored Cam's faith in himself. No wonder he'd loved her back.

11.

Don't call. Don't write.

Three days pass after Cam's cremation without a word from Ursula. Eleanor tells herself not to call. But she has this bowl filled with ashes sitting on the mantel. What's she supposed to do with them? More than this even, there's the matter of the wooden hat.

Years ago, a very old woodworker Cam met up in Vermont gave him a piece of cherrywood he'd been saving for years. Cam made a hat out of the block of wood—hand turned, sanded down so thin that except for the grain you'd think the hat was made of felt, and light enough that a person could actually place it on her head.

The night Cam brought the amazing wooden hat into the house from his woodshop to show the family, they'd passed it around the table, each of them stroking the finely sanded finish, the perfectly turned curve of the brim. Toby, not yet three years old, had rubbed his cheek against the wood, purring like a kitten. Al—always the serious one—had remarked that they should donate the hat to a museum. Eleanor—though she'd admired Cam's work as much as any of them—had quietly calculated the number of hours of work Cam must have devoted to the hat's creation.

"We're two months late on the mortgage and my husband just spent a hundred hours making a wooden hat," she told her friend Darla the next day. (Darla, whose husband had recently broken her arm, remarked that things could be worse.)

When the wooden hat reached Ursula's hands, she didn't waste time admiring the workmanship. Five years old, she placed the hat on her head like a crown. It was way too big—covering her eyes, with only the tip of her nose visible.

"Someday can this be mine?" Ursula asked her father, placing the hat back on the table.

"You got it, baby girl," Cam told her.

Ursula never forgot that. Neither had Cam. A few days before he died he had reminded Eleanor. His voice was so soft by this time she had to bend low over the bed to hear. "The hat goes to Ursula," he told Eleanor.

So now she picks up the phone. Her body stiffens slightly as she does so, as if preparing to receive a blow. How have they gotten to this place where the act of dialing her daughter's number makes Eleanor's palms sweat?

Ursula lives up north with her husband, Jake, and their two children. She works at a progressive private school in a small town filled with moneyed émigrés from New York City. Though Jake has been in Ursula's life since the two of them were teenagers, the person he's become remains a mystery to Eleanor—a quiet, brooding man who coaches soccer and collects guns and in recent years has begun to speak of Mexican Americans (a group that includes Al's wife's family) as "illegals." Jake was Ursula's junior high school boyfriend, her first and only. Her choice to marry him the day she turned twenty-one was the first sign of the increasing distance she put between herself and her family, with the exception of Cam.

The last time they'd spoken—actually spoken as opposed to exchanging text messages—was a few days before Cam's death. Ursula had made the long drive down to see him at the end of her workday, as she did every week without fail over those last months of her father's life. Seeing her daughter looking even more ragged than usual, Eleanor had put her arms around Ursula. Or tried to.

"We're not at that place, Mother," Ursula told her. "I need you to respect my boundaries."

Ursula speaks a new language now—the vocabulary of therapy. As busy as she is, she never misses her appointment with Adrienne.

"Fair enough," Eleanor said to her daughter. (*Take a deep breath,* she reminded herself. *Don't react. Your daughter doesn't want to hear about how hurt you feel. Remember how much better it is now than a couple of years ago, when she didn't speak to you at all.*)

Eleanor knows what not to do mostly because she's made all the mistakes in the past. Crying, sending letters. Telling Ursula how heartbroken she is at not getting to see her, how much she longs to see her granddaughter and, now, her grandson. Calling Ursula to suggest she could drive up and take her out to dinner. Or lunch. Coffee. Anything. She can't afford to sound needy or desperate even if she feels that way.

"I'd go to your therapist with you," she has told Ursula. Eleanor gathers, from a previous conversation, that Adrienne has expressed, to Ursula, her view that Eleanor displays tendencies of narcissistic and possibly bipolar behavior.

"Adrienne's my therapist not yours," Ursula told her. "Though she and I agree you would benefit greatly from doing some serious work on yourself."

Count to ten. Deep breath.

"This woman hasn't met me," Eleanor said. "How does she know who I am?"

"I don't think this conversation's going anywhere," Ursula told her. She hung up then.

In the last few years, Eleanor has read many books on the subject of parental estrangement. She has attached a group of file cards to her refrigerator (the one back in Brookline, but she made a set of cards to keep handy in Akersville now, too, naming the five most common mistakes of estranged parents from *The Rules of Estrangement* by a psychologist named Joshua Coleman and a second list, "Ten New Rules for Parent–Adult Child Relations.") Sometimes, when she's had some kind of difficult interaction with Ursula, she takes the cards down and reads every item on one of the lists out loud, to remind herself. In her days as a young mother, Eleanor had never been one to consult a lot of parenting books. It's ironic that now, in her fifties, with her children grown, she finds herself needing to do this.

"*Mistake #1: Believing that reconciliation should be based on fairness.*" Eleanor reads from the card, with nobody but herself in the room.

Eleanor studies the photograph she keeps on the refrigerator, next to the estrangement tips, of Ursula holding her daughter, Lulu, and newborn son, Orson, in Vermont just after Valentine's Day earlier this year. Though she has seen Ursula surprisingly often since—times she drove down to Akersville to visit Cam—this was the last time Eleanor got to see her grandchildren.

Lulu's four years old now. Orson's not yet one. Though Eleanor has been allowed to see them on occasion, she has never spent more than an hour in their company, always with Ursula monitoring closely, as if Eleanor might kidnap one of them, if Ursula doesn't keep an eye out. As beleaguered as her daughter appears to be by her job and her responsibilities at home, with a husband who seems always to be off playing soccer, Ursula invariably declines her mother's suggestions that she could take the children for a weekend, a night, even an hour.

"I'd love to give you a break," Eleanor tells Ursula, every chance she gets, not that there are many of these. "Maybe I could take Lulu to buy a book. Or go for ice cream."

"Thanks," Ursula always responds. "But we've got everything under control. Lulu doesn't feel that comfortable with people she doesn't know all that well."

People. She was one of those people. A woman her grandchildren did not know well enough that she might care for them. And if she never saw them, how would that ever change?

12.

Woman of the Year

Here's what Eleanor has learned in the years since she packed up a U-Haul and set off for the condo in Brookline, that winter Cam told her he'd fallen in love with someone else:

The story of a divorce gets written early and only once. In Ursula's version, Eleanor played the role of the villain. For three terrible years—directly following the birth of her first child—Ursula did not speak to her mother. Of all the hard things Eleanor has experienced, and survived, none delivered greater pain. Short of one of her children dying, she can't imagine anything harder than this.

The idea that any of her three children might cut her out of their life would have seemed unimaginable to Eleanor once. Of the three, that the one to do so had been Ursula would have seemed the most unfathomable. Always, in the past, it had been Ursula who displayed the greatest devotion to her mother, the most fierce and unshakable brand of love.

Ursula was the one who always called Eleanor back for one more kiss at bedtime. When she was six she made a birthday card for her mother proclaiming that she was more beautiful than Dolly Parton and better at cooking than (the only chef whose name she knew) Julia Child.

"My mom can do anything," she wrote. The front of the card featured Ursula's rendering of the cover of *Time* magazine, with a drawing of Eleanor and the caption: "Woman of the Year." Ursula always adored her father, but even when young, she understood that Cam could be unreliable. It was Eleanor she'd recognized as the linchpin. "When I grow up," she told Eleanor, "I want to be just like you."

Ursula had been seven when her parents sat the three of them—her, Al, and Toby—down to tell them they were separating. The divorce had involved both parents, but somehow Cam had emerged, in Ursula's eyes, at least, as its victim. As she saw it, the responsibility fell to Ursula to rescue him.

More than twenty years later, when she sat beside her father's bed that last day, her tears appeared to speak to more than grief over the loss of her father. In some way Eleanor did not understand, Ursula seemed to be weeping for herself and for the life she'd lost when her mother left the farm. Of the three children Cam and Eleanor raised (as a couple for that precious handful of years, then apart) Ursula had been the one most attached to the dream of their family and the most shattered by its rupture.

It was Ursula who could not let go of the picture of the five of them, together—snow days building their forts and tumbling back into the house for hot chocolate after, making art projects, gathering around the table for a dinner of Eleanor's spaghetti carbonara, holding hands and singing "Simple Gifts." Ursula was like an immigrant who, decades after getting off the boat in a new land, still yearns for the old country, even if it's a place that no longer exists, a world to which she can never return. Like her brothers, she had carried on with her life and made a family of her own, even—a family she would sooner cut off her arm than tear asunder as hers had been. But she had never gotten over what was lost.

Ursula still put her arms around her mother when they saw each other—a brisk, cool hug, like a visiting dignitary to her host, conducting state business with some minor government official.

Eleanor, who seldom missed anything that concerned her children, recognized something else: Ursula's eyes, taking in the sight of her mother, betrayed no trace of warmth or affection. Her mouth, in repose, remained set, lips drawn tightly together, without the trace of the smile Eleanor knew so well from the old days.

This might have broken Eleanor's heart, and for a while there it almost had. But it turned out she would survive this, as she had survived so much else. She no longer uttered a silent prayer that things with Ursula would return to how they'd been. Her prayer was simpler now. "Let Ursula be happy." From where she stood, she doubted that was so.

The thing was, Ursula had always been the happy one. The easy one. The one who adapted to Al's sullen moods and Toby's wild explosions. Maybe that had been the problem, Eleanor thinks now. Her daughter was always so good, so perfect. It must have been a hard role to play. But after the divorce she didn't just give up on being Happy Ursula. She gave up on her mother.

Eleanor can still see Ursula at age six, dressing Toby up—Toby, as he was before the accident—in some wild costume made from scarves and old rubber gloves and the head of their mop and a pair of swim goggles—to perform in a circus she'd put on, with herself as ringmaster. Toby was the monkey. Also the clown, and the lion.

"Ladies and gentlemen!" Ursula announced to her audience. (This consisted of Cam and Eleanor. Al was elsewhere, cringing no doubt.) "Announcing the greatest show on earth. Starring. . . . *MY*

LITTLE BROTHER! The amazing, the incredible, the lovable, the one and only . . . TOBY!"

Ringmaster was a role that suited Ursula well. She was not, herself, possessed of her little brother's gifts of imagination and invention, or sense of humor. Ursula was earnest, dogged, literal—a person who appreciated order and structure, while Toby lived to obliterate whatever stood in his path. Her pride in Toby, for possessing talents she did not have herself, knew no bounds. She didn't want to be a star. She loved it that her brother was one.

Then he wasn't anymore.

Just turned seven years old when Toby had suffered his brain injury, Ursula had taken on the responsibility to fix what had been broken in their family, which amounted to just about everything. She'd studied that book *When Bad Things Happen to Good People,* underlining the parts that might help and writing them down, even—leaving Post-it notes on her mother's desk with quotes from the book. Observing the tension in her parents' marriage, after, she had prepared a surprise candlelit dinner for the two of them of grilled cheese sandwiches and a chocolate bar. The look on her face, as she set their plates in front of them—a heart-shaped hole cut into the middle of each sandwich—made Eleanor's heart hurt. She who would do just about anything for her child could not deliver what her child wanted most, which was that her parents stay married to each other.

For Ursula, their family meant everything. When their family seemed to be falling apart, she did everything she could to hold it together. For Ursula—brave warrior Ursula, their little bear—there was no differentiating who she was from who she was as a part of the unit of the five of them.

The divorce shattered her.

For the first seven years of her life, Ursula had maintained an unshakable faith in Eleanor's ability to solve any problem, make everything all right. Even Toby's accident had not changed this perception. Then a problem confronted them (the worst one possible, in Ursula's world: the divorce) that her mother could not solve. Eleanor had failed to keep their family together. For Ursula, this failure served as evidence of the worst betrayal imaginable.

13.

Eggshells

W hen Eleanor left Akersville for Brookline and let Cam keep the farm, she told herself she was making things easier for the children by sparing them a fight over the property she and Cam had shared. But to Ursula, her mother's departure from the farm looked like nothing less than an abandonment of their father. Worse than this—an abandonment of their whole family.

Eleanor had chosen to protect the three of them from the part of the divorce that had to do with Coco—the kiss she'd witnessed by the waterfall the day the *Challenger* exploded, followed by Cam's announcement that he didn't want to be married to her anymore.

All Alison and Ursula and Toby knew—all they saw—was that U-Haul truck taking away their mother's things, and Cam (Cam alone, no evidence of Coco in the picture at that point, though she was a big part of the story) rattling around by himself in their old farmhouse, stoking the woodstove, heating up a can of Campbell's tomato soup every night, ripping open a packet of Annie's mac and cheese. At the ages of six, eight, and ten, the children felt so sorry for their father that by the time his relationship with Coco was out in the open—more than a full year after their parents' separation— they displayed no resentment toward their former babysitter for stepping into the role of stepmother, only gratitude that Cam had someone to love him again.

Al and Toby left it there and got on with their lives. Only Ursula seemed unable to let it go. Of the three of them, the child who was quickest to champion their father and condemn their mother was the one who had probably loved Eleanor with the most steadfast de-votion before.

The narrative Ursula constructed after the divorce—and now, in therapy—portrayed Eleanor as an ambitious, hard-driving, and unforgiving woman, impatient with her husband's easygoing ways, who'd grown restless with small-town life in her little New Hampshire farmhouse and sought out the excitement and career opportunities only a big city might offer. She'd left their heartbroken father to struggle on alone while pursuing fame and fortune.

Three days after the birth of Ursula's first child, Louise, Eleanor attempted to set the record straight about the divorce, delivering to Ursula the story, so long hidden, of Cam's affair. Her timing was terrible.

Hearing this revelation so long after everything happened, Ursula responded with a new and unprecedented level of contempt toward her mother—more than that, outright rage. Though things had not been good between the two of them for a long time, this was the moment when Ursula cut Eleanor out of her life as well as that of her newborn daughter.

"Don't call. Don't write. I don't want to see you anymore," Ursula told Eleanor. "Don't plan on seeing your granddaughter ever again, either."

That day Ursula sent Eleanor away—from her house, from her life—was the one Eleanor named, after Toby's accident, as the worst of her life. When she called the house, Jake told Eleanor that Ursula didn't want to talk with her.

Two days later came a letter. "I honestly don't want to hurt you," Ursula had written, "but I've come to the conclusion it is not healthy to have you in my life anymore, or in the life of my family."

Eleanor wrote a letter back to Ursula—then many more—begging Ursula to give her a chance, to let her come see her. Talk it out, apologize. The letters came back unopened.

Months passed. A year, then another. When Eleanor ran into women she had known in the old days—days they were all raising their children—they always took out photographs of their children's children and talked about how wonderful it was being a grandparent. On these occasions Eleanor said nothing.

"Wait a second, didn't Ursula have a baby a while back?" one of them asked her.

"A girl," Eleanor told her. The less said the better. "She's adorable."

No doubt she must be. Except for one brief, disastrous visit right after Louise was born, Eleanor hadn't laid eyes on her for three years. Now and then Elijah, who maintained an easy, friendly connection to his older sister, would show her a picture of Louise. "They call her Lulu," he told Eleanor.

Lulu. Eleanor had studied the picture on Elijah's phone, of Ursula holding Lulu, as if maybe, if she looked long enough and hard enough, some deeper understanding might come to her of how it could be that a child who had once meant the world to her—a child to whom she had meant the world—could dismiss her so swiftly and utterly. It was as if Ursula had picked up the X-Acto knife they'd used when they made their Valentines around the dining room table long ago—running the blade around the edges of a photograph on the pages of their Burpee seed catalog, excising the image of a rose or a zinnia or a sunflower—except it wasn't pictures of flowers and vegetables Ursula had excised. It was Eleanor. *Rip, cut, slice. Gone.*

For Eleanor, unlike some women, the period of absolute estrangement from her daughter had lasted just three years. (Just? An hour seldom went by, over those years, that Eleanor didn't feel the ache of this, and think about the granddaughter she hadn't seen since she was three days old.)

At Al's wedding, where they'd all gathered on the farm (for Eleanor, her first time back in years), Ursula and Eleanor had made an uneasy truce. Eleanor was grateful, but it had not been the dreamed-of reconciliation when the two of them might have fallen into each other's arms to say how sorry they were for all the time they'd lost, the pain their separation had inflicted, the joy of their reunion.

But here was something she'd learned over those three terrible years of Ursula's silence: Once your adult child has cut you out of her life, the possibility will always be there that she might do it again.

"This is your grandmother, Lulu," Ursula had told her little girl—now three years old—at the wedding that day they'd made their careful, tentative reconnection, her voice firm and cool. "She won't hurt you." As if that were even a possibility.

Lulu had settled into her grandmother's arms as easily as she had that one time Eleanor got to hold her as a newborn. Those women Eleanor used to know who told her about the joys of grandparenthood weren't wrong. What she felt at that brief moment, holding

Lulu, was pure love. She would do anything to keep this child in her life. Her granddaughter, and the baby brother who'd followed her.

A little over a year later—a year that has seen Cam's diagnosis, Eleanor's decision to move back to the farm to care for her children's father, and now his death—Eleanor still walks on eggshells in the company of Ursula, choosing her words carefully or simply saying nothing out of fear that what she might say could serve as evidence of some new offense.

She knows now that it could all blow up again in an instant. One misguided remark, one thoughtless action, and Ursula could disappear from her life again, along with the grandchildren. This time possibly forever.

14.

The wooden hat

There was a time when Ursula used to tell Eleanor she wanted to be just like her when she grew up. Now the governing principle of her life appears to involve putting as much distance between how her mother's life has played out and what she intends for her own. Ursula, as she is now at thirty-two, possesses a resolute determination to do what Eleanor had failed to achieve: maintain her marriage and the stability of her family at whatever cost. For her, the idea of getting a divorce is unacceptable, no matter what. Much like Eleanor's own younger self, Ursula manages to fit in the requirements of her career, and any aspirations she might once have had for her own life, around meeting the needs of her children.

In those last weeks of Cam's life, Ursula made the long drive down from Vermont at least twice a week and sometimes more than that. She barely spoke to Eleanor on those visits beyond asking—as she brushed past her on the way to Cam's hospital bed—if her father had eaten anything. She'd spend an hour alone in the room with Cam. (Never longer. She had to get back to the children.)

After her time with Cam, Ursula headed for the car. If she said anything before she left, it was only to remind Eleanor when the next dose of morphine was due.

Standing by the door at the end of those visits, taking in Ursula's chilly goodbye and the cool gaze that accompanied it, Eleanor tried to locate some trace of the little girl she remembered, the one she'd raised, who told her once she was the best mother in the solar system.

It came to her then that Ursula was not the only one of the two of them who'd undergone a transformation. So had she. She, who believed it was her central and sole purpose in life to keep her children safe and happy, has had no choice but to face the fact that even if a person has tried the best she could to do those things, she may not succeed. She wishes she could tell her daughter this. *Oh, Ursula,* she would say. *I wish you could give up trying to be perfect. I wish you could give up on the idea of making your children's lives perfect. You think you can protect them from all the hard things in life. You can't.*

It took Eleanor a long time to learn this lesson but she has: that in the end, her children's happiness, or sorrow, is out of her hands. She, the mother who had once ripped their house apart in search of Ursula's lost Barbie shoe, but could not save her marriage, had failed at protecting her child from far greater forms of grief. It was probably too late to tell her daughter: *No parent on earth can do what I set out to accomplish. Loss happens. So does grief. The best we can do is to know, when it does, that it's survivable.*

The only person whose happiness lay in one's own hands was one's own self.

This is what Eleanor reminds herself, as she stands in the kitchen, looking at her phone, holding the precious wooden hat in her hands. At the time he'd made that hat, Eleanor had failed to appreciate its beauty, but she does now. Ursula had always seen it.

Call now, Eleanor thinks. *Tell her that.*

The phone rings for a long time. Eleanor is just about to hang up—feeling a certain relief that she won't be subjected again to Ursula's harshness—when her daughter picks up.

"What do you want?" Ursula's opening line.

Eleanor should be used to this by now, but the coldness in Ursula's voice on the other end of the line still unnerves her.

"I thought we should talk about your father's ashes. It's up to the four of you, naturally. But I wanted you to know they're here."

"Thank you."

"We could make some kind of ceremony. Bury them down by the pear tree maybe. Your call. Yours and your brothers'."

"I know that."

"Maybe this is a bad time," Eleanor says. "I could call back."

"It's as good a time as any," Ursula tells her. "I just don't know what there is to say. My father's dead. I feel shitty. End of story."

"He wanted you to have the hat," Eleanor says.

"Hat?" It takes Ursula a moment to understand. Knowing how busy Ursula is, how she never sits down or stops working (who does this remind Eleanor of?), Eleanor guesses her daughter might be folding laundry or sitting at her desk, going over faculty evaluations, or nursing Orson, if she even nurses him anymore. (It saddens Eleanor to realize she doesn't know the answer to this. Or it would sadden her, if there weren't so many other aspects of Eleanor's relationship to Ursula that make her sad. So much else she doesn't know, because they never talk about anything anymore.)

"The wooden hat Cam made. He wanted you to have it."

"Oh, right."

On the other end of the line, Eleanor can detect a certain softening in Ursula's voice, but she doesn't kid herself that this has anything to do with her daughter's attitude toward herself. It's about the hat, and Cam. Here's one more of the ten million things Ursula loved about her father: that he'd make a wooden hat, and that he'd make sure, after his death, that it would be hers.

From another room in the house, Eleanor can hear the sound of cheering. Jake's watching a game, no doubt. Jake's always watching a game. From Ursula, no words. Eleanor thinks maybe her daughter is crying a little.

"I'll drive down to pick it up," Ursula says.

"You'll bring the children?"

"Lulu gets carsick," Ursula says. "I don't like messing up Orson's nap schedule."

"I could drive up and bring it to you," Eleanor tells her daughter. "That way maybe I'll get to see Orson and Lulu."

"Do what you want," Ursula says. How can it be that something as simple as the tone of a person's voice can have the effect of a knife slicing into your heart? It can have that effect if the person is someone you love, and they're speaking as if you're a stranger to them now. A stranger you gave birth to once, a million years ago.

PART 2

The Family Moves On

15.

Does Scarlett Johansson like rocks?

Much as, when he was small, Toby gave names to the cork people they used to construct, now he gives great thought to the naming of his goats.

He knows every one of them as well as a person might know the members of his family—knows, for instance, that Harriet favors a particular patch of clover out behind the barn, and that the sight of Toby, approaching with his wheelbarrow, inspires in Vivian a kind of joy that causes her to run in circles. He knows that Janice likes Patty and dislikes Bernadette, while Gladys rejects the company of any goat other than Rita. "I think they're gay," Toby suggested once. If so, he's fine with that.

Some people have a hard time distinguishing one goat from another. But Toby can tell you whose tongue bears an interesting black stripe down the middle, whose nose features a single white dot, and which goat seems a little depressed. He knows all their birthdays. He knows who loves eating chicory and who needs to steer clear of it.

While milking his goats he often whistles to them (Johnny Cash or Hank Williams, tunes he learned from his father, and sometimes tunes he makes up). The goats need milking for over ten months of the year, but even when they don't, they still need daily care. There is no vacation from caring for goats, not that Toby would want one. He likes having a routine.

Though she hadn't intended this to happen, in the days since she's been back on the farm—most particularly, the days since Cam's death—Eleanor has one, too. Sometimes now, pinning the laundry on the line, Eleanor can hear her son carrying on conversations with the goats in the odd, slightly flattened tone of voice that has been Toby's since the accident—the short, simple sentences, sometimes drifting into wordless humming, combined with what often come across as curiously philosophical musings.

"You need more grain, Patty?" "Sleep okay, Bernie?" "I know you don't like that fence, Harriet. But remember what happened when you got out? And that coyote almost got you?"

"I wonder if trees have feelings. I wonder if Scarlett Johansson likes rocks. I wonder if fish hear birds."

"I think I died once. That day in the pond. I think I saw God. Either God or a cloud."

16.

The Make Your Own Cork Person kit

Toby loves his goats. He also misses his father. When Cam was alive, the two of them—he and Toby—would play cards by the woodstove or look at catalogs featuring machine parts or daffodil bulbs, or study Toby's mineral books together. They watched reruns of *Gilligan's Island* on Nickelodeon. (Toby's favorite was Gilligan. Cam's, the Professor.) The two of them played Parcheesi and checkers for hours at a time, or cards.

Tonight, Eleanor takes out a deck of cards. "How about a game, Tobes?" she asks him. Toby looks happy, but a little dubious.

Though she's tried, Eleanor has never been very good at playing games with her son. For so many years now, she's been running so fast that somewhere along the line she stopped knowing how to sit still, go slow.

Now she sets out the game pieces. She doesn't want to, but she checks her cell phone in the middle during Toby's turn, much as, in the old days, she'd find herself adding up numbers in her check register during a game of Operation to figure out if they had enough money that week to replace the head gasket on Cam's truck.

These days money is no longer the source of worry it used to be when she and Cam were raising their children, but the old habit of keeping constantly on her guard dies hard. There's always some piece of business to take care of: a talk at a book conference, the French translation of one of her Bodie books, a meeting with the toy company in New York that has licensed the rights to manufacture kits for children, inspired by the books. At the moment, the Make Your Own Cork Person kit occupies her thoughts.

Back when she and her children made cork people together every spring, the materials they'd used were fabric scraps and matchsticks, snaps and buttons from her sewing box, stuck onto wine corks with a glue gun. Now a company based somewhere in California is planning to charge $19.95 for a cardboard box containing all the materials needed for fans of the animated *Cork People* television series to make their own cork people.

In Eleanor's opinion, nobody should have to buy a kit to make a cork person. But it seems that so many parents these days would rather hand over their charge card for a box containing the parts, along with an instruction book and a tube of glue, than assemble the materials with their children themselves.

She's just meditating on this—Toby, having recently snagged her ten of clubs to round out a hand of tens—when her phone rings. On the other end of the line, a low-level toy company executive is explaining to Eleanor that unfortunately the company has been unable to implement her recommendation that the packaging of their cork people kit include the advice that children might gather things like seed pods and pine cones in the woods to use to make their cork people.

"We're sticking with plastic," the toy company executive tells her. Eleanor studies her phone, constructing her response.

"Your turn, Mom," Toby says.

Eleanor's mind is elsewhere.

"No plastic," she says. "These cork people should feel to a child like real woodland characters. Nothing made of plastic ever feels magic."

On the other end of the line, the executive says he'll get back to her on this. The issue here is numbers. Replicating cork people on a vast scale. When you're talking tens of thousands of units, there's no way to put a pine cone or an acorn cap in every kit.

"Mom?" Toby is saying. It's Eleanor's turn. "*Mom. Mom. Mom. Where did you go?*"

17.

If Gilligan ever got off the island

Wintertime now. The woodstove's lit. Eleanor and Toby sit at the kitchen table—Toby playing solitaire, Eleanor on her laptop, as usual.

"I wonder how Gilligan would feel if he ever got off the island?" Toby says to his mother. Or maybe to himself. "I wonder if he'd be happy if they rescued him. He might end up missing his old life with his pals."

This much about Toby, at least, has not changed entirely from the boy she'd known before the accident. At age thirty, he still asks more questions than anyone Eleanor has ever known.

"Maybe he's just going to die there." Toby again.

"Who's dying?" Eleanor says. Immersed in writing her letter to the president of Wonderland Toys, she's missed Toby's earlier remarks. She has no idea what he's talking about.

"Gilligan. Not now. But someday. Like Charlotte."

They drive to New York together—a meeting with the chief of marketing at the company that has just paid a ridiculously large amount for the rights to manufacture and distribute the plastic cork people kits. Eleanor might have preferred to make the trip alone, but Toby wanted to join her today. On the ride to the city, they listen to the audio book of *Charlotte's Web* together. This is probably Toby's all-time-favorite book.

Toby speaks of Charlotte like a friend—as real as one of his goats or one of the men he shoots the breeze with at the bowling alley. He loves the family's triumphant visit to the fair with Wilbur, the day Charlotte spins the words "Some pig" in her web. Today—just as Eleanor's car is heading over the George Washington Bridge—they've reached the part of the story where Charlotte dies. In the seat beside Eleanor, her son begins to weep.

He's thinking about the death of Charlotte, but also of Cam, no doubt. In the months since his father died, Toby still talks about him all the time, generally in the present tense.

"My pops and me like to play Parcheesi," he says, looking dreamily out at the Hudson River.

"My pops and me do yoga."

"My pops lives in a different galaxy now."

Today though, he speaks of Cam in the past tense. "My pops is never coming back," Toby says. "He's dead. Like Charlotte."

"Maybe we shouldn't listen to this tape anymore," Eleanor says to Toby. Hands on the wheel, eyes on the road. "It always makes you so sad."

"It's okay to be sad," Toby says. "Life is sad sometimes. Just not always. It's a combination."

They drive in silence then, over the bridge.

"You're sad sometimes, too, Mom," Toby says. "You're probably sad about Ursula. She's not very nice to you these days."

"You're right about that," Eleanor tells him. She hadn't expected to discuss this with her son, but of course he's noticed. Toby notices everything.

"The thing is," he says, "I don't think my sister's mad at you, really. She's mad at the world. You're just the person it's easiest to blame."

"Why is that, do you think?" Eleanor asks him.

"Because you just care so much," Toby says. "You probably can't help it. But you just care so much all the time."

18.

I'm calling him Spyder

For close to a year, the house that had belonged to their neighbors Walt and Edith has remained vacant. With Walt gone, their son Walt Junior had moved Edith to a nursing home. Then Edith died. All that winter, snow piled up against the door.

Late that summer, not long after Cam's death, Eleanor notices a car in front of the old place. On her walk to the waterfall a few days later she sees a young woman kneeling on the ground out front, planting a flat of petunias (spaced so far apart and in such a shady spot that it's clear this person knows nothing about gardening).

The woman—more of a girl, to Eleanor—appears to have connected a boom box to an extension cord. It's propped next to the patch of dirt she's digging in, blasting a song Eleanor recognizes from Zumba class at the Y. Eminem, a duet with Rihanna.

The girl can't be more than eighteen. She's skinny, but when she gets up Eleanor sees that she's pregnant.

"I'm your neighbor," Eleanor says. "For now anyway." No need to explain the rest.

"Raine," the girl tells her. It takes a moment for Eleanor to understand that this is her name, not a forecast.

"You're living here now?" Eleanor offers. Maybe Walt Junior has decided to rent the place.

"Walt and Edith were my grandparents," she says. "My dad's letting me hang out till I get things together."

That might take a while.

A memory comes to Eleanor then, of a time long ago when she stopped by Walt and Edith's sometime after the divorce on a rare visit to the farm. Walt had been standing in a patch of sunlight in the yard holding a very small infant.

"Can you believe it, I got myself a granddaughter?" he said. That must have been Raine.

Now Eleanor studies the girl's small, pale face, those impossibly thin arms, with a tattoo of Johnny Depp on one, an image of the Pringles potato chip logo on the other. She takes in the car in the driveway, with its back bumper dragging. So much rust it's hard to tell what color it started out.

Raine seems to read her mind. "I only drive at night," she says. "That way the cops don't notice."

Eleanor asks when the baby's due. "Sometime next month?" Raine speaks in that style Eleanor recognizes from young people she's met lately who end every sentence as if it were a question. Prenatal care does not appear to be part of her plan.

"I'm having a home birth?" she says. That lilting cadence again.

"My children were born at home, too," Eleanor tells her. "Of course that was a long time ago."

Different in other ways, too, she guesses. There appears to be no sign of a partner in this picture. No prenatal vitamins on the kitchen shelf, probably. In the last weeks of her own first pregnancy, she and Cam had painted a scene of forest animals on the wall of the bedroom they'd fixed up for the baby and hung a mobile Cam had made from seed pods and acorns over the crib. She'd sewn a patchwork quilt from cut-up dresses and a pair of Cam's overalls. For all the months of her pregnancy—but more so, as the date approached for the birth—Eleanor had been consumed with making their home ready for the child on the way—canning fruit, knitting tiny caps and booties.

Standing in the dirt now, Eleanor studies the girl with the trowel in her hand. From the boom box next to the flat of petunias, Eminem is yelling *"I love the way you lie."*

"I hope you've got a good support team," Eleanor offers. Raine looks momentarily baffled.

"I found this tape at the Swap Shop," Raine tells her. "It's all about having a baby underwater. The only catch is, this place doesn't have a bathtub."

The next day Eleanor stops by with a basket containing fresh zucchini from her garden, a jar of spaghetti sauce she'd canned the summer before, a box of pasta, and a bar of lavender soap. She has set a slice of lemon meringue pie in the basket, left over from the one she'd made with Toby the night before. She'd dug a couple of baby sweaters out of the box she'd found at the house—odd that Cam held on to them, or maybe it was Coco who did. She'd set a couple of these on top.

Raine lifts one of the sweaters from the bag and examines the buttons. Except for her belly, she could be playing with doll clothes.

"This comes from back in the day, right?" she asks Eleanor. "I love vintage."

All that month Eleanor makes a point of dropping off groceries for Raine. Sometimes she just sets the bag on the porch, but after a few times, Raine asks if she'd like to come in. "I've got some Diet Coke," she tells Eleanor. This seems to be her drink of choice.

She keeps the radio on, very loud. Also the television. She has a cage with a canary in it who doesn't look well and a litter box that suggests the presence of a cat.

Eleanor wouldn't have expected this: The kitchen is spotless. Whether or not Raine has a doctor at the moment, she must have visited one at some point. An ultrasound image of a fetus in the early stages hangs on the wall over the sink over a framed photograph Eleanor remembers—one of those portraits from Sears, she guesses—from back when Walt and Edith lived here, of the two of them years back.

"You've got your plans all set for when you go into labor?" Eleanor asks Raine. She doesn't want to pry, but you had to wonder.

"We're cool," Raine tells her, patting her belly in a way that suggests the other individual involved in this project—the only other one—is her baby.

Sometime in the night Eleanor wakes to what sounds like fireworks going off, only it isn't that. Out the window she sees Raine, leaned up against her car with the motor on. Backfiring loudly.

Eleanor throws on her bathrobe. By the time she gets outside, Raine is doubled over and making noises like a wild animal caught in a trap.

"I think it's coming," she cries out to Eleanor. No need to elaborate.

Toby appears in the doorway. Toby, who might not be that familiar with the multiplication tables, but knows all about birth from nights in the barn helping goat mothers deliver their kids. The two of them help Raine into the house. Even giving birth, she looks around fourteen years old.

Cam's hospital bed is still set up. Raine lies down on it. Eleanor dials 911. Toby's already washing his hands. Eleanor helps Raine out of her underpants.

Things are happening fast, in a manner totally different from anything Eleanor knows from her own deliveries. Already the head is crowning. No way the ambulance will get to them before the baby arrives.

Some women in labor might have expressed resistance to the presence of a man in the room who wasn't a doctor—particularly one wearing bright green sweatpants and a Teenage Mutant Ninja Turtles T-shirt—but Raine, though she has not met Toby before, seems to have no problem with his being there. Toby has always occupied his own category. Not boy or man, just Toby. Now he's stroking Raine's head and murmuring softly. He looks into her eyes. She's looking back into his as if her life depends on it.

Eleanor stands at the foot of the bed holding Raine's knees. She's crying out even louder now, if this is possible, but Eleanor hears another sound in the room, coming from her son.

An odd thing has happened. In the minutes since Raine lowered herself over the bed, the sound of breathing—Raine's and Toby's—seems to have become perfectly synchronized. Raine is panting, then pushing, exhaling long and slow, then panting again, faster than ever. Breath for breath, Toby matches her. They exchange no words, but the two of them seem as perfectly tuned to each other in that moment as a couple of musicians singing harmony. The Everly Brothers. "Bye Bye Love."

This is an aspect of Toby everyone in their family knows well—the way he connects so deeply with a person, sometimes, that he seems almost to become them. Whenever Eleanor watches a movie with Toby, she can count on the fact that if she looks over at him with his eyes on the screen, his expression will perfectly mirror that of whatever actor he identifies with in the film. If the movie's one of his favorites, that he's seen many times, he'll soundlessly mouth the words the actor speaks along with him.

Now comes a long, low grunting sound, the sound Eleanor has made, herself, only three times ever: when pushing each of her babies out into the world. Raine is making that sound. From deep in his diaphragm, so does Toby.

"Check for the cord, Mom," Toby tells her. He knows this from his life in the barn.

A moment later there's the head, crumpled up and folded in over itself like a walnut before somehow, miraculously, seeming to inflate before their eyes, then sliding into Eleanor's hands—head first, then shoulders, arms, torso—smooth, damp . . . A whole baby, with a red and screaming face, his eyes staring out at them with a look of utter amazement and maybe terror. Wailing.

A boy.

"I'm calling him Spyder," Raine tells them.

Eleanor bends over to hand her the baby. Raine shakes her head. "Not yet," she says. "I need a minute to chill."

So it's Toby who holds him first, Toby who stands there beside the same bed where his father had left the world only a few weeks earlier, wrapping a towel around the red and squirming infant. Humming softly, counting the baby's fingers, weeping in a way that would have made a person think—if they didn't know—this must be the baby's father. Not some neighbor who'd met the mother twenty minutes earlier.

"Spider, like in *Charlotte's Web*," Toby says.

"We'll spell it with a *y*," Raine tells them.

"I think he'll be my friend," Toby says. "My little pal."

Eleanor looks at Raine, lying on the bed, having just delivered the placenta. "Oh, gross," she groans, as it slips from her body into the salad bowl Eleanor has grabbed to catch it. "Nobody told me about that part."

Nothing in her expression suggests joy or any shred of maternal connection. She's chewing her nails and studying her stomach. She isn't happy with what she sees.

"I thought once it came out I'd look normal again," she says. "I'll tell you one thing. I'm not going to eat anything but carrot sticks and celery till I get back to a hundred and five pounds."

19.

Talk funny

As much as anyone could know, observing from outside, Al and Teresa appear happy in their marriage and fulfilled in their careers. Their success in the world of tech start-ups has given them a mid-century modern house on Whidbey Island and a pair of BMWs in the driveway, all courtesy of their start-up, Lyricon. The month after their honeymoon in the Maldives they took a vacation to Martha's Vineyard. Over the Christmas holidays, they rented a yacht with a crew to sail around the British Virgin Islands. When Al came to see his father over those last months—once with Teresa, two other times on his own—he'd flown first class.

But their wealth has not provided Al and Teresa what they want most: a baby. Eleanor loves Teresa. She has no doubt Al would be a wonderful father. As a person who started out life with ovaries, not testicles, he just lacks the biological material to make fatherhood possible in the traditional way. It seems to Eleanor a sad irony that a person like Walt and Edith's granddaughter, Raine, who displays so little enthusiasm for her son, could have made a baby so effortlessly, while Al and Teresa remain childless. So far the world of adoption has shut them out not once but three times.

They're still young, of course. They haven't been married long. But the two of them—Al, at least—display a kind of urgency about becoming parents that one might expect only in an older couple who'd been trying for years. Maybe because Al has gone through his life as an outsider in the world, he approaches the experience of parenthood as his way of becoming fully a part of the society from which he's always felt excluded.

In all other ways that Eleanor can determine, the life Al and Teresa have made for themselves in the Pacific Northwest seems rich and full and—to a woman like Eleanor, whose own youth was spent caring for children to the exclusion of so much else—enviably free. One time, when they were off on one of their vacations, Teresa texted her from Hawaii to share footage of Al, standing up on a surfboard after his first lesson. Three weeks later they attended a music festival at Red Rocks in Colorado. And still, Eleanor knows, Al would give all that up for the chance to become a father.

Al's life provides a stark contrast to that of his younger brother, whose main adventure at this point, except when birthing goats, is his weekly night at the bowling alley with his mother. You can always count on Toby to be home—which has made him, since Raine's delivery of her son, a trusted babysitter to Spyder. Given her general approach to parenthood, Raine would have left her baby with Toby whether he seemed trustworthy or not. But in fact, Toby would sooner cut off his arm than let any harm come to that baby.

A number of times over the years, Al has suggested that he and Toby take a trip together—camping in Idaho, or to the Grand Canyon, Alaska. Toby has never wanted to go. Then one night, on the weekly call between Toby and his brother, Al tries again, only this time the destination he proposes is Seattle.

"Come on out for as long as you can persuade Mom and Ralph to cover for you with those goats," Al tells him. "Teresa and I will take you out on the town."

More important than nightlife, for Toby, probably, is what Al says to him next. "I'd like to spend more time with you."

Maybe it's Cam's death that has changed things. At some point, not far from the end, Cam had evidently expressed the opinion, to Toby, that he should see more of his brother. As many people as there were who might have suggested that Toby would need Al more once their father was gone, Cam had seen it differently.

"You know what my dad told me?" Toby reported to Eleanor, after the last time Al had come to see his father. "He said Al's going to need me. My pops asked me to help him."

In an odd way, Eleanor understood what Cam had meant. Maybe this came from all the years Al had spent concealing his sexuality, or trying to—followed by what he was doing now, which was creating a company in which investors might confidently invest millions of dollars. Al can't afford to betray doubt or sadness. For all his success out in the world, Al is a person who has a hard time opening up. Where Toby knows no other way to be.

"I'm Toby," he says, when introducing himself to someone new. "I talk funny because I have a brain injury."

For Al, even now, no similar level of disclosure occurs concerning his history. As much as Toby lays his cards on the table, Al keeps his close to the chest.

Though he's never been on a plane, and has always had a fear of flying, Toby surprises Eleanor by accepting Al and Teresa's invitation to visit them in Seattle. He spends a day choosing his wardrobe for the trip, and another three days briefing Eleanor and Ralph on the fine points of dealing with each of the girls. It's the time of year when milk production has gone way down, and none of the girls is due to give birth for another month. Still, leaving for the better part of a week requires a lot of advance preparation.

One more time, on the drive to Logan airport, Eleanor talks her son through the process of getting to his gate. She'll be there to check him in, but he'll have to do the rest on his own. She stands at the entrance to security, watching him move along the line with his fellow passengers. He's chosen to wear the Day-Glo orange vest Cam always put on when he walked in the woods during hunting season and a bright red beret Eleanor brought home one time from France.

"Wish me luck," he says as he hugs Eleanor goodbye. "Some flight attendant might fall in love with me."

Maybe he's making a joke. Maybe he believes this to be a possibility. Even now, when dealing with Toby and his damaged but surprising brain, Eleanor never knows how much her younger son understands of the world and his place in it. Or how much the world will understand him. This is the greater worry for Eleanor. She tries to imagine the flight attendant—or anyone, never mind her profession—who could recognize what Eleanor does about Toby.

Her son is a rare treasure. Nobody knows better how to love than Toby. Nobody has more love to give.

20.

A $6,000 blown-glass sculpture

During the five days of Toby's trip to visit his brother and sister-in-law in Seattle, Eleanor resists the impulse to call. If Al and Teresa run into problems—or if Toby himself does—they'll let her know. Making her way out to the barn every morning just after sunup to check in with the goats, she offers up a silent prayer.

Let nothing bad happen to Toby. The dream of a flight attendant who might recognize her son's large and beautiful heart seems beyond reach, but maybe, for that brief stretch of days he spends in the care of his brother and his brother's kind and loving wife, Toby might experience a taste of being out in the world in a way he has almost never known. Just that.

On the baggage claim level, where she's come to pick him up, Eleanor stands at the foot of the escalator, studying the passengers as they descend. Her heart lifts when she catches sight of him. He's wearing a Nirvana T-shirt and a Seahawks hat. He's talking to an elderly woman he must have met on the flight. "I'll be right with you, Mom," he tells Eleanor. "I just need to help Roberta with her suitcase. She's been visiting her grandchildren. And guess what, she likes goat cheese!"

In the car on the way home, Toby fills Eleanor in on the rest—Al's house, the surround-sound media room he and Teresa built, Teresa's Pilates class, which he attended with her, the upholstery in Al's car, and what they ate for breakfast every morning. They're halfway home when he mentions he's spent his entire savings—$6,000— on a piece of blown glass for Eleanor from the Chihuly Garden and Glass. He's so excited to show it to her he can't wait till they get home. There in the front seat he lifts the package from his backpack.

What he discovers, when he opens it, concerns Toby less than it would anyone else. The precious bowl must have broken on the trip. There must be a few hundred pieces of glass in the package.

"Never mind," Toby says, lifting the pieces up one by one to catch the setting sun. "We can keep them on the windowsill. They'll make rainbows."

About the rest of his visit, Toby remains vague. His favorite part of the trip seems to have been a fish taco he and Al shared at Pike Place Market. He liked the ferry they'd taken him on, and the Space Needle, and—knowing Cam had gone to Woodstock, and sometimes played him the soundtrack album from the movie, with the Hendrix version of the national anthem—he tells Eleanor he wished his pops had been there when they visited a museum dedicated to Jimi Hendrix.

It's dark when they reach Akersville. Almost more than seeing his goats, Toby's anxious to see Raine's baby, Spyder. "I bet my little pal missed me tons," Toby says.

Now, with darkness setting in as they turn off onto their road at the end of his long day of traveling, her son asks if they can stop by Walt's old house on their way home, to say hello to Spyder. He's brought Bigfoot T-shirts for both of them—Raine, as well as Spyder.

"Jesus, it's about time you got back," Raine says when she sees Toby in the doorway. "Spending all day alone with this kid like I've been doing I thought I was going to lose my mind."

Back at the house after, he pays a visit to the girls in the barn, but only for a moment. He's tired.

"I like Seattle," Toby tells Eleanor before heading to bed. "But there's too many people. It's good to be home."

Home. For Toby, a refuge. For Eleanor, increasingly, the house on the old farm feels like a box she's outgrown but sees no way of escaping.

21.

No pancakes. No waffles.

Then there's Ursula. Though things between Eleanor and her formerly sunny, once-loving middle child are better than they had been during that terrible stretch of years when Ursula no longer spoke to her, she still keeps her mother at a wary distance.

It's a fact of her life Eleanor has come, slowly, to accept, that Ursula seems to have closed the door to her heart where Eleanor's concerned. What Eleanor yearns for now—the best she can hope for, she figures—is a connection with her daughter's children, Orson and Lulu, who carry no grievances toward their grandmother, never having spent enough time with her to acquire them.

Orson's still a baby, but sometimes Eleanor allows herself to imagine how it would be if Orson and his older sister were allowed to come for a sleepover one day at the farm—an idea Ursula has vetoed every time Eleanor suggests it. Or just Lulu could come, Eleanor suggests to Ursula. If she thinks Orson's too young.

She pictures the meal she and Lulu might prepare together if Ursula allowed it, and after, how they'd curl up on the couch with a stack of her children's old books. In the morning she'd make pancakes or waffles and let Lulu squirt whipped cream on the top.

Maybe not whipped cream. Ursula wouldn't approve.

"You and Jake could go away for a romantic weekend, or just a night even," Eleanor told her one time. Never mind the two-hour drive. She'd welcome it. "I'd love to look after the kids."

"Thanks, Mother," Ursula tells Eleanor. (*Mother.* Somewhere along the line, back when she was a teenager, Ursula stopped calling Eleanor Mom. She's *Mother* now.)

"But even if we could afford some kind of getaway, Jake and I don't leave our children with people," Ursula told her.

As hurtful as it is being on the receiving end of Ursula's chilly behavior, and living in fear of the possibility of getting cut off from Ursula altogether again, as she did before, what saddens Eleanor most is the sense she gets on those rare moments when she and her daughter speak—recognition of the fact that Ursula's unhappy. Even from a distance—their conversations never going beyond weather and school schedules—it's not hard to recognize that Ursula and Jake are having trouble in their marriage.

Shortly after the birth of Orson—in the last months of Cam's life—Jake was laid off from his job coaching basketball at the same private school where Ursula's star has been rising rapidly. She's an assistant principal now. Jake collects unemployment.

A year later, Jake remains home every day, on the computer mostly, from what Eleanor gathers. On the basis of a single short visit to Vermont, Eleanor has observed that he watches TV a lot, having developed a disturbing allegiance to Rush Limbaugh and Sean Hannity, whose politics could not be further from Ursula's. No longer out on the soccer field with his players, Jake has put on weight. He's drinking a lot. Eleanor knows well—as a woman who was once, herself, a young mother responsible for paying the bills—

what it could do to a marriage when one partner earns money and the other doesn't.

Around Orson's first birthday, Jake and Ursula drive down to Akersville to pick up some of Cam's tools. Over dinner that night, Jake holds forth on what a loser Barack Obama is. "He's giving all the jobs to foreigners," Jake says. "Him and his angry bleeding-heart wife. What do you expect from a guy whose middle name is Hussein?"

Eleanor studies Ursula's face as her husband says this. If Ursula registers a reaction, she keeps it to herself. Ursula keeps a lot to herself these days, as she has for a long time now. Including, it seems to Eleanor—at least where her relationship with her mother is concerned—her heart.

Back when Cam and Eleanor first told the children they were separating, nobody had tried harder to save Eleanor and Cam's marriage than Ursula. When her efforts had failed, she blamed her mother. As much of a flake as her father could be, it seemed to Ursula that the greater crime was Eleanor's, for her inability to forgive him.

"Everyone makes mistakes," Ursula told Eleanor. "Can't you get over it?"

To Ursula, it was Eleanor's fault in the end. It was Eleanor who had moved to a condo, of all places, in a suburb full of rich people. Leaving her dad to fend for himself on the farm while, over in Brookline, Eleanor brought home sushi, the deluxe assortment platter. Her dad was the one who tried so hard to help Toby's brain get better—and he had. While her mother sat at her desk, writing those books about some little girl who went off to Antarctica to see penguins. This is how it looked to Ursula, anyway. All she knew to do was make it up to her dad the best she could by being the most perfect daughter ever. To him.

From the day they'd left the farm and moved into the condo, Ursula had hated Brookline. She hated her new school full of kids who dressed in J.Crew and went out for gelato together every afternoon after school but never invited her. She hated it that her father was off by himself on the farm now without his kids, eating a sweet potato for dinner. She hated going back and forth all the time: Brookline on weekdays, weekends at the farm. Her real home. No question about that.

She hated what had happened to her little brother, of course. Hated the sound of her mother's voice on the phone to some friend of hers, late at night when she thought Ursula couldn't hear, complaining about her father not paying the bills. This was her dad they were talking about.

She never said anything. Ursula wasn't that type. She just sent out her silent hate-waves in her mother's direction. They hit their mark.

22.

Like a pair of parentheses

Weekends when Ursula got dropped off at the farm, after the divorce, she tried to cook for her dad. Eight years old when the new routine began—the back-and-forth—she found a Betty Crocker cookbook at a yard sale. Every weekend, she picked out a different recipe—simple meals, pigs in a blanket, celery sticks with cream cheese dip—and made extra so he'd have leftovers to get him partway through the week. With her mother gone, she figured someone needed to take care of her father. That person would be her.

When her dad and Coco had gotten together, Ursula registered relief. She didn't have to work so hard anymore, trying to make her father happy. Someone else had that job now. She was off-duty, almost. (Except she wasn't. Not once Jake came into the picture, and there was a whole new man to look after. Not to mention the two children who joined them soon after.)

It was definitely weird at first that Coco had been their babysitter. Maybe her father was a little old to have a wife who'd graduated from high school only a few years before, but the good news was, he wouldn't be lonely anymore. Ursula wouldn't have to worry about him so much now that there was someone else to do that. Maybe she'd get to be happy again, too, if that wasn't too much to ask for.

And they'd all loved Coco. Even Eleanor had, once. Coco had been hanging out with their family, going on their annual trip to Maine with them even, and always there at her dad's softball games, cheering when he did something good, which her mother probably never even noticed anymore. Coco was always fun, unlike Eleanor, who stayed at her desk, even on Saturdays, working on her greeting cards and children's books, and a bunch of other things Ursula couldn't keep track of. Eleanor had a worried look on her face from the minute she got out of bed in the morning. How was that for a crazy situation: that her serious, no-fun mother, whose mouth stayed in a straight line, used to draw a *comic* strip—*a comic strip!*—not to mention it was about their family.

Here was a thing Ursula noticed about her mother, as she was during those years following the divorce. She always had these two lines on her forehead. Not her forehead exactly. In that place between her eyebrows. Like a pair of parentheses, a frown that never went away. Unlike Coco, who always looked happy. Unlike her dad, who never looked worried about anything. Most likely because he wasn't.

23.

Basically, my family's a mess

The year Al turned thirteen, Eleanor and Al had a big blowup—something about a Guns N' Roses CD he was playing too loud. Al called their mother a bitch. Eleanor slapped him. Next thing you knew their dad's truck had pulled up in front of their condo and Al was throwing his bag in the back.

Al moved home to the farm. Ursula, not quite twelve, stuck it out another six months before she did the same.

Once Ursula left Brookline and moved back in with her dad—her dad, plus Coco and Elijah now—things were better, only now she had to deal with her mother looking sad and hurt every time she came to see them, as if she was the world's biggest victim. She didn't have to listen to her mother's late-night phone calls with her friends anymore, but she knew what Eleanor would be telling them. The number one theme: what a terrible person her father was.

Ursula was thirteen years old—Jake one year older—when they met. It was the beginning of eighth grade, the year after Ursula had left Brookline and moved back to Akersville.

She'd gone to a basketball game with her friend Cassie. Cassie had a crush on the star player on the team, a popular boy named Ranger. Jake wasn't tall like Ranger, or particularly handsome, but she could tell by just watching him on the court what a good person he was. That first time she spotted Jake, Ursula knew he was the one for her.

He was the shortest on the team, a point guard. He handled the ball as if he'd been born with it in his hands, but that wasn't the thing that made him stand out most on the court. What Ursula had noticed about Jake was the way he encouraged the other players, how he'd call out "good job" and "way to go" any time one of his teammates made a great play.

Ursula didn't know much about basketball, but she knew enough to understand that Jake was one of those people who didn't feel a need—the way Cassie's crush, Ranger, did, for example—to get the glory and be the star. What mattered for Jake was the team—working together to get the ball to the other end of the court and score points. Jake's job was defending the basket and later—when he switched over to soccer—the goal.

After the game, she and Cassie met up with a bunch of boys on the team. The others were all showing off for the popular girls. Jake paid attention to Ursula. "You were at another school before this, right?" he said. "Me too."

It turned out they had a lot in common. Messed up parents, top of the list.

Jake's mother had moved to Akersville right around the time Eleanor had left. She'd rented a crummy apartment over the laundromat after his father took off for Florida with a woman he'd met at work who was only twelve years older than Jake.

Not only had Jake's dad left Jake's mother—as Ursula believed her mother had left her dad. It got worse: Jake's dad had a set of twins with this person. From the day he left, Jake never saw his father again. His mother started drinking a lot. Money was a problem. Jake got himself to soccer practice—he played baseball and basketball, depending on the season—and when he came home after a game or practice it was up to him to make dinner.

"Your lousy good-for-nothing father," Jake's mother used to say to him, as he stood at the stove, stirring the spaghetti sauce or frying the hamburgers. "Your lousy father fucked his secretary and left me holding the bag."

Jake never understood exactly what that meant—*holding the bag*—but it wasn't good, obviously. He was only fourteen years old, but in addition to knowing how to play basketball, he could cook. He'd taught himself.

"Your lousy no-good father's probably eating steak tonight," Jake's mother would say as he served her dinner—rice, beans, canned vegetables. Ursula could relate. Her mother never complained about her dad to her face, but she conveyed, to her children, that same sense of perpetual disappointment.

"Don't you hate it when parents want you to take sides?" Jake said to Ursula.

Oh God, did she ever. Why couldn't they all just love each other the way they used to?

"When I have kids, I'm never going to be like that," Jake told her. It was odd for a fourteen-year-old boy to talk about being a father someday, but Ursula liked that about him. "One more thing. I'm never getting a divorce. Not in a million years."

"Me neither," Ursula told him. It was the number one topic they agreed on.

In an odd way, the role Jake played on the basketball court and the soccer field reminded Ursula of the one she played in her family. *Team player*, they called Jake. The same could be said of Ursula— always looking out for the others, trying to make sure they were okay, encouraging them, backing them up, same as Jake did in games. Jake was never the star, but he was always there when his team needed him, passing the ball to the right person.

In the old days—meaning the days her parents were together—Ursula might not have actually called out "way to go" to her father if he did something nice for her mother, or "good job" when her mom made her father's favorite dinner, but she had kept an eye out at all times—urging Al to be nicer to their father, offering to read to Toby when he got wild and she could tell her mother needed a break.

Her specialty was offering positive reinforcement. She'd learned this term from an article she'd read in one of her mother's magazines, while she was sitting on the toilet. "Positive reinforcement." She wrote the words on her wrist in ballpoint pen, to remind herself. *Point out the good things instead of the bad,* the article recommended. *Look at life like a glass of lemonade. Not half empty. Half full!*

Only once her parents got divorced, there was nothing positive to reinforce anymore. The two of them might as well have lived on two different planets after that. Two countries, anyway. At war with each other. With Ursula and Al and Toby stuck in some kind of no-man's-land, having no idea which way to run.

Away, was the main thing. Away from the person who reminded her best of everything she hated about her life, which was mainly just one big awful thing: that her parents had gotten a divorce.

"Basically, my family's a mess," Ursula told Jake, the first time they'd really talked with each other (for three hours), which happened to be two days after she'd watched him on the basketball court and decided, then and there, he was her destiny.

"My little brother's brain got messed up when he almost drowned in a pond," she told Jake. "My older sister wants to be a boy. My mother hates my father. My father spent a bunch of time being sad because my mother left and he didn't get to be with us anymore and now he has a wife who used to be our babysitter and they have a new baby, so he's happy again. And when my parents got a divorce I had to leave my friends at my old school, and I hated living in Brookline, and then I left and my mother put this big guilt trip on me. And I did everything I could to make it better but none of it worked."

"I'll be your friend," Jake said to Ursula. Then he kissed her.

"We should get married someday," Jake told her.

Eight years later they did.

24.

An amazing invention

From the day he was born, when his parents put him in a pink sleeper suit, no doubt, Al hated being Alison. Young as he was, he knew the truth about himself and who he was, really. Which was a boy.

Early on he had made it clear to his parents and everyone else that he had no intention of putting on a dress ever again. (His parents accepted this, more or less. His grandmother kept sending frilly outfits. Generally pink.)

Then he cut off his hair. Not long before his parents' divorce, he'd made the announcement that going forward, his name would be Al, not Alison. But even that failed to address the core problem. It wasn't simply that Al wanted to be like a boy. He knew he was one already. He had been born into the wrong body was all. Nobody understood this. He was all alone. The only place he got to be himself was when he was working on his computer. Writing code.

Until Toby's accident, Al kept his true identity secret. He chose the name Ali as a kind of neutral middle ground. But after his parents' marriage had exploded, all bets were off. Nothing was the way it used to be anyway: not Toby, not their parents' marriage, not the world. If everything was going be different, Al might as well be different, too. He stopped pretending to be Alison. He was a boy now. Simple as that.

Nobody noticed. Everyone was so busy being sad about Toby, nobody cared all that much about what was going on with Al, off in his room, lifting a couple of bricks he kept hidden in his closet to make his muscles grow bigger, wrapping bandages around his chest before any breasts started to grow there, as if he could head them off at the pass. Dreading the day he knew was coming, when he'd start to menstruate. Pretending, when it happened, it was just some strange injury, like maybe he'd jumped over a fence and got cut by barbed wire. The kind of thing that might happen to a boy.

Al didn't say anything about this part, but in his own head, he thought of himself only with male pronouns now. His strategy was to keep a low profile, attract as little attention as possible. Duck and cover, which translated into *Stay in your room. Just come out for meals, and even then, only when absolutely necessary.* That song they used to sing every night before dinner, "Simple Gifts," felt like a bad joke now, made worse by Eleanor's insistence that they hold hands while singing and pass a silent squeeze around the table.

To bow and to bend we shan't be ashamed, to turn, turn, will be our delight, till by turning, turning, we come round right . . .

Al had always loved computers and programming. Now he found his solace there, and something else—a world where it didn't matter what your body looked like, or who people thought you were. All that mattered was the code you wrote, and if you were good at that, that was as much identity as you'd ever need.

Al was good at writing code. All those hours he spent in his room now, Al read magazines like *BYTE* and the book that had become, by age ten, Al's bible: *The C-Programming Language.* When they'd announced a science fair at school—eighth grade—he came up with his big idea.

His teacher, Mr. Earle, had handed out a list of possible science fair project ideas to the class. Grow bean plants in four different locations, measuring the height and recording the foliage color of each. Breed fruit flies. Divide planaria. He'd even suggested that old chestnut for the more research-minded students—or those most lacking in imagination—to construct a papier-mâché volcano and write a report on volcanic activity around the globe.

That night Al had a dream about Toby. In this dream he saw Toby's old violin—the one he'd loved to play in the bathroom before the accident—sticking out of a trash can. Al and Toby were back in Suzuki class, only Toby kept telling their teacher "I can't play this anymore. I don't know how. My brain got messed up."

This was how it came to Al: The idea for a machine he'd build using his programming skills—a piece of equipment capable of creating musical notes and reproducing the sound of a wide range of instruments, employing a device he'd read about recently in one of his computer magazines, the Nav-vector board.

Ursula wasn't the only one in the family who set out to rescue their family after the disaster of Toby's accident. Al did, too. Just differently. His invention couldn't restore Toby's brain to how it had been, but it might actually allow his brother to make music again. He called his invention the TB-10, for Toby's age at the time.

Al's dream revealed everything to him—not only the function of his invention but the actual specifications for building it. To house the Nav-vector boards, Al would create a cylinder of plexiglass, cut with a hacksaw. His father had one in the studio. Cam was so distracted by the Toby situation that when Al asked to borrow it he hadn't even asked what he wanted it for.

"While you're at it," Al said, "could you lend me a drill?"

All that month and the next, alone in his room, Al labored over his invention. He said nothing about it to his family, and no one asked. Then came the great day when he charged it up.

The concept was simple enough. The boards encased in Al's cylinder, roughly the size of a football, emitted a vast range of sounds—actual musical notes that varied depending on the pitch and yaw at which you tipped the device.

But there was more. A person holding the TB-10 could totally alter the notes as well as the timbre of the sound, also the volume, by tipping the device at various angles. This gave it surprising and unexpected potential as an object people might take with them onto a dance floor and toss back and forth to one another, even, so long as they didn't drop it. With two TB-10s operating simultaneously, it should be possible to create harmonic sound. Music! Without knowing the first thing about playing an instrument.

Al had no interest in dancing himself. But he was in love with the device he'd constructed. His invention obsessed him. He spent every moment he had now—late into the night—perfecting it, resenting the time he had to spend at school.

Now and then, Ursula or Toby would make some comment about strange noises coming out of Al's room. He concealed them by playing a particularly abrasive and—to Al's ears—obnoxious Guns N' Roses CD at top volume while working (in the privacy of his closet) on the TB-10. It had been this, his mother's objection to his constant blasting of Axl Rose, that led to Al's showdown with her—the slap, the confiscation of his boom box, the call to his father (*my mother hit me*) and his father's arrival in Brookline an hour and a half later to take him away.

For this reason, Al's invention never made it to the science fair. By the time the fair took place, Al was living back on the farm with his father. The truth was, he had never cared about winning a prize for his project. For Al, the TB-10 had been about one thing only: making it possible for his little brother to participate in making music again. Bringing the old Toby back to them.

The part about his fight with Eleanor passed swiftly. Unlike the bitterness his sister displayed toward their mother, Al's anger toward her over the slap had been short-lived. Levelheaded and objective as Al was, even when young, he knew he'd deserved it. The larger issue between them—Al's recognition of his true gender, and his mother's failure to recognize it—remained unaddressed. He chose not to make an issue of it. He said nothing when his mother called him Ali and referred to him as her daughter. By the time he returned to the condo, just to pack the rest of his things, before moving back to the farm with his dad, he had given her a brief but affectionate hug.

"Don't take it personally, Mom," Al told her, on his way out to the car. (Cam was waiting for him out front in the truck.) "I just need to get away for a while."

He was biding his time until high school graduation. Then he'd be gone. His family might think he was simply heading to college, but there was a far greater journey ahead. Al was already planning his transition from girl to man. Soon enough, the person known as Alison would disappear forever. Goodbye and good riddance.

Meanwhile, Al kept his head down, stayed under the radar. His specialty. No need for discussion concerning his gender or what he planned to do about it. That day he'd returned for his things Al had actually admitted to his mother that he wasn't much of a Guns N' Roses fan.

"It wasn't really about you," he told her. "I was just mad in general. Sometimes when a person's feeling that way, it helps to turn the music up."

The reason he'd been playing the *Appetite for Destruction* CD that day had less and less to do with loving Axl Rose—and nothing to do with his issues concerning his sexual identity. He'd just wanted privacy. He'd wanted to surprise Toby with the invention he'd created. He'd had to drown out the sounds it made while he was still building it. Guns N' Roses, played at top volume, accomplished that.

Al spent much of high school perfecting the TB-10. He revised and refined the design a hundred times. This wasn't just a way of helping Toby. Al believed his invention would open up the world of music for disabled people everywhere, for whom playing an instrument had previously seemed impossible. The TB-10 would help those with cerebral palsy or MS, those missing a limb or suffering spinal cord injuries that severely limited the use of their hands. Now all those people could make music again. Again, or for the first time in their lives.

Finally, after two and a half years of working on it, the great day came for Al to unveil his invention to Toby. He set the stage with care, waiting until Ursula was off at a basketball game. He set the TB-10, fully charged, on a table in his room, a glass of chocolate milk beside it.

"Come in my room, Tobes," Al said. "I have a surprise for you."

Toby was always happy to spend time with Al. So often Al was too busy for him.

"Sit here." Al indicated a pillow in the corner. He handed his brother the chocolate milk. He picked up the TB-10. "Listen."

The demo started slowly. At first Al just moved his device from side to side, letting the notes come. Just a low tone to start off with, like the sound a conductor might make when an orchestra was tuning their instruments. One long note, soft at first, then louder. Richer. Filling the room. (Al took particular pride in the speakers he'd built into the TB-10. With little space to operate in, he'd managed to give them a surprising sound.)

He shifted the device sideways, slightly. A different note came out. From his spot on the pillow, Toby sat motionless, taking it in. He took a sip of his chocolate milk.

Then Al moved the TB-10 from side to side, transferring it between his hands, lowering it to the floor, tipping it sideways. A single musical phrase emerged, then a tune—almost otherworldly, as if, off on a mountaintop somewhere, a milkmaid were humming. Coming closer now, as birds surrounded her.

He waved the device over his head. He moved it up and down like a painter making brushstrokes in the atmosphere. What came out of it sounded like a song, one neither of them had ever heard.

As much as Al cared about the performance of the TB-10, the true object of his focus remained his brother. Toby seemed to be mirroring the motions of Al's body with his head, nodding along with the up-and-down of the device, the sideways motion. Times when the TB-10 held steady, so did Toby, waiting for the next note. His eyes remained fixed on the magical cylinder as he listened to the sounds emanating from it.

Al took a seat on the chair beside his brother, but did not stop moving the device. From his spot on the pillow, Toby leaned to lay his head on Al's knee. He set down the glass of milk. He closed his eyes. For a moment, Al allowed the TB-10 to rest motionless. It appeared his brother might have fallen asleep.

"Don't stop," Toby murmured. "I love the music. Keep playing."

"You take it now," Al told him. "It's for you. You can make music, too. That's the point. That's why I made it."

He set the TB-10 into his brother's hands. For a moment Toby just sat there staring at Al's amazing invention.

"You do it," he said.

"I don't know how."

"It's easy. I'll show you." He wrapped Toby's fingers around the plexiglass cylinder and moved his hand for him. A single tone came out of it. Another.

A look of confusion came over Toby's face. Toby was seldom a fearful person, but he was frightened. He let go. The TB-10 dropped to the floor. A sound came out of it. Not a pleasant one this time.

"I like when you make it go," Toby told Al. "I just want to listen."

"Give it a try," Al said. "You'll like it once you get the hang of it."

Toby sat there, holding the TB-10 in his hands. "This is a really nice invention," he said. "I think you should give it to someone else. Ursula maybe."

"Remember how it was at first, getting on your bike," Al said. "You didn't used to like pesto, but now you do."

Toby shook his head. In all the years, Al could not remember a time when his brother had expressed anger, but now he did.

"I told you no," Toby said. "I like to listen to music. I don't want to play music. I can't do that anymore."

"You always loved music," Al said. They had an unspoken rule in the family that they did not speak about Toby as he'd been before.

"Remember your little violin?" Al said. "Our Suzuki lessons? How you played in the bathroom because that's where it sounded the best."

"*Stop it,*" Toby said. "I told you already. I'm not that person anymore."

As he spoke the words, Al had been moving across the room, waving the TB-10 through the air and flailing his arms as odd, discordant notes came from the speakers. Now he set it down. The device went silent.

"I'm sorry," Al said. If anyone should understand what it was to have your family try to make you into a person you weren't, he of all people should have understood. "I'll never do that again."

25.

An encounter with Bill Gates

Al put the device away but never forgot about it.

The summer he graduated from high school—1995 now—he'd boarded a plane for Texas to attend a conference sponsored by

Microsoft at the Dallas Hilton. He'd earned the registration fee—
$250—by mowing lawns the summer before and selling a gold
heart locket his grandmother had given him for his thirteenth
birthday—an item he had no interest in wearing. Ever.

Al had read about the conference in *Programmers' Monthly*. The
title of the event was "Neural Networks as They Relate to Genetic Al-
gorithms." To someone like his mother, or equally his father, these
words would have meant nothing. For Al it was a thrill just reading
them.

As a person who had felt like an outsider all his life—loving his
family without ever feeling he belonged, not even called by the
name he had chosen, or the gender that accompanied it—Al had
wondered whether it could be possible that here in this place so
far removed from his New Hampshire farmhouse, he might locate
what he had longed for always: a community. His tribe.

He was eighteen years old. In preparation for the trip, Al bought
three pairs of chinos and two identical button-down shirts. He
wore different clothes until he reached the airport. He waited until nobody else appeared to be occupying the men's room and then
changed clothes there—pants belted, shirt tucked in.

When the plane landed, he took a taxi straight to the conference.
His heart was racing as he stepped into the ballroom. Scanning the
hall, with its endless rows of tables set up for laptops, all facing a
giant screen and a podium where the first presenter would deliver
the keynote address, Al found a spot near the back.

His fellow attendees were a diverse group—mostly young, though
a few appeared as old as forty. With a handful of exceptions—a guy
in a purple jumpsuit, one wearing a kilt—most wore nondescript
clothes, generally sweatpants. Some wore baseball caps. Nobody
appeared to have given any concern to their appearance.

Within minutes of taking his seat he understood that here at
last, in this vast ballroom, he had found a place where he might be
recognized for the one thing shared by every single person here:
a passion for everything to do with technology. Nothing else mattered.

There was one other distinctive aspect to the people in the ballroom that day. Every single one of them was male. In this room, for the first time in his nearly two decades of life, Al felt like one of the boys.

The first presenter, Doug Planter, was a Most Valuable Player from Microsoft and no more than ten years older than Al, probably, speaking on the topic of object-oriented programming. "Microsoft has this field all sewn up," he said, from the front of the room, his voice practically trembling with excitement. He was wearing Nikes, and paced the floor of the stage, waving his arms.

Doug Planter directed those in attendance to turn to their screens. Their registration fee to the conference had entitled them to a download of a brand-new program about to be released by the company. "You're welcome to follow along as I talk you through the software," Doug told them. "Let's have some fun!" From the floor below, the rows of attendees manning their desktops clicked furiously on their keyboards.

A couple of hours into the day—partway through the second presentation—a thrilling event occurred. At first all Al heard was a murmur from somewhere behind him, the voice of someone—a fellow attendee—crying out, "Oh my God!" Then others joining his. A ripple—electric—of excitement. One whole table of conference participants had stood up now, then another, all of them cheering. From where he sat—then stood—it took Al a moment to understand what was going on. Then he did.

Dressed in a manner closely resembling the majority of attendees—chinos, button-down shirt not unlike Al's—Bill Gates himself had entered the ballroom. Nobody introduced him, but recognizing the commotion his entrance had created, he called out to the crowd, "Don't let me interrupt what you're up to, guys. I'm just here to observe."

Bill Gates did not approach the podium. He wandered through the aisles along the many tables filled with the laptops of those in attendance, all of them at work implementing the new material they'd been given to work on. Nobody who might have entered this room—Madonna, Michael Jordan, the president—could have inspired comparable excitement. At one table, a cluster of particularly enthusiastic attendees had gotten up from their seats to get closer to their man.

With a friendly smile, Bill Gates waved them off. "Down dogs!" he called out. They obeyed.

Then an extraordinary thing happened. Just as he reached the section of the table where Al sat over the laptop he'd worked for two years to purchase, working on the program they'd all just been given, Bill Gates stopped. He leaned in over Al's laptop, studying the code Al had been inputting.

"Crackerjack, man," he said. "I can see our program is going to work for you. You're one of us."

Bill Gates did not linger long. A moment later he was on to the next person. But Al had received his gift, and it would change everything. Here in this hotel ballroom, in a city he'd never visited before, surrounded by men whose names were mostly unknown to him, Al found what he'd been looking for all his life.

"One of us," he'd been called, by the man who was the closest Al had to a god. There was a place he fit in. He'd never leave it. He was home.

26.

Dancing at Olive Garden

That fall Al enrolled in the systems engineering program at Stanford. Like Bill Gates, he chose not to complete his studies at college. He went, for a semester, to Oxford—mostly to put as much distance between himself and his family at a time when he needed to separate himself from the life he'd lived with them and the person he'd been when he was living it. Choosing not to let his family know his whereabouts—a hard choice but a necessary one, to keep them in the dark while he was figuring things out—he returned to Boston, working for a data-base provider called Sybase. He liked the work well enough and it was good getting a regular paycheck. He was going through his transition now. The surgery had not come cheap.

The year he turned twenty-four—his transition complete at last, with a full beard courtesy of the hormones—Al reached out to Microsoft introducing himself and suggesting that he come for a job interview.

"I'm going to be in Seattle next month," he wrote to the head of the division where he saw himself—design and innovation. A letter came back to him, with a date and time to show up at the company's headquarters.

Al was ready to take on whatever they might offer him. But he also had a file of ideas to present, if given the chance. Among these— though he recognized this fell well outside Microsoft territory—was the TB-10. He still had the prototype and hoped he might show his device to someone there.

It was the post-9/11 world now. Al understood, before flying west, that to a TSA screener the TB-10 would look too much like a bomb to be allowed on the plane, so (not without trepidation; this was an item whose construction had occupied years of his life) he chose to ship it ahead to the address of the hotel where he'd booked a three-night stay.

The company executive with whom Al had met, Rick Magnuson, offered him a job on the spot. After, he took Al around the office and introduced him to a number of other programmers there. Everyone was young—some younger than Al, even. One of them, Harry, invited Al to join him and a group of others on his team for lunch.

They went to Olive Garden. It didn't matter how much these men were earning. (Plenty, probably.) They were not the kind to care deeply about the meals they ate.

That morning, on his way to the interview, Al had stuck the TB-10 in his backpack. He had little expectation that he'd have an opportunity to demonstrate his device to anyone at Microsoft, but he had brought it with him just in case.

There in the restaurant, gathered around the table eating their sandwiches, one of the guys had mentioned that he'd attended a show the previous weekend, the Foo Fighters.

"God, I'd give anything if I could play guitar like Dave Grohl," he'd told the group. That was the first time, all day, that Al had heard anyone exchange an observation outside the topic of technology. In the time the men had spent talking animatedly over lunch—strictly the language of programming—nobody had mentioned girlfriends or partners, hobbies outside work, trips, books they'd read, pets. Now, hearing Joe express regret at his inability to play music, Al reached for his backpack. He set the TB-10 on the table.

A respectful silence came over them. These were men who recognized a piece of innovative technology when they saw one.

Suddenly Al felt a wave of freedom—joy, even—he had seldom if ever experienced. It came to him in the company of six men he had not met until an hour before. It came to him because he knew he'd be accepted here.

He took the TB-10 in his hands and stepped away from the table. "Let me show you something," Al said. "I made this for my little brother."

He cradled the plexiglass case against his chest. "Let's start with guitar," he said. He clicked a button. Then with his right hand outstretched like Peyton Manning preparing to throw a pass, he raised, toward the ceiling, the invention he had first constructed almost a decade before. Now he waved the device in the air, tipping it from one side to the other. Quietly and slowly at first, then in rhythm with his rocking device, a song emerged—the Shaker hymn his family had sung before dinner every night of his childhood, "Simple Gifts." Now came a gently strumming guitar, then something resembling a sad violin, then a cheerful flute, a raucous saxophone, a wailing clarinet—but different. The music produced by the TB-10 was like nothing any of them had ever heard. Like sounds emanating from another planet.

Under any other circumstances Al would never attract attention to himself as he did at this moment. He could do this because it wasn't him performing. It was the TB-10. In Al's hands, the instrument filled the air with magic. The whole restaurant was listening, and when the song ended the patrons burst into whistles and cheers.

In the midst of it all, the lead guy from the Microsoft gang at Al's table hollered, "Hey, genius boy, give me that thing!" Pretty soon the TB-10 was getting tossed around the table. The song started again but quickly turned into squawks and louder squawks. When the manager approached, Joe handed the TB-10 back to Al. The programmers went silent, though they were all grinning as Joe signed the check.

As they got up to leave, they all patted Al on the back. "Welcome aboard," Joe told him.

Al returned to Boston that weekend, only long enough to pack up his apartment. He would have liked to say goodbye to his parents, and Toby, all back at the farm. But Al wasn't ready yet for them to meet the New Al. He sent them a card instead: "Got a job in Washington State. Moving this week. Love."

He was back in Seattle ten days later. He was here to stay.

27.

If I married a man who didn't love me

Al's design for the TB-10 went no place, but his invention had served Al well. Almost six years after he was hired at Microsoft, having proven himself as a valued and trusted worker as well as a brilliant one, Al was put in charge of overseeing the technical presentation of a software product, the SQL Server, with the plan of pitching it to Boeing. He spent two months on the project, staying at the lab past midnight, sometimes. Falling asleep at his desk. Waking a few hours later to get back to work.

When the day came to make his presentation, the company provided Al with a chauffeured limousine to bring him to Boeing headquarters. He'd been informed that a young woman from the marketing division would accompany him for this important event.

He bought a good sports coat and new shoes for the Boeing pitch, and also opted for a step up from his usual white tube socks. The woman assigned to go along with him, the Microsoft VP of marketing who would propose the terms of the contract—worth nearly a million dollars in the first year alone—met him in the lobby of

Microsoft headquarters. She wore a suit, perfectly fitted. Conservative but classy. Though Al normally paid little attention to this kind
of thing, he could not help but recognize her elegant legs, the turn
of her calf. As fully as he'd made his transition to manhood, Al had
never been with a woman. He'd never kissed a woman. Here now
was a woman he wanted to kiss.

"I'm Teresa," she said. There was only the slightest indication of
an accent in her voice.

"Let's go get 'em," Al told her. Six years at Microsoft had taught him
a way of speaking that would once have felt like a foreign language.

In the car on the way over to the offices where they were making
their pitch, Al and Teresa planned out their approach. As the technical lead on the project, it was up to Al to walk the Boeing IT techs
through what made Microsoft's product superior to IBM's. Teresa
would take over the meeting when the time came to discuss the
contract. Their conversation seemed not simply easy but effortless.
More than once, Al had found himself doing something rare for
him. Smiling.

The presentation went well. When it was over, the head of the
Boeing team showed them around their offices, introducing the two
of them. "It's not official yet," he said, "but I think we'll be seeing
more of these two."

In the car on the way back to their company's offices in Redmond,
Al made a suggestion—out of character for him.

"What do you say we go celebrate?" he asked Teresa. "You name
your favorite kind of food."

That would be Mexican.

She told him much more over dinner. Her parents had come from
Michoachán as teenagers. The two of them worked as strawberry
pickers in Texas and raised their daughter and sons to have what
they had not—a college education. The youngest in her family, Teresa was a rising star at Microsoft—smart, funny, and beautiful. It
was her goal, she told Al, to earn enough money to buy her parents a
house and make it possible for them to retire. She was almost there.

In the middle of their dinner, he had interrupted their conversation to take a phone call. After, he apologized.

"I'd never do that under normal circumstances," he told Teresa. "But when my brother calls I always pick up. He has special needs. My parents look out for Toby, but I guess you could say I'm his person."

"Maybe you need to go?" she asked him. "That sounded important."

He shook his head. "He'll be okay. He was just sad about something."

How was someone supposed to explain—in the middle of a dinner in which they were celebrating the apparent success of a deal that would earn a few million dollars for Microsoft, and a significant bonus for the two of them, no doubt—that one of Toby's goats had gone into labor that morning? A stillbirth.

Only he did tell Teresa. It was unlike Al to say anything about his personal life at work, or anywhere else, for that matter. Something about this woman made him feel he could.

They'd talked until the waitress came over to let them know the restaurant was closing. In the car, bringing Teresa back to her apartment, Al told her he needed to explain something about himself. A block from where she lived, he asked the driver to let them off. They'd walk the rest of the way.

It was the first time Al had ever felt able to reach out to a woman as he did now. Though he'd been living as a man for several years by this point, he hadn't gone on a date with anyone.

"I was born with a female body," he told her. "I always knew I wasn't who people imagined."

He had not planned this. But he could no longer imagine not letting Teresa know the truth about himself. The two of them looked out at Elliot Bay, the lights of the city glittering before them. The sound of a ferry horn—deep and low—cut through the night. For a few minutes, neither of them spoke.

"So I'm not who you thought," he said.

"You are exactly who I thought you were," she told him. "An honest man."

They were married two years later on his father's farm back in New Hampshire, with both their families in attendance—his parents, also his sister and brother and his sister's child, and Teresa's mother and father and brothers, along with a Catholic priest Teresa's parents had requested to officiate. A mariachi band came all the way from Texas to play.

At some point early on in their relationship, Al had asked Teresa if her family had a problem with her choice of a husband.

"My parents would have a problem if I married a man who didn't love me well," she said. "My parents would have a problem if I wasn't happy."

Her parents had no problem, she told Al. They gave the couple their blessing.

28.

To babies

Cam has been dead for over a year by the time—late fall now, the water in the pond not yet frozen, leaves long gone from the trees, branches bare, frost on the ground, and Eleanor still living on the farm—the family finally comes together to celebrate Cam's life and mark his death. They've agreed to make it a small gathering. Only those who'd meant the most to Cam. Eleanor qualifies.

Al and Teresa make the trip from the West Coast—flying in on a Saturday with the plan of leaving Sunday afternoon to be back in Seattle for meetings Monday morning. Though Eleanor knows from Teresa that she and Al have been trying IVF now, she doesn't ask how it's going. But at their family dinner Eleanor notices that Teresa, who has always enjoyed wine, has refrained from drinking. Ursula must have observed this, too, but unlike Eleanor, she brings it up.

"Just club soda, Teresa?" Ursula says, passing her the large bowl of the meal that was always the family favorite, spaghetti carbonara. "What's the story?"

The others at the table look surprised and embarrassed. (All but Toby. Toby is never embarrassed.) It's Al, not Teresa, who responds.

"We were going to hold off till the holidays to tell you all," he says. "But since we're all together we might as well share our news. With everyone feeling sad about Dad, this is probably good timing. The IVF worked on Teresa's first cycle. The baby's due next summer."

There's a lot of whooping then, with hugs all around. Elijah, who has driven all night from a gig in Pennsylvania to join them, pats his brother on the back. "With a couple of brainiac parents like you two," he says, "this kid will probably be heading up a computer empire by the time she's in fifth grade." Nobody reminds him that given the circumstances, there is no way Al has contributed to the gene pool for this baby.

For Eleanor, the IQ of her future grandchild is immaterial. It's enough to know that her son and his wife will have the thing they wanted more than anything in the world. They get to be parents.

When they raise their glasses—champagne for everyone but Teresa and, in solidarity, Al—it's Toby who offers the toast.

"To babies," he says—his words echoing through the room as the others repeat them. What did it matter in the end, if a child grows up to run a software company or raise goats? Whoever this child turns out to be, a baby represents the future.

First, though, they need to honor the past.

29.

Great hair

𝔅 ury my ashes under the pear tree," Cam had told Eleanor, one night not long before the end. This much they'd done—just Toby and Eleanor, the summer before, knowing the others couldn't make it. Cam had made it clear that they didn't need to make a big deal of this.

"But save out a few for when all the kids can make it back to the farm," he said. "Scatter a few handfuls at the waterfall. For old times' sake."

There's snow on the ground by the time they manage to pull this

off—a gathering with all four of Cam's children, three of them Eleanor's. It's early December, and there's a stiff wind blowing, but they
choose to go by foot.

Eleanor must have made this particular half-mile walk a thousand times—starting when she was not yet twenty, on her own—
that time she first met Timmy Pouliot fishing for trout—then with
Cam, then with Cam and the children. Back in those days she always kept an eagle eye on Toby, knowing how wild he was—the one
of their children who could get into trouble faster than anybody.
In the end, of course, it wasn't in the swirling water of those falls
where trouble found him, but the shallow pool of their own quiet
little pond. A person never knew where danger might lie. Seldom
where she anticipated it.

This was the place where, every March, they'd brought the little
boats and the people they made to ride inside them to launch in the
brook. Over the years Cam had accompanied Eleanor and the children less and less for the launching of the cork people. After those
first few years he stayed in his woodshop or headed off to craft fairs.
In a manner not so different from what happens when rushing water cuts through a stream bed—eroding the edges, deepening the
divide—the gulf between him and Eleanor had widened.

Though in the normal course of events they made their trips to
the waterfall in warm weather, Eleanor had brought the children
there on the day the *Challenger* exploded. Wanting to be somewhere
she loved, someplace that reminded her that some things remained
solid and unchanging, even at a moment when it felt as if nothing
would ever be the same, Eleanor had stopped at the falls on the way
home from picking the three of them up at the bus. There was nothing any mother could do at such a moment to take away the grief
and confusion, but she'd wanted to keep her children close that afternoon. Maybe she wanted to convey to them a silent message: Here's a
part of your world you can count on. This, at least, will never change.

Only things did change. Everything, as it turned out. What could
a person count on, really? A pile of rocks? A stream, racing past, roaring so loud you couldn't hear the sound of your own voice telling your
youngest child, "You're too close to the water. Hold my hand."

Eleanor and Cam had known their troubles before Toby's accident. They'd drifted apart—so slowly you'd barely notice—in the way people so often do when they're raising children together. Eleanor can still remember the thought coming to her, the strange irony that accompanied the state of parenthood. First there's just the two of you, and if you're lucky, as Cam and Eleanor had been, it's this wild love you feel for each other in the beginning that inspires you to want to make a child together. (And maybe another after that. Two more, in their case.)

Then it begins. You end up falling in love with your child, and before you know it she's become the object of all the energy and passion you used to devote to the person who made you want to have the child in the first place.

If they aren't careful, the two people who started the whole thing off may lose sight of each other, and what's left of all the love that started things off are the children.

Toby's accident had caused a terrible rift. Then came the day Eleanor found her husband parked by the falls with Coco in the front seat of his truck.

Look at them now. Twenty-five years earlier, when it seemed to Eleanor that her family had been blown apart as irretrievably as that space capsule, she would not have imagined that the day would come when she'd stand in this spot on the rocks with their three grown children and Cam's son by the woman who came after her, to scatter his ashes. As sad as this moment feels, she's grateful she can be here, grateful to share it with the children. Making the familiar walk with them now, the thought comes to Eleanor, that a profound shift has occurred in her feeling about her children's father and the family they once occupied together.

She knows now, as she did not once, what matters and what really doesn't. At fifty-eight years old, Eleanor has reached a stage in her life when it no longer makes sense to revisit all the old grievances or to hold on to bitterness that hurt nobody as much as one's self. She has forgiven Cam for all the ways he disappointed and hurt her. She has had to forgive herself, too, for her own vast catalog of shortcomings and failures, poor choices, damage incurred to those she loved and to herself. She knows now what she did not before, that every family's history is made up of many stories—all probably possessing some element of truth, but none of them, individually, containing all of it.

There could be no repairing the old mistakes. All a person could hope for was to do better in the future.

Eleanor has put on a dress for this event. Toby must have felt a similar need to mark the occasion; he's wearing a vest and a top hat Ursula gave him once, in honor of their old days when they'd put on their circus extravaganzas for the family. Al's brought a good camera. Ursula, looking harried as usual, has left her children home with their father—the reason, she says, that she needs to take off as soon as they're done here. She has made it plain to Eleanor that her decision to stay at the farm the night before was a one-time-only event.

"Lulu's been suffering from anxiety and Jake can't even remember where we keep Orson's diapers," she explains to them. "I have to get back."

One other person is expected to join them today. Coco. "Are you sure you don't mind?" Elijah asked Eleanor, before inviting Coco.

"She was an important part of your father's life," Eleanor told Elijah. "Not to mention, she's your mother."

Over all the months of Cam's illness, Coco had never shown up to see him or to say goodbye. Because driving long distances was hard for her since her accident on the motorcycle—her hip, never right again, and then there was the metal rod in her left leg—her son had offered to pick her up and bring her to the farm. Cam himself, sick as he was, had asked his youngest son if Coco was planning to come to the farm to see him.

According to Elijah, Coco had told him she'd get there eventually, but the visit never took place. For Eleanor, that was just as well.

Eleanor can remember, still, those summer evenings she'd round up her children and haul them over to Cam's softball games to cheer for the Yellow Jackets. Coco could not have been older than twelve—a gangly adolescent, not yet the beauty she later became—when she used to gather the kids of the various players on the team around to French-braid the girls' hair (they were all mesmerized by her) and taught them how to do cartwheels across the ball field. Back then Eleanor had never thought to question what this girl was doing at her husband's softball games, though one of the wives had pointed out that Coco was always shooting glances to right field.

"Looks like somebody's got a little crush," she had said. At the time, it all seemed harmless and even amusing.

Eleanor had never known the moment that her husband had crossed the line. On one of those rare Saturday nights she and Cam went out on a date, maybe. They would have driven to Concord, shared a bottle of wine and a movie. Eleanor had probably put on lipstick that night. Driving home, she would have felt the stirrings of desire.

One night in particular she remembers. They'd gone to see *Body Heat.* The two of them hadn't talked that much on the way home, but the movie, and the rare experience of being out together that way, just the two of them, had taken them to a place they hadn't occupied for a while, of wanting each other. Cam had put on a cassette tape of Peter Gabriel—*So*—clicking through the songs to get to one in particular, "Red Rain." In the old days, that album had been their favorite to play while making love.

"*Red Rain is pouring down,*" Peter Gabriel sang. Cam's hand was on her thigh. Inside it. "*Pouring down all over me.*"

Eleanor can still remember how she'd felt as she and Cam pulled up to the house that night—how ready she was to take off her clothes, get into bed with her husband, touch him. Feel his touch.

"Back in twenty minutes," Cam would have called out to her on his way out to the car to drive Coco home. She charged a dollar fifty an hour, but would probably have babysat for free, just to spend time with him.

Funny how it worked in those days, when a babysitter was part of every evening they spent together, if they wanted to go out. There was always Coco, at these sexy, desire-filled end-of-the-evening moments—waiting in the living room, watching TV while working on her splits or changing the color of her nail polish, offering up a report on the children's activities. Who had given her a hard time brushing his teeth. Who had spilled her hot chocolate. At the end of it all, it was Coco sharing the front seat with Eleanor's handsome husband as they headed out into the darkness.

By the time Cam made it back to the farm, Eleanor had fallen asleep.

On which of those nights, Eleanor used to wonder—after—had her husband first kissed their babysitter? Thinking about it used to drive Eleanor crazy.

The good news is, enough time has passed now—enough other things have happened—that the answer no longer matters much. If at all.

Water under the bridge. The phrase applies particularly well at the moment, considering the fact that Eleanor and the children are standing on one now as they look out to the waterfall—the same bridge she used to bring their children to when they were small. One time, as they stood there, a stiff gust of wind had lifted Toby's cowboy hat right off his head and deposited it in the water below.

Al snaps a picture. Ursula holds the bowl containing Cam's ashes. Elijah places his hand on Eleanor's shoulder. Toby drops a stone in the brook. No sign of Coco.

As things had worked out after the divorce, Coco had stayed with Cam only about as long as Eleanor had—just a little over ten years. All Eleanor ever knew was that one day she had moved out, leaving Elijah. Not long after came the news of the motorcycle crash. The horror of it, for Eleanor, lay less in the fact that Coco was on the back of the motorcycle than the discovery of who had been driving it. The man was Timmy Pouliot, Cam's onetime teammate on the softball team and later Eleanor's lover, a man who once vowed—in the lonely aftermath of her divorce—to love Eleanor forever. He probably would have, too, if Eleanor had let him.

Timmy died instantly in the crash. The doctors had managed to save Coco's leg—that long, wonderful leg Eleanor still remembered from watching her execute all those cartwheels—but she limped badly and walked with a cane after that. Eleanor knew, from Elijah, that Coco worked at a spa somewhere up north, though giving massages as she'd done once was no longer possible. She sat at the desk. She'd be past forty now.

For a while Elijah had tried to help his mother get sober, but after she met her most recent boyfriend, Jesse, things had gone downhill fast. Jesse was an addict, too. A dozen years younger than Coco, he had a seven-year-old son named Patrick who sometimes lived with them and sometimes didn't.

"It's crazy at my mom's apartment," Elijah had told Eleanor on one of his visits at the farm. "Jesse's kid sleeps on the couch. When he's hungry he fixes himself a bowl of ramen. When I took him out for a hamburger you would have thought it was filet mignon."

Eleanor thought of Raine then, another young mother, lost. As a woman whose failures involved doing too much for her children, one who paid too much attention, probably—she had a hard time imagining the world of a mother who paid so little. They all had their story. This much Eleanor knows now.

"She's still your mom," Eleanor told Elijah. "She still loves you. I have no doubt you love her. She's been through a lot of hard things."

"You have, too."

"She loved your dad," Eleanor said. "And look . . . she made you."

They stand on the rocks now—Eleanor and the children, all grown up. Toby has found a piece of mica he's holding up to the light. Al adjusts the lens on his camera. Ursula checks her watch.

"Maybe she hit traffic in Concord," Elijah says, speaking of his mother now.

"Let's give it another minute." This is Al.

Toby's off in another world, having picked up a feather. Ursula looks as if she's just bitten into a lemon. "Jake will throw a fit if I'm not back in time for him to take off for poker night," she says, checking her watch.

"Let's just get things started," Elijah tells them. The others have been waiting in deference to their brother, but if Elijah's okay going ahead without Coco, so are they. Eleanor cues up her cell phone to a John Prine song—one of the funny ones. Cam would have wanted that. She pushes *Play.* Over the sound of rushing water comes a guitar and a familiar voice.

"Please don't bury me down in the cold cold ground," John Prine sings. *"No, I'd druther have 'em cut me up and pass me all around."*

"He's talking about us," Toby says. "That's kind of what we're doing for Pops. Only we didn't cut his body up. We burned it."

"Hush," Ursula says. The way she speaks to her brother now reminds Eleanor of how she talks to Lulu when she spills her milk. Or Jake, when he does pretty much anything.

"It's okay, Urs." Al places a hand on her shoulder. "We're not in church or anything."

In a way, this is Eleanor's church—the closest she has to one: this waterfall, this bridge, these rocks, with ice just forming on the rocks and John Prine singing, Toby humming along. Cam would have liked this.

A car pulls up—the kind that could never pass inspection, music blasting out the window. It takes a moment to recognize the person who emerges from the driver's seat—slowly, and not without effort—to make her way down over the rocks. Though always slim, her body seems to have withered (the expression takes on a new and vivid meaning to Eleanor now) to nothing but skin and bones. *Coco.*

"I couldn't find my shoes," she says. "I meant to get here sooner."

Elijah helps her to their gathering place by the water. "No problem," Al tells her. "It's good you could make it."

"We were all just going to say a few words about Cam. Maybe you have some thoughts," Eleanor offers. She can feel her throat tighten, but this is the right thing to do.

"Oh jeez," Coco says. "I never did this before. I should've looked up a poem or something. Some inspirational quote."

"That's okay," Toby tells her. "We're all just saying whatever we feel. Things we liked best about him."

Coco stands there for a moment, biting her lip. Eleanor studies her face. You can still find the remnants of her former beauty, but something—the presence of constant physical pain, maybe— appears to have altered her features. There's a sharpness to how she looks now. When she opens her mouth Eleanor sees she's missing some teeth.

"Oh, God," Coco says. "I could really use a cigarette."

Nobody offers one.

"The guy had great hair, and not just because it was red," Coco says. "With most people, when you cut their hair, it looks funky until the cut grows out, but with Cam, whenever I gave him a haircut, it looked great from the first day."

"You two had some good times together," Elijah adds. How has it turned out that this boy whose birth, twenty-one years before, represented the final reminder of her husband's betrayal has turned out to be someone Eleanor deeply loves?

Nobody says anything for a while then. They stand there listening to the water crashing over the rocks. Coco speaks again.

"I know I screwed up," Coco says. "I shouldn't have done what I did in the first place."

Is she talking about getting together with Cam? (The term Darla had used at the time: *homewrecker*?)

"You seemed like such a great family," she says. "Always doing these interesting projects and things. Baking pies. Making people out of corks. I used to watch the way you were together, softball game nights, driving off at the end of the game, looking like you all loved each other so much. I just—I don't know—wanted to be part of it."

She starts to cry.

Eleanor does something she would not have anticipated then. Standing there on a patch of moss below the bridge, taking in the picture of this sad, lost woman, huddled by the waterfall, snorting into a piece of Kleenex, Eleanor opens her arms and wraps them around Coco. No longer young or beautiful, she seems to Eleanor, at this moment, like a lost little girl in need of a mother.

"All that's over now," Eleanor says.

Hearing herself speak these words, Eleanor realizes they're true.

30.

Maybe you forgot about bowling night?

Christmas comes—a day Eleanor marks with Toby alone over a meal of grilled cheese sandwiches and chocolate ice cream. A little after New Year's, Eleanor's friend Jason drives up from

Cambridge. He's never visited the farm before. It's the day after a snowstorm—the fields blanketed and glistening in the sunlight, ice just starting to form over the pond. In the house, Eleanor has cranked up the woodstove and made a pie.

"So this is the famous farm I've been hearing about all these years," Jason says to Eleanor, after she's given him the tour. (The barn. The studio. The frozen pond. Toby's rock and mineral collection.) "Of course it's very sweet. But I can't see how this works for you, staying on in this place. You're not Laura Ingalls Wilder. What's a person supposed to do for a social life in a town like this?"

"Maybe you forgot about bowling night," Eleanor says. "For your information, Moonlight Acres is a happening place in this town. The Akersville police force bowls on our same night and I get the feeling the chief has a soft spot for me."

"That could come in handy if you ever have a run-in with the law," Jason says. "But maybe you should set your sights a little higher?"

"He's a good guy, actually," Eleanor says. "I'm just not interested. I'm fifty-eight years old."

"You may not believe it, but fifty-eight is still young, " Jason tells her. "You deserve a good man in your life. Take it from me. There's nothing like one of those."

She can't come up with a response. The idea of finding a partner seems as distant as the prospect of making her way back to her daughter, as distant as the moon. "I've got Toby," she reminds her friend. "And my work. The new book."

Jason isn't leaving it alone. "This should be your time, finally, El." He places his hands on her shoulders and looks her square in the eye. "You've waited long enough."

"I know you're right," she tells him. "I just don't see how to find the exit door." How to leave this place, she means—the thing she wishes she could do, the very thing that had once devastated her, when she did it. Twenty-five years earlier it had nearly broken Eleanor's heart when she left for Brookline. Now she longs to get back to her life there but sees no way of making it happen.

"You can always find an excuse to put yourself last," Jason tells her. "For once in your life take care of your own self."

She loves this about her friend: that he stands up for her, even when she cannot do that herself.

"Your children are grown up now," Jason tells Eleanor. "They'll survive without you. Even Toby."

Easy for Jason to say: As a gay man without children, the same age as Eleanor—having cut his successful therapy practice in Cambridge back to half time—he and his longtime partner, Hank, maintain a comfortable and astonishingly low-stress life for themselves, traveling to Martha's Vineyard every August and Portugal in the winter. They function as a pair of benevolent uncles to their niece and nephew, who seem to prefer the two of them to their own parents. Nobody in their lives has ever accused them of having been responsible for their PTSD or manifesting "toxic pathology."

"If I'd never gotten to be a mother, I would have grieved that forever," Eleanor observes. "And of course I'm going to tell you I wouldn't have missed it, getting to be a parent. But I don't kid myself about the other side of the story: the hardest things I've faced come from having children."

"The good news is, your job is basically done," Jason tells her.

"I barely even know what I might want for myself anymore," Eleanor tells Jason. "I can't stop myself from worrying about what *they* want, what *they* need."

"Whatever it is those children of yours need at this point," Jason tells her, "they're probably not going to get it from you."

31.

Whiskey in the baby bottle

O ver the course of that first winter she'd spent back at the farm, Eleanor had been so focused on Cam she hadn't noticed all the other things that were hard about living there besides caring for a dying man. A year and a half after his death, she knows them well.

It's lonely, for starters.

Back when she was caring for Cam she'd been busy all the time—bringing him to doctor's appointments, fixing protein shakes designed to keep weight on him, not that it worked, helping him sort through piles of finished and half-finished woodworking projects in his old studio, selling off his physical therapy equipment and his tools.

The house is eerily silent now—Toby out in the barn or the cheese room with Ralph for days on end. Days go by when the only people she sees are Toby and Ralph and Raine. And Spyder.

She spends most of the day at her drawing table. At night she stokes the woodstove, or Toby does, but mornings when she gets up it's still so cold in the kitchen that she can see her breath. The snow, that had glittered back in December, has turned crusty and gray now. Out in the studio, she keeps an electric heater going so her fingers don't go numb. By four o'clock it's dark, and the wind whips over the field. She and Toby eat early—six o'clock at the latest. She's usually in bed with a book by eight thirty, asleep by ten.

Raine comes by often to drop Spyder off, times she knows Toby will be in from the barn and available to care for him. Walking now, though unsteadily, Spyder is a pale, regretful-looking baby—with large sad eyes that look too big for his face. He cries a lot and when he does, Toby is the only one able to quiet him.

Even before Spyder started teething he was a fussy baby, whose face bears a worried expression much of the time, as if he's asking himself, *How do I get out of here?* Even in the care of Toby, he hardly ever smiles. Sometimes, looking at her son, walking around the house with Spyder in his arms, humming to him, it seems to Eleanor as if the baby is holding on to Toby for dear life—almost as if he knows, even at this young age, who is least likely to let him down.

Normally Raine barely says a word when she drops the baby off, she's in so much of a rush all the time. Then one day she asks Toby if she could speak with him.

"I got a job at the nursing home," she says. "Night shift, ten to six. I was wondering how you'd feel about taking Spyder. On a regular basis."

The truth is, Toby's already been caring for Spyder more days than not.

"I'd pay you," she says. "They're only giving me minimum wage but I'd give you a buck fifty an hour. It's nights. With luck he'll be sleeping."

That last observation seems unlikely, but never mind. "I'll take him," Toby tells Raine. "You don't have to pay me anything." Raine must be happy to hear this but says nothing.

The first night of Raine's job, she shows up a little after nine thirty to drop Spyder off before her shift starts. "I heard about this great trick for if he wakes up hollering," Raine tells Toby. "You just put a few drops of whiskey in his bottle. Works like a charm."

Toby will not be putting alcohol in Spyder's bottle, Eleanor knows. He has a different method for getting Raine's baby to sleep. Toby wraps his arms around Spyder and hums to him, all night when necessary. Now and then, when Eleanor gets up to go to the bathroom, she sees the two of them in the rocking chair by the woodstove— her large, awkward son in his sweatpants and an old flannel shirt of his father's that doesn't button but he wears it anyway, with Spyder in his arms, pressed up against his chest. Toby will be stroking Spyder's back, probably, or resting his cheek against his small pale head, with its downy fuzz. Sometimes on these occasions she can see Spyder's small hand wrapped around one of Toby's large, rough fingers, his head on Toby's shoulder. Now and then Toby will be talking to him, telling a made-up story involving Smurfs and Ninja Turtles, with Spyder featuring as the hero every time. Eleanor sometimes stands in the doorway to the kitchen watching and listening. Her son never notices. His focus is always on the baby.

"Did you know, Mom," he says to Eleanor one night, from where he sits in the chair, holding the baby, "one of Spyder's ears is different from the other one. It's got this little folded-over part, like an elf."

Toby notices everything.

32.

Scarlett Johansson. Address: Hollywood.

More than anything she might hope for in her own life, Eleanor wishes Toby could fall in love with a woman who'd love him back. She tries to imagine a woman capable of this—a woman (no doubt an unconventional one) who might see, in her younger son, his sweetness and tenderness and capacity for loyalty beyond all bounds—a goodness of heart like nothing Eleanor has observed in another human being, ever.

On a trip to Manchester—the year after Cam's death, Toby nearing his thirty-first birthday—they drive past a store selling wedding gowns. "Someday my bride will wear a dress like that on our wedding day," Toby tells Eleanor.

He writes a letter to Scarlett Johansson. Eleanor knows this because the letter gets returned, marked "undeliverable." Though Toby had put one of Eleanor's return address stickers on the upper left-hand corner, he'd simply addressed the envelope with Scarlett Johansson's name and the word "Hollywood."

Toby wants to be somebody's husband. He'd love to be somebody's father, too. Goats are great, but he longs for a real, human kid in his life. He loves his visits with Spyder, times Raine drops him off when she goes to work—and sometimes just for whatever it is a nineteen-year-old could find to do in a town like Akersville at seven thirty on a Thursday night, or two o'clock on a Sunday afternoon. Next to the photograph he keeps by the bed, of Scarlett Johansson, Toby keeps one of Spyder. But far from satisfying his longing, his times with other people's children seem only to intensify the yearning for one of his own.

"I love babies," Toby says. "I just wish there was one I got to be with all the time. Not just in the night, but always. Like in a family."

What's Eleanor supposed to tell him? Give her son false hope? Suggest that a scenario might be possible that seems unattainable?

"It's not easy being a parent," Eleanor tells him.

"You probably don't think I'm smart enough," he says. "But a person doesn't need to be a genius to know how to love somebody."

In the twenty-seven years since the accident that robbed Toby of a portion of his brain cells, Eleanor has frequently witnessed the curious moments in which her son displays the depth and perceptiveness of a man who sees things in the world around him that most other people miss entirely. Somewhere deep within his sturdy and ungainly body, Eleanor detects a remnant of the funny, magical little boy he had been once, the spark of sheer brilliance that had burned so bright.

Toby had been a beautiful child. To Eleanor, he is a beautiful man. But at the end of the day, it doesn't matter what Eleanor thinks about Toby or what she knows about the uniqueness of his gifts. Who else but his mother would watch closely enough, spend the time necessary, to understand these precious and irreplaceable aspects of Toby? Who else but his mother could overlook his odd way of walking, his unusual taste in clothing, the strange, off-kilter way he speaks? Who else but a writer of fiction—a woman who makes readers believe that a ten-year-old orphan named Bodie might travel all around the globe on her own, having adventures—could believe that a man like Toby might ever become some woman's lover and husband? But she does.

33.

A Farrah Fawcett poster and a waterbed

As difficult as it is to imagine a partner for Toby, the idea that she might ever again have one, for herself, is beyond Eleanor's imagination. That night at the bowling alley, when the police officer—Quince was his name—had suggested they go out sometime, he might as well have suggested the two of them go trekking in Nepal, or skydiving. She's that far, now, from the idea of being with a man again, let alone falling in love.

Eleanor has not forgotten what it felt like on those sweet nights long ago, after the divorce, when she used to stop by Timmy Pouliot's apartment—how his face lit up when she walked in the door, and how, after he'd drawn a bath for her, he'd sit next to the tub with a washcloth in his hand, and the two of them would talk, and after, how they made love on his waterbed. The pizza boxes everywhere, and the trophy he'd won long ago in a fishing derby with his dad, his poster of Farrah Fawcett—though there was never any question who Timmy's dream girl had been, really. It was Eleanor.

Sometimes, alone in bed now, she still summons a memory of a winter night after she and Timmy had made love on that ridiculous waterbed of his after dropping her children off with their father. Knowing she had to drive back to Brookline that night, he had thrown on sweatpants and a parka and run downstairs to warm up her car for the long drive home in the night. That is what she remembers best about Timmy Pouliot—the care he'd shown, the attention he paid to the small details like setting her boots on the heating grate when Eleanor came by on winter nights so they'd be warm when she left. She might miss that more than the sex part, though she misses the sex part, too.

Most of all she misses her own self—the person she had been when she was young and hopeful and in love. Maybe what she misses is something she never had. For those brief interludes with Timmy Pouliot—only a few hours at a time—Eleanor had gotten a glimpse of what it might be like to know her desires and honor them.

Did anyone ever give birth to a child without relinquishing some part of herself? Had any woman ever truly managed to meet her own needs while raising a child?

"You wouldn't know what to do with a morning to yourself if you had one," Cam had told her once, on a morning he was heading out to go mountain biking, when she'd asked, "When do I get a morning off?" As dismissive as his words to her may have been, he had probably been right about that.

That's what love represents to Eleanor now: you find a lover, you lose yourself.

She's done with that.

34.

$1,200 pants. Penguins, trending.

Springtime now. The *Cork People* television series has been so successful that the producers approach Eleanor with a new project: a feature film adaptation of a children's book she'd published years before, as part of her series about the little orphan girl, Bodie, and her solo adventures around the globe. This one will center on Bodie's trip to the South Pole, but with a focus on Bodie's quest to address the ravages of climate change. The idea, as the producers see it, is to make a movie that will not simply entertain children but educate them about what's happening to the planet. Speaking to Eleanor from her office in Los Angeles, the producer, Marlys, assures Eleanor that to avoid leaving audiences feeing hopeless they'll approach the story "with an eye to the positive."

"We don't want to get kids depressed about the future," she tells Eleanor in their conference call with the studio. "The idea is to inspire them to learn about the danger of melting glaciers. Turn them into little climate change activists."

It's a well-intentioned concept, though probably unrealistic, but Eleanor is willing to go forward with the idea. Given her responsibilities in caring for her son, she explains to Marlys, a trip to Los Angeles seems out of the question, but she'll give the project her blessing.

"Oh, you've got to come to L.A.," Marlys says. "We want you involved at a personal level. For all those hundreds of thousands of Bodie fans out there, you are the face of the Bodie books. It will mean so much to us all to have you on the team."

They make a plan for Eleanor to fly to California for just a couple of days. Ralph has agreed to stay with Toby.

As the date of her trip approaches, Eleanor's excited to be going somewhere other than the grocery store and the bowling alley. In her life before Cam got sick, she traveled back and forth to New York and even, on occasion, to Los Angeles regularly for work—and to Mexico once, on a vacation with Al and Teresa and her parents, and to France to promote translations of her books there. Now two years have passed since she's gotten on a plane. She hasn't put on a pair of high heels in ten years.

The studio has arranged for a car to pick her up at the airport, and for a room in a hotel with a Dale Chihuly sculpture in the lobby. ("I have one of those," she says out loud to no one in particular, seeing it. "Sort of.") There's a gift basket of fancy cheese and nuts and a bottle of champagne waiting in her room. Eleanor hasn't considered this kind of thing for a long time, but the thought comes to her, how good it would feel if there were someone to share it with.

That night over dinner in Santa Monica, Marlys lays out the studio's plan for *Bodie Goes to Antarctica*. In the updated version of Eleanor's story, the little girl—an animated character—arrives at the South Pole to discover that the ice sheets are melting. A friendly old scientist working at a weather station there explains to Bodie what's happening: global warming has raised sea levels to a point that will soon result in massive flooding over the planet. Despite Marlys's assurances of the movie's ultimately uplifting message, Bodie will also discover—from a wise Indigenous woman—how the retreat of arctic ice will threaten the survival of the very wildlife she has come to discover: seals of course, the showy sheathbill, the giant petrel, and—Eleanor's particular favorite—the emperor penguin.

Eleanor would like to believe that Marlys's interest in this project is rooted in environmental concern, but over the course of their dinner (at an Italian restaurant in Beverly Hills whose menu omits the prices) she recognizes the more basic truth about why she's been summoned to Hollywood and why a movie studio is suddenly so interested in adapting her children's book for a film.

A few years earlier, the documentary *March of the Penguins* had enjoyed massive success. Even with the passage of time, the South Pole remained hot. "And when I say that I'm not just talking about climate change!" Marlys adds, taking a bite of a dish with the impressive name of Sous Vide Steak with Apricot Gochujang and Cauliflower Blueberry Shrub Foam. "The box office potential is massive."

Penguins are trending. The market for feel-good entertainment with a positive message about the environment is exploding.

Listening to the producer and her partner lay out their vision, Eleanor—though she's been gone just a day—suddenly misses the farm, and her son. The picture comes to her of her garden and her clothesline. Her son, off in the barn, whistling to his goats or sitting by the woodstove humming to Spyder, tunes from an old Burl Ives record she used to play for him.

"We've got a surprise for you," Marlys says as their waiter sets down their dessert: green apple sorbet with smoked salt meringue. "Tomorrow we'll be meeting with the world's leading activist working to save the Antarctic ice sheet. Guy Macdowell. Guy's spent the last thirty years in the front lines of the war on climate change. Before most of us even knew it existed, Guy was traveling in a Ski-Doo, assessing the collapse of the ice and working to save the penguin habitat."

"This man lives in Los Angeles?" It seemed unlikely. Everything about this meeting did.

"God no," Marlys says. "You wouldn't believe the hoops we had to jump through to get Guy to work with us. He's flying in from Ush-uaia, Argentina, tonight but until the day before yesterday he was at a field camp someplace on the middle of an ice sheet where the only means of communication is a satellite phone. It took us a week and a half just to get our invitation to him."

The studio has made a substantial contribution to Guy Mac-dowell's foundation, naturally. But for him the real motivator is the idea of reaching the next generation with the importance of address-ing climate change.

"When I told Guy about your book and what a huge following you have with kids," Marlys tells Eleanor, "that was what persuaded him to work with us. We're talking about a man who keeps his car-bon footprint as low as possible. Guy was super-reluctant to get on a plane."

"Actually, I never saw myself as writing a book about climate change," Eleanor says. "I was just telling a story about a girl who loves penguins."

Marlys nods vigorously. "That's how we rope in our audience," she says. "First, we give them some strange birds with wacky personalities and an adorable kid. Then we hit them with the message that keeps their parents happy."

When she gets up the next morning, Eleanor calls Toby. "How's Hollywood?" he asks her. "Have you seen Scarlett Johansson?"

"No, but I'm meeting a man who spends a lot of time with penguins," she tells him. She and Toby have watched the penguin documentary many times. Toby loves that it's the male penguins, not the females, who sit on the eggs. "That's like me with Spyder," he told her last time they watched the video.

The meeting with Marlys and the other studio executives is set for ten o'clock that morning. A car comes to pick Eleanor up. Walking into the building—glass and stainless steel, pots of orchids lining the hall, a collection of original Norman Rockwell art lining the entryway—her reflection in the mirrored wall catches her up short. What was she thinking, packing these outdated clothes? Her jacket has shoulder pads. How is it that all this time—even as recently as the dressing room at the boutique—she's failed to notice her hair, which is more gray than brown now, and the deep lines around her eyes? This is what happened to a person who spent all her time worrying about her children.

After the meeting, Eleanor spends a couple of hours walking around Beverly Hills. There was a time, after her divorce, when her children were staying with Cam, when she had briefly lived in Hollywood, developing the *Cork People* series, and for a brief period she'd kept company with a man who lived near Venice Beach. That feels like a long time ago now.

For no particular reason she stops in at a boutique and tries on a pair of white silk pants just to see what it feels like to wear something like this—the perfectly cut legs, the feel of the fabric against her skin. She doesn't check the price tag until she's zipping them up: $1,200. She puts them back.

That night the studio is throwing a party, with Eleanor and Guy Macdowell as the guests of honor. As she walks in the door to the room where the event is underway—wearing a Laura Ashley dress from the eighties—a young woman, wearing a fitted blazer and a pair of silk pants that look identical to the ones Eleanor had tried on a few hours before, approaches her. She introduces herself as Kiki. She's an assistant at the studio.

"Oh my God," Kiki says. "You have no idea what a thrill it is meeting you. I just got off a project with Ashton Kutcher. But frankly, movie stars mean nothing to me compared to someone like you who's a real artist. I have so much respect for writers."

Eleanor never knows what to say at these moments. But there's no need to say anything. The young woman is still talking.

"I read every single one of the Bodie books when I was a kid," she says. "*Bodie Under the Sea?* I probably had that one memorized. The part where she meets the octopus killed me. I'll never order grilled octopus again." This young producer ends her sentences with the same lilting question mark employed by Raine, back home.

"My younger son was obsessed with undersea life for a while," Eleanor tells her. Just speaking of Toby, here in this place, feels strange, and oddly comforting. "Every afternoon when he came home from school we used to watch all these old nature videos together. We still do, actually."

Kiki is still talking when Eleanor spots him across the room: the only person here who looks even more out of place than she does. She knows before anyone introduces them that he must be Guy Macdowell.

For a man who's been spending his time in tents on an ice shelf, riding snow machines full of beef jerky and biofuel across frozen tundra for the last three decades, Guy Macdowell has done a surprisingly good job of dressing for the party—unlike Eleanor. But in other ways it's clear Wilshire Boulevard must be as foreign a place to Guy Macdowell as it is to Eleanor. The skin on his face—with its strong jaw and aquiline nose—is red and very dry.

Eleanor remembers something she read about Guy Macdowell on the plane: that the ultraviolet rays he'd been subjected to on his 220-day hike across the desolate frozen landscape had turned his eyes a different color. They'd been hazel once. Now, as Marlys steers him in Eleanor's direction for the introduction that is no doubt about to take place, Eleanor can see that his irises are the pale blue of an Alaskan husky's.

"This man's been to ground zero," a man to Marlys's right—also a studio executive probably—tells Eleanor. "I'm telling you, when I listened to Guy's TED talk, I cried like a baby."

Guy extends his hand to Eleanor. This is not the first time she's shaken the hands of a man who works hard out in the elements. So does her son Toby. So did the man she'd been married to, and the man—Timmy Pouliot—who had loved her after that. But she has never experienced the touch of a hand like Guy's—its roughness or its strength.

"I should have warned you about my finger," he says. She has registered this of course: the fourth finger on his right hand is missing.

"Frostbite," he tells Eleanor. "The final North Pole expedition in eighty-seven. I was skiing across an expanse of sea ice when it happened. Nothing much to do but keep on going. That was a long time ago. I was an idiot, not to wear better gear. I've learned some things over the years."

"Me too," Eleanor says. "I made a lot of mistakes in 1987. Also 1988. You name it. I've made a lot of mistakes."

The minute she says this she regrets it. What is she doing, offering up an admission so nakedly personal—also trivial—to a man she's just met at a Hollywood cocktail party, who will probably win the Nobel Prize someday for saving the world? But hearing her, Guy Macdowell appears genuinely interested.

"Maybe sometime you'll tell me about yours," he says, those pale unblinking eyes looking straight into hers. The way he looks at her—the intensity of his gaze—reminds Eleanor of Cam on the last night of his life, when he'd called her a good woman and thanked her for taking care of him as she had.

Then Kiki's back, taking hold of Eleanor's arm. "I'm going to steal Eleanor away from you, Guy," she tells him. "So many people want to meet her. Same as they want to meet you. Meet and greet, you know."

In her years publishing books and going to festivals and conferences, Eleanor became familiar with the concept of working the room. Rusty as she is now, she does it, steered by Kiki and Marlys— shaking hands, answering the question, more than once, concerning how her flight went and the other question that people so often ask her, "How are things in Vermont?" Sometimes she lets them know that things are probably fine in Vermont, but actually she lives in New Hampshire. On this particular occasion she lets it go.

A young man who introduced himself as the head of the studio's animation division brings her a second glass of champagne, or possibly a third. A woman named Cleopatra tells a man Eleanor recognizes from the movies, whose name escapes her, that this project will do more to reverse the dangers of climate change than any film since Al Gore came out with *An Inconvenient Truth.* "We're not just making a movie here," she tells Eleanor. "We're launching a revolution."

At some point in the evening, Eleanor wanders out on the vast deck overlooking Sunset Boulevard. She's standing there with her champagne when he comes up alongside her. Guy.

"You too, huh?" he says. Those eyes. Even in the darkness, their pale blueness burns into hers.

"I don't attend events like this very often," she tells him. "Like . . . ever."

"Me neither. I'd sooner wrestle a polar bear. Well, maybe not. But you get my drift."

"I probably should have known better than to make this trip." She takes another sip of champagne. Is it possible she's on her fourth glass?

"I'm glad you did. You were a big part of the reason I came, you know."

What is he saying? A shiver passes through Eleanor. Also panic. *Change the topic. Go somewhere safe. Safe and domestic.*

"I had to leave my son. His father died a year and a half ago. We have all these goats. He makes cheese and takes care of a baby named Spyder."

She must sound like a crazy person but Guy smiles.

"I'm sorry to hear about your husband."

"He wasn't my husband anymore," she tells him. "Actually, he left me a long time ago for our babysitter."

Champagne always does this to Eleanor, on the rare occasions she has the opportunity to drink it—makes her talk more than she normally does. Maybe it's also something about Guy's eyes that has this effect on her. Of wanting to tell him things she usually keeps to herself.

"What do you say you and I get out of here?" he says. "Do you think there's such a thing as a plain old coffee shop in this town?"

There's a reassuring firmness to the way he takes her arm and steers her to the door. For a woman who's had to be in charge of nearly everything nearly always, it feels good to be with a man who makes it plain that he's comfortable running the show.

"I think we did our part," he says, as they get into the elevator. "Now they can say they've teamed up with Guy Macdowell and—oh God, this is embarrassing. I should know your name."

Eleanor, she tells him.

"Well, Eleanor," he says, placing his hand on her cheek as he leans in close. Her back is pressed against the wall of the elevator. His body is pressed against hers. "I'm feeling this overwhelming need to kiss you."

35.

Not one of those ne'er-do-well polar explorer types

Because—in this town filled with boutiques selling white silk pants and diamond-studded pet collars and eighty-dollar onesies for newborns—Eleanor and Guy cannot locate a coffee shop, they go to her hotel, which turns out to be his hotel also. The lobby is noisy due to a wedding party of Brazilians. "I don't want to be forward," Guy says. "But if we want a quiet place, I'm thinking my room would work better."

She follows, saying nothing. This isn't like Eleanor. Nothing about what's happening feels like her life. That is the good news.

Guy Macdowell appears to have traveled with a single backpack—less luggage than Eleanor, even. There's a thick parka of a sort you would not expect to see in Los Angeles draped over a chair, the down lining repaired with many layers of duct tape. The label on his shirt says Armani.

"You're probably wondering what that's doing here," he says. "The thing is, where I took off from day before yesterday it was twenty below zero."

He's kissing her again. Harder now. No longer just on her mouth but her neck, and the place where she's wearing her locket, with the photographs of Lulu and Orson in it, the place between her breasts. "Are you all right with this?" Guy asks her. All Eleanor can do at the moment is nod.

"I want to look at you first," he says. Those eyes again. Head to toe, he studies her.

Timmy Pouliot had looked at Eleanor that way, but Timmy always felt to Eleanor less like a man than a boy. Timmy had been so young, with so little in the way of resources of his own, there was nothing he could give her but his heart. Physically strong as he may have been, Timmy was fragile. The man in whose hotel room she stood now had walked to the North Pole and fallen into a crevasse when the ice gave way under his feet. And pulled himself out. Where Timmy Pouliot's world had been the size of a one-bedroom apartment, Guy's spans an entire continent. Two of them. Guy Macdowell might be the first man in Eleanor's life stronger than she is. It's a good feeling, though unfamiliar.

An extraordinary thought occurs to Eleanor. *This man chose me.* The party at which they met earlier that night had been filled with beautiful women—most of them younger than Eleanor, dressed in the kind of clothes women bought in Beverly Hills boutiques, all wanting a few minutes in the company of Guy Macdowell. And still, amazingly, the person he sought out among all of them was her.

They stand there saying nothing at first. Then he's kissing her.

Then that large, leathery hand is unbuttoning her blouse, lowering her onto the bed, with himself beside her.

"In case you're under the impression I'm one of those ne'er-do-well polar explorer types who hop from one bed to another, loving and leaving women all across the ice sheet, I'm not," he tells her. "I can't remember the last time I made love to a woman."

After that, no more words. They are just two bodies then, a man and a woman wandering across a vast and lonely landscape who unexpectedly found each other at the same cocktail party in Beverly Hills. When the sun comes up, they are still wrapped in each other's arms.

"I want you to hear something," Guy says, as they lie together. There's a tape recorder beside the bed. Old-school. He pushes *Play*. The room fills with a joyful sound.

"That's a South Georgia pipit, in case you didn't know," he tells her. "The southernmost species of songbird. Soon to be extinct if we don't do something about it."

It's not a sound you'd expect to hear in a luxury hotel suite off Wilshire Boulevard. This might be the first time, ever, such a sound has been heard in such a place.

"Birders dream of the colorful, the magnificent," Guy says. "And they've got a point. There's nothing like an emperor penguin or a wandering albatross to get your heart beating faster. But for my money, no sound is sweeter than the song made by this little bird. If you want to hear it for yourself, there's nowhere else on the planet to do that but the South Georgian Islands of Antarctica."

She studies his face. It's hard to guess the age of Guy Macdowell. All those years he's spent on ice cutter boats and cross-country skiing over ice sheets have taken their toll on his skin. Still he's a very handsome man. Around Eleanor's age, if she were guessing. She strokes his cheek.

"You gave me something beautiful last night," he says. His hand reaches to touch her again. She falls back onto the pillows.

"You may be well acquainted with ice," Eleanor says. This next might have sounded like a line, though it isn't. "But here's what it looks like when a woman melts."

36.

How to save the world

He isn't actually a bird man, he tells her. He's an ice man. A protector of ice. For virtually his entire adult life he's been haunted by the knowledge that the glaciers are retreating. Once they go, it's not just a disaster for Antarctica. It's a disaster for the planet.

"I don't want to come off as self-important," he says. "But someone's got to do something. And until somebody else comes along, that person seems to be me."

"I haven't made much of a contribution myself," she tells him. What has Eleanor ever done for the planet, beyond making sure to separate her recycling at the town dump?

"It's not for everybody, a life like mine," Guy says. "It's not for anybody, probably. Other than me."

They order room service, and over coffee and fresh-pressed orange juice, they talk, finally. As little experience of morning-after conversations as Eleanor possesses, she doubts they generally go as this one does. Two hours earlier, they'd been touching every inch of each other's bodies. Now, still in his hotel bathrobe, with a cigar in his hand, the topic is saving the world.

Thirty years earlier, as a young man, Guy Macdowell had met his hero, Jacques Cousteau. He made a promise then to devote his life to trying to rescue the collapsing ice shelves on the last truly pristine continent on the globe. He would do all he could to alert the world to their importance. Even thirty years ago, time was running out, not only for Jacques Cousteau but for the planet.

Guy will be returning to Antarctica next year, he tells Eleanor. As soon as he's sufficiently recovered from his hip replacement surgery, he's headed there. Within twelve months, he says. Sooner if possible.

Eleanor listens closely. Measured against the challenges faced by Guy Macdowell, Eleanor's problems—the necessity of caring for Toby, her own loneliness and frustration living on the farm, even her estrangement from Ursula—seem inconsequential. This is not

118 ••• JOYCE MAYNARD

a sad feeling. Just the opposite. It feels oddly reassuring that the issues in her own life, which loomed so large a day before, appear so small by comparison.

As for the other part—that Eleanor has fallen hard, already, for a man who has just announced to her his intention to take off for the South Pole within the year—it doesn't sound like a deal-breaker. Mostly because they have no deal. Whatever it is that has just taken place with this man, she carries no expectation of future commitment. It's an unfamiliar experience to Eleanor—and a good one—to realize she doesn't need a commitment from him. What she had experienced in that hotel room with him the night before was enough.

Up until now, most of Eleanor's conversation with Guy Macdowell has centered on his projects, his commitment to saving Antarctica, his plan to return there as soon as possible. The two of them are getting up to go—Eleanor to a meeting with Marlys, Guy to a presentation for a wealthy supporter of his foundation—when he speaks of the night they spent together and what it meant to him.

"I was married a long time ago," he says to Eleanor. For nineteen years, Guy tells her, he'd tried to keep a connection alive with his wife in between his solitary trips across sheets of ice and monitoring the glacier. Eight years back she'd given up on him.

"Who can blame her?" he says. "What woman wants to sit around waiting for a man who makes it home every six months, when the sunlight disappears, only to check himself into a hospital for another joint replacement surgery? Then watch him go off again on a lecture tour to raise money so he can get back out on the ice.

"Over the past quarter century I spent more time with emperor penguins than I did with the woman who loved me," he tells her. Eleanor notes how Guy puts this. *The woman who loved me.* Not *the woman I loved.*

His words to her convey something else maybe. A cautionary message. Eleanor might choose to fall in love with Guy Macdowell. It might not even be a matter of choice. It might just happen. If so, she'd better understand where he's headed: In twelve months he'll be off to the coldest continent on the planet, and the most brutal. *Proceed at your own risk.*

37.

I can't stop thinking about you

As little inclination as she feels to leave Guy's room one moment earlier than she has to, Eleanor dresses and makes her way back to her own room—to the untouched bed for which the studio probably laid out many hundreds of dollars, and the gift basket, with its note from the studio. "Welcome to Beverly Hills!" Fifteen minutes later she's walking into the hotel restaurant, waving to Marlys and Kiki.

"What did you think of him?" Marlys asks. "Guy." For a moment, it feels to Eleanor as though this woman knows everything.

She doesn't, of course. Marlys would not guess that a woman like her—unfashionably dressed, straight off the farm, with streaks of gray in her hair that she never gets around to coloring—would have spent the night in the arms of a world-famous explorer. A man—the phrase comes back to her—*acquainted with ice*.

"So inspiring," Eleanor tells them.

The conversation shifts to the movie project then, though Guy is part of this, too. "He can't be involved in the day-to-day, naturally," Kiki explains. "But we're hoping he'll be motivated to keep a close eye on what we're up to. The man's vision is so important. His passion."

Oh yes.

"What we're hoping is that you can be a real member of the team here, Eleanor," Marlys is saying. "Everybody's super excited to have you on board."

"I can't say I know anything about making films," Eleanor tells them. "But I do know my little character, Bodie. She means a lot to me. I've been writing books about her since I was nineteen years old."

Since before Guy Macdowell met Jacques Cousteau, probably. Before he set out on his heroic quest.

Guy the conqueror. Her mind goes to a scene of the two of them as they were the night before. Guy's rough hand moving over her skin.

"We all have utmost respect for what you created," Kiki assures her. "We couldn't be more excited about what's down the road for this collaboration."

"Me too," Eleanor tells the two of them as she gets up from her chair. There's a car waiting for her.

I have a lover, she thinks to herself, as she heads to the airport. *I am somebody's lover.*

Back home that night, Toby has dinner ready for Eleanor. He's made one of his odd concoctions, a meal of stir-fried vegetables with popcorn and radishes on the side and hot chocolate. He must have biked into town for the ingredients: He has also purchased a helium balloon with a yellow smile face that says, *Have a Great Day.* Eleanor pictures her son riding home with the balloon tied to his handlebars. A wave of love sweeps over her, and an odd little twinge of guilt that for the forty-eight hours of her trip to California she barely thought of him.

By the time Eleanor climbs into bed that night it's close to midnight. She peels off her pantyhose and pulls on her pajamas. The night before, she was naked in the arms of a polar explorer. Thinking of his hands in her hair, his mouth moving over her body, she shivers as deeply as a person might at the 86th parallel—the place, he'd told her, where his hip had given out and he'd dropped onto the frozen ground, writhing in pain, the place he'll return soon to resume his quest.

Eleanor tells herself that what she experienced in that L.A. hotel room was a wonderful interlude, just that. She'll get back to her work now, and her life with her son, her small, tentative efforts at connection with her grandchildren in Vermont, and the anticipation of Al and Teresa's baby, due to be born in Seattle a few months from now.

A person should not be greedy. *Be grateful for what you have,* she tells herself.

From the table next to her bed, her phone vibrates. Tired as she is, she might have chosen to ignore it but she looks at her screen. A message from Guy.

"I can't stop thinking about you. When can we see each other again?"

38.

A too-low neckline at the Harvard Club

While he's recuperating from his most recent knee injury, the foundation that funds Guy's work in Antarctica has set up a speaking tour—every night a different city. It turns out he's coming to Boston in two weeks.

Meet me there, he texts her.

Except for a single email alerting Eleanor to the time and place of his talk, she and Guy do not communicate over the days before the event. Every morning she notes exactly how many of these days remain before she'll see him.

The afternoon of his speech at the Harvard Faculty Club, Eleanor drives to Cambridge. She sets out a list for Toby, reminding him to tamp down the woodstove when he goes to bed. She leaves a roast chicken in the refrigerator and a package of Klondike bars, his favorite. Also a drawing of Toby with one of the goats. "Have fun with the girls," she writes.

Her trip to L.A. has confirmed for Eleanor that Toby can manage on his own for a night or two. She's bought a blouse for her visit to the Harvard Club and colored her hair—not, as she's done in the past, by herself, with a bottle of L'Oréal, but at an actual beauty salon. Checking herself in the rearview mirror it comes to her how long it's been since she's done anything like this.

Never, actually. In the years since her divorce, Eleanor has gone on a few dates—a couple that were disastrous, one or two with genuinely nice men, a couple of whom became, briefly, someone with whom she kept company for a time. But the feeling she experiences now, driving over the Tobin Bridge and winding her way along Storrow Drive toward Cambridge to see Guy—the thrill she registers in her body—is one she has not known for a long time. Since those nights with Timmy Pouliot, probably.

Stepping into the crowded foyer of the Harvard Club, Eleanor looks around the room to a sea of blue blazers and women in Talbots dresses. Her choice of outfit is all wrong, she sees now. Her hair looks too recently blow-dried, the evidence of too much effort, too easily apparent. She runs her hand through the curls the stylist created, trying to flatten the look she just paid fifty dollars to achieve.

Eleanor finds a seat in the back row of chairs, her eye on the podium. She scans the room for Guy without success, imagining the scenario of what will happen when they see each other. Eleanor doesn't want this reunion to take place in front of all these people. Better to find a spot as far away from the front as possible. Let him greet his followers first. Their time can wait.

A professor from the university introduces Guy. She's an extremely attractive woman wearing an understated suit of the sort Eleanor now wishes she'd chosen to wear tonight. Listening to the Harvard professor speak, the thought comes to Eleanor, *What if I got it all wrong?* Maybe Guy never expected she'd actually show up. Maybe he'll be embarrassed and at a loss for what to do with her— this desperate-seeming fan who's just driven an hour and a half to see him, wearing a too-short skirt and a blouse whose neckline (low) she deeply regrets. She has put on perfume for this event. Too much of it, from a bottle that must have sat unused on her shelf for years. Eleanor is out of practice in every way. Worse, she was never *in* practice.

Guy's talk is brilliant and inspiring, of course—a presentation that probably has the effect of leaving the young people in the room, the Harvard students, ready to commit their lives to saving Antarctica, and the older ones, the alumni, ready to take out their checkbooks.

After, a crowd assembles around Guy. The professor who spoke first—at least twenty years younger than Eleanor, a climate scientist— steers Guy through the crowd, introducing him to the people who appear to be particularly important.

At the back of the room, Eleanor considers the possibility that she should leave. If she heads to the parking garage now, she could be back on the farm before midnight.

Then there he is next to her, leaning close, whispering in her ear.

"I couldn't wait to see you." No need to discuss where they're headed.

39.

A bottle of perfume and three dozen oysters

𝒯he next morning they go shopping together. "We need to find you a bottle of perfume," he says. "Good perfume this time. French."

"Forget about those big department stores and duty-free shops," he tells her. "I'm taking you to the absolute best place to choose perfume. Every woman needs the right scent. It's not a casual decision."

Guy brings Eleanor to a store in Harvard Square called Colonial Drug. It's an old-fashioned shop, with bottles and testers filling every available surface and little silver containers holding paper for trying out the hundreds of perfumes they carry—classic and obscure.

"I don't normally get to do things like this," he says. "Not exactly part of my routine. But we need to find you the perfect scent."

We. Eleanor notices this.

"The first thing you need to know is to take your time," he tells her. "There's no rushing this decision."

The shop is small, the woman behind the counter very old and a little forbidding, but never mind. The only person who matters to Eleanor here is Guy. When she's drawn to a perfume—for no better reason often than the look of the bottle, or the name—Guy unscrews the top and dips the little white paper into the bottle before touching it lightly to Eleanor's wrist or neck, lingering an extra second as he does so. More than once, bringing her hand to her nose to breathe it in, she tells him this is the one. He shakes his head.

"You have to wear a scent for at least an hour to see how it lives on your skin," he tells Eleanor.

How does a man who's spent a significant portion of his life on one of two frozen continents, where he was more likely to keep company with penguins than women, acquire this information? Eleanor wants to ask him but something holds her back. He seems to read her mind.

"When a person spends as much time as I have over the years on a virtually uninhabited continent," Guy tells her, "he's got a lot of time to fantasize. If he's got an active imagination. I used to like thinking about what I'd do with a woman, when I found one I wanted to spend time with."

The two of them examine the bottles, reading the names and the descriptions that accompany each of them. When they discover a perfume they like (it's important that Guy like the scent as well as Eleanor) they have to give it time to sit on her wrist for a while, or her neck, see how the scent holds up over time. They leave the shop and walk around, look in store windows. Get a drink. They study the newspapers at the kiosk outside the subway from all over the world—places Eleanor's never been that Guy seems to know well. Then they return to Colonial Drug. They repeat this process more than once.

The two of them spend most of the day walking around Harvard Square. Every few minutes Guy reaches for Eleanor's hand and brings it to his nose to smell her wrist, each bearing a different brand. He leans in to her neck, brushing her hair aside, lingering to take in the scent he applied there an hour or two earlier. "I feel embarrassed," Eleanor tells him. "I'm not accustomed to so much attention."

"You should be," Guy tells her.

It's late afternoon when they finally make their perfume decision—a scent called Portrait of a Lady. "A sumptuous and symphonic perfume that required hundreds of trials to balance its expressive formula," reads the card next to the bottle. Portrait of a Lady turns out to be among the most expensive perfumes in the store, but Guy insists on buying it for her.

After, they go for oysters. Three dozen. Then to the hotel.

40.

They never talk about who does the dishes

Over the months that follow their time together in Cambridge Guy and Eleanor meet in a surprising number of cities. Guy sends Eleanor plane tickets to Atlanta, Chicago, Dallas. Not Los Angeles, oddly enough; now that work is underway on the Bodie film, the movie studio's interest in involving the two of them in their project seems to be waning. Not that Eleanor has a problem with that. The person whose interest she cares about now is Guy Macdowell. Just when she thought she was done with all that.

They seldom spend more than a single night in each destination, which is about as long as Eleanor feels comfortable leaving Toby. On a couple of these occasions she and Guy may only have a dozen hours together. They spend them well.

It doesn't even matter so much that two weeks or three might pass between one hotel rendezvous and the next. Between these visits the two of them seldom speak. For them it's all about physical touch, nights in their hotel bed, mornings waking up together before they head back to the airport.

Here's the thing Eleanor learns from flying off to whatever city Guy's speaking in that night as she does now: It isn't only the times they have together that matter so much. The simple fact of Guy's presence in her life—the knowledge that at some point in the next weeks or months they'll meet up again somewhere—transforms her days. It turns out to be different, for a woman living alone with her son in a farmhouse at the end of a long dead-end road, when she knows that somewhere on the planet there is a man who can't wait to see her.

She'll say it: *a man who loves her.* He doesn't need to tell her. She feels it.

How Eleanor spends her time, home on the farm with Toby—engaging in her strained, stiff, infrequent conversations with Ursula, checking in with Al and Teresa out west about the pregnancy and impending birth, fixing ginger lemon tea for Raine when she stops by to drop off her son (and smelling the alcohol on her breath)—remains surprisingly unchanged. Work at her desk, trips to the store, meals, laundry, conversations with her editor, meals again . . . a walk to the waterfall when the weather's warm enough, carrying in wood for the stove when it isn't.

But now when Eleanor pins a sheet on the clothesline, or when she drives the trash to the dump or pushes the vacuum cleaner over their old rug—times she sits at her drawing table working on her newest book or answering fan mail from readers of her Bodie books or *The Cork People*—she can summon the memory of Guy's hands on her belly, her hair, her neck. His lips kissing her.

She doesn't tell her children about Guy. She tells no one. The part of Eleanor's life that involves Guy Macdowell is her secret. She can't think when she had a secret, before this. It feels like a good thing that there is one part of Eleanor's life now that belongs to her alone.

When she was young and newly in love with Cam, her dreams had been all about making a home and populating it with babies. For Eleanor now, as she approaches age sixty, all of that has fallen away. She and Guy are two people who have lived utterly different lives for over half a century. What it is they care about most—besides each other—has taken them in utterly different directions and this matters not at all, because everything they've done in their lives up to now has brought them where they are now, made them who they have become: two people who adore each other.

It occurs to Eleanor, when she contemplates the nature of her relationship with Guy and the powerful hold he has on her, that this may be what she loves: They don't live together. They don't share children or a household. They never talk about bills or dental appointments or whose turn it is to clear away the dishes. What they have found with each other exists away from all the stuff of domestic life that filled Eleanor's days for a couple of decades. It doesn't matter to Eleanor that he doesn't read the books she writes or ask her about her children and her day. Guy and Eleanor ask nothing of each other, carry no expectations but what they find in those rare and precious moments they get to be together.

She tells herself that she wants nothing more than what they have now. She almost believes it.

41.

Somebody's grandmother, somebody's lover

Al calls from the hospital in Seattle. Teresa's in labor. Everything looks good.

They've chosen not to learn their child's sex in advance. Identification of gender, for Al, represents a complicated topic. Simpler, maybe, is Teresa's reason for not wanting to know the baby's sex. "It should be a surprise," she says. "Whoever this baby turns out to be, we're going to love them." This was true for Eleanor, too. In the case of her own firstborn child, it just took her longer than usual, learning that child's true gender.

After Al's call, Eleanor keeps her phone in her pocket, of course. When she goes to bed that night, she puts it on the pillow beside her. It's early morning when Al calls with the news. He and Teresa are the parents of an eight-pound baby girl.

Alone in her bedroom at the farm—the bedroom that used to be Cam's—Eleanor speaks the name of the new baby out loud, though no one hears her. *Flora*, she says. She's trying it out, wondering what this baby's nickname will turn out to be, if they'll give her one, and what Flora will call her. She remembers the night of Al's birth, thirty-five years ago. Cam waltzing around the bedroom with Al in his arms—he had another name then—singing "Isn't She Lovely." The two of them had all kinds of ideas then about their future, and the future of their newborn child. Most of them wrong.

We don't tell our children who they should be, Eleanor knows now. They tell us.

Here's the thing about the day a baby's born—if you're lucky, and her health is good. For that one moment in time—never again, probably—a parent can still believe that everything is possible. Everything can be perfect. Just as well new parents don't know all the hard things that await them. For this one brief moment anyway, everything remains possible. Eleanor feels this now.

Flora. *Our little flower,* Eleanor says. She thinks of Cam then— Flora's grandfather whom she will never know. Like Toby, Cam loved babies. He would have loved being a grandfather to this one. Locating the pure joy he took from spending time with young children was something he was uniquely good at. Maybe because he didn't worry so much, as Eleanor always did, about all the practical details of taking care of things, he did better at that, probably, than she had.

Now, as Eleanor thinks about this new grandchild, and the two already born, she's ready to do better, if her children will allow her to. Maybe Ursula's reluctance to let Eleanor into her life, and that of her children, stems from this—her memory of how wound up and occasionally out of control her mother could be on occasion, those times Eleanor thinks of as her visits to Crazyland. She understands now how much those times must have scared her children— Ursula most of all, maybe. Eleanor wishes Ursula could know that she doesn't pour wine over her head as she did on more than one occasion when her children were young. But Ursula's spent so little time with her mother in the last many years, she barely knows who Eleanor is anymore. Ursula does not know Eleanor, as she is now.

Eleanor has never again done what she did that Christmas morning when the children were small, and she was frustrated with Cam for watching a ball game while she worked, and just plain exhausted from yet another attempt at creating, for her family, the appearance of a happy Christmas: she picked up the *bûche de Noël* she'd just finished constructing for their big holiday meal and smashed it into the garbage.

Becoming a grandparent means getting a second chance to do it right, Eleanor thinks. Getting to love and to spend time with another child, without the exhaustion and stress of doing it all day, every day. Never a break. With Flora, she thinks, she might finally be able to do what she has not been able to with Lulu and Orson. *Just be there.* Get to know her slowly and quietly, a little at a time.

At another moment in her life, Eleanor would have jumped on a plane to Seattle. But her experience with Ursula has taught her to take care and not overdo it. Teresa's parents are there to help out, also one of her brothers and her brother's wife. There will be time to get to know her granddaughter. *Take it slow.*

And maybe there is this, too, affecting Eleanor's choice to hold off a few weeks on a visit: The woman she has been for so many years— despite her career success—defined herself as a mother, above all else. With Guy's arrival in her life Eleanor's sense of her identity has shifted. She will always be her children's mother, and she will never fail to love each of them. This includes Ursula, whether or not Ursula chooses to love her back. She knows, without having met her yet, that she will love this new granddaughter as she does the two who came before her, and she will be the best grandparent she can.

But Eleanor is changing. She's a woman who puts perfume behind her ears now, even if nobody's there to breathe it in—because she will, anyway. She's a woman with a life of her own apart from her family.

It's possible, it turns out, to be both somebody's grandmother and somebody's lover, all in the same lifetime.

42.

The great thing about a sixty-five-year-old boyfriend

As she does almost every evening now, Raine shows up just as Eleanor's getting ready for bed to leave Spyder with Toby for her shift at the nursing home. Most evenings she's in the door and out, all in a minute, but this time she lingers.

"I've got a boyfriend," she tells them. "His name is Herb."

They're in the kitchen—Eleanor putting away the last of the dinner dishes, Toby already in the rocking chair with the baby, their favorite spot.

"Where did you meet him?" Eleanor asks.

"The home." Meaning the nursing home.

"He works there, too?" Or maybe Herb is the son of someone who lives there. Grandson, more likely.

"He's one of my clients."

"Clients?"

"He lives at the home. He's, like, a resident?"

Sometimes when Eleanor's at a loss for words, it's Toby who steps in with the observation another person might have kept to herself.

"You mean he's an old-timer?" Toby said. "Like . . . Jimmy Carter?"

The former president is one of her younger son's heroes. One of Toby's most treasured possessions is a book Cam gave him a long time back, to celebrate his being able to pass a reading test: *Inspirational Sayings for a Better Life*. He keeps it open to the page with a quotation from Jimmy Carter. "I have one life and one chance to make it count for something . . . My faith demands that I do whatever I can, wherever I am, whenever I can, for as long as I can, with whatever I have to try to make a difference."

"Not so much like President Carter, maybe," Eleanor suggests. She thinks about a picture she saw recently, of Jimmy and Rosalynn, working on a Habitat for Humanity house. She thinks about Guy—roughly the age of Raine's boyfriend, Herb—dedicating his life to saving the glaciers.

"Herb's not like . . . ancient or anything," Raine says. "The one problem is, he's got diabetes, and it messed up his circulation, so they had to chop off one of his feet. Other than not being able to drive anymore he's doing pretty good, considering."

"How old is he?" Toby again. Most of the time, when Spyder's around, his attention remains focused on nobody but the baby, but Raine's news has him worried.

"Sixty-four. Well, sixty-five actually, but he just had his birthday a couple months ago. Not to mention it's kind of great that he's sixty-five on account of he gets Medicare now, and senior citizen passes at the movies."

Eleanor's been sweeping the kitchen floor. Now she leans the broom against the counter. She wants to choose her words carefully but Toby needs no time to consider his.

"This guy's too old to be your boyfriend," he says. "Twenty-five would be okay. Maybe twenty-seven."

Raine has more to say then about the immaturity of boys her own age—Spyder's biological father, gone from the picture, being a prime example. "Guys my age are all peckerheads," she says. "They've got one thing on their mind."

Herb has all this great life experience, Raine tells them. He knows a ton about the Civil War and ham radios, for one thing. Also horse racing. Back before he went on disability, he operated an excavator. A few years ago he won the lottery. He wasn't one of those big winners, but with his earnings he went to Puerto Vallarta and Expo 67 and bought a professional deep fat cooker that he used to take to carnivals to sell fried dough and curly fries. You wouldn't believe what a person could pull in on a weekend when they had one of those.

There's something missing in this story. Eleanor has a guess, but it seems better to let Raine do the talking.

"The thing is, I can't keep living at my grandparents' house forever," she tells them. "My dad's going to start charging me rent. I've got to think about my future. Mine and Spyder's."

This is the first time Eleanor has observed any sign on Raine's part that she has given thought to her life as a parent, or to what her son might need beyond a supply of diapers and formula and, now that he's eating solids ("with the poops to prove it!" Raine has told them), baby food.

"I know what you're thinking, but Herb wants to take care of us," she says. "He's got a really great RV. He bought it before they amputated his foot so he can't take it anyplace. It's just been parked there out behind the American Legion, but we're thinking of taking a road trip together, the two of us. Plus Spyder naturally. Herb's great with kids."

"You'd drive?" Toby asks her. He and Eleanor have observed the way Raine tears down the driveway, times she drops Spyder off, and how she peels out even faster once she hits the road.

"I love driving," she says. "Herb says we'll go to Gettysburg. Also Knott's Berry Farm and Six Flags."

The RV has a great sound system. Raine's always wanted to see California. Also Las Vegas. There's this great song Herb played for her, she tells Eleanor. Has she ever heard of a group called the Mamas and the Papas? "California Dreamin'"?

"Going on a trip with this guy's a bad idea," Toby says. Eleanor's never heard her son speak this way. He sounds almost angry. He's holding tighter than usual to Spyder, as if Herb, with his one foot—and a walker, no doubt, or who knows, a peg leg?—might burst in at any moment and try to snatch him away.

"Let me fix you a cup of tea," Eleanor tells Raine. "I think we should talk about this. What does your father say?"

Raine's mother's dead, that much she knows, and in the months since she moved in down the road there has been no sign of her father, Walt Junior. But from all Eleanor can tell he's nothing like his father, Walt Senior, who would never have charged his grand-daughter rent. If Walt Senior were alive, and he'd heard about some old geezer trying to take his granddaughter off in an RV, he would have had plenty to say, none of it good.

"I haven't told my dad," Raine says. Suddenly she sounds about thirteen years old. "I don't have his number anymore."

"And what about Spyder?" Toby again. "This won't be good for Spyder. Spyder needs to stay here where we can help take care of him."

"I know what you're thinking," Raine tells them. "But before you know it, it's going to be winter again. You know what it costs to heat that house? Not to mention there's nothing going on in this town. Nothing for me anyway. I want to see the world."

Eleanor studies Toby's face. He's shaking his head and rubbing his temples, as if he might summon the brain power to figure out a way to keep this from happening.

"Plus there's the social security check," she continues, addressing her arguments to Eleanor now, having recognized she'll never convince Toby. "It's crazy, all the cash these guys get every month just for still being alive."

"You're nineteen years old," Eleanor says. "When I was nineteen, I had all these ideas that turned out to be wrong, about who I was or what I wanted. I thought I knew a lot that I didn't."

Toby, over in the rocking chair, is still taking in the part about the baby going away. He's holding on to one of Spyder's feet and stroking his earlobes, that one elf ear. His arms are locked around the baby as if someone might try to grab him from Toby's grasp.

"Don't go," Toby says. "Don't take him away."

"Maybe you could take this a little slower, Raine," Eleanor says. "I'm sure you care for this man. But liking a person is different from going off with them to live together in a camper. Ten years from now you could end up being Herb's unpaid health aide, helping him to the bathroom or changing his Depends."

"If you want to go to California, I'll give you money for a plane ticket," Toby adds. "You can leave Spyder here. I'll take care of him."

"Herb bought me a ring," Raine tells them. "With a real diamond. I bet if I hawked that thing I could get five hundred bucks for it, easy."

When Eleanor and Toby drive past Walt and Edith's old house two days later, there's a pile of Raine's discarded possessions out front: an old suitcase with clothes spilling out, the crib Eleanor had given them, her old Swyngomatic baby chair.

Toby is not a person to cry, but he asks Eleanor to pull over for a moment. From the car she watches as her son climbs out from the passenger seat and lumbers over to Raine's trash pile. Slowly, with a kind of reverence, like a man visiting a gravesite, he kneels on the ground. He fishes one of Spyder's stuffed animals out of the pile. That and a blue rubber pacifier on a piece of string.

"I hope she remembers to rub that place on Spyder's belly," Toby tells Eleanor. "He always likes that."

Toby's different after Raine and Spyder take off. He still goes out to the barn every morning to milk the goats, and again around sunset. He still does his farm chores. He talks with his brother in Seattle sometimes, holding the phone close to his ear to take in the sound of baby Flora making gurgling noises. But Eleanor hardly ever hears her younger son humming or whistling anymore. There's a heaviness to his step. At least once a day, usually more than that, she catches him staring out the window and knows, when she does, who it is he's thinking about.

"I wonder what my little pal is doing right now," Toby says. "I wonder if Spyder misses me.

"That's the thing with babies," Toby says. "You can't explain things to them. If somebody they're used to seeing all the time isn't there anymore, there's no way you can explain to them what happened. They're going to think you stopped loving them."

"We'll write," Eleanor tells him. "We'll send postcards."

43.

A bona fide member of the Akersville Volunteer Fire Squad

A notice runs in the *Akersville Gazette*. They're looking for volunteer firemen. It's not a paying job, but that doesn't matter. All Eleanor wants is for her son to be engaged again in something that matters to him, that gets him out of the barn now, where he spends his days with the goats, and puts him in the world of human beings.

Over Eleanor's many years of bowling nights with Toby—starting when he was ten or eleven—the two of them have developed a friendship with the Volunteer Fire Department bowling team, who bowl on Tuesday nights along with all three members of the Akersville police force. Now she calls the captain of the volunteer firemen, Marty. Years ago, he played on Cam's softball team, the Yellow Jackets.

"You know my son has brain differences," she tells Marty. "He can't drive and you might not want him operating your equipment, but I was wondering if there might be a place for him down at the fire station. Cleaning maybe? Hosing down the trucks? He'd be so happy just to be around a group of guys. Since his father died it's been hard for him." The part about Spyder she keeps to herself.

"I remember Toby back from softball days," Marty says. "That boy of yours was a pistol." This would have been Toby before the accident.

"He's different now," Eleanor tells him. "But he'd do just about anything you asked him."

"Bring him down," Marty says.

They put Toby in charge of polishing the brass. That and a job he's born for: When they host groups of children at the fire station, as they do every week or two (sometimes a day care group, sometimes elementary school kids), Toby's in charge of serving the refreshments—fresh-baked cookies he brings from home or Klondike bars. Every time a school or daycare group pays a fire station visit, Toby lifts each child, one by one, into the cab of the fire engine to blow the horn and work the windshield wipers. They've given him a badge and a jacket with the insignia of the Akersville Volunteer Fire Department. He wears it every day, even when milking the goats.

Toby loves everything about his job. Most afternoons now he rides his bike to the station to say hello to the guys and see what jobs needed doing. The brass on the fire engine has never shone as brightly as it has since he started cleaning it. But Toby's favorite times are when the children visit the station house. Nights back at the farm, he tells Eleanor about his day there.

"There was this one little girl, Olivia, that was afraid of climbing ladders," he reports. "So we did it together, the two of us." After, he had given her a stone he'd particularly loved from his collection, to keep on her windowsill—a piece of granite with a tiny garnet chip embedded in it. "Anytime you're afraid of something, you can put this in your pocket," Toby told her.

Another child, Jessica, had shared with Toby the story of a night her father came home drunk and hit her mother, and how the police took him away. She told Toby she had bad dreams in the night. "I told her I sometimes get bad dreams, too," he explains to Eleanor. Then he told Jessica what he does when it happens. Whenever he wakes up from a nightmare, he thinks about someplace he knows that makes him happy and calms him down. He goes there in his head.

Yoga class at the senior center with his dad when he was little is one of those places. So is the goat barn. Then there's the waterfall. For Toby, the fire station has become such a place.

"A kid named Max wet his pants today at the station," Toby tells Eleanor another night. "He was scared the other kids would see."

"What did you do?" Eleanor asks him.

"I pretended to spill a glass of water on him," Toby says. "So he'd be wet all over. That way nobody ever knew."

"If anyone ever says something about how you aren't smart enough, just tell them that one," Eleanor says to her son—she, who did the same thing one time, for a child of her own, when he'd wet his pants at a ball game.

"Nobody's perfect," Toby says. Though if anybody is, Eleanor reflects, it might be Toby.

44.

First your heart gets broken

It's a little after noon, less than two weeks before Christmas. Toby's down at the firehouse, as he is most afternoons now, as soon as his chores in the barn are completed. Eleanor is at her drawing table working on her newest book—the story of Bodie's latest adventures in Mongolia, where she teams up with an eagle huntress. Her editor loves the idea of this latest in the series of Bodie stories because it presents not simply one strong female character but two.

Eleanor looks out the window. A few days earlier flurries covered the field but the day has turned unseasonably warm, with grass showing through the snow. Out under the pear tree, a mother deer and her fawn graze on last season's fallen fruit and overhead a hawk circles. The radio is tuned to the Americana station Eleanor listens to most when she works. Patty Griffin's singing about a woman working at a pie-making company, remembering the love of her youth killed in a war. A voice interrupts the broadcast:

This just in. Earlier today, an unidentified gunman entered an elementary school in Newtown, Connecticut, carrying an

AR-15 semiautomatic assault weapon, opening fire on a classroom of first graders and their teacher, later turning the gun
on himself. Authorities report that twenty-six people have been
killed in the attack, twenty of them children. Before the deadly
assault, the twenty-year-old shooter is believed to have shot and
killed his mother, who had purchased the weapon.

Eleanor sets down her drawing pencil and turns off the radio.
She'll have time enough to learn the rest later.

The picture comes to her of her own children at the age of those
who'd been murdered that morning, and of her grandchildren. Lulu
is seven now, the age of many of the victims.

Eleanor lays her head on her drawing table.

That night she and Toby sit together on the couch listening to
President Obama as he addresses the nation about the tragedy.
Speaking of the murdered children he bends his head, and for a
moment he stands silent at the podium. Eleanor wonders if the
president might break down in tears.

After, washing the dishes from a dinner neither of them felt able
to eat, Toby stands at the sink running water and staring out at the
snow-dusted field. "How do those parents go on living?" Eleanor
says out loud. Maybe she's talking to Toby. Maybe to herself. She's
thinking of the parents of the dead children, but also of their brothers and sisters, their grandparents. Not only those, but the children
who were in the classroom that morning, or in other classrooms
at that elementary school, or in other elementary schools in other
towns. Anywhere. How does anyone hold on to hope in the face of
something like this?

"I don't know," Toby says, still standing there, washing the same
dish. "Your heart gets broken. Then you pick up the pieces."

On the windowsill, the shattered glass bowl.

Eleanor knows Toby's approach to life. Toby's and Jimmy Carter's,
probably. You mourn what's lost and locate good where you can. You
might find it in a goat barn or a fire station or maybe a church—in a
woodshop making hand-turned bowls or with your boots planted on

a vast expanse of ice and your telescope focused on a male emperor penguin standing guard over his eggs. You might even find it at the town dump, sorting your bottles from your cans at the recycling section, shooting the breeze with your fellow townspeople and the guys who work there, stomping their feet on the frozen ground to fight off the cold.

Later that night Al calls—a rare event. Though, unlike his younger sister, her older son bears no rancor toward Eleanor, he's so busy with his company and with his infant daughter that weeks go by sometimes in which she doesn't hear from him.

"I guess I just wanted to hear your voice, Mom," he tells her. "Teresa and I were just sitting here listening to the news and feeling like the world's going crazy. How are we supposed to bring our little girl up in a place where a mentally ill young man, barely out of his teens, can just walk into a classroom with an assault weapon and open fire? How are we supposed to protect Flora against something like that?"

There was a time when Eleanor believed that she could do that: protect her children from grief. She'd locate the lost Barbie shoe and everything would be all right again.

"I think you just raise your daughter to be as strong a person as possible," she tells Al. "That's all a parent can hope for." Children were cork people, bobbing down the stream. Terrible things could happen—and would—over which even the most loving parent had no control.

Eleanor's love had not saved her son from landing face down in the pond and lying there long enough to kill off a significant number of brain cells. Eleanor's love had not spared her oldest child the agony of feeling he was born into the wrong body.

And just because you love your daughter with your whole heart doesn't mean she might not decide, at some point along the line, that she no longer wants to have you in her life for anything more than the most superficial and strained relationship—or simply wants to cut you out altogether. Loss took many forms, for a parent, as it did for a child. Seeing your son or daughter in pain—witnessing trouble coming her way—was worse than anything you could imagine happening to your own self.

All a parent could do was protect her children the best she could for as long as she could, knowing that in the end there was no such thing as a safe place. In a fair world, children would get more than five years on the planet before having to learn this lesson. Parents would get more than five years with their child before they discovered it.

Eleanor learned this earlier than most parents she knows. Nobody needs to tell her anything more about the futility, for a mother, of supposing she can keep her children safe forever.

That December night, as she climbs the steps to bed, Eleanor also knows that nothing anyone says, not even the president of the United States, can serve as consolation for the parents of the murdered children. She has never lost a child as those parents have, but she has known what it is to have a child—one close to the age of those murdered today—whose life is changed forever by the events of a few unspeakable minutes. And though she also knows the Newtown parents would give anything right now if their children had been brain-injured, rather than killed, she has learned a few things about surviving loss over the twenty-seven years since the day they found Toby face down in the pond.

You carry on because there is no alternative. You carry on because you have other children who need you, and because it will be a part of your job now to go out in the world and tell your story in the hope that other parents' children might escape what yours did not. Somewhere along the way, if you work hard at this, you might find a path through the darkness.

45.

Getting together with a guy

S ummer again, 2013 now. Eleanor has turned sixty, Toby's thirty-two. Ursula continues to keep her distance from Eleanor, who has managed a couple of brief visits with Lulu and Orson—times she's driven up to Vermont for some event at their school. No other invitations forthcoming.

Unlike her daughter, Eleanor's daughter-in-law, Teresa, speaks with her often, and easily, about what's going on—with Flora always the most important topic, naturally.

"I guess you heard about Ursula's job," Teresa says to Eleanor.

"New job?"

Teresa is aware of tensions between her mother-in-law and her sister-in-law, but Eleanor tries to keep the rest of the family out of it as much as she can.

"You know how long she's been hoping for this position," Teresa says, though Eleanor hasn't known, actually. "Al and I just hope Jake doesn't resent all this success she's having, with him still unemployed. You know how he can get."

This much Eleanor does know, actually. More and more, she gathers (from Al, and Teresa, and even Elijah has noted this) Jake seems to be embracing a view of himself as a man suffering from oppression at the hands of immigrants, liberals, and strong women. On the rare occasions when Eleanor gets to talk with Lulu over the phone, or Orson, she can hear the television in the background. Fox News, no doubt.

From Ursula, Eleanor hears nothing. Whatever grief she's feeling over the state of her marriage—and Eleanor guesses it's a lot—she keeps to herself. She's staying married. That's all there is to it. (*Unlike you, Mother*: her daughter's unspoken message.)

Eleanor has her own off-limits topic. For her, it's Guy. The two of them have continued their hotel suite assignations for a year and a half now, the passion of those early nights barely diminished, but except for her vague explanations to Toby when she goes away for the night—"I'm getting together with a guy"—she has yet to tell any of her children about him.

It's not like Eleanor to keep a major part of her life from her children. It may be part of what she loves about her relationship with Guy: how unlike her it is, to be doing any of this.

46.

A person's grandmother

Guy flies to Europe to raise money for his next Antarctica expedition, in which he hopes to bring attention to the imminent collapse of the Brunt Ice Shelf, whose disintegration threatens to eradicate an entire population of penguins.

But he's having knee trouble.

"It's looking like I might have to put my expedition off another year," he tells Eleanor. Hearing this, she felt concern as always, for Guy's heath, and the realization of how disappointed he must feel. But she couldn't pretend she wasn't relieved to think of him staying around longer. If you can call Guy's being in Europe "staying around."

He calls her one night from Berlin to say he's thinking of her. (Nighttime in Berlin, anyway. Late afternoon on the farm.)

"I wish you were in this bed with me," he says, his voice low and a little husky, as if he were whispering in her ear. "I could send you a plane ticket." But Eleanor has a book deadline to meet, and after that she's made plans to visit Al and Teresa and Flora out west. With all that they've got going on, it's been difficult keeping connected. Flora's almost five months old. It's about time Eleanor met her. For the first time in their relationship she tells him she can't join him.

Nobody understands better than Guy the part about a person needing to do their work. The part about wanting to meet Flora, not so much.

"She's just a baby," he points out. "She won't even know who you are. She won't remember."

"But I know who she is," Eleanor says. "It's about being in a family."

"Ah, family." He sighs. "I never got that part down."

There's silence on the other end of the phone for a moment. Then he's back. "Tell me what you're wearing," Guy says. "Perfume?"

In fact, what she's got on is an old Lanz nightgown, due to the weather, which has grown surprisingly chilly for October. Flannel. High neck, with lace trim, like something a person's grandmother might wear.

I am a person's grandmother, Eleanor thinks. Three persons, in fact. But she is someone else now, too.

The visit to Seattle goes well. Though Flora was conceived by IVF with a sperm donor, nobody would question Al as her father. Their mouths look surprisingly similar, though Flora's coloring is closer to Teresa's.

"Can you believe it?" Al says to Eleanor, as she studies her new granddaughter—the soft fuzz on top of her head, that Teresa has managed to gather into a pigtail. "She even has hair."

"Your brother's going to love her," Eleanor says. This would be true, with or without hair.

"I know," Al says. "We'll get out back to the farm when our schedules allow. We're just working so hard all the time now.

"I didn't know," he says, "how precious all the days were back when we were young, and it felt like we had all the time in the world."

47.

Fish and Whistle

Finally, right around Flora's first birthday, Al and Teresa come to visit, and Ursula drives down with her family—only the second time she's set foot in the house since Cam died.

Eleanor has no illusions about Ursula's reasons for paying this visit, after all the dinner invitations she's turned down from Eleanor over the years. Ursula wants to see her brother and his wife and their daughter, that's all. When she calls to announce the visit, her voice is cool and clipped as ever.

"Don't go to trouble over dinner, Mother," Ursula had told her before the visit, but Eleanor does, of course. Two kinds of lasagna: regular and vegetarian. Simple buttered pasta for the children. Salad, corn on the cob. Three kinds of pie. It's an old habit of Eleanor's, doing too much.

Seeing the array of dishes when she steps into the kitchen, Ursula shakes her head. "I told you not to," she says to her mother.

"You know me," Eleanor says.

"I do," Ursula agrees. Is it possible the smallest flash of a smile crosses her face? Her eyes scan the counter, the components of the family dinner Eleanor's always dreamed of pulling off. For Eleanor, it's about so much more than food.

"You made strawberry rhubarb," Ursula says. "My favorite."

"I know you, too."

While not without its tensions (Orson spills his milk on Lulu's dress and she cries; Jake asks Al how much money he makes; Flora spits up) the evening they spend together gathered around the farmhouse table feels like the closest Eleanor has known in years—since Cam's death probably, but not even then—to a happy family evening with her adult children and their children.

A happy family evening. Not what Eleanor might have imagined once, but she's learned to lower her expectations. Coached by Ursula, Jake has refrained, for once, from discussing his favorite topic, undocumented aliens crossing the border from Mexico, without any apparent concern for the fact that the family of his sister-in-law, Teresa, comes from Michoachán. The first time he brought up his theories about keeping immigrants out of the United States, Teresa and Al had pushed back hard and Lulu had started to cry. This time they're prepared to leave the room if he starts in, but to everyone's relief—Ursula's in particular, probably—Jake refrains from discussions of the wall, for once.

Over dessert, Toby tells a long story about something that happened down at the fire station, when one of the kindergarteners who visited recently told him that her grandmother died.

"We don't use that word," Ursula says to Toby. "It upsets the children."

"*Grandmother?*" Toby's not the only one looking baffled.

"No. *Died,*" Ursula whispers. "Lulu gets anxious."

"Right," Jake says, his voice very loud, possibly from having consumed multiple beers. "So, when I was driving to the store last week, and the engine on my truck gave out . . . I'm supposed to say it was *indisposed*."

This is the moment Al announces he's brought presents—T-shirts with the logo of his company on the front, and a goofy hat featuring a different variety of fish for each of them. Even Jake, who often retreats to the den on social occasions to turn on the television, puts his fish hat on. All evening a flounder sits on top of his head. After, they play a round of charades. When it's Lulu's turn, she staggers around making funny noises.

"Who do you think I am?" Lulu asks.

"Your father, after his second six-pack?" Ursula suggests. An uneasy silence follows as Lulu continues to portray the character whose name they have yet to guess.

"I know. You're Flora!" Toby calls out. Bingo. Lulu has, in fact, re-created almost perfectly the first steps of a toddler making her way across a room.

As Al clears away the dishes, Lulu approaches Eleanor, an anxious expression on her face. She leans in close so only her grandmother can hear.

"My dad doesn't really drink that much beer," she whispers. "One six-pack maybe. Hardly ever two.

"Also," she says. "I don't really think he hates Mexican people. He's just saying stuff he heard on TV."

From the limited times she gets to see her granddaughter, Eleanor can see Lulu is a sensitive and anxious little girl. Maybe she was born this way, but it seems to Eleanor (though she would never say this out loud) that Ursula reinforces her daughter's fearfulness as a way of keeping her close. Lulu worries about germs and strangers, and has been known to burst into tears if a daddy longlegs touches her arm. One time when she was five, seeing her mother swimming in a pond, with only her head above water, she burst into tears, afraid of where the rest of Ursula's body had gone. At school, as her class was learning alphabet sounds, she expressed the concern that she might forget the difference between *G* and *J*. "It's okay if you do,"

Eleanor told her. "Six-year-olds aren't supposed to know everything. That's why you go to school."

The year before, when Lulu's class put on their annual show at the end of first grade, and they sang "Itsy Bitsy Spider," she asked her teacher if she could be sure to stand somewhere on the stage where she'd be able to spot her mother in the audience at all times.

Her mother, the only person she fully trusts. Strange to think that Eleanor used to be such a person for Ursula.

Now, though, in the glow of the candlelight as the game of charades winds down, Lulu surveys the assembled group—uncles, aunt, cousin, grandmother, brother, parents—and offers a shy little smile. Al, in his salmon-head hat, is teaching Orson an old John Prine song, "Fish and Whistle," Cam used to sing to the children when giving them their baths. Toby's holding Flora, who's fallen asleep in his arms. Ursula's leaning her head on Jake's shoulder, even. Jake rubs her back.

Stop time, Eleanor thinks. *Hold on to this moment.*

"I wish we could always be together like this," Lulu says. "I wish we could always be this happy."

The morning after the big family dinner, Ursula and Jake drive back to Vermont. Al and Teresa stay at the farm three more days, during which time Flora falls in love with Toby, as babies always seem to do, but Flora even more so than any of the others. Though just starting to walk, and far from steady, she wants to follow her uncle everywhere he goes, and particularly loves hanging out with him in the goat barn. By the time Al and Teresa are ready to leave, she's making goat noises and calling Toby To-to.

It's a two-hour drive to the airport. As Al loads their suitcases in the back of Eleanor's car for the drive, Toby comes running out from the barn with a pound of goat cheese for them.

"Come back out to see us in Seattle," Al tells Toby, as they hug goodbye. "We can take in another Mariners game and get more tacos."

"It's not the tacos I care about," Toby tells him. One last hug for Flora. Then they're gone.

48.

As if someone just walked over her grave

Where does the time go? Another full circle of the seasons passes—the familiar rituals of snow followed by thaw, planting the garden, blackfly season, picking blueberries, first frost, first snow, stacking firewood, burning it, starting over. Two years have passed since the night Eleanor and Guy met at that party in Beverly Hills—a passage of time she can measure in gifts of perfume. As costly as the fragrance is that Eleanor and Guy picked out for her, she wears it every time she sees him.

Eleanor's lost count of the number of hotel rooms the two of them have shared, the number of cities she's traveled to for one of their rendezvous, but she still can't bring herself to tell anyone about their relationship. Everything else about her life is well known to all of them—her children, her editor, all those devoted readers of her Bodie books. This is the one thing that feels as if it belongs to Eleanor alone.

There's probably another reason she keeps her relationship with Guy a secret. There's always a part of Eleanor afraid it could end. Between herself and Guy there remains, to Eleanor's amazement and gratitude, a level of excitement not discernibly diminished from the first time he kissed her in that elevator the night they met. This itself sometimes feels odd to Eleanor: that though they don't slip backward in the level of desire they feel for each other, neither do they move toward any different place from the one they inhabited at the beginning. Guy's still raising money for his final expedition back to Antarctica—still held back by joint problems. (This time, his right knee requires replacement.) Eleanor's still looking out for Toby and wishing things were better with Ursula. Ursula's still quietly resentful of Eleanor. The ice shelf has continued to break up. More all the time. Sea levels are rising around the planet. At this rate the Maldives will disappear.

Sometimes Eleanor allows herself to wonder: *What's going to happen to us?* Unlike Guy, she's not thinking about the future of the planet when she asks this question. She's thinking about the two of them. Whether they have a future. She always says that with Guy, she lives in the present. But the present bleeds into the future, doesn't it? What then?

One night in Chicago, lying next to Guy in their king-size hotel bed, a question comes to her. Not the big question—"Where are we heading?"—but an oddly small one that keeps coming into her head at odd moments. Who knows why.

"Colonial Drug," she says to him now. "The perfume. Walking around all that time before choosing the scent. How did you know about that?"

"There was a woman once," he tells her. "She brought me there one time."

"What was her name?" Eleanor asks.

"You know the funny thing," he says. "I don't remember."

For a moment there, a chill comes over Eleanor. A phrase comes to mind. *As if someone just walked over my grave . . .*

Imagine two people who cared enough about each other once to spend a day together choosing perfume. (Two people like herself and Guy. But not her. Somebody else.) Imagine the time coming when one of them no longer remembers the other's name.

49.

Like a priest

It's a Friday night in early fall—the days getting shorter, leaves turning color. Eleanor's home—as she nearly always is, except for the occasional trip to Brookline and those times, every month or two, when she's off in some city where Guy's speaking to spend a night with him. Over these years they've met up in well over a dozen cities, places known to her only by luxury hotel rooms and four-star restaurants. (As much as Eleanor cares about art, she has not visited the Art Institute of Chicago or the Kimbell in Fort Worth or the Atlanta Botanical Garden, though she's passed through all those places more than once in the last couple of years, in a taxi on the way to meet up with Guy. What she knows are the linens in the Four Seasons Hotels in those cities. The champagne.)

Tonight though, Eleanor's settled into bed with a book—Toby asleep in the bedroom next to her, a record playing, a candle flickering by the bed.

Jason calls, having recently returned with his partner, Hank, from their annual trip to Portugal. "Next year you should come join us," he says.

"Not likely," she tells him.

Jason knows nothing of his friend's getaways with her lover. As far as Jason knows, apart from their occasional dinners together in Boston, Eleanor hardly ever goes anywhere.

The movie studio seems to have lost interest in its original promise to keep her involved at every step of adapting her book into an animated film, now titled *Bodie and the Penguins*. Her French publisher has invited her to Paris again for a book tour, but she can't see leaving Toby long enough for that.

"I don't get it," Jason says now. "What are you doing, spending your life in a town full of—no offense—deadbeats, where the big event of the week is some lecture on loon habitats at the library? When are you going to get a life?"

She wants to tell him she has one actually. Instead, she chooses to tackle Jason's dismissal of her town and its residents.

"The people who live in Akersville aren't deadbeats," Eleanor tells him. "Most of them just haven't had the advantages you and I did. Take that young woman, Raine, who used to live down the road, until she took off with a man from an old folks' home. You know what? Her mother died when she was seven. From what I gather, her father was pretty checked out. She got pregnant when she was seventeen to a guy who beat her up. Everyone's got their story."

Eleanor thinks about her friend Darla—dead for almost ten years now. There would be people—and Jason might be one—who would have called Darla a loser for her failure to leave her abusive husband. But if they knew her, as Eleanor did, if they knew the challenges she'd faced, they'd look at her differently. She'd done the best she could with a pretty bad hand.

"I'm sorry. I'm just worried about you, that's all," Jason tells her.

Jason is Eleanor's best friend. Still, until this call she has not been able to bring herself to tell him about Guy Macdowell. As a therapist, he'd probably say she's got serious issues, conducting a relationship as she has for all this time with a man who's always got not simply one foot out the door, but two.

He's not leaving yet, anyway. Eleanor holds on to this. The date Guy has projected for his departure to Antarctica keeps shifting forward. As of now, he's saying he'll get there when light returns next November. It's not tomorrow anyway.

Maybe Eleanor's afraid that if she tells Jason about Guy, he'll judge their relationship and tell her all the reasons she should end it—reasons she has considered but doesn't want to hear. But what kind of friendship is it, where a person can't tell her best friend the truth?

Eleanor takes a breath and refills her wineglass.

"Actually, there's a man I've been seeing," she tells Jake now. "We don't get to be together that much but when we are things feel . . . pretty wonderful." Saying this, relief floods her body. She's finally done it.

"What do you know?" Jason says. On the other end of the line, she can imagine him grinning. "It's about time." He wants to hear everything, naturally.

She describes how it is for her and Guy, those nights they get to be together. Not the whole story. But enough. When she's finished, her friend is uncharacteristically quiet. Finally, he speaks.

"So . . . it's always you that adapts to this guy's schedule, right?"

"You could put it that way."

What she finds in those hotel rooms is worth it, Eleanor wants to tell him. But saying this—even to her friend of so many years— feels scarily intimate, almost dangerous. What if, by revealing the precious secret of how it is between herself and Guy, she ruins everything they have? It's as if they came up with a secret formula they must never reveal, or the whole thing would be lost.

"I don't get it," Jason says. "What's a climate change activist doing flying first class all over the world raising money so he can ride around in a skimobile ? Why doesn't he come to the farm and spend time with you there for a change?"

Eleanor has asked herself the same question. She always comes up with an answer, as she does now for her friend.

Research missions like the ones Guy has conducted in Antarctica and plans to conduct again—or any trip to Antarctica—cost tens of thousands of dollars, Eleanor explains. Hundreds of thousands, for a man like Guy, who brings state-of-the-art camera equipment and videographers with him, by ice cutter ship, to record what Eleanor now knows to call "the calving" of glacial masses and the rate of what Guy refers to as "glacial retreat." Three years ago, Eleanor might not have been able to say whether Antarctica lay at the top of the globe or the bottom. Now—because it matters so much to the man she loves—she's an expert. She has studied Guy's photographs and films of his trips—the vast scale of the landscape, its staggering beauty, and the potential for devastation that would take place if radical action is not taken soon. Eleanor can practically recite his fundraising speech by now.

"Guy is like a warrior," she says. "Or a priest. When you listen to him talk about the effects of climate change on our future, the things I used to think were so important seem so small."

"A priest who stays in five-star hotels," Jason observes.

"I know how it sounds. None of that really matters to Guy. He just has to maintain a certain image."

"You know I just don't want to see you get hurt," Jason says.

"You'd understand if you heard one of Guy's presentations. When people walk out of the room they're practically on fire." Eleanor's seen this over and over. Every night he delivers his speech, in whatever city it might be this time, people line up to shake his hand. Sometimes they're weeping. Many of them write checks to his foundation.

"Time is running out," Eleanor tells Jason. "We all probably know this already. The majority of people just choose to look away. Guy has dedicated himself to bearing witness."

"So where do you fit into this grand plan of his?" Jason asks her.

"I don't try to figure it out," Eleanor says. "I'm just grateful to have this man in my life."

"You're sure you aren't just experiencing, I don't know, hero worship?" Jason asks her. "You love this man, right?"

Of course she does.

"And he loves you? He's told you this?"

It's not Guy's way to talk about love, except when speaking of the planet, the environment, a species (many of them) at risk of extinction. But Eleanor has no doubt that Guy loves her. His actions speak loudest. The way he looks into her eyes with those pale blue, ozone-damaged irises of his. The way he touches her. The bottle of the perfume they'd chosen together. A year into their relationship, on one of their nights in some city whose name she no longer remembers—having noted she was getting near the end of the one he'd bought for her—he'd tucked a new bottle of the scent into her overnight bag.

"Don't take this as a carry-on," he'd told her.

"He loves me," Eleanor tells her friend.

50.

A bite of rotten fruit

December. Two weeks before Christmas. More than four years have passed now since Cam's death—five since Eleanor moved back to the farm. As she did in her old life in Brookline, Eleanor continues to work on her books and drawings—a graphic novel even, and a couple of brief consultations with the movie studio about *Bodie and the Penguins* that felt to Eleanor like the producers' way of checking off a box.

Where she works now that she's living on the farm again is in the space overlooking their old pear tree that used to be Cam's woodworking shop, and then the place he saw his physical therapy clients. There's a woodstove in the studio that she stokes every few hours in winter. In summer she takes a break now and then to dip into the pond. Late afternoons she heads into the house to make dinner for herself and Toby. Simple meals are fine with him.

Eleanor has found a kind of rhythm to her days here now. Every Saturday Toby and Ralph sell their cheese at the farmers' market. Every Sunday Eleanor takes the trash to the dump. One night a week she and Toby go bowling—one lane over from the Akersville police and fire team. The chief, Quince, still asks her out now and then. Eleanor never elaborates on her reasons for turning him down. Every month or so—every six weeks, at most—she flies off to see Guy for a night. Between those times, she works at her drawing table and drives into Boston now and then to see her friends.

One night the phone rings. Ursula. "I've got an appointment in Concord," she says. "I was wondering if I could drive down to the farm with the children and drop them off for the afternoon."

Of course she can. "Is anything wrong?" Eleanor asks.

The question is a mistake. "Do I have to tell you my life story? I just thought I'd take an afternoon off and visit my friend Kat. She used to work at my school," Ursula says.

"Kat. Have I met her?"

"Probably not. Believe it or not, Mother, I have a life that doesn't involve you. Kat and I are working on a grant proposal. Do you have a problem with that?" Ursula's voice is clipped. "Can't you ever just . . . give me some space?"

Here comes one of those moments—and there are many of these—when Eleanor might register hurt, but she's learned not to. Ursula doesn't want to hear about Eleanor's feelings. She's got too many of her own, probably.

"I get it," Eleanor tells her. "I'll take the children anytime."

After this first visit, it gets to be something of a pattern in Eleanor's life—a welcome one. Not every week, or every month even, but now and then Ursula calls up to say she's heading to Concord. Can Lulu and Orson spend the day with Eleanor and Toby at the farm? The answer is always yes. Ursula doesn't get out of the car when she drops the children off, and doesn't take Eleanor up on the offer of a meal or a cup of tea. But getting to see her grandchildren as she has on these visits—and simply catching a glimpse of her daughter— represents a vast improvement from how things had been going before.

"I'm glad to see you getting a little time for yourself," Eleanor says, one time when Ursula returns to pick the children up after they've spent the afternoon with her.

"What's that supposed to mean?" Ursula says—the old sharpness in her voice again, a look on her face as if she's just taken a bite of rotten fruit. When she's with Eleanor, it seldom leaves her. "You act like I've got some kind of problem. Everything's fine."

"I just meant—" Eleanor doesn't know how to end the sentence. "I hope you had a nice afternoon."

"It was fine. I checked in with Kat about our grant proposal and did some shopping. No big deal."

Lulu comes out to the car then. She's carrying the stack of potato print notecards she and Eleanor made this afternoon and a plastic tin of Orson's favorite cookies. "See you later, alligator," she calls out, as the car pulls away. Eleanor stands in the driveway watching them go—Orson turning back to wave, Lulu rolling down the window to call out "I love you, Grammy." When was the last time Eleanor heard words of affection like those from Ursula? So long, she can't even remember, but never mind. She gets to see her grandchildren anyway.

51.

What happiness felt like

In the kitchen one morning, making coffee before heading out to her drawing table, Eleanor's eyes go to the windowsill, the row of broken glass pieces from the expensive Dale Chihuly bowl that Toby brought home from Seattle after his first trip there.

Sometimes the fragments of the bowl look like nothing but a bunch of broken glass. But occasionally, when the light hits them right, they fill the kitchen with rainbows. Now is one such moment.

It's like that with her family, Eleanor thinks. Not all the time, or often—just now and then—the light hits the pieces of colored glass just right, and for what may be just a fleeting moment, everything looks beautiful. If a person doesn't ask too many questions about what happened yesterday or what's going to happen next. If she can just look at this one brief moment in time, without asking for more. It's the sunlight hitting the glass. Catch it if you can.

A few months back there was a visit from Al and Teresa—a single night—when they called to say they were on their way to a software conference in Boston with Flora; could they stop by? Teresa made tamales and Flora went out to the barn with Toby to see the goats. And another night: a call from Ursula to say that Jake was off on a camping trip and Ursula had a day full of meetings and Lulu had come down with chicken pox. Was there a chance Eleanor could drive up to Vermont and watch her? There was.

The two of them got to spend the whole day together, snuggled up on the couch with a stack of books. (*Ramona the Brave. Ramona and Her Mother. Ramona and Her Father.* Lulu loves Beverly Cleary at the moment, though Ursula's concerned by the absence of persons of color in her books.) When Ursula got home, the two of them had fallen asleep with a copy of *Beezus and Ramona* open on Eleanor's chest. A perfect day.

Here's what you did—if you were wise. You held on to these small, good moments, the small, good things, and tried not to be greedy for more. They're like the pieces of expensive broken bowl lined up on the windowsill that catch the light. The times when it hits the glass might be rare. You never knew where you'd find one of these moments, or when. Best not to go looking for them. Keep your eyes open and they'd appear. And for one fleeting moment anyway, you remembered what happiness felt like.

The memory comes to Eleanor of a night not long ago, one of the best. Elijah was on tour with his band, Dog Blue. He called from Providence. "We've got a night off between gigs," he told her. "I was wondering if I could drive up to the farm for the night."

Two hours later Elijah and five members of his band had tumbled out of the van together—guitar cases; amps; microphones; mandolin; two jars of the kimchee made by their Korean bandmate, Duri; a disco ball they'd picked up at a yard sale on the drive. While Eleanor made up the beds, Elijah showed the other members of the band around the farm.

"I can't believe you got to grow up here," the drummer—Crash—told Elijah. "This has to be the coolest place ever." At the end of a dirt road like this, a drummer could play as loud as he wanted and never worry about the neighbors. But the part about the farm that Elijah's friends loved best was the pond. Within minutes the five of them had peeled off their clothes and jumped in the water—naked, shivering, whooping and calling out to each other like a bunch of ten-year-olds playing Marco Polo.

After, Eleanor made dinner for everyone. Not having expected company, she had taken three jars of last summer's tomato sauce down from the pantry shelf and fixed a giant pot of pasta, followed by apple pie.

Sitting around the table after the meal as they took out their instruments and tried out tunes (a little Bob Dylan, a little Tracy Chapman, a Hank Williams song whose words she knew, as Elijah's band members did, too, unexpectedly), a thought had come to her, not for the first time: You may not get what you asked for. Then a gift appears that you never expected—in the form of a band of very young and skinny rock-and-roll musicians, two with dreadlocks, all with tattoos, in the company of her ex-husband's son by his second wife—and before you know it everyone's gathered in the living room singing harmony on "I'm So Lonesome I Could Cry."

It's the light coming through the window at just the right angle, just for a moment there. You wish it never ended but you know it will. Take joy in those moments the sun hits the broken pieces of the Dale Chihuly bowl just right, and never mind when it doesn't. Leave it at that.

52.

Does my mom like you?

Ursula has another appointment in Concord, so she drops Lulu off at the farm. Just Lulu this time. Against Ursula's wishes, Jake has taken Orson to a motorcycle race. So it's just the two of them, Lulu and Eleanor, working side by side in the garden, planting tulip bulbs together. Lulu looks up from the patch of dirt where she's digging a hole. For a moment, she looks so much older than age eight.

"Does my mom like you?" Lulu asks her.

Eleanor's grandchildren, Lulu in particular, have felt it, of course—how could they not?—their mother's coldness toward their grandmother. Now Lulu studies Eleanor's face waiting for an answer. Looking anxious as she so often does.

"Even people who love each other sometimes get on each other's nerves," Eleanor tells her granddaughter. "I probably get on your mom's nerves sometimes, that's all."

"You never get on my nerves, Grammy." Lulu reaches for a bulb and places it in the hole. "But my parents do."

Better to wait for a moment before responding, Eleanor thinks. *Just listen.*

"Sometimes when my dad drinks too much beer my mom gets mad at him." Lulu digs her trowel into the dirt again. "Then my dad gets mad at my mom," she says.

"They don't sleep in the same room anymore." Lulu speaks in a low voice, as if she were worried someone might overhear. But it's just the two of them here.

"Married people have problems, like everybody else," Eleanor tells Lulu. "But one thing for certain is how much they love you and your brother. That's never going to change."

"Somebody always gets mad at somebody," Lulu says. "Things never work out like in Ramona books."

53.

Missing people

More than three years have passed since Raine disappeared with Spyder, but Toby still speaks about him often. "I wonder what my little pal's doing right now," he'll say, when he and

Eleanor drive past the house where they'd lived. Still unoccupied. "I wonder if he remembers me."

Spyder would be five years old now, roughly the age of Orson, though the similarity between the two of them ends there. Eleanor knows how much her son always hoped that when Spyder was old enough he'd work with him in the barn, milking the goats, and in fact, even as a baby, Spyder had loved going out to the barn, much as Flora did when she came to visit. Orson and Lulu, not so much.

The good news is that Ursula has been driving down from Vermont on a regular basis lately—every week almost—to drop off the children to have a day to herself. Somewhere around six o'clock, usually, Ursula returns from her day on her own to pick up the children. On these occasions she'll give her brother a quick hug, then busy herself packing up the children's things. Lulu always asks if they can stay for supper. The answer is always no.

"I wish the kids lived closer," Toby says after one of their visits, as he and his mother stand in the driveway—the sun going down over the field, the house quiet again—watching Ursula's car drive away with the children buckled in back. "I miss them already."

"It's hard missing people," Eleanor says. "But just think how much harder it would be if you had no one to miss."

54.

Make hay while the ozone layer disappears

The other person Eleanor misses—though she has told herself she wouldn't let this happen—is Guy. The rhythm they've established over the years since they met—three of them now—continues, unchanged. Guy sends Eleanor a plane ticket. She flies out to see him, and they spend the night together—sometimes, on rare occasions two, never more than that. Between these nights weeks might go by—sometimes longer—in which the two of them barely communicate. Eleanor understands this, or says she does anyway. When the man you love is trying to save the planet from destruction, you don't expect a nightly phone call from him asking how your day went.

After many delays, the animated film adaptation of Eleanor's book—the movie that had brought the two of them together in the first place—is set to go into production, finally, with plans for a big spring release the following year. Over the years since the project got underway, Eleanor has received occasional updates from Marlys, the producer, or more typically from her assistant, Kiki. Nobody involved in the film appears to have a clue that Eleanor and Guy have had anything to do with each other since that one evening in Los Angeles when they met, and they prefer it that way.

For Guy, it appears, there seems nothing extraordinary about the way he and Eleanor conduct their relationship. He's lived a substantial portion of his adult life alone on one pole or the other, hiking across a vast ocean of snow in the company of climate scientists who share a single passion—to protect some of the most fragile regions of the continent of Antarctica and possibly the planet's entire ecosystem. Guy has told Eleanor that after his marriage ended—and in truth, it had ended years before the divorce papers were signed—he never supposed that anyone other than another polar explorer could understand, let alone accept, his passionate obsession, or the long and grueling absences it required. These years in which he and Eleanor have been conducting their odd, intense, geographically challenging relationship constitute the longest consecutive period of years in which Guy has stayed away from one or the other of the poles in his entire adult life. He's getting restless, and Eleanor knows this.

Guy has taken pains to explain to Eleanor the difference between the work he does in Antarctica and that of the scientists he consults with. Guy's an explorer, an adventurer—cut from the mold of Ernest Shackleton and Captain Robert Falcon Scott, but with the particular mission to bring awareness to the crisis of the retreating ice shelves. Guy's most recent estimate for when he means to resume the final leg of his conquest—the last seven hundred miles of his trek from the coast to the interior of Antarctica—calls for a departure date a year into the future, more or less. Eleanor reminds herself that Guy's projections are as shifting as the glaciers themselves. He might leave in one year. Might leave in two. He'll leave at some point. This much she believes. But not forever. More than Eleanor has intended, she holds on to this thought.

"There may come a day when it no longer makes sense to you, putting up as you do with an old bastard like me, obsessed with melting ice," Guy tells her. "If so, I'll understand. Meanwhile, let's treasure whatever time we get."

"Make hay while the ozone layer disappears," he says. "Bad joke."

They're in New York City, spending the night together at the Four Seasons—a place as far removed from a tent on the 92nd parallel as any, probably. The two of them are lying naked on the one-thousand-thread-count sheets with all of Central Park stretched out below them—as green as Antarctica is white. Guy has a look on his face that Eleanor has come to recognize. He's thinking about glacial melt.

"There's something important I'm going to ask you to do for me," she says. She positions her face so there's no way he can avoid her eyes. In all this time, she has hardly ever asked this man to do anything for her beyond what he chooses. Now she does.

"I need you to come to the farm," she tells him. "I need you to see my world. I want you to meet my son."

She means Toby, of course. Who's probably out in the barn at this very moment, saying good night to the girls.

A while back she started offering Toby the simplest of explanations for her occasional absences from the farm, times she leaves for her overnights with Guy. "There's a man I go see," she has told Toby. "*Guy.*"

Maybe the name confuses him. Probably not. Guy is a guy. Simple as that. But recently Toby has raised a question that, like so many of the things he asks Eleanor, makes perfect sense.

"Why don't I ever get to meet this guy?" Toby asked her. Capital *G* or small, it hardly matters. "Doesn't he want to meet me?" If

Toby hadn't asked this, it's possible Eleanor never would have. She's grown so accustomed to the terms of their relationship and to its boundaries (*boundaries*! There comes Ursula's term) that she never questions them—for fear of the answers they might yield.

She has told Guy about Toby, of course. He's heard about Al and Ursula and Elijah. Guy knows about Eleanor's art studio, her garden, Raine and Spyder, the Akersville Volunteer Fire Department, the bowling alley, the waterfall. Where the landscape Guy inhabits, vast as it is, remains virtually uninhabited, Eleanor's life includes a whole cast of characters known only to Guy as names in her stories.

Guy has no children of his own. His most meaningful human connections are those with fellow climate activists and board members of the foundation that funds his work. What could he know of a brilliant and driven son who used to be her daughter, carving out a life for himself and his family on the West Coast, a daughter who still blames her mother for a divorce that happened a quarter century before, a granddaughter who wakes up in the night crying from another dream about men with guns coming into her second grade classroom? What could he know of a brain-injured goat farmer who lifts preschoolers into the cab of a fire truck and shows them how to work the windshield wipers? Eleanor wishes Guy could know them all. But the one she most needs him to know is Toby. The place she needs him to see is the farm.

"I want you to meet my son," Eleanor says to Guy, again. "Just one time, would you come to the farm?"

Guy's response surprises her. She has imagined that if she were lucky, and Guy appeared open to her idea, they'd make a plan for a visit months in the future.

"Tomorrow's a free day," he tells her. More so than most anyway. He can cancel his lunch appointment and a conference call with the board.

"I'll rent a car and we'll drive up," he says. "We'll leave the city early enough that I can spend the afternoon there. I've always wondered how they make goat cheese."

55.

A newborn goat and a Tesla

Guy rents a Tesla for the drive up to the farm from New York City. It's a little after two o'clock when the car pulls down the long dirt road to the place where Eleanor's old farmhouse used to sit.

"Here's where my children were born," Eleanor tells Guy, as the spot comes into view. Eleanor knows better than to expect much response to this information from Guy. The birth of babies—humans, not penguins—is not a life event Guy registers in a big way.

He pulls the car up alongside the spot where the new house stands. "Toby and I live here," Eleanor tells him. She points out her garden and the pear tree and beyond that, her studio and the goat barn. Her heart is pounding. Until now, she hadn't realized how important it is to her, that he see this place.

A Tesla is an incongruous sight here. For a moment Eleanor imagines what Cam would say if he came back from the dead to see a hundred-thousand-dollar sports car parked outside the woodshop where he'd made his burl wood bowls.

"I wasn't expecting it to be so beautiful," Guy tells her. Eleanor feels a rush of pride.

She has promised herself she will not be greedy, but this is her secret, though she tells no one: She longs to integrate her two worlds—longs to connect the days with her family with the nights she and Guy spend together. Never enough of them. *Imagine*, she thinks. *Having both.*

She has called ahead to let Toby know they're coming. He appears in the doorway now, wearing one of his special outfits in honor of Guy's visit—a suit he'd found at Goodwill. The original owner must have been taller than Toby, and significantly wider, but to Toby these are minor details. The suit is made of seersucker and came with a vest. He's wearing his Town of Akersville Volunteer Fireman badge. Not having a handkerchief, he's stuck a bandanna in the breast pocket.

"Nice car," he says to Guy. He reaches out his hand. "So you're the guy."

"I've heard a lot about you," Guy tells him.

"Did my mom mention I'm a volunteer firefighter?"

She did.

"She probably told you about my accident, huh?" Toby tells Guy. "I used to be smarter but that's okay. Brains aren't the only important thing in life."

"There's different kinds of smarts," Guy says. "You're probably smart about some things I don't know anything about."

"My mom told me you spend a lot of time walking around in the snow."

"You could say that," Guy tells him.

The two of them—Eleanor and Toby—show Guy around the farm, pointing out all the highlights—Toby and Elijah's old tree-house, Eleanor's herb garden, the spot Toby, Ursula, and Al buried their time capsule when they were young, the place where lady's slippers come up every spring. Toby shows Guy his rock collection and the barn, of course. He introduces Guy to the girls, checking on Bernadette, who's pregnant, due in a few days from the looks of her. They inspect Eleanor's drawing table, with the colored pencils lined up in their rows, arranged by color family, and drawings for her new book tacked on the walls along with the pictures Eleanor and Lulu made recently for a story they're writing together about a pair of talking shoes.

"I understand there's a waterfall down the road," Guy says to Toby. To a man who has spent a lot of time studying water—frozen or melted, but preferably frozen—water is a perpetual source of interest.

"You want to see it?" Toby says.

Guy does.

On the drive up to the farm, Eleanor had wondered how it would be for her son to see her with a man who wasn't his father, as he never has until now. Now the three of them walk down the road together to the falls—Guy in his beautiful cashmere sport jacket. Toby in pinstripe seersucker. Eleanor between the two of them.

"You like my mom, huh?" he asks Guy. "Everybody should have someone they love. I hope I have a girlfriend someday."

The three of them stand together on the stone arch bridge looking down at the racing water, the rocks.

"It's funny," Guy says. "I wouldn't have guessed this but in some ways this spot reminds me of places I know in Antarctica. Open water under ice. That's one of the things that makes it so challenging walking across an ice sheet. You never know what's happening under your feet, or when the ice could give way."

"My dad's here," Toby says. "His ashes. People call them ashes, but really they're more like little pieces of bones."

"Not a bad place to end up," Guy says. "When the time comes, I hope my ashes make it to Antarctica. When they cremate me, I want to be wearing my best polar boots and gloves and my sheepskin hat."

"You should always have a good hat," Toby says, tapping his head. His cap is bright orange—to alert hunters, no doubt; Ursula has made sure of this. "My sister made mine."

"A good hat is important," Guy agrees. "And a good sister."

Toby has made dinner: grilled cheese sandwiches and sardines, celery sticks with peanut butter, raisins, and pickles. He explains to Guy that he biked into town to pick up his favorite dessert, Klondike bars.

After, they sit in the living room. Guy asks if Toby would like a cigar, and when Toby says yes, he takes out his case. He's brought along two particularly fine Cubans.

They stand outside the barn, looking up at Cassiopeia—a constellation that appears upside down, viewed from the pole—with their cigars in hand. Toby coughs a little. Nobody's saying anything or feeling any need to do so. Eleanor takes a puff of Guy's cigar—not inhaling; she just likes the smell.

"I'm like James Bond," Toby says, blowing a smoke ring.

"I should probably take off," Guy tells them, after they've finished the cigars. "I've got a five-hour drive back to the city and a meeting with a big donor in the morning."

Just then, from inside the barn, comes a sound unfamiliar to anyone who hasn't raised goats. A low moaning—not the human kind.

"I'd better check on the girls," Toby says. But he already understands what this means. *It's Bernadette.*

She's lying on her side, emitting sounds of extreme discomfort. From the rear end of her, just underneath her tail, a bulge that looks at first like the water balloons Eleanor's children played with long ago on hot summer days is coming out of her. Just barely visible at first.

"Bernie's having her kid," Toby says. From her behavior that day, he'd recognized the time was close but thought she had another day or two to go. This is her first delivery. No telling yet if she's carrying one kid or two.

Toby hands Eleanor his suit jacket. He kneels beside the laboring goat, Eleanor beside him, stroking Bernie's haunches. Guy stands back for a moment before joining them in the straw.

"What do we do?" he asks.

"Nothing," Toby tells him. "I only step in if she gets into trouble."

The goat is breathing heavily now. He strokes the spot between her ears—a tuft of stiff, wiry hair that reminds Eleanor of Toby's cowlick back when he was young.

"You're doing great, sweet pea," Toby tells Bernadette. She looks at him with her dark, soulful eyes. So different from the blue of Guy's.

Then one hoof is out. Surprisingly, considering how many baby goats have been born on their farm over the years, this is only the second time Eleanor has joined her son in the barn for the actual moment of birth. Goats give birth in the night, mostly. The last few times one of the girls delivered her kid Eleanor was away visiting Guy.

The sight of Bernadette's kid emerging from the body of its mother—though with a single foot coming first, not the head—is not all that different from what Eleanor observed, and will remember always, of the night Raine delivered Spyder on the bed in their living room. Goat or human, it's a moment that makes a person hold her breath and pause at the wonder of the world. She can make out the face of the kid now—mostly white, with a black patch around the nose and the ears—but her eyes, or his, remain shut, and from its mouth no sound comes. No movement except the bleating of the mother, pushing hard against the straw, her face reaching upward to the rafters of the barn as if in some form of supplication. *Get me out of here.*

Then comes another foot. Now Bernadette stands on all fours, leaning against the wooden slats of her stall, her kid dangling, wet and bloody, like a piece of meat, sliding out from the soft pink opening in her body. There's still no sign of movement from the newborn goat. Eleanor can feel her stomach tighten. She looks at Toby. No evidence of panic, but he looks worried.

"The baby's not doing anything," Guy says. "What do we do?" There's no question who's in charge here.

"Give her a minute," Toby tells them. "Sometimes it takes a new kid a little longer to know they're in the world."

The kid has dropped in the straw now. This should be the moment, Eleanor knows, when a healthy newborn goat rises on her own four feet and makes her way to her mother's teat. This one just lies there.

Toby knows what to do. Just as Guy pointed out a few hours earlier, there are many forms of intelligence. One might involve knowing how to calculate the rate of glacial melt on the polar ice cap. Another: knowing what to do for a goat kid not yet breathing.

"Molasses," Toby says. From the jar he evidently keeps handy in the barn, he puts a drop on his finger, then puts his finger in the mouth of the newborn goat, rubbing the inside of her cheek. Another goes in the mouth of Bernadette, who's not in danger, but clearly upset. Though Toby's not generally a person who does things fast, there's a sense of urgency in his voice at the moment that brings to Eleanor's mind the awful day when the one who lay motionless on the ground, not breathing, was her son.

Now Toby has wrapped his jacket over the baby goat. Guy sits next to him, taking it all in. Then, as gently as he would if what he cradled in his arms were the most precious treasure—and to Toby, it is—Toby lifts the baby goat from the straw, his strong hands clasping firmly but not too tight to her belly. For the first time, she opens her eyes. She has a look on her face as if she's angry, and her whole body's trembling. But she's breathing.

"I will never forget this night," Guy says. He, a man who has sat to the right-hand side of the president at a White House dinner.

It's close to midnight when he gets in his car to make the long drive back to New York City.

Toby and Eleanor stand outside the house watching as the Tesla disappears down the long dirt driveway.

"Nice visit, but short," Toby says. "He seems like the kind of guy that likes to keep moving."

Toby doesn't need to tell her. He likes to stay put.

56.

Kids. Both kinds.

Somewhere around 2:00 A.M.—Toby, Bernadette, and the new kid all resting no doubt after their eventful night in the barn—Eleanor calls Guy. She's in bed. It's an unspoken rule in their relationship that they hardly ever call each other between their hotel nights, but in the aftermath of Guy's visit to the farm, a powerful feeling has come over Eleanor. She misses him.

He'll still be out on the highway—somewhere between New Hampshire and New York City—so there's no danger of interrupting an important meeting.

"I loved seeing you today," she whispers into the phone, with Toby asleep, or getting there, in the bedroom beside hers. "Now when you're off raising money or pulling some sled across a sheet of ice when it's fifty below zero, you'll be able to picture me here."

"I loved watching you in the barn. You looked beautiful. Glowing."

It should make Eleanor happy, hearing him say this. The hard part is knowing—as she has come to understand more clearly in the last few months—that for Guy, an essential aspect of their relationship is not simply about being together but equally, perhaps, about the romance of being apart. He does not say—and Eleanor knows he wouldn't—that he wishes he could be on the farm with her.

"Your son's a great kid," he says. "He's doing so well for a person with a brain injury."

For a moment, it's as if she's on the phone with a man who doesn't even know her. Doesn't know her son. Two hours ago, they had kissed each other goodbye, but Guy might as well be in Antarctica now.

So many years have passed since the day of Toby's accident, she never thinks of him as brain-injured anymore. He's just Toby, a person who functions differently from others. A person whose brain, whatever injury it sustained long ago, seems to grasp much that the brains of those with so-called normal brain function do not—Guy, a prime example. As smart as he is, and knowledgeable about so many things—climate change, endangered species, the best brand of boots for hiking in subzero temperatures—to Eleanor at this moment, Guy seems clueless, but there's probably no point in trying to make him see. How does a person begin to explain something as boundless as what she feels for her son?

"Maybe you can't understand because you aren't a parent."

"It's a funny thing," Guy tells her. "In all these years, even when I was at the age when people I knew were getting married and having children, I never thought about what it might have been like, having one myself. It was never part of the picture I had of my life."

"I could never have imagined my life without my children," Eleanor tells him.

Guy's silent for a moment. She can tell, because she knows him so well, that he has another cigar in his hand.

"An idea came to me while I was driving," he says. "Inspired by my tour of the farm."

"Let me guess. You want to raise goats. Or build a treehouse." Still shaken by his observation about Toby, all Eleanor can do is make a joke. He seems not to notice.

"Maybe someday I could bring you with me to Antarctica. Show you my world the way you showed me yours."

She pictures the two of them setting their backpacks down in one of the special superinsulated tents she's seen pictured in the slide shows Guy presents at his fundraising lectures, one of the places he and his crew stay when reporting on the work of scientists measuring the rate of ice mass loss—an event Guy calls "a global catastrophe" of a scope barely comprensible.

But it's not the findings of the scientists Eleanor thinks about. She sees the two of them at the end of the day standing in front of a tent, taking in the night sky—more vast than anything she's ever witnessed, even the ocean. One time during his South Pole hike, he has told her, he'd stood on an expanse of unbroken snow the size of the entire United States. Nothing but snow and ice in every direction for three thousand miles. Nobody else to see it but him. Guy and only Guy.

She pictures the two of them unzipping the flap that forms the door to the tent, a gas heater glowing in the semidarkness, pictures them stepping in out of the cold, peeling off their clothes—their naked bodies under a pile of thermal blankets, the clouds their breath would make in the frigid arctic night.

"I wouldn't expect you to go with me on the long hike of course," he says. "We'd just stay at base camp for a few days. If you spent a night under those stars, you'd know why I keep going back."

There are many reasons that Eleanor will not accompany Guy to Antarctica, and when she considers these, she realizes that the challenge of leaving Toby for more than a night or two does not represent the insurmountable obstacle. Eleanor has never loved cold weather—even what passes for cold weather in New Hampshire—but she could deal with that part. She knows, too, that Guy could work out all the details, find her the perfect boots, the ultimate parka, the best gloves. She could sleep in the most hostile environment on earth if he were there next to her. She's done harder things.

It comes to Eleanor that as much as Guy has felt a need to offer the prospect of this trip together, if she were actually to take him up on his invitation, it would never work. As much open space as exists on that frozen continent, there's no room for Eleanor there. As little as Guy understands about who Toby is to Eleanor, that's how little Eleanor will ever understand what Antarctica is to Guy.

She has lost count of how many times she's sat at the back of some lecture hall, seeing the slide come up on the screen with the picture of Guy in his Cub Scout uniform at age ten—a boy who'd never ventured farther than Cincinnati—and heard him tell the story of finding a book in his small-town library about the adventures of Admiral Scott and his team from a hundred years before. Every man on that expedition had died less than three miles from their destination at the pole.

"And that was the moment," Guy always tells the audience—leaning close to the microphone, closing his eyes as if he's summoning the memory for the first time—"when I made myself the promise that one day this small boy from a mining town in eastern Ohio would accomplish what Admiral Scott and his men had failed to do. Set foot at the southernmost place on earth."

She could give the speech herself now—not just about the hundred-mile-an-hour wind, the weeks Guy spent cross-country skiing over the treacherous terrain, but also his years of work conferring with climate scientists, measuring the thickness of the ice, recording its recession as the sun bore down on the ice sheet. Word for word, she knows the story of Guy's life-altering encounter, when he was young, with Jacques Cousteau, and how the great explorer had put a hand on his shoulder and spoke the words that shaped his destiny.

"It's up to you, young man, to carry on the work I've been doing."

It was Cousteau himself who had entrusted Guy with responsibility for seeing to it that no oil rig ever plumbed the depths of Earth's one remaining pristine continent, the place on which one of the planet's most vital ecosystems now depended.

"The worst failure of any human being," Guy tells his audience at the end of every one of his presentations, "lies not in what we do, but in the willingness of some to do nothing." From her seat in the back of whatever room he was speaking in, Eleanor often mouthed the words along with him.

"Together, we can save the planet," Guy tells his audiences. "It begins tonight."

The line always gets a standing ovation. There's always a swarm of admirers surrounding Guy after, wanting to shake his hand. He never needs to tell Eleanor not to approach the podium. This is his moment to confer with donors. Their time—his and Eleanor's—comes later.

Antarctica is Guy's world as much as the farm has become Eleanor's again, and when he finally returns there—as he says now he is finally ready to do, once he completes the rehab on his new knee—the last thing he'll want is a woman at his side. If Eleanor were there with him, they'd end up hating each other.

It's 3:00 A.M. now. Guy's probably almost back to Manhattan. In the morning, he'll return the Tesla and get on a plane. Denver maybe. Or Toronto. She's lost track.

"We'll talk about the Antarctica trip another time," she says to him. But she knows this: they won't.

57.

Wheel of Joy

Springtime returns. The daffodils Eleanor and Lulu planted the previous fall come up, followed by the lilacs and after that, lupine. Years before, on a trip to Maine when she and Cam were still together, Eleanor gathered a bunch of lupine seed pods to bring home and scattered them around the edges of their pond. Now they bloom every year, lining the edge of the water—a glorious border of pink and purple against the dark water beyond.

Toby and Ralph have taken care to set out the portable goat fencing in such a way as to protect the flowers from being eaten. The baby goat born the night of Guy's visit to the farm, later named Molasses—along with her twin sister, Scarlett, delivered directly after—now grazes in the field, leaping over rocks and munching on grass.

"Do you think, if I ever got Scarlett Johansson to come to the farm, she'd take it the wrong way, me naming a goat after her?" he asks Eleanor. "Do you think it would hurt her feelings?"

Toby nuzzles his face against Scarlett's flank and scratches her head—a place she loves, between her ears. "The thing is, Scarlett's the most beautiful of all the girls," Toby says. Scarlett the goat, he means. Though he'd say the same of Scarlett the movie star.

Things on the farm are going well. At an agricultural fair in Brattleboro, Toby's cheese—Wheel of Joy—wins first prize in the Artisanal Goat Cheese division. After goat-birthing season is finished, Al and Teresa once again buy Toby a ticket to visit them in Seattle. As they did on his first visit out west, they take him to a Seahawks game and—because Toby loves traditions—to the same food truck where, on his previous visit, he ate what he considers to have been the best fish taco of his life. But mostly what he talks about when he returns home from his three days out west is Flora. She's beginning to speak in both English and Spanish. She calls Toby mi amor.

At the fire station, too, he's the favorite of the groups of schoolchildren who come on field trips. In the thank-you notes their teachers have them send to the volunteer firemen after these visits, the children nearly always single out Toby as their favorite part of their visit. The drawings they send to accompany their thank-you notes nearly always feature Toby prominently. "I wish Toby was my uncle," one of the children wrote. "I wish I had a dad like him."

Children always adore Toby. Orson and Lulu among them. But there remains one child more than any other, closest to his heart. Flora. "There's something special about her," Toby tells Eleanor. "We understand each other."

For Toby, who is not always easily understood, this is the best thing.

58.

Inch by inch

ulu's class is putting on a show and she's invited Eleanor and Toby to attend. Two of the goats are due to give birth any day, so Toby can't get away. But Eleanor has made the drive to Vermont.

She sits with Ursula and Jake, of course—Ursula, looking tense as usual. Orson climbs on Eleanor's lap and takes out his tablet. Jake smells like beer.

The curtain opens on the scene of a barnyard, Lulu dressed as a baby chick. As one of the smallest children in the cast, she's been positioned in the front row, which makes it easier for Jake, who's making a video, to capture the event. The children are singing a song about gardening that Eleanor taught her own children long ago. *"Inch by inch, row by row, going to make this garden grow . . ."*

("I don't get it," Lulu pointed out to Eleanor, earlier. "Chickens don't plant gardens." "Never mind," Ursula told her. "It's just a show.")

The children have learned hand gestures to go along with the song. Onstage now, they're acting out *"all it takes is a rake and a hoe"* and patting the floor when they get to the part about planting the seeds. Eleanor keeps her gaze on her granddaughter—that earnest, hopeful look she remembers as Ursula's once. The old Ursula who, like Lulu now, always kept an eye on her parents to make sure everything was okay. Always intent on making her family happy and doing a good job.

After the song is over, some of the children bow and wave. Lulu looks out to the audience, searching for her family. When she spots them, she allows herself a small, shy smile. After, they gather around with the other parents and grandparents to celebrate their new graduate. Eleanor takes them all out for ice cream.

"I wish you could come to our house for a sleepover," Lulu tells Eleanor. "I could show you my terrarium."

Eleanor studies Ursula's face, looking for a sign.

"Grammy's probably busy," Ursula tells Lulu. "Plus, Uncle Toby needs her back home."

This might have been the moment for Eleanor to say that she isn't that busy, actually. Toby can manage fine without her—something she's learned from the many times over the last few years when she's taken off to see Guy without repercussions on the home front. But Ursula knows nothing of these trips or the reason for them. Even now that she's dropping the children off at the farm on a semi-regular basis, Ursula always appears to be on the lookout for evidence of her mother's deficiencies and mistakes in judgment. Eleanor's relationship with Guy would probably fall into this category.

"You know, I'd love to have a sleepover," Eleanor says to Lulu. "But I should probably head home."

She hugs them goodbye. The children and Jake first. Ursula last.

"I wish it was easier between us," Eleanor says, softly enough that only Ursula can hear her.

The look on her daughter's face then is not so much angry as sad.

"It's not a great time right now," Ursula tells her.

59.

A common misconception about polar bears

With Al, busy as he is, things are good. On Memorial Day weekend, he and Teresa pay another short visit to the farm, where Flora gets to see a baby goat. "You pick her name," Toby tells Flora. The name she chooses: Amor.

June now. Guy's invited to speak at a climate change symposium in Seattle. He buys Eleanor a plane ticket. Though always before, the occasions when they meet up had been reserved for each other, this time she suggests that they have dinner with Al and Teresa.

"There's a man I've been seeing," she tells the two of them over their weekly phone call a few days before the trip. "I want you to meet him."

"You deserve a good partner, Eleanor," Teresa says. "Who is he? Where does he live?"

It's easier than Eleanor anticipated, telling her son and his wife about Guy—his work, and how they met—though she avoids the part about how long the two of them have known each other—going on five years now, with no mention of his existence until now.

"We're working together on a film adaptation of one of my books," Eleanor tells Al and Teresa. Couching it this way, the relationship feels safer, less crazy. No need to add it's been a year since either of them has been consulted on the project, let alone heard a word about where it stands.

Al's question to her about where Guy lives is harder to explain. Between speaking engagements he stays in the homes of wealthy patrons and board members. Otherwise, he lives in hotel rooms around the world, when not in a yurt on a rapidly melting ice shelf. Guy lives everywhere and nowhere.

It's not so surprising that Eleanor has said as little as she has about her get-togethers with Guy. If they had a more conventional relationship—meaning, if they lived together, shared friends, projects, mundane activities—there'd be all these aspects of their day-to-day experiences Eleanor might share with her children. When two people conduct their relationship exclusively in hotel rooms—in one-night increments—there's no way of concealing how much the whole thing must involve sex.

This much Eleanor understands. Nobody's adult children—even Al, a reasonable and nonjudgmental person—want to imagine the sexual life of their mother. But her reasons for withholding the full story of her time with Guy go deeper. Telling Al and Teresa about Guy, at last, Eleanor has had to confront a hard truth that didn't come up in the same way when she introduced Guy to Toby. As much as her relationship with Guy means to Eleanor, a part of her never fully trusts that it can last. She's afraid of announcing that she's in love with Guy only to have to tell them and her son, later, that it hasn't worked out. He's heard that story before. All three of her children have.

The visit with Al and Teresa goes off with surprising ease. Eleanor's son and his wife greet Guy warmly. Al wants to hear about the final leg of Guy's ski adventure cross Antarctica, the differences between the two poles. He's curious to know what kind of computer programs the National Science Foundation uses to track glacial melt. Teresa's curious about the animal life in Antarctica.

"It's a common misconception that polar bears and penguins cohabit," Guy tells her. He goes on to explain that polar bears inhabit the North Pole exclusively, while penguins are confined to the south. "If penguins occupied the North Pole, polar bears would have no issue with their food supply," Guy explains. "And penguins would have evolved with the ability to fly instead of acquiring flippers for swimming."

Guy's in his element discussing the topic of the two polar regions. It's what happens on all those other continents between them—the one where Eleanor lives, in particular—that challenges him.

"The South Pole is colder than the North," he goes on to tell Teresa, who looks genuinely interested. "Not that temperatures in the North Pole can be described as balmy." Antarctica is basically an ice formation over an ocean, he explains—melting so rapidly now that many portions of the ice sheet over which he once trekked could no longer be reached on skis.

For this reason, all of Guy's work now focuses on the southern polar regions of Antarctica, whose rich stores of oil place the continent in grave danger of drilling that, if allowed, would ultimately destroy it.

"Call me an obsessed and driven man," Guy tells Al and Teresa. "I can't argue with that. Time is running out."

For decades, Guy explains, a treaty has been in place, preserving Antarctica's resources, but that treaty is due to expire in the year 2041. "If we don't do anything to protect those resources before then," he says, "oil rigs and tankers will move in and the last pristine place on the planet would be lost forever."

Eleanor has heard this speech countless times before. Every time she hears it, though, she feels Guy's passion. Greater, she knows, than any other he may possess. This includes his passion for her. He tells Al and Teresa how, on his most rigorous trek at the North Pole, his eyes had actually changed color from lack of protection.

"They weren't always blue," he tells them.

This, too, was a familiar story, one of Guy's best, though Eleanor must have heard it fifty times.

"I so admire what you're doing, Guy," Al says, "I'd love to see how our company might become involved."

Guy hands Al his card. He's never without one.

Dinner's over by eight thirty; her son picks up the check. "So when are you going back to Antarctica?" Al asks Guy, as they head out to their cars.

"We haven't set the date just yet," Guy tells him. The four of them stand there outside the restaurant, waiting for the valet to come with their cars. *We still have more time,* she thinks.

More than she anticipated, Eleanor feels happy that she has been able to introduce her older son and his wife to the man who has become so important to her. Even more, she loves it that Guy met them.

Al and Teresa would not imagine, probably, the longing Eleanor felt over the course of that dinner to get back to their hotel room. To Eleanor's son and daughter-in-law, no doubt, Eleanor and Guy are a couple of almost-senior-citizens keeping each other company, passing the time together discussing climate change and books, probably. Eleanor never ceases to feel gratitude that at the age of sixty, she still feels excited every time she walks into a hotel room with him.

Some things are important for a parent to share with her children. Some not.

In the car heading to their hotel, Eleanor waits to hear what Guy has to say about their evening with her son and his wife.

"Great couple," he says. "If I didn't know Al was born a girl, I never would have guessed. He seems like a totally normal man."

A chill comes over Eleanor. There are so many things a person might have observed about Al after spending an evening with him. His kindness, his obvious devotion to his wife, his passion and modesty concerning the work he does and, more so, the interest he showed in Guy's work as well as his mother's. Of all the things Guy might have noted about Al, is that what mattered most?

"I don't even think about that anymore," Eleanor says, as he pulls up to the valet parking at their hotel. She can hear the sharpness in her voice, though Guy appears not to have noticed it.

"Let's focus on you and me now, shall we?" he says, as they head to the elevator. He kisses her neck. Perfume there, naturally.

60.

Goat relationships and Japanese ceramics

It's late September, the temperature unseasonably hot. Three of Toby's girls are in their fertile period, which means a trip to the stud farm. It's a two-hour drive, goats in the back. Eleanor at the wheel, her son beside her, humming.

Over the years, Toby has brought his goats to a number of different farms for stud, but Hans Verlander's place is his favorite. For many goat farmers Toby knows who raise breeding stock, the process of inseminating female goats from operations like Toby's is about business, pure and simple. In years past, Toby has told Eleanor, he and Cam visited farms where the male goats weren't even given names, just numbers, with computer-generated profiles posted on the farm's websites listing statistics involving the productivity of their past offspring.

Hans Verlander runs his place the old-fashioned way, which suits Toby better. Smelly as they are, and frequently aggressive, Hans displays obvious affection for each of his eight prize-winning bucks. They all have names. More than this, Hans can tell Toby about particular traits—pro and con—in the bloodlines of each. Not from any printout. He's got goat stories involving each of them. (In Toby's world, these are the best kinds of stories to have.) Hans has made his goats a beautiful pasture to play in with the sweetest grass and plenty of boulders to climb. His barn is so clean, Toby himself would have no problem sleeping there. Even Eleanor could.

Hans is working on his tractor when Toby and Eleanor pull up to the farm. Seeing their truck, he looks up briefly, then returns to his work on the machine. A widower for many years, Hans has never been a man for small talk, or talk of any kind, from Eleanor's experience. Maybe his daughter has something to do with this.

June's the youngest of the three adult Verlander children, and the only girl, but she's the one who has chosen to stay on the farm, when her two older brothers left long ago to pursue more lucrative forms of employment. There are easier ways to make a living than goat farming.

From the looks of her, June's probably in her early thirties. She's deaf.

Eleanor knows, from a conversation she had one time with Hans's older son, when he still worked on the farm, that back when she was pregnant with June, Hans's wife, Velma, had contracted rubella. Though by the year of June's birth vaccines had largely wiped out German measles, Velma had chosen to forgo vaccines for reasons having to do with her distrust for Western medicine. Sometime around June's first birthday, after learning that the rubella had left her child unable to hear, Velma fell into a deep depression. When June was four years old, she'd taken her life, leaving Hans and her two older sons to take care of the farm, and June.

June communicates exclusively in sign language. Though she reads lips, she makes no attempt to speak. She spends her days with goats, mostly. And her uncommunicative-seeming father.

June's tall, like her father, and slim as a reed—from all the time she spends chasing buck goats probably—with a single braid that goes down almost to her waist. Nobody would call her pretty, but there's an arresting and mysterious quality to her, as if she might have just stepped off a spaceship and doesn't know how she ended up here. Very briefly, that first time Eleanor accompanied her son to the Verlander farm, Eleanor had held out a certain hope that Toby and June might take a romantic interest in each other, but it had swiftly become apparent to her that June had no interest in this. Except for leading the bucks into the breeding pen for him, she barely acknowledges Toby's existence.

One thing about bucks. In addition to smelling terrible, they're noisy. The noisy part is not a problem for June Verlander, of course. From where she stands in the shade of the barn, trying to avoid the heat, Eleanor can see June now, carrying a bucket of water in the direction of the goat pen—her plain, intent face seemingly off in some other world. Eleanor positions herself in June's line of vision, to wave to her. June appears not to notice.

"She's not your average kind of person, my girl," Hans tells Eleanor. "There's probably some kind of music going on in her head none of the rest of us know about. I like to say our June's just tuned to a different frequency."

Eleanor knows something about this. She might have said the same thing of Toby.

Today, as Toby leads his girls down the ramp from the truck, one at a time, and into the enclosure Hans Verlander has constructed to facilitate breeding sessions, it's June, not Hans, who assists him. Toby has selected the goat he wants to breed with Violet—a smaller-than-average male with brown markings and a winning personality. June holds him steady while Violet enters the pen. Once the two are safely enclosed, Toby and June step away. "Time to let nature take its course," Hans observes, returning to his work on the tractor. Though the buck Toby has chosen to breed with Violet is ready, Violet ignores him.

The buck urinates on her. Then snorts. Then urinates again.

"It's not exactly romantic, the way they do this," Eleanor observes to her son.

After it's over, Eleanor and Toby follow Hans into his house—a ramshackle place that seems to be under renovation, though in the six years Eleanor's been making this trip, nothing appears to have changed.

The two of them, and Hans, sit at the kitchen table. He sets out a pitcher of lemonade.

As Eleanor's just writing the check for stud services, something on a shelf over the counter catches Toby's eye. It's a strange-looking bowl. Strange and beautiful.

"What's that?" he says. He rises from his chair to get a better look.

"My daughter made that," Hans tells them.

Toby's standing at the counter now, studying the bowl. "Is it okay if I hold this?" he asks Hans.

"Be my guest. The thing's broke already. That's kind of the point."

He's talking about the cracks running through the bowl—a few dozen of them, as if it had been broken and glued back together, except that in every place where two pieces of pottery show evidence of having been reconnected, a vein of gold runs along the broken part.

"My daughter-in-law took June to a museum in Burlington one time where they had a pottery show," Hans tells them. "That's how she got acquainted with this kind of thing. She got a book. Next thing you know she signed up for a pottery class. She was breaking bowls right and left just so she could put them back together. If that doesn't beat all."

"But with gold," Toby says quietly, running his finger over one of the thin, spidery threads of gleaming lacquer on the bowl he's been admiring.

Hans takes out his wallet. "I wrote down the name someplace," he says. "For what they call it. I keep it on a card so I won't forget. *Kintsugi.* I never get it right, so June wrote down the explanation."

He reaches for a sheet of laminated paper on the shelf where the bowl had sat. The words are handwritten in a round, almost child-like hand, though what they say is not childlike.

Toby's not much of a reader, but he studies the laminated page for a long time, taking it in.

The art of kintsugi is based in the idea of repairing broken pottery in such a way as to transform it into something more beautiful than the original piece. Instead of attempting to mend shattered fragments together seamlessly, concealing the evidence of damage, a kintsugi artist views the visible evidence of the repair as an essential element in the finished work. The process of making these repairs calls for the artist not simply to glue the pieces together but to employ a particular kind of resin in the work of mending. In the crucial final stage of the work, a thin gold lacquer is applied to the places where the repairs have been made, creating fine, spidery filaments of gold that run through the work like veins.

"My daughter doesn't wait around for a bowl to show up broken, mind you," Hans says. "She breaks each and every bowl on purpose. First she works like the dickens to make the thing. No sooner does

she take it out of the kiln and let it cool down then—*bango bango*—
she smashes it. Then puts the whole thing back together."

This is the moment June herself comes into the kitchen. She's
probably just getting a cool drink herself, on account of the heat.

"You know what they say," Hans tells them. "'Stronger in the broken places.'"

"I never saw anything like this," Toby says, his voice almost a
whisper, as if there might be a baby here that he doesn't want to
wake. He's still holding June's kintsugi bowl. Running his fingers
over the golden veins.

"I love this," Toby says to June, handing it to June with the reverence a man might display when holding out an ancient chalice, or
a baby, newborn. He knows she can't hear him, of course. He has
positioned himself in front of her face, no doubt figuring she'll get
the idea.

June hands the bowl back to Toby.

"She wants you to have it," Hans says.

"We couldn't take this," Eleanor says. "It's a valuable artwork."

"My daughter's not one to hold on to things," Hans says. "Once
she's made a bowl, she's ready to let it go."

"What should I pay her?" Eleanor asks Hans.

"I think it's okay, Mom," Toby speaks with surprising forceful-
ness. Maybe he's thinking about his father, who was always ready to
give away the work he made—bowls made from wood, not clay—the
way Hans Verlander's goat-farmer daughter just did.

"My girl's not one for socializing," Hans tells them. "She's probably spent too much time around bucks. Except for her brothers and
me, she doesn't think that much of the male of the human species."

It's getting late. They've finished their lemonade. Eleanor and
Toby have a long drive home.

In the passenger seat of the truck heading home, Toby cradles the
precious bowl on his lap, holding tight. Hans has wrapped it for him
in a bunch of old *PennySavers*.

"I won't let anything happen to this," Toby says—remembering
the Dale Chihuly sculpture, maybe. "This is the best present anyone
ever gave me."

On the drive home, he cradles the bowl in his hands as if it were a nest of baby birds. The longer a person studies this bowl, Toby tells Eleanor, the more he sees.

61.

Borrowed time

She's living on borrowed time with Guy now. That's how Eleanor feels. He's going to leave. Only he doesn't. Yet.

Seasons again. Snowstorms. Tomato crops. Leaf raking. Mud. Lilacs. Baby goats. Blackflies. Geese flying south. Robins returning.

Plane tickets. Hotel rooms.

How can it be that all these years have gone by since the night Guy and Eleanor met at the studio cocktail party and fell into each other's arms back at his hotel?

She remembers how, in that first speech she heard him deliver, he'd announced his plan to return to Antarctica the following November—the mission that had defined his life.

Every year he sets a new date, then postpones the trip again. At first the issue was that he was raising the money while recuperating from his hip replacement. Then came problems with his right knee. Then his other knee showed signs of giving out. *Bone on bone,* the orthopedist told him. Another surgery. Another stint of physical therapy.

Guy has never suggested to Eleanor that she might be the reason he keeps delaying his expedition, but she likes to believe she's been a factor. "All these years alone in my tent, I hardly ever thought about the touch of a woman," he tells her. "Now I know what I was missing."

Times they meet up now—in whatever hotel room, in whatever city he's speaking in that night—they make love with as much longing for each other as they ever possessed. He still brings her perfume—the same exotic and mysterious scent they chose together that day at Colonial Drug. She still feels a shiver every time he unbuttons his beautiful white shirt and lays it on the bed, then unbuttons her blouse. They still make love for hours—till the sun comes up, sometimes.

But now, as Guy approaches the final stretch of physical therapy from the latest surgery, Eleanor registers a shift in him. When he books a hotel for them now, he makes sure it's one that has a gym so he can work out. He's getting into shape for the long expedition ahead.

Nobody who doesn't know Guy would detect this, but Eleanor can sense it: that state of mind a person occupies when they haven't yet moved, but they're starting to pack their bags. Eleanor sees it in his pale blue eyes—the way he looks to the door sometimes now or stares off into space in the middle of a conversation. In the middle of their lovemaking, even. He's feeling the pull of that frozen continent, that endless expanse of ice and snow.

He's ready to be cold again. He misses putting on his all-weather hiking boots and facing the wind. It feels to Eleanor as if Guy's whole being is pulled to the polar regions, like the needle on a compass, compelling him to venture one more time, and one more time after that, as far south as a human being can go.

62.

Adam and Eve

On the plane flying back to Boston after a night with Guy—first class, as usual—a memory comes to Eleanor. Maybe it surfaces now, of all times, because she's just spent a night with a man with whom she shares almost no history—none besides a long series of hotel room nights.

What does it mean, to have no past with a person, and no clear idea of your future with him? What does a person do with all that history she shared, with a man who's dead?

She was twenty-three years old, newly pregnant with Al. These were the first early days of their marriage, when she and Cam had been practically drunk on the excitement of having made a baby. Every afternoon back then, a little before sunset, the two of them would walk down to the waterfall together, and if no one was there—as was often the case that late in the day—they'd peel off their clothes and dive off the rocks into the swimming hole just below the falls. Then they'd head home to make dinner together, which was nearly always a stir-fry or pasta. They had so little money then. It mattered so little that they didn't.

Sometime in late summer—August probably, or the first week in September—the weather had turned very hot, so hot they slept naked on top of the sheets, though never so hot they didn't press their bodies up against each other. Those were the days, still, when Cam and Eleanor could barely keep their hands off each other. Their hands, and all other body parts.

It was a full moon night. Even at night the temperature hovered in the nineties—almost unheard-of for New Hampshire. Lying in their bed with the moonlight streaming in the window, Cam had whispered to her, "Let's go swimming."

This was before they'd dug the pond on the farm. He meant the waterfall, the swimming hole.

Eleanor was only a couple of months pregnant at this point, but the act of carrying inside her body the person who was forming there—Alison, then Al, though they didn't know who their child would be yet, of course—left her more tired than usual. Still, she had loved this about Cam—his boundless energy for adventure. In those days, the adventures he liked best were always with her.

They threw on their clothes. They didn't need much: a sleeveless dress for her, a T-shirt and shorts for Cam. The moon was so bright they had not needed a flashlight.

It had rained that week. The water—often slow by this point in the season—was roaring so loudly they had to yell to hear each other. Cam took Eleanor's hand as they made their way to the highest boulder at the edge of the swimming hole. Since she'd been pregnant, he'd displayed a new level of tenderness and care Eleanor had not known before, ever. (Not with her parents. Or anyone else.)

As fast as the water raced over the rocks, Eleanor felt safe with her husband's arm around her waist. In those days Eleanor believed that with Cam at her side, nothing bad could ever happen. In those days Eleanor believed he would be there always.

They set their clothes on the rock and dove into the water, the spot they knew was deep enough that no danger existed of either of them hitting their head. Not even Cam, tall as he was.

They stayed in for a long time—the water swirling, the moon directly above the two of them, its light shimmering over the surface. Cam dove under, kissing her breasts, her belly. Knowing that inside, at that very moment, cells were dividing into someone who would become their child.

When Cam surfaced, he placed his hands on either side of her face as if he were studying one of his precious wooden burls in its raw, uncarved state, taking in everything about the form, imagining the bowl it would become in his studio. All these years later, Eleanor can still summon that picture of her young husband—Cam, with his hands encircling her face, as if she were the raw material of an artwork, and he the one to create it.

They'd kissed, of course. A very long kiss. She remembers thinking, as their mouths pressed together, *Remember this moment.*

Well, she has.

As they were kissing she became aware, though just dimly, of a car pulling up alongside the falls, the engine stopping, the lights cutting out. She could hear voices—a man and a woman, she thought.

She might have been frightened but wasn't. It was probably another couple like the two of them—oh, but there was no couple like the two of them; that's how Eleanor felt then. No doubt, like herself and Cam, they had also been drawn to this place by the heat of that night, the moonlight.

Cam heard them, too, then. "We'll stay in the water," he said. No need to whisper; the roar of the falls drowned out their voices.

Neither of them was particularly modest, but they were naked. Their bodies—the fact of their naked skin—felt wonderfully, magically intimate, a secret for themselves and each other alone.

From a ways off they heard laughter. The two people who'd shown up were not getting in the water. More likely they'd opened a beer. Eleanor could make out the sound of conversation, though not what they were saying. More laughter.

After a few minutes the couple must have returned to their car. Cam and Eleanor heard the sound of the engine starting up. The headlights came on. Then came the sound of car tires on the dirt road, the car backing up, then driving away. Quiet now. It was just the two of them again.

"I guess we should head home," Cam said. They had no idea how long they'd been in the water but the moon, though still fully visible, was lower in the sky now.

Eleanor was the one who climbed out onto the rocks first. She reached down to get her dress. Not there.

She looked around. Maybe they'd set their clothes on a different rock than she'd remembered.

Nowhere.

Now Cam pulled himself out of the water, too. The two of them stood naked in the moonlight. His skin seemed to glow. Dark as it was, she could make out the red of his hair.

"I guess we know what happened," he said. Whoever it was who'd just taken off hadn't even left them their shoes.

"We're like Adam and Eve," Eleanor said.

"Without the shame," Cam told her. He placed a hand on her belly, just barely showing the signs of pregnancy, though her breasts had filled out already. "I'll never forget how you look right now," Cam told her.

The walk back to the farmhouse was less than a mile, though slow going, barefoot.

"You know the worst part?" Cam said to Eleanor. "Those were my favorite flip-flops they took."

"I never liked those shorts," Eleanor said.

Cam and Eleanor had already decided that if they encountered a car they would not hide. Whoever the person might be, out on this back road at such an hour, they'd have a story to tell later, about what they'd seen well after midnight on that narrow dirt road, miles from the nearest town. But they encountered no one.

It was sometime around 2:00 A.M. when they made it back to the house. They fell onto the bed, their arms spread wide, laughing.

This was a story they never told anyone, not even Al, though it could be said Al had been there with them.

Thinking of that night now, so many years later—Cam dead, her body much changed from the one that had faced him in the moonlight, the youngest of their children older than she and Cam had been at the time—it occurs to Eleanor what one of the saddest parts is about a person dying, with whom you had once shared your life.

Once that person is gone, there's nobody left to remember the things you shared with them. Eleanor carries the picture of that night alone now. The day will come when there's nobody left who knows the story. Oh, maybe those two people might, who'd stolen their clothes. Maybe they've entertained friends with it over the years—the night they ran into Adam and Eve. Who knows, maybe all those years back they'd hidden at the edge of the road, watching Eleanor and Cam as they made their way up the hill back to their house.

She almost hopes this is so—that somewhere in the world, somebody other than herself still carries a memory of that night.

With herself and Guy, she thinks, who even knows the story of their love affair?

What will remain, after Guy leaves for Antarctica? If a person goes away, and hardly anybody knew he was ever there in the first place, how do you grieve that he's gone?

63.

Crevasse

Guy and Eleanor are in Aspen—a climate change conference—when Guy tells her the news. He's booked his trip back to Antarctica. Six months from now he'll be heading south.

Once he leaves, Eleanor understands that Guy will be gone for at least a year—six months in Ushuaia, preparing for his mission, and another six months out on the ice. The trip will be brutally difficult, also dangerous—more so all the time as the ice continues to melt. Just this summer, one of the scientists who advised Guy over the years died when he got caught under the ice on a scuba diving mission. Guy himself had a narrow escape when the Cessna he was flying in hit whiteout conditions and came within moments of crashing.

Knowing Guy, Eleanor believes he can survive the dangers of the trip. For Eleanor, the question is what happens after? A man like Guy is never going to settle down in some comfortable place—sit by the woodstove with her on long winter nights, or work beside her in the garden, or go along when she takes Lulu and Orson or Flora blueberry picking.

His mission now is to traverse all five of the most imperiled ice sheets on the continent of Antarctica. When Guy tells Eleanor the date of his departure for what he anticipates may be the final leg of his quest, she just nods. How can she love this man and know his passions without wanting, for him, that he succeed in covering those last few hundred miles? When you love a person, you want him to realize his dreams. Same as you hope he wants you to realize yours. Of course, first you need to know what they are.

64.

I could have been anybody

Elijah's band, Dog Blue, has been traveling around Scandinavia for six weeks. From what Eleanor can tell from Elijah's Instagram feed, they're pulling in great audiences wherever they go.

And Elijah is in love. The year before, he met a woman named Miriam, also a musician, originally from Nigeria. This year she's joined them on the tour with her mbira—an unlikely instrument for a bluegrass band, but they're making it work.

Now he calls Eleanor from the hotel they've been staying in to tell her he's asked Miriam to marry him. She said yes. He's thinking they might get married on the farm.

"Have you told your mother?" Eleanor asks him.

"I'll let her know eventually," Elijah says. "The two of us aren't speaking at the moment."

Things between Elijah and Coco have been bad for a few years. (It's odd how this works, Eleanor reflects. She, herself, has a grown child who cut off communication for a few years and still keeps a chilly distance. And all the while, another woman's son—Elijah—calls to tell her he's getting married, while not speaking with the woman who gave birth to him.)

Eleanor knows from Elijah that back when she first suffered her injuries from the motorcycle accident in which Timmy Pouliot had died, Coco had started taking oxycodone. In the beginning, taking the drug was a way of dealing with terrible pain from the accident and her many surgeries after. But for the last few years, she's evidently been displaying all the signs of opioid addiction. Coco had always been a thin person, but the day she made her brief appearance for the scattering of Cam's ashes at the waterfall, Eleanor observed that Coco was down to skin and bones. Her arms were sticks. According to Elijah, she sleeps till noon and gets up with dark circles around her eyes. More than once after a visit from his mother, Elijah told Eleanor, he'd discover after she left that money was missing from his wallet.

"The thing is, she could have asked me for the money," Elijah tells Eleanor. "What made me so sad was that she just took it. Like I could have been anybody. Like the only thing that mattered was getting her hands on that hundred-dollar bill."

65.

Good enough to be in commercials

A car pulls up in front of the house at the farm—a Gremlin (who knew any of those were still out on the road?) with one blue door and one purple. Coco gets out.

Eleanor has not seen Coco since the day, a few years back now, when she blew into town for the scattering of Cam's ashes. She knows from Elijah that his mother has been living over a friend's garage, working for a company that sells some kind of miracle pill endorsed by Dr. Oz that's supposed to make you lose all your belly fat. ("Coco's a great representative for the product," Al commented when he'd heard this. "I don't know what was keeping her jeans up at the memorial service that day.")

Coco's parents, Evan and Betsy, got divorced a while back. Evan remarried a much younger woman from the Philippines with whom, Eleanor has heard, he has a bunch of young children. (She remembers how Coco had always longed for a sibling. But not now. Not these.)

Betsy joined a religious community that teaches its followers the value of cutting off all connection with family members from the past who may hold them up in pursuing their spiritual growth. Elijah pays visits to his mother when he can but Eleanor gets the impression that things between them are not easy.

Who am I to judge? Eleanor thinks.

When Coco left Cam for Timmy Pouliot and told him she wanted a divorce, Cam had taken out a loan on the farm to pay her a lump sum for a settlement so he could hold on to the property. Eleanor knew this all too well; after Cam's death, she and Al had paid off the bank to spare Toby the responsibility of a mortgage payment he'd never be able to keep up with.

It's a fair guess, based on what Eleanor's heard of Coco's activities in recent years, that the money Cam paid her for the farm is long gone now. The sight of her as she was that day they scattered Cam's ashes—a forty-two-year-old woman in a forty-year-old car, leaning on a cane—came as a shock. Not so many years ago, when Eleanor ran into Coco at one of Elijah's shows, it was still possible to see in her—even as she was after her accident—traces of the lithe and beautiful teenager Eleanor remembers from long ago, who'd had a crush on her husband since the age of twelve. Now Coco's cheeks have that caved-in look from all the places where she's missing teeth. Her skin is weathered and deeply lined. As she approaches—even outdoors—Eleanor can pick up the smell of cigarettes.

Something about the way Coco stands there—the set of her mouth but more so something about her eyes—makes Eleanor reluctant to invite her in. This is the mother of a young man she cares about and loves, her children's brother—Elijah. She's known Coco since the day she and her mother, Betsy, stopped by the house with a loaf of banana bread when Eleanor was in labor the first time, with Al. She can still remember the sight of her as a teenager, viewed from out the window of her studio, playing soccer with her children and Cam while Eleanor worked, leaping across the improvised goalposts they'd set up in the field, whooping when she made a save. In the years since, Eleanor has wondered, were Coco and Cam having sex together even then? If so, she no longer needs to know.

Eleanor greets Coco. She does not ask how Coco's doing. The answer's obvious.

"We need to talk," Coco says.

This is a surprise. It's hard to imagine what these two women might have to talk about.

"It's about your son."

Eleanor has two sons. Though this has not always been the case, that's how it is in their family now. Nobody—not even Jake—questions this.

"I'm talking about Toby. I thought you should know."

For a moment, Eleanor just stands there, taking in the hard, vaguely feral face of the woman in front of her. Time was, Coco used to sit out here on summer afternoons, French-braiding Ursula's hair. Ursula had worshipped Coco then. Even Al, who hardly ever liked anyone in those days, had a soft spot for her. Toby even more so.

The memory comes to Eleanor of a day—Coco must have been thirteen at this point—when she'd accompanied the family on a camping trip and somewhere along the highway she'd whispered to Eleanor that there was blood in her underpants.

"Don't tell anyone," she told Eleanor as they made their way into a rest stop ladies' room.

The two of them had squeezed into a cubicle together. Eleanor had a tampon in her purse. She took off the wrapper and showed

Coco how to insert the tampon, then crouched beside her on the floor until Coco got it right.

Now Coco stands by the doorway of the house that was once her home. She's leaning on a cane. Her hair is stringy and her eyes seem sunken into the sockets, her pupils opaque.

"Depending on what you decide to do, I may have to report Toby to the authorities."

"Authorities? Toby?"

"I'm talking about your son Toby . . . and children," she says. "How much he likes little boys."

For a moment, Eleanor thinks she might throw up. Leaning on her cane, Coco looks at her with a strange expression. Almost a smile. Not the good kind.

"I don't know what you're talking about. Everybody who ever met Toby knows he loves children and children love him back. It's not a sexual thing. He's the gentlest person anyone ever met."

She wishes she hadn't said this. She hates that she just dignified the charge with a denial.

Coco leans on her cane. She's looking out to the pond. *She can't look me in the eyes,* Eleanor thinks.

"Let's just say someone reported him," Coco says. "What if they said Toby touched their kid?"

"No one would believe that," Eleanor says. She can feel her heart pressing against her rib cage. She's never hit anyone before, but she knows now what it feels like, wanting more than anything to do it.

"Suppose a little boy reported him?" Coco says.

"What little boy? Who?"

Coco leans on her cane. She does this thing Eleanor remembers from long ago: She slides her tongue over her lower lip. Licks it. She used to do that a lot, back when she babysat for them. The children used to imitate the gesture affectionately.

What she reminds Eleanor of now is a small rodent, licking its chops. Templeton the rat, from *Charlotte's Web.* Coco's enjoying this moment and is in no rush to elaborate. She likes making Eleanor wait for the next part.

"My boyfriend has a kid," Coco says. "Patrick. He needs this asthma medicine and it doesn't come cheap."

Asthma medicine? What is she talking about?

"I think it was on one of those school field trips. To the fire station." Coco looks out in the direction of the field where Eleanor has planted her garden. There was a time when Coco had played Red Light Green Light with the children there.

"I think we're done with this conversation," Eleanor says. "Toby would never do anything to hurt a child."

"Maybe he would, maybe he wouldn't. My boyfriend and me are thinking it wouldn't go over too big with people around here if Patrick and his dad said something about your retard son putting his hand down Patrick's pants and playing with his you-know-what. Not to mention what that would do to that little cheese-making business of his. What's it called? Wheel of Joy? Oh, and by the way, congratulations on them making a movie out of your book. My girlfriend read about it in a magazine. They probably paid you a lot of money for that, huh?"

The picture comes to Eleanor of her son back in the days when Raine dropped Spyder off for her shifts at the nursing home, before she ran off with one of its residents. Rocking that colicky baby back and forth because if he stopped, Toby knew, Spyder would cry. All night long, Toby sat there in that chair, rocking that baby and humming to him.

"What do you want from us?" Eleanor asks Coco now.

"It's not just money for the medicine," she says. "My boyfriend has a great opportunity to invest in a weight-loss product franchise. I'm planning on opening a party and event-planning business." Coco's been looking at these chocolate fountains where you dip a piece of fruit on a stick in the melted chocolate. She's planning to buy a photo booth, too.

"All we need to get it off the ground is five thousand dollars," she says. "By this Friday. Then we'll leave you alone."

There it is. As angry as she feels, and nauseated, what Eleanor registers now is an odd brand of sorrow over the low ambitions Coco has set for herself in her new career as an extortion artist.

Five thousand dollars for a weight-loss franchise and a machine that pours melted Hershey bars out the top to make chocolate-covered strawberries? Is that as far as her imagination takes her?

Although the day is cool, Coco's wearing high-heeled sandals, open toe, evidence of nail polish having been applied, but not recently. She studies her foot in the dirt. Still not meeting Eleanor's eyes. "Five thousand dollars," she says again. "It's probably nothing to someone like you."

Eleanor doesn't need to think about her response to any of this. She has already stepped back toward the door, preparing to return to the house. A house that, for a brief stretch of years, had been Coco's. Coco's with Cam.

"My family and I won't be having anything to do with you, Coco," Eleanor says. "You need to leave now."

Coco appears surprised, and a little shaken. From the look of her, it seems she had not anticipated this.

"You'll be sorry," she tells Eleanor, her voice a low hiss. "Your messed-up son could land in a shitload of trouble."

"Someone in this story is messed up," Eleanor tells her. "But it isn't my son."

"If you got a load of Patrick, you'd know to be scared. The way he tells the story. This kid's so good he could be in commercials. He can turn on the waterworks easier than some people turn on the shower."

Eleanor shakes her head. She's walking toward the house as Coco calls after her.

"I just want to protect other innocent children," Coco calls out. "Someone like that kid of yours shouldn't be allowed out in the world with normal people."

Eleanor turns to face her one more time. These will be her last words to Coco.

"My son is not a child molester," she says. "But if you actually believed someone was doing the kind of things you want to pin on Toby, what does it say about you and your boyfriend that you'd be willing to keep your mouth shut and leave other kids at risk for five thousand dollars?"

"We were going to make it easy for you," Coco says.

A minute later she's gone down the driveway, tossing a cigarette butt out the window as she rounds the bend.

66.

He'll never get elected

She calls Jason. (Jason, not Guy. Guy is not a man to whom a person brings the struggles of daily life. Even if those include the threat that your ex-husband's former wife might report your son for sexual abuse. Even if he weren't occupied now with preparations for his expedition, Guy would not be the person you'd call for advice or assistance concerning your ex-husband's ex-wife.)

"You know what I think?" Jason tells Eleanor. "That woman's not doing anything. She was just out trolling money to buy drugs. From what you've told me about Coco, I'm guessing she's not much on the follow-through.

"Hank and I are heading to the White Mountains for the weekend," Jason tells Eleanor. "Unless you're planning to meet up with this boyfriend of yours in someplace like Dubai, you should come with us."

Partly to get her mind off Coco's visit—and no doubt surprising him, since she normally turns down all invitations but Guy's—Eleanor says yes. In a few months, Guy will be off in Antarctica. She'd better figure out a way to deal with his absence. For too long now, weekend trips were about one thing and one thing only: Guy.

The three of them—Hank, Jason, and Eleanor—spend the afternoon hiking, with a trip up the cog railway to the top of Mount Washington. Eleanor pictures how it would be if Guy were with them. Only she can't picture it. Her life with Guy, and the rest of her life, occupy two utterly different places for Eleanor. Sometimes she loves this about their relationship. Sometimes she hates it. Right now, she wishes her life didn't feel split down the middle as it has been.

Late that afternoon there's a forum scheduled in Plymouth, with visits from the presidential candidates vying for votes in the upcoming New Hampshire primary set for that winter. Eleanor and her friends head over to hear them speak.

Unexpectedly, she spots her daughter and Jake there, with the children. Ursula's there to pass out literature for the Bernie Sanders campaign. The greater surprise is seeing Jake, knowing his political views.

"Bunch of idiots," he says. "Lulu talked me into coming so we could have a family dinner out, after."

"You could come, too, Grammy," Lulu tells Eleanor. Ursula doesn't look pleased, but what she says to her mother is, "Sure, if you don't have anything else to do."

Jason and Hank join them. They know about Eleanor's problems with Ursula, of course—and about Jake, whose views concerning the LGBTQ community are pretty much the same as his views on undocumented immigrants, pro-choice, Alexandria Ocasio-Cortez, and Bernie Sanders, among others. At the restaurant, they try to avoid discussion of the upcoming election and the positions presented by the candidates that afternoon, but Eleanor can feel the tension between her daughter and her husband. For once, Ursula's irritation with Jake exceeds that she more frequently displays toward Eleanor.

As the evening progresses, Jake—under the influence of many beers—calls Bernie Sanders a communist and a liar, before loudly extolling the policies of his preferred candidate, Donald Trump. From across the table, Eleanor can feel the room go cold as surely as if someone had opened a door and a stiff gust of icy wind passed over them.

"Mom said we aren't supposed to talk about him," Lulu announces to the group.

Lulu's ten now, still inclined to anxiety. More so than ever, probably. Lulu's always on the lookout for potential trouble between her parents, same as Ursula used to be during the last year of Eleanor's marriage to Cam. Like the child version of Ursula, Lulu just wants everyone to be happy.

It's never that difficult to spot trouble between Ursula and Jake when the topic of politics and the election comes up. That, or Jake's drinking. Or his failure to find a job, his growing obsession with Fox News and video games. His stupid friends, who share his politics.

Her father's hero worship of Donald Trump invariably leads to a fight between Jake and Ursula. Lulu tries hard to head them off at the pass, but tonight her efforts aren't working.

"*Dad, Dad,*" she says, stroking his arm. "Tell Grammy about that baby fox we saw last week. Right down the road from our house."

Nobody's paying attention, except Eleanor, probably.

"I can't believe you admire that idiot," Ursula says, waving her fork at Jake. "He's worse than an idiot actually, because he's smart. Smart and evil. The worst combination."

Jake raises his hand for the waitress. He's ready for another beer.

"How about the time your hero called Mexican Americans drug dealers and rapists? Mexican Americans, Jake. That's my sister-in-law's family. *Flora's grandparents.*

"How about the time, on some podium in front of his fans, when he did an imitation of that newspaper reporter who had a disability? Waving his arms around and talking in a crazy voice?"

"*Mom. Mom Mom,*" Lulu's saying. Pleading, more like it. "We're having a nice family dinner."

The idea has been to get away for a night from all the trouble surrounding the accusations about Toby. Have an easy, quiet night.

Jake gets up from the table, heading to the bar. "I think I'll check on the ball game," he says. He's slurring his words.

After eight beers (Ursula's counting, as Eleanor has been, and Lulu, too, probably) Jake's not entirely steady on his feet. Eleanor studies Ursula's face, watching him go. For once, Eleanor isn't the object of her daughter's greatest scorn, but this brings little comfort.

"The crazy thing is, Jake actually believes Donald Trump is a champion of the little guy, the down and outer," Ursula says. "A millionaire real estate developer with a reality TV show."

"He'll never get elected," Jason says.

67.

If anyone knew Toby

A week passes. Eleanor almost allows herself to forget about Coco's visit. She's planning to meet Guy in Atlanta that weekend. This is what she's thinking about when she picks up the phone.

It's Marty from the firehouse. "Listen, Eleanor," he says. "We've got a problem. There's been a complaint concerning Toby."

Until now, Eleanor has held out the hope that if Coco and her boyfriend ever followed through on their plan, Toby's fellow firefighters would be wise enough to realize what was going on. *Extortion,* plain and simple. If there's anyone who knows Toby's nature—anyone other than his family—it's the other volunteer firefighters who hang out with him nearly every afternoon and see him with the children.

"None of us believes what this person is saying about Toby," Marty tells Eleanor. "But there's a protocol to these things. We're legally obligated to investigate. Until we do, I have to let Toby know he's suspended. Pending review."

"You know what this will do to him, right?" Eleanor says. "Those times at the fire station are the happiest parts of my son's life."

"It's just for a while. As soon as we get some social worker out to talk with the kid who's saying this shit, I'm betting the whole thing will blow over."

68.

"Diminished moral capacity"

Sometime that week an investigator named Clarice Jennings shows up from the state division of sex crimes. It's bad luck that Eleanor's in Vermont that day, attending one of Orson's games. If she'd been home, she would have known not to let Clarice Jennings into the house, but Toby did, of course. And fixed her a grilled cheese sandwich while he was at it, if she knows her son.

As much as she can determine from what she learns after, Toby showed the woman his rock collection and introduced her to the goats. He pointed out his kintsugi bowl and the wall of pictures of his nieces and nephew, along with the one of Scarlett Johansson, explaining that she isn't really his girlfriend. He played her a cassette of her singing. "Everybody thinks Scarlett Johansson's just a movie star," he told Clarice Jennings. "But she's got a really beautiful voice, too."

Al groans when Eleanor tells him, over the phone, about the investigator's visit. "I'm flying home," he says. "It doesn't matter that the charges are baseless. These people will never understand someone like Toby. We need to get him a lawyer, fast. In the meantime, don't let him talk to anyone again."

After reading Clarice Jennings's report concerning the visit with Toby, Eleanor understands the wisdom of Al's insistence that they hire an attorney. They should have done it sooner.

The report describes Toby as "adult male, age 34, suffering from moderate brain injury resulting in diminished intellectual and moral capacity."

He'd told Clarice Jennings about Spyder and Lulu and Orson and Flora, making a point of how he and Flora had connected from the first time he met her, and how—when Spyder had colic—he'd learned that it helped to rub his stomach and back.

"With a little kid, it helps to make skin contact," he was quoted as having told the investigator.

"Subject appears fixated on touching children," Clarice Jennings had written in her report. "Also noted was subject's strong interest in animal reproductive behavior." At some point during the visit with the investigator, Toby had evidently gotten into an explanation of goat insemination techniques, in a manner she had termed "disturbingly obsessional."

Several times in her report, she quoted remarks made by "subject" over the course of their interview.

"I love kids," Toby had told Clarice Jennings. "I just like to cuddle them."

About his work as a volunteer fireman, Toby had mentioned that his favorite times at the firehouse were those involving visits from schoolchildren. "Most of the time there's one little kid that's different from the others," he was quoted as having told the investigator. "Those are the ones I like spending time with the most because someone like me understands what it's like being different. I can make them feel good. I make them happy."

Reading the report with Al the night he drives up from the airport in Boston, Eleanor can almost hear Toby's voice saying these things. For Eleanor and Al, it's not difficult to imagine what he meant. But you have to know Toby. You have to understand how he takes in the world, and the people in it.

Toby sees a woman standing on his doorstep with a clipboard in her hand and sees a friend—someone he'd invite to share a grilled cheese sandwich and a visit with the goats. Clarice Jennings studies the wall of photographs of young children in Toby's room and sees a potential predator.

69.

A problem with children

The attorney they've hired is named Barbara Cohen. She'll be challenging the legality of the investigator's having questioned Toby without an attorney present. According to the authorities, he'd been advised he could remain silent, but Barbara Cohen will make the argument that Toby does not possess the intellectual capacities to understand the consequences of speaking for the record as he did that day.

Barbara Cohen's words to them that Toby "did not possess the intellectual capacities"—delivered in the presence of her younger son—are painful for Eleanor, but at a moment like this, Eleanor knows, they're in no place to argue with their attorney. Toby, sitting beside her, shakes his head. "I understood why she came to see me," he says. "I just wasn't worried because I didn't do anything bad."

"Precisely my point," Barbara Cohen says. "Intellectual capacities precluded accurate assessment of legal jeopardy."

Al finds Barbara Cohen's assessment encouraging. Eleanor less so. Her approach might keep Toby out of jail, and there's comfort in that. But none of the legal challenges they might make, based on technicalities, will alter the fact that once word of these charges gets out in the small town where he's lived all his life, Toby is likely to be viewed by many as a person who molested children.

Up until this moment, Al and Eleanor had hoped that once they met with Barbara Cohen, she might reassure them that they have nothing worry about. After Eleanor lays out the story for her, the attorney shakes her head.

"Listen, it doesn't matter that all these people have is the testimony of one well-coached child whose father's girlfriend has some kind of axe to grind," she tells Al and Eleanor, when they sit together in her office with Toby, going over the case. "Any time a judge gets wind of possible sexual violation of a child, people go crazy. And I'm not saying they're wrong to take this kind of allegation seriously. It's just a hard situation for a person like Toby—knowing how the D.A. can use some of the things he said to the investigator when she talked with him.

"At the end of the day, it's going to be Toby's word against Patrick's," Barbara tells them. "We just don't want the other side submitting additional evidence that points to anything that could look to a judge like an indication that Toby has a problem with children."

Hearing her say this, Toby looks confused. A problem with children?

What's the problem with children?

70.

They misspell "traumatic"

]I[n the two weeks since the child, Patrick, and his father, Jesse, showed up at the police station accusing Toby of sexually violating a minor, Jesse has given an interview to a radio station in

Manchester and another in Keene. A woman named Bonnie Diamond, whose name Eleanor dimly remembers as a high school friend of Coco's, has published a letter to the editor for the *Union Leader* about the importance of protecting children from sexual predators, citing a case involving "a mentally retarded volunteer fireman in Akersville." A man who calls himself "a concerned friend" of the accuser's father reaches out to Eleanor, with a note left in her mailbox, asking if she might have reconsidered the family's suggestion that Eleanor handle the matter with what he referred to as "a small donation that might be applied to the boy's therapy and other expenses related to the traumatic event." Misspelling "traumatic," he has included his phone number and email address at the bottom of the card. Eleanor won't be responding.

71.

Nobody has an appetite

The days are getting shorter. Normally this would be the season Eleanor and Toby would be inviting the guys from the fire station over for their annual dinner of Chicken Marbella and apple pie, but nobody has much of an appetite. Toby spends most of his time in the barn now. No sound of humming. Setting a stack of folded laundry on his bed one day, Eleanor notices her son has taken down the picture of Spyder that used to sit next to his bed, along with all his pictures of Flora and Orson and Lulu.

"I didn't want anybody getting the wrong idea about me," Toby says. He's even thrown out his Scarlett Johansson poster.

Though Eleanor seldom speaks with Guy between their nights together, she calls him. Though the evening is cool, she chooses to do this outside on the porch rather than risk letting Toby overhear. With just four months to go before his departure for Antarctica, Guy's in Vancouver to give a speech—a trip he has not mentioned until now. His voice, speaking to her from his hotel room, sounds far away. Farther than British Columbia, even.

"This must be hard for you," Guy says. "I'm glad you've got a lawyer you trust."

"I'm scared," Eleanor tells him. She may never have spoken those words before.

"We're talking about a couple of two-bit lowlifes," Guy tells her. "I'm sure your attorney will know how to get rid of them."

"I think it's personal at this point," Eleanor tells him. "Now that she's not part of our family, some part of Coco wants to destroy us."

"I wish I could stay on the phone," Guy says. "But I've got to meet someone. Keep me in the loop."

After she hangs up, Eleanor sits on the porch, looking out to the field and above it, the stars. Nothing Guy said to her in his response to her account of Toby's troubles—which are Eleanor's, too—was unreasonable, or unfeeling. Still, she feels disappointed. Though, from the beginning of their relationship, she has named, as one of its strengths, that the two of them make no demands on each other—expecting nothing but that each shows up for those magical nights of theirs—she wishes Guy could have offered her something tonight beyond bland words and vague assurances that things would work out.

"You're a strong woman, Eleanor," he said to her before signing off. This is a good thing, of course. And he's right. But sometimes she wishes she didn't have to be so strong all the time.

72.

The cost of a person's reputation

Eleanor has heard no more from Coco since the day she came to the farm asking for money. Now her boyfriend, Jesse, reaches out to her. A late-night phone call.

"Five thousand dollars is pretty cheap to save your son's reputation," he tells her. "Get us the cash by Friday and my boy won't say *boo* about anything anymore."

Eleanor hangs up. After, she asks Al if he thinks she made a mistake. Maybe she should have just given Coco and her boyfriend the money.

"We all know Toby didn't do anything wrong," Al says. "If we write them a check it will be like saying Toby did what they claim. Once we start paying off crooks to keep them from spreading lies about our family, where does it end?"

73.

No more cheese customers

The investigation continues. They do not arrest him, but life for Toby, and for anyone who loves him, turns very dark very fast.

Ursula stops making her trips to the farm. "I just can't take one more thing right now," she tells Eleanor. "Also, it could look bad for me at school, if people hear about these kinds of charges against my brother."

Looking back to the time when her daughter didn't speak to her at all, Eleanor tells herself she should be grateful Ursula even says this much, but the coolness in Ursula's voice is unmistakable. Al offers comfort, but he's back in Seattle, busy with his family and his company.

The *Akersville Gazette* runs an item: "Local man under investigation for sex crimes." A television station in Manchester picks up the story. A group that call themselves "Parents Against Perverts" stands outside the fire station with signs—never mind that Toby has already been removed from the volunteer roster—demanding "accountability." One woman publishes a letter in the *Gazette* stating that "given reports of immoral activity on the part of her son," the town library should remove all of Eleanor's books from its shelves.

The Saturday morning after the story breaks Toby sets his table up at the farmers' market, same as always. Eleanor goes with him to the market this time.

"I don't need help selling my cheese," Toby says.

They know within minutes of putting up their sign and laying out the wheels of cheese that everything's different now. Gretchen, the woman selling handmade soap at the table next to Toby, who has always called out to him on Saturday mornings, says nothing when he greets her. When Toby offers her one of the doughnuts he's brought, she turns away. Seeing Toby's table next to theirs, the couple selling maple products relocates their stand to another part of the market.

Toby stands with his hands in his pockets for most of the morning. No customers. Finally a woman stops by his table.

"I don't actually eat cheese," she says to him. "Lactose intolerant. I just thought I'd come by and say hello."

She has remembered a time, the year before, when she brought her granddaughter to the fire station because her cat got stuck in a tree, and how kind Toby had been to the child that day.

"Her name's Jasmine, right?" Toby says. "The cat was . . . wait a minute . . . Puffball."

The woman turns to Eleanor. "You have a good son here," she says. "I won't let anyone tell me differently."

After she leaves—having bought a Wheel of Joy cheese for her daughter-in-law—Toby turns to Eleanor.

"Let's go home," he says. Two hours remain before closing time, but she doesn't argue.

74.

A hotel room cigar. A late-night phone call.

She had told Guy what was going on back when the charges were first filed against Toby, but since then the two of them have not spoken, and knowing how busy he is out on the road, she seldom calls. But her worries about Toby have made it hard to sleep. Late in the night, she dials Guy's number. He sounds surprised to hear her voice.

"Something wrong?"

"It's just this situation," Eleanor says. "Things have gotten worse."

"Situation?" She pictures Guy sitting outside the home on Martha's Vineyard where he's been staying lately, owned by one of his board members. Ocean breezes. Lobster in the pot, maybe. Or maybe—she's lost track—he's at a hotel somewhere, just cutting the tip on one of his Cubans. There were rules against smoking in hotel rooms, of course, never mind smoking cigars, but as far as Guy is concerned, they don't apply to him.

"The situation with Toby. The boy."

It takes Guy a moment but now he remembers. "What a mess," he says. "Fuck the bastards."

Eleanor had hoped for something more from him, though what that might be she could not have said.

"I feel so helpless," she tells him. This is unlike Eleanor. As bad as things have been at other times in the past she has always come up with a plan.

"Maybe you need more of a heavy hitter representing your son," he says. "That person you hired might be out of her league. I could refer you to my attorney. He's based in L.A. but he has a branch in New York."

It's not about a lawyer. She doesn't know how to explain. Eleanor suddenly feels tired.

"Listen," Guy says. "I don't want to offend you or anything but someone should probably ask you this. Are you one hundred percent confident there isn't some element of truth in the kid's charges?"

"It's probably better if we talk some other time," she tells him.

75.

All about saving those glaciers

ΙΕ lijah has heard nothing about the problems on the farm. Eleanor has chosen not to tell him. For the first time in his years as a professional musician, his band has managed to put together a tour where they are not the opening act, but the lead performers. Dog Blue enjoys particular popularity in Sweden and Denmark.

From what Eleanor can tell, following Elijah's Instagram feed, good-sized crowds are turning up to hear them, and of course he's in love, though he and Miriam have yet to set a date. Elijah's on top of the world. Eleanor sees no point in ruining his big moment.

Al feels differently.

"Elijah's Coco's son," Al says. "If he asks her to get her boyfriend to drop the charges, maybe she'll listen to him. She could tell the police the whole thing was a mistake. If Coco and her boyfriend convinced a little kid to tell a made-up story about Toby, they can just as easily get him to change it."

"It's probably too late for that, even if Coco agreed to walk away from this," Eleanor points out. "A lot of damage has already been done."

The original plan was clearly about money. What Al doesn't understand—none of them do—is what has motivated Coco and Jesse to pursue their campaign against Toby even after it has become clear that Eleanor and her family aren't offering any payoff.

In late fall, Coco publishes a letter in the *Akersville Gazette*, warning local residents about the danger, to their children, of visiting the fire station. She doesn't name Toby in her letter—someone must have explained to her about slander and libel—but anyone reading her words will know who Coco is talking about when she mentions the volunteer firefighter who "messed around with my boyfriend's kid." A talk radio show in Nashua picks up the story and invites Coco on as a guest. A group called Concerned Parents Against Child Sexual Abuse has evidently invited her to speak at a dinner they're hosting to raise awareness of the issue and honor "warriors in the fight to defend children."

In the end, it's Al who reaches out to Elijah—somewhere in Norway now—to tell him what's going on. On the other end of the line, Elijah says nothing for a moment.

"I hate what she's doing," he says. "I'm so ashamed."

"Not your fault, buddy," Al tells him. "You know we all love you."

"Here's the thing about Coco," Elijah says. He does not speak of her as his mother. "She was always intimidated by your mom. Eleanor was so much stronger than she was. With everything that happened, Eleanor did a better job than my mom of keeping her head above water. Even though my dad left Eleanor to be with Coco, I always got the feeling Eleanor was the one he really loved. Even that thing with Timmy Pouliot. I think she got some kind of kick out of being with a guy who used to be Eleanor's boyfriend. Any time I'd see the two of them hanging out, Timmy would want to know how Eleanor was doing."

Coco must have acquired her own brand of disillusionment with Cam over the years—much as Eleanor had, though for different reasons probably. Or maybe she just got restless and bored. When Timmy Pouliot had shown up on his motorcycle—and odds were high Coco had been the one who'd sought him out—it hadn't taken much to persuade her to hop on the back.

After the accident, she was like an old woman all of a sudden. Cam was gone. Timmy was dead. One of her amazing legs was shattered. There she was sitting behind the counter at a cut-rate day spa handing out bathrobes and bars of soap—a stash of pills close at hand.

"This plan those two cooked up," Elijah tells Al. "If you ask me, it's about a lot more than some kind of payoff. Coco wants to bring your mother down, and she knows the best way to do that is to wreck Toby's life."

Coco is doing a good job of that. The day before, a Hollywood trade publication had gotten hold of the story that the son of one of the producers of a big-budget animated children's film slated for release the following spring was under investigation for sexual assault on a minor.

"Under investigation" was not the same as being charged, but to the studio this was enough.

A call comes from Eleanor's agent: Marlys has put her on notice that for reasons Eleanor can surely appreciate, it will be necessary for the studio to sever their relationship with the author of *Bodie Goes to Antarctica*. To further distance themselves from potential scandal going forward, the heroine of the film will no longer be named Bodie—a change necessitating significant work in postproduction. They're calling the character Zoe now and taking Eleanor's name off the credits. Her agreed-upon compensation will remain intact. But lawyers have advised Eleanor that she should no longer speak of any involvement with the film project.

"We wish Eleanor and her family all the best going forward," Marlys has written, in care of Eleanor's agent. "We're confident that she'll appreciate the potential negative impact an event of this nature could have on a project so dear to all our hearts, and that she will share our view that the film's message concerning climate change must not be compromised by any hint of scandal."

The producers will still keep Guy Macdowell's name in the credits, of course. "No doubt this new development will sadden him," Marlys has written. "But let's keep our eye on the prize here. We're all about saving those glaciers!"

They're ice sheets, Eleanor says, to nobody but herself. Guy has taught her this, and so much more.

Guy and Eleanor are due to meet up the following weekend in Kansas City. Now—in part because of the crisis involving Toby, but maybe too as a result of Guy's disappointing reaction—she cancels the trip. "Too much going on," she tells him in a voicemail message. She'd been surprised at how readily he appeared to accept this.

Soon after, Guy calls from Toronto to tell her about his day. "I wish you were in this bed with me right now," he whispers. "You know what we'd be doing right now."

Eleanor can picture the scene. Never mind the city: The good linens, the room service scotch, Guy's Armani shirt draped over a chair.

His silver cigar case and trimmer would be on the dresser, along with the tooth he takes with him wherever he goes, from a seal he and his team found trapped on an ice floe, with fishing line wrapped around its neck. They'd succeeded in capturing the seal in order to free it from the line, but the seal had bitten Guy, leaving a tooth embedded in his arm. Every night when he delivers his speech, he holds up the tooth.

Eleanor makes no further attempts to explain to Guy what's happening with Toby, or with herself. She knows how inconsequential her crisis must seem to a man like Guy—up against nothing less powerful than the rays of the sun burning through the ozone, the steady overheating of the planet.

Volunteer firefighters? Letters to the editor of the Akersville Gazette? *Eleanor's books removed from the library? Some stupid remark about cuddling baby goats?*

On the other end of the line, Eleanor can feel Guy's attention drifting. He's checking his email, probably. In less than three months he'll be in Antarctica.

76.

Play hardball back

Barbara Cohen has recommended to Eleanor and Al that they hire a private investigator to look into the background of Jesse St. Pierre. Eleanor hates this idea. Al overrules her.

"They're playing hardball with Toby," he says. "We have to play hardball back."

Two weeks later, Eleanor gets a call from Barbara. "Are you sitting down?" she says.

Three years before, Jesse was involved in a different case involving his son. He filed a claim against an amusement park outside Rehoboth Beach, Delaware, accusing them of operating a ride that resulted in an injury to Patrick's neck that caused headaches and dizziness and "ongoing medical issues." The park owners settled the case for twenty-five thousand dollars.

That was not the only lawsuit Jesse filed in which he named his son as a victim. When Patrick was three, Jesse claimed to have found rat droppings in a burger purchased at a Rhode Island McDonald's. It appeared that in this case, too, the company had chosen to offer a small settlement rather than pursue litigation.

The case that interests Barbara Cohen even more is one Jesse pursued when his son was just two years old. He filed suit against a day care center in Providence, Little Angels, charging that one of the staff members at the center had fondled his son's penis while changing his diaper. His witness to the alleged event was his girlfriend at the time, a woman named Marie Budd, who also worked there.

In the criminal case resulting from the charges, the day care worker had been charged with second-degree child molestation, though later the charges were dropped on the grounds of insufficient evidence. In the civil suit Jesse St. Pierre filed against the day care center afterward, for psychological damage to his son, he was awarded twelve thousand dollars.

"If these damages were real, that's a pretty small settlement," Barbara Cohen tells Eleanor. "This guy specializes in low-budget lawsuits. Take the money and run."

The investigator they'd hired pursued the case further, Barbara adds. He tracked down Marie Budd, now living in a religious community on the coast. When he asked her about the case, she told him she'd prayed for this day. Ever since finding God, she had wanted to undo the damage she'd done back when she lived with Jesse St. Pierre and his little boy.

"We made the whole thing up," she told the PI. "Well, Jesse did. I just followed along. When a guy's beating you up every night, you do what he says."

Marie Budd doesn't go out in the world much anymore. She works on the farm at Angels of Mercy, tending soybeans. But she's prepared to sign an affidavit. She'll even testify, if necessary. She wants to make it right with God.

Within days the New Hampshire Division of Child Protection Services announces its decision to suspend its investigation of Toby on the grounds of insufficient and unreliable evidence. When Barbara calls Eleanor with the news, she runs out to the barn to tell her son.

Hearing the news, he weeps.

77.

The 45th President of the United States

It's the night of the election, and Eleanor's throwing a party. Back in the old days when she and Cam were married, they often had friends over to the farm—charades nights, poker night, bonfires in winter down by the pond where, if the ice was right, they might bring down a boom box and lace up their skates or organize a hockey game. One year, for their annual softball picnic, Eleanor created a luau.

She hasn't thrown a party for longer than she can remember, but Toby's reprieve, combined with the idea that finally, after all these years, the country is about to elect its first woman president, seems like reason to celebrate.

Jason drives up from Boston, sharing the ride with a woman Eleanor met in her book group back in her Brookline days, Gloria. She's invited Toby's teacher, Errol, from the days when Toby attended his special school for brain injured children, and Annette, the mother of one of his classmates there, a girl named Gigi who'd briefly had a crush on Toby but drifted away from the friendship when her recovery from a milder form of brain injury allowed her to go back to regular school, as Toby never did. Long after Toby and Gigi no longer saw each other, Eleanor and Annette have stayed in touch.

Eleanor has invited two young women, Mindy and Chris—volunteers from the local Democratic headquarters—to her election night celebration, too. During the terrible months when Toby was under investigation, Eleanor had felt unable to work on the election, but in those final weeks before voting day, after the charges against her son were dropped, she canvassed door-to-door, her hopefulness restored. Mindy and Chris are college students who took the semester off to bring out the vote. It's the first election in which they've been old enough to cast a ballot themselves.

"I'm so excited I don't know if I can eat," Mindy says when Eleanor tells her she's making her spaghetti carbonara. "Someday I'll be telling my grandchildren about this night we elected the first woman president."

Eleanor has also invited Ursula to join them. Not that she has much hope her daughter will accept the invitation, but she recognizes how uncomfortable things are likely to be at Ursula's house as the vote comes in, knowing where Jake's loyalties lie. Ursula is voting for Hillary, of course, but she has not gotten over the defeat of her candidate, Bernie Sanders. For Ursula, it seems, this feels like another in a growing list of disappointments. For once it has been impossible to pin this one on her mother.

"Actually, I might drive down with the kids," Ursula tells Eleanor. "My friend Kat invited me to watch the returns with her and some of her friends in Concord."

Maybe Eleanor would look after the children?

For Eleanor, this is a rare chance to have her grandchildren for a sleepover. She loves the idea of getting to spend such a historic night with them. In the morning she'll make waffles with maple syrup and whipped cream to celebrate Hillary's victory.

"Stay at Kat's house as long as you like," Eleanor tells Ursula. "Maybe we'll be inspired to make a mural featuring great women through history or something. Or just play board games and eat popcorn."

Eleanor's guests started arriving just after dark—everyone in a celebratory mood. Eleanor has decorated the house with candles and American flags and an old storm window she's leaned against the television with a hammer alongside, meant to represent the glass ceiling they'll be breaking later. She's made a mixtape for the occasion. ("Living for the City" by Stevie Wonder. "Get Up, Stand Up" by Bruce Springsteen. "Everyday People" by Sly and the Family Stone. Bill Withers, "Lovely Day.") From his collection of interesting costumes, Toby has put together something vaguely resembling an Uncle Sam suit. Red, white, and green.

The television is on, of course, though at this point in the evening CNN has little to report. The polls out west wouldn't close for several hours. The map on the screen, meant to indicate which states go red, which blue, remains totally white.

With everyone gathered around the table, Jason makes a toast. "To the future," he says. "*To women*. Where would any of us be without them?"

"We wouldn't even be born," Mindy offers.

Just a few weeks have passed since the release of a tape in which Donald Trump can be heard recounting how he's put the moves on a woman who was not Melania. If his campaign wasn't doomed already, this surely represents the nail in the coffin.

"That part where he started talking about popping a Tic Tac in his mouth before he started kissing her," Chris says. "How gross can you get?"

"And when he said if you're famous you can do anything you want." This is Annette.

"This election will send a message," Gloria says. "Men can't talk like that and get away with it anymore."

Long ago, Eleanor had her own experience at the hands of an older and more powerful man who'd felt entitled to do what he wanted with her. If not for her choice to speak about him, years later, Matt Hallinan might have been among the candidates running for office tonight. He had been an up-and-coming Republican congressman at one point. The last she heard he was a real estate developer in Rhode Island.

"Better days," Eleanor says, raising her glass. Lulu and Orson, in their pajamas, say good night to everyone.

Around nine o'clock the map on Eleanor's television indicates a surprisingly strong turnout among Trump voters. A few states everyone assumed to be in the Democratic column are showing up on the screen as leaning red. The conversation gets quieter. Several of Eleanor's guests pour themselves another glass of wine. Jason goes straight for the Jack Daniel's.

By ten thirty, red is creeping across the map like a leaking wound. Pennsylvania's a tossup. The big surprise is that Michigan looks like one, too.

"Hillary should have spent more time there," Jason says, staring into his glass. "She took that state for granted." None of them have much to offer after that.

Eleanor has saved dessert for later, with the plan of cutting into the pie when the Clinton victory becomes clear. When she finally brings it out, nobody is hungry anymore.

When CNN announces that Donald Trump has taken the state of Ohio, Mindy begins to cry. When Florida goes the same way, several others join her. The older ones in the group—those, like Eleanor, who have lived through plenty already—sit stiffly on the couch or find a devastated younger person to hold as they weep.

By the time Pennsylvania goes to Trump all of Eleanor's guests have gone home. "No need to stick around for the last act," Jason says, screwing the top on what is left of his bottle of Jack Daniel's, which isn't much.

Alone in her living room, Eleanor clears away the dishes— unfinished plates of spaghetti carbonara, untouched pie. As she is often moved to do, at hard moments, she steps out onto the porch, looks to the stars. There's Orion. Cassiopeia. Venus. She takes her phone from her pocket and dials a familiar number. Guy's.

"I just wanted to hear your voice," she says.

"Not one of the better days," he offers.

"I can't believe it yet. I keep thinking there's been a mistake."

"It's real all right. How are you doing?"

"About the way you'd think."

"Ah, darling," he says. "I wish I could put my arms around you."

There he is. The brilliant, handsome, passionate, elusive, hot, cold, difficult, irresistible man she loves. She knows all the worst things about having a relationship with Guy but this never changes—the feeling she has, when she's with him, that for this moment anyway, which lasts only as long as they're in the same place together, they're the only two people in the world.

They're not even in the same place tonight—he's in Dallas, she's on the farm—but Eleanor feels it now, too. Somewhere on the planet, a thousand miles away, there's a man who loves her. Just when she's started to think it's hopeless with Guy—that he's self-absorbed and emotionally distant and they have no future together—she'll hear this tenderness in his voice, and the thought will come to her: *How could I ever live without him?*

Guy doesn't understand Toby or Al, doesn't understand why it's so hard on her that Ursula speaks to her as if she were someone who'd just stolen her parking spot. Guy doesn't know any of her friends, can never get the names of her grandchildren straight, never spends more than two nights in the same place, unless it's a tent surrounded by a few million acres of unbroken ice. Still, she'd be there with him now if she could. She'd run away with him, if she could. Tonight, more than ever, she thinks this.

It's a little past midnight when Eleanor climbs the stairs to bed. Her room is dark.

It takes her a moment to notice a small figure on one side of the bed. Sometime earlier in the evening Lulu must have climbed in. Now, as Eleanor pulls the covers around the two of them, Lulu opens her eyes for a moment, blinking dreamily. Ten years old, still in that place a child inhabits partway through the night—not asleep, but not really awake yet either—she looks over to her grandmother beside her in the semidarkness. She presses her face against Eleanor's ear and whispers into it, as if there might be someone listening.

"The bad guy won, didn't he?" she asks her grandmother. This would be the man her father voted for, but that hadn't changed her opinion.

"It's looking that way, Lu," Eleanor tells her. Later she will search for optimistic things to say—about how this is only going to last for a few years (small comfort for a child who has only been alive a few years) and how there will still be so many good people out there working hard to do good work. Tonight, though, she can do nothing but stroke her granddaughter's cheek as Lulu presses her body as close to Eleanor's as possible. A single bed would be sufficient for them that night, they hold each other that close. The two of them lie there this way for a while, awake in the darkness.

In the end it's Lulu, not Eleanor, who finds the words.

"We have to keep trying, don't we, Grammy?" she says. "Even when terrible stuff happens. We have to keep hoping things will get better. We have to keep trying."

PART 3

When the Light Goes Out

78.

Rats on the loose

December comes, and the world turns bitterly cold in ways that have nothing to do with weather. Marty has called many times, reminding Toby that the guys at the fire station are looking forward to seeing him back, but even though all the charges against him have been dropped, he hasn't wanted to go there anymore. When Eleanor brings up returning to the farmers' market, once the season begins again, he tells her, "I think I'll pass." Ralph can handle the sales.

From what Eleanor can gather, the movie based on her book, whose main character now goes by a different name, is coming out sometime the following year, but nobody's been in touch to say when, and Eleanor no longer cares. Guy has mentioned the studio's plan to make a short promotional video tie-in for the film's release. They want to shoot him with a flock of penguins, talking about climate change. The threat to the planet has never been greater, once the new president takes office.

He hasn't even been inaugurated yet, and already she feels a change in their world. When she goes to the store or the library—where her books are back on the shelf—or on her weekly trip with Toby to bring their trash to the dump, it seems to Eleanor that she can see the effects of the election on everyone's face. Not just the ones whose candidate was defeated, but in another way, on the faces of those who voted for the winner. Eleanor has never felt this before but it seems to her now that the election has brought out a mean-spiritedness in people she had not known to exist—even her neighbors, people she'd known since they were all young, as if the behavior of the man they elected has suddenly provided them license to look out for no one but themselves and to sneer at those foolish or weak enough to think differently. Maybe it has been there all the time—this dark side she's been noticing—but the triumphant expression of the man who now presides over the country seems to have revealed, in her fellow human beings, a form of ugliness Eleanor never knew to have existed until now.

She remembers, from her time in Brookline, a project known as the Big Dig, in which vast expanses of the city's underground were uncovered in an effort to upgrade Boston's subterranean transit system. One consequence the engineers and contractors who'd overseen the project had failed to anticipate were the teeming hordes of rats, previously hidden away underground, suddenly let loose on the city, scurrying along Boston's beautiful streets, the Public Garden, past the golden dome of the State House even, and the mansions in Back Bay.

These days they're living through now offer a similar picture. The rats must have been around forever, Eleanor thinks. It's just that they've emerged from the darkness. Now you can see their glowing little eyes, not simply in the person of Donald Trump, but in all those others, wearing their red hats and waving their "Fuck Hillary" signs, chanting "Lock her up!"—seemingly ordinary people with whom Eleanor has rubbed shoulders for years, for whom the election appears to have unleashed previously concealed forms of self-interest, bullying, greed, and downright cruelty. The message they seem to proclaim—that only the strong deserve to survive, and everyone else is a loser—would have offended Eleanor, regardless of her own personal story, but as the mother of a man like Toby, a man whose body and brain function differently, it's painful to realize that he is precisely the kind of person this president would mock relentlessly. There will be no room in Donald Trump's America for a person who struggles.

It's going to be every man for himself now. One person unlikely to make the cut will be Eleanor's younger son.

79.

Set him up for bumper bowl

It's Tuesday at Moonlight Acres, Eleanor and Toby's bowling night. The two of them are just lacing up their bowling shoes (something that takes Toby a very long time) when a couple of young men and a young woman—late twenties, from the looks of them—take their seats in the spot where she and Toby are preparing to bowl.

"My son and I were just starting to bowl our string," Eleanor tells them. Not unpleasantly, just stating the fact.

The young men laugh. "Why don't you take that feeb someplace they can set him up for bumper bowl," one of them says, setting down his bag directly in front of Eleanor. "We like this lane."

Eleanor looks to the lane—one over from theirs—where the Akersville police and firemen's bowling team are settling in for their first game of the night. It's their night off; she doesn't want to involve them. She considers complaining to the management, or simply picking up a bowling ball and letting it go down the lane—but doing that would only embarrass Toby.

"Let's get a pizza," she tells her son. "I'd just as soon not deal with people like that."

Only she does have to deal with them, more and more. They seem to be everywhere now. It may show up as nothing more than someone pulling his car into the parking spot she's been waiting for and giving her the finger as he slips into the space, or Orson—now a first grader—reporting to her on a recent visit that a boy in his class said people who don't speak English shouldn't be allowed at their school.

One person Orson chooses not to mention in these conversations is his own father, Jake, for whom the election seemed to have unleashed a new flood of bitter invective about immigrants, homeless people, senior citizens, gay people, liberal softies who spend their time trying to protect endangered species, Black Lives Matter and LGBTQ (Al?) and the disabled (his brother-in-law among them), Mexicans (Teresa?)—all, according to Jake, looking for handouts and living off the backs of hardworking Americans like himself.

Turning on her laptop every morning before getting to work on her book, Eleanor considers simply avoiding the news. She can never stick to her promise to herself to steer clear of what's going on now in this increasingly unfamiliar new world, the latest painful chapter. Barack Obama—the president still, for a handful of days—seems suddenly to have grown thinner, grayer—not defeated exactly, but nothing like the bold and optimistic young man who'd been sworn into office eight years earlier, with his wife and two little girls at his side.

Michelle as she appears now, in the days leading up to her husband's departure from the White House and the arrival of the man replacing him, continues to look powerful and fierce—"angry," some people say of her—code word for *Black*.

For eight years, Eleanor has found dependable solace in the presence, at the White House, of a family who, whether you agreed with every stance they took or not, seemed undeniably decent. She has loved watching videos of Barack and Michelle dancing together— the clear evidence, when they do, of genuine affection and more. She has studied videos of Obama bending down to child level, when greeting a three-year-old, and seeming to actually pay attention to the child. She loves the images of Michelle in the vegetable garden she's created, teaching kids about healthy eating. It seems to Eleanor now as if a giant bulldozer is plowing through the lettuce and tomatoes she planted there, crushing everything, with a gloating thug at the steering wheel.

Eleanor has always believed—as she knows Toby does—that the world is full of more good people than the other kind. When she was a teenager, she kept, tacked to her wall, a line from Anne Frank, written from her hiding place in the annex, as the Nazis who would eventually murder her stormed the streets. "In spite of everything I still believe that people are really good at heart."

Could she say this still? Could anyone?

Now when Eleanor passes a car on the road with a Trump sticker on the bumper, and their two vehicles pull up alongside each other at a stoplight, she finds herself staring inside, studying the face of the person at the wheel as if it might reveal something, offer a clue to what's going on in her town, in her country. What did a person who truly believes the things this new president they'd elected is saying look like?

It turned out most of these people look just like everyone else.

80.

Kiss every inch of you

P hone conversations with Guy never worked all that well for two people whose connection seemed so grounded in the physical. They had to be in the same room together to locate their true connection. In the same bed, preferably.

Between those times, they continue to live lives that seem to have virtually no common ground other than their feeling for each other. After their call the night of the election, Guy and Eleanor had hung silent on their separate ends of the line for a few moments before heading off to their separate worlds.

It's a new year now. 2017. Almost four months have passed since Eleanor and Guy have seen each other. For a while their not meeting was the result of Eleanor's need to focus on Coco and Jesse St. Pierre's allegations against Toby. She was meeting with the lawyer, standing guard over her son, then—after he was vindicated—she was canvassing voters. Largely because of this, Eleanor's newest book is months overdue. She's still trying to pull Toby out of the bone-deep sadness that seems to have taken hold over what he'd endured.

Guy has been occupied, too. Though in the past he's made a point of separating himself and his foundation from political campaigns, in the final months before the election—his last few months before taking off to complete the final leg of his expedition—he'd stepped up his speaking engagements, hoping to bring attention to the urgency of electing a candidate who, though hardly Guy's idea of a champion for the environment, offered a far better shot at addressing climate change than her opponent.

In January, shortly before the inauguration of the new president, Guy calls Eleanor. "Meet me in Los Angeles," he tells her.

He doesn't speak of the other part, that the date of his return to Antarctica—once the days grow longer at the southernmost part of the globe—is closing in on them. Guy's new knee is fully functioning. He's ready at last to complete the final brutally challenging few hundred miles of his quest to the last three glaciers he has yet to explore—and to venture farther than Admiral Scott or Ernest Shackleton ever made it on their epic quests more than a century before. He'll be heading to Chile at least three months before the expedition gets underway to prepare equipment and meet up with his team, but he has said little about this to Eleanor, and she doesn't ask.

The plane ticket Guy sends her for the Los Angeles trip—first-class, as always—arrives the next day. Eleanor receives a press release: the movie project that brought her and Guy together—delayed many times—is scheduled for release in the spring, but Eleanor has no desire to see the film. She and Guy choose not to alert Marlys or any of the other studio executives on the project to the fact of their imminent arrival in town, and in Eleanor's case, she knows she's no longer welcome at the company offices. Apart from a sum of money that had made it possible for her to share, with Al, the bill for Toby's attorney, and the fact that the project brought Guy into her life, Eleanor has no further interest in involving herself with a movie that no longer bears her name or even that of the character she created.

They meet at a hotel in Malibu just off the beach, waves crashing on the shore as Eleanor hands the keys of her rental car to the valet. Before entering the lobby, she runs a hand through her hair (he likes it a little messy) and sprays their perfume—this is how she thinks of it, *theirs*—behind her ears.

Guy is already in the room when she gets there. As is his way at these moments, he wraps his arms around her, breathes deep, and buries his face in her hair. There's a place on her neck she loves to be touched. Neither one of them says anything.

"I just want to kiss every inch of you."

Every other time they've met like this, Eleanor has registered an equal measure of excitement, but something feels different to her now. The shiver of anticipation that has always accompanied their reunions is missing. She takes his hand that has reached out to stroke her breast and holds it in hers, instead.

"So much has happened," she tells him. "I think I just need to lie down next to you for a few minutes. Find my way back."

It's as if he hasn't heard. His hands are still reaching for her breasts. He runs his fingers along her spine. He reaches for her top button. She doesn't want this to happen but her body stiffens.

"We need to take it slower," she says. "I'm in a different place. I can't explain, but I'm not ready."

Until now, he hasn't actually looked at her. He's been too occupied with touching her. Now he studies her face. His eyes, that cool ice ozone-baked blue, with thin threads of filament radiating out from their centers, like fried marbles.

"What happened?"

"I don't know. Everything. My son. My daughter. Lawyers. Neighbors. Grandchildren. Goats. Donald Trump. Life."

"We both have a lot going on," he says. "That's always been so."

"Maybe it all caught up with me." For the first time in five and a half years, after all their nights together, she feels nothing.

"It's about Trump," he says. "Everyone's in shock. But we can't let the asshole ruin our lives. Not tonight anyway."

"That's not it." Eleanor shakes her head. "You'll be going away soon. I don't know what that means. I don't know what it's going to feel like when you're off on this whole other continent." There's more to it, but she doesn't go there.

"It will feel the way it always feels when we're apart." He strokes her arm. Less forcefully now, he reaches for the zipper on her skirt. "We've always understood how it is for us. Times we're together. Times we're not."

"Maybe I just need to talk for a while first," she says. Over all these nights—all these years of nights—they've done less talking than might have been supposed. They're always so busy touching each other's bodies that large aspects of their lives remain, like that frozen landscape at the edge of the world, unexplored.

Guy lets out a long sigh. He's a man largely unacquainted with the condition of weariness, but he displays it now. *"Talk, talk, talk."* He sighs. "God, I'm so tired of talking. Night after night up on some podium or other. All I ever seem to do these days is talk."

"But not with me."

"Can't I just kiss you for a while first?" She has loved this about him—his hunger for her. The fact that even as a woman closer to sixty-five than sixty (as if sixty were young!) she possesses for him, at least, a kind of sexual power she might have supposed to have lost long before. She knows what a rare thing this is. Rare and precious.

"I can't," she tells him. His hand is on her rib cage. Then her thigh. She has to push it away—something she's never done before. Not with him. For a moment, he won't release his grip. For a split second she registers something like fear.

The picture comes to her of her high school friend Patty's brother, Matt, in the front seat of his car, times he'd pick her up from work, take her down that dead-end road, unhook her bra, pinch her nipples as he thrust his erect penis into her. But this is Guy, the man she loves. What's the matter with her?

He sits up on the bed. "What do you want to talk about?" She can hear the faintest tone of impatience.

"I don't actually know. I just need something from you. Other than your hands. We've . . . gone through a lot."

"Okay, let's talk." It's unmistakable now. Not just weariness but anger. "You actually want to discuss the election? Now of all times?"

She shakes her head.

"What's going on?"

"Toby, for one thing."

"Oh God. Don't tell me you're turning into a mother on me?" He speaks the word as if it were an obscenity.

"What he went through was awful."

"I thought that was all settled. They dropped the investigation, right?"

There'd been so much more to it. How, all those days, as the investigators were interviewing schoolchildren—looking for evidence of wrongdoing on the part of her son at his beloved fire station—Toby sat in the kitchen, staring out the window. All those weeks he never whistled anymore or got on his bicycle. Driving in the car with him, passing the fire station and seeing the men—his old friends—out in front, hosing down the truck. His crumpled-up Scarlett Johansson poster in the trash.

"Scarlett would probably hate me now," he'd told Eleanor.

One time when the two of them were at the supermarket a child had dropped his blanket and Toby bent to pick it up. When he handed the blanket back to the boy's mother, she had first smiled and then—recognizing him—recoiled.

No more trips to the bowling alley. Not even the dump. It's over now, Eleanor tells Guy, but her son hasn't gotten over what happened. He used to view the world as a good place. He doesn't anymore.

As much as events of the last few months have changed Toby, they have changed Eleanor, too. Lying on the bed beside Guy for the first time since the accusations were first leveled against Toby, she registers a new distance between the two of them. She felt more connected to Guy that first night they spent together than she does now.

"We went through a lot," Eleanor tells Guy. "It's not a part of my life I share with you. But it's a big part. Maybe the biggest. The part about being in a family."

Guy sighs deeply again. His fingers, that reached for her hair before, now rake through his own.

"Listen, Eleanor." His voice sounds weary. "The world is full of people who live ordinary lives. They wake up every morning in the same bed together. They go about their day. Somebody turns the television on. Somebody goes shopping. After dinner, they watch more television and go to bed. Now and then they may even fuck."

This is how he talks. She doesn't mind it. This is Guy, a man who can deliver a speech to a roomful of powerful corporate donors or world leaders even, or to a group of society types at a private club and jet off with them the next day in a private plane to some island they own in the Caribbean. He's also a man who can say "I want to fuck you all night long."

There have been times when she found the rawness of Guy exciting but now what she needs is to talk about what happened with someone who is, himself, a parent. Lying next to this man she has loved for five and a half years now, a surprising thought comes to her.

She misses Cam. She misses her fellow parent, the red-headed man who'd been there for the birth of their red-headed son, the only person who'd loved Toby as much as she does, probably. As he did

Ursula and Al. As he would have loved their grandchildren, if he'd lived to know them.

"I guess I can't expect you to understand," Eleanor says.

"I've never pretended to be the domestic type," he says.

He reaches to touch her again. He reaches for her hair—only a strand—and wraps it around his rough, leathery finger. She studies the space where the other finger used to be. The one lost to frostbite.

"You and I aren't like regular people," Guy tells Eleanor. "What we have, what we've gotten to experience with each other, is rare and precious."

She would not disagree. Only all of a sudden it seems a little pointless, maybe even ridiculous—the two of them coming together as they have in expensive hotel rooms around the country even as Guy spends the evenings directly before talking the moneyed elite into making large donations to support his efforts to save the planet. After the sex part, taking their showers, putting on their thick terry-cloth hotel robes, ordering caviar and room service champagne.

"What we've been doing all this time feels like a fantasy," she says.

"What's wrong with a fantasy?" he says.

"It's not real." Also difficult to sustain. "And it lacks . . . substance."

They do not make love that night. They lie there on the bed next to each other for a long time, bodies not touching. Even now, when, for once, the urge to make love no longer stands in the way of their talking, they have surprisingly little to say to each other.

Sometime in the night—one A.M. maybe, or two—Guy gets up and puts on his jacket. Over the few hours they've spent in this hotel room neither one of them has taken off their clothes.

"I think I'll head to the airport," he says. "There's this flight to Buenos Aires that leaves at five. I was invited to a symposium. I thought I'd miss it but what the hell, why not go?"

His back is to her as he gathers his things. His backpack. The silver cigar case. Eleanor could pretend to herself that they have simply experienced an off night, that once more time has passed, things will be the same between the two of them as they'd been before. She knows otherwise.

Standing at the door to the hotel room—Guy's backpack already on his shoulder—they tell each other the obvious things. The word "love" is mentioned. There is simply nothing further either of them knows to do.

"I need to go," he tells her.

"I guess I should give you this," he says, reaching into his backpack. She recognizes the shape of the package. The twenty-eight-ounce size.

Just after the sun comes up Eleanor drives her rental car back to the airport. Able to change to an earlier flight, she's home in time to make dinner for herself and Toby.

"You could have stayed longer with that guy if you wanted," he tells her, over a dinner of raw cauliflower, peanuts, tomato soup, and toast. In all this time, Toby has never quite gotten it straight, the part about Guy's name, though he remembers well the night they spent together in the barn—part of a night, anyway—when a baby goat was born. Two of them.

"I can actually take care of myself okay now," Toby tells her. "Me and Ralph and the girls." He means his goats.

Toby is right about this. The thing Eleanor had wished for so long, that had seemed for so long unattainable—that her son might one day no longer need her there to take care of him—has come to pass. She can leave him, in fact. More all the time. She just doesn't have a place to go.

"I think I'll just stay home for a while," Eleanor tells her son.

She climbs the steps to her bedroom then. The room that had been hers and Cam's once. Then Cam and Coco's. Then Cam's alone as he lay dying. Eleanor's room now.

This is when she opens the package Guy gave her as he headed out the door to the airport.

It's perfume all right. But not the scent she loves, the one he'd always bought for her. She stands there studying the bottle.

For more than five years, he had always bought her the same very good French perfume. They'd chosen her scent together. He'd known it well. This is not her brand.

81.

Getting off the *Orient Express*

There have been, over the years, a number of dividing lines that led Eleanor to view her life in terms she thought of as "before" and "after." The first, when she was sixteen, was drawn the night her parents died. They were driving home (drunk, no doubt; they often were) after a weekend of skiing in Vermont while she'd been away at boarding school. As an only child—an uncle she'd met only once, her sole relative—she no longer had a home or a family, which no doubt contributed to what has been her lifelong obsession that she would one day have both.

For a while, after her parents' death, she'd spent her vacations with the family of her roommate, Patty. It was over her summer at the home of the Hallinans, in Rhode Island—the first summer she was an orphan, the summer Neil Armstrong walked on the moon— that Patty's older brother Matt had started driving her to her restaurant job every day. The memory never leaves her: Of Matt Hallinan, leaning across the seat to open the car door for her when he picked her up after her shift was over. The fork in the road, right turn to the Hallinans', left-turn dead end to nowhere. Matt, taking the left turn that first time. Then every day after that. Pulling up her skirt, pulling down her pants. The abortion she had that fall—paid for by Matt—probably makes the list of before and after divisions in Eleanor's life.

Before Matt Hallinan. After Matt Hallinan.

Then there was meeting Cam, and once again a line cut across her history up until then: Life as it was before they met. Life once they fell in love. At the time, she had believed that there were no more dividing lines as important as this one. *Before Cam. After Cam.* After, meaning once she got to be happy at last, living on the farm with a man who loved her. For the rest of their lives, she thought. Only it hadn't worked out that way.

Then came parenthood. Before the babies. After the first one.

Becoming a parent was like walking into a room you never knew existed in a house you've lived in all your life.

The before and after that defined everything was Toby's accident. One day Eleanor was the mother of a wild, hilarious four-and-a-half-year-old who played his quarter-sized violin in the bathroom and recounted to the family his conversations with God and Mr. T. One day later, a child who resembled that boy was lying on a hospital bed hooked up to a wall of machines, and though eventually he learned to walk again, and to speak, and to ride his bike and tend the goats—learned how to make cheese, even—the child she had known before had disappeared.

There was before and after the divorce, of course. Before, when Coco was her children's babysitter. After, when she became their stepmother. Before and after Eleanor moved away from the farm—a place she loved too well to stay. There was before and after Al's decision to transition. (Before, she had two daughters and a son. After, two sons and a daughter.) Before and then after Ursula cut Eleanor out of her life.

Before Cam's death. *After.*

Now here comes another.

Eleanor crossed a line that night in Los Angeles when Guy first reached out to shake her hand—that firm grip, the space where a finger should have been but wasn't. After: There was a man in her life who sent her plane tickets that took her to hotel rooms where they got to leave the world for a while. What the two of them found there was a place Eleanor never knew existed before. A state of being. A kind of physical connection she'd never known until then. Other things those hands of his could do, even with just nine fingers.

She has reached the *After-Guy* stage now. She used to hope she'd never go there, same as she'd dreaded she might.

The surprise, for Eleanor, is how differently she experiences the loss of Guy from how she experienced certain other losses she's known. This one bears no resemblance to the loss of the shining star who had been the old Toby once, or the loss of her marriage, or the farm. The sorrow she feels now bears no resemblance to what she felt that day Ursula sent her away and told her she never wanted to see her again.

Always before, when one of those dividing lines split Eleanor's story in two parts, it had been the circumstances that changed, not Eleanor herself. This time is different. With Guy suddenly no longer a part of her life, it seems briefly to Eleanor that what she's lost is not so much the man himself as the woman she became with him.

Guy had reminded Eleanor of a person she'd been once, long ago—a woman who walked home naked from a waterfall in the middle of the night, with her naked husband beside her. Until she met Guy, she'd lost sight of that woman—a risk-taker, a lover. He brought her back to life.

Once—was it in Chicago? St. Louis?—she had hung a "Do Not Disturb" sign on the door of their hotel suite and spent an entire day naked in bed with Guy. "I never do things like this," Eleanor told him then.

"Well, you just did," he said.

Not right away, but a few weeks after that last night they spent together at the Malibu hotel—realizing that she's not heartbroken after all, not playing an endless loop of Sinead O'Connor singing "Nothing Compares 2 U"—the thought comes to Eleanor, what Guy's true purpose was in her life.

Guy reawakened the part of Eleanor that wasn't the wife of a husband, author of books, mother of children. Whatever he'd failed to offer her—including permanence, including his simple presence on the same continent she inhabited—he'd given her something precious.

He's gone now. Whatever Guy's future plans may be, she won't be part of them. But with or without Guy in her life—with or without any man in her life—the part of herself that he reawakened won't go back to sleep.

Eleanor can't regret anything that happened between them. The time they spent together—fewer than one hundred nights over a little less than five years—seems to her now like some once-in-a-lifetime trip she went on. She'd had a first-class ticket on one of those train cars on the *Orient Express* with windows in all directions, including the roof, to take in the most glorious vistas, visit the most spectacular sights. "Visit," the operable word. Nobody stayed forever in a first-class railway car. At some point a person has to get off the train.

82.

Not the good kind of funny

It was January when she and Guy met up that last time in Los Angeles. It's February now, Valentine season. Eleanor will turn sixty-four this year. Her health is good. She doesn't suffer the aches and pains, and worse, of so many people she knows around her age. But she's conscious now, as never before, that her time is finite. This is true for everyone, of course, but it's so much more real to Eleanor now than it was when she was the age her children are. She felt as though she'd live forever in those days. It's not a bad thing, this awareness she carries with her all the time now, that she won't. It gives her a new appreciation for her days. Even the difficult ones.

Now that Donald Trump has been elected, Jake's behavior is more obnoxious than ever. He never misses his Make America Great Again meetings and Order of the Patriots rallies. He still drinks a lot. More than ever, probably. Eleanor knows this from Orson, who has also confided in her that his father takes a lot of pills for his back pain. They make him act funny sometimes, Orson says. Not the good kind of funny.

83.

X's and O's

The rest of Eleanor's family members carry on with their lives much as before. Toby has made another trip to the Verlander farm for the usual purpose. No further sightings of June Verlander, but he's got four pregnant goats to show for the trip, and when he left this last time, Hans Verlander presented him with another kint-sugi bowl.

"My daughter wanted you to have this," he says, placing the second bowl in Toby's hands. This one's green, with gold running through in all the places June put the broken pieces together. "She told me you appreciate the work she does."

He didn't elaborate, but Eleanor understands what June meant. Her son is the type of person who looks closely at a bowl. A person who looks closely at everything, in fact.

Toby pays attention. To people as well as goats.

Evidently June Verlander is the type of person who notices this.

Toby has started visiting the fire station again, finally, though he steers clear on days when school visits take place—the thing he had loved best about being there, once. Come summertime when the baby goats have been delivered, he'll get on a plane for his annual visit with his brother and sister-in-law and their daughter, Flora—who recently turned five years old. Now that she can write a little, she sends him postcards covered with X's and O's, mostly of their favorite Seattle hotspots and incredibly large salmon.

Lulu's eleven now, and still worries a lot. Orson's seven. Ursula continues to keep Eleanor at a careful remove as she has for so many years now, making her occasional day trips to Concord to work on some project she's developing with her friend Kat, that Eleanor knows better than to ask about. It's rare now for the children to accompany Ursula on these trips, to visit their grandmother as they used to for a while. Orson's on a T-ball team, also in a peewee soccer league. Lulu's got Girl Scouts and 4-H and violin lessons and gymnastics. When they have a free afternoon, they mostly want to spend it with their friends. They love their grandmother—this she knows. But they're moving on with their lives, as children should feel free to do.

The question for Eleanor is how to move on with hers. Or maybe—here is a new thought—it's not about moving on. It's about making peace with where you are. The messy, imperfect, frustrating, lonely, and occasionally beautiful place a person carves out for herself. For

Eleanor, it's a farm in Akersville, New Hampshire. Despite her long resistance to the idea, she knows this now. This is her home.

84.

Goats don't break your heart

It's a Friday night. Eleanor and Toby are out for dinner at Thai Garden. He's put on his favorite shirt for the occasion. Day-Glo paisley, and a vest. For the first time, Eleanor notices a few gray hairs on her son, mixed with the red. There's gray in his beard now, too. Her youngest child turned thirty-six in December.

"Scarlett got divorced again," Toby tells her, looking up from his spring roll. As little as he knows of the world beyond the farm, he always keeps tabs on Scarlett Johansson. "I wonder if she's dating anyone."

"Maybe she is, maybe she isn't," Eleanor offers. "But I'm not sure she's your type."

"I don't think I'll ever get to meet her," Toby says. "I was just kidding myself."

The first time the actress had gotten married, Toby was sad for a week. Then she got divorced, and though Toby would never be one to celebrate anybody's divorce, he'd allowed himself to become— briefly—hopeful again. Years after she'd come out with her album, he used to call the radio station in Boston several times a day, requesting that they play the song "Anywhere I Lay My Head." Not that they did. Every time a movie of hers comes out, Toby and Eleanor are there the first night, to grab the best seats.

"I was stupid, thinking I had a chance with her," he tells Eleanor. His voice is steady, level, realistic. This could almost be Al talking, or Ursula. "She's way out of my league."

Eleanor could be relieved that Toby appears to have given up his Scarlett Johansson fantasy. But what she feels, taking in what her son tells her, is a stab of sorrow. As worried as she used to be once, over her son's unrealistic hopes and dreams and the disappointment they were likely to bring him, she realizes now that the saddest thing comes when a person gives up on his dreams. Saddest of all if the dream he's giving up on concerns love.

Who Toby wants to spend time with, he says, are his goats. A goat—even a particularly lovable goat, and to Toby, every single one of his goats is lovable—is a lot less likely to break your heart.

85.

Taking out her colored pencils

lijah has been out of the country almost a year. He and Eleanor speak fairly often on FaceTime. Back in the fall, when the charges against Toby were dropped, Eleanor called to tell him. They spoke again after the election, and after things with Guy ended. Oddly enough, at the time, the one of the children with whom Eleanor had felt able to talk about what happened had been Elijah.

Now Elijah has gotten a gig in Boston on a night she's in Brookline to see a matinee at the ballet. He shows up on the doorstep of Eleanor's condo, straight from the airport, guitar case in hand. Standing next to him, his fiancée, Miriam, with her mbira—a beautiful young woman with a single long braid wound around her head.

"Mind if we crash here?" he asks.

It's after eleven o'clock but the two of them haven't eaten, so Eleanor fixes them an omelet. They sit in the kitchen. Eleanor opens wine.

"I'm so sorry about what Coco did to Toby," he says. "To everyone."

"It's over," Eleanor says.

"I don't even recognize her anymore. The person Coco is now." Elijah reaches for another piece of the apple crisp Eleanor's made for them.

"Maybe someday if she gets off the drugs, you'll get your mother back," Eleanor says. "If she leaves that bad-news boyfriend. Jesse."

"I should have been there for Toby," Elijah says.

Eleanor puts a hand on Elijah's shoulder. "You couldn't have done anything," she tells him.

From when he was very little—it was Toby who looked after Elijah. Then it was Elijah who looked after Toby. Elijah—the only one of the children who had never known the old Toby, or suffered the loss of him as the others had. Maybe it was Elijah's ability to see Toby, from the first, as the person he became after that day at the pond, rather than the person he had been, that allowed the two of them to form the happy, uncomplicated connection Al and Ursula had struggled to maintain with Toby. Toby and Elijah are probably the closest of all the siblings. Neither one of them speaks of the other as his half brother, only his brother.

They talk about Miriam and Elijah's wedding plans then—no big event, just a small gathering, but they'd love to do something at the farm. Meanwhile, they're taking a road trip. Miriam has never traveled to the United States before. She wants to see New York City, of course, and because she has always loved Dolly Parton, she wants to see Nashville. Dollywood maybe. Their ultimate destination: Seattle, to visit Al and Teresa and Flora.

It's after midnight when Eleanor makes up the bed for the two of them. They're heading to the club in Arlington the next day to set up for their sound check.

Next morning, after they leave for the club, Eleanor sits at her desk for a few minutes before getting to work. The room seems still to be filled with the nearly electric energy of a young couple in love heading out on their next big adventure.

Eleanor was such a person once. She's come so far from those days. After all those years in which she was longing for something or other—the love of a man, a baby, money to pay the mortgage that month, her son's health restored, her husband's affection, the farm she'd given away to him, Ursula's forgiveness and the presence of her grandchildren in her life, Toby's reputation restored, a woman in the White House, a night with Guy—the thought comes to her that at this particular moment, at least, she's content. She felt happy to see Elijah and Miriam arrive and she's equally happy to see them leave. She has friends to see and a book to finish. She loves her work.

For so long, Eleanor has placed her life as an artist close to the bottom of her list of priorities. The well-being of everyone else in her family always came first. If her husband was depressed, if one of her children was in trouble or registering some measure of pain, as someone nearly invariably was, she'd found it impossible to focus on anything else.

For so many years she had imagined that the central meaning and purpose in her life would come from her marriage, and later, after the divorce, from her children and then her grandchildren. This has changed.

As much as she loves her family, they are all off living their lives now—even Toby, though he remains on the farm. Large problems may face him still, as they do for all three of her children. But whatever the issues are they struggle with, they're not for Eleanor to solve. She will celebrate their triumphs and do what she can to support them during their hard times. But she no longer supposes she has a central role to play in the stories of their lives as they play out now.

Where does this leave a woman who, for so long, poured her energy into attempting just that? Cam's words to Eleanor long ago—*You wouldn't know what to do with a morning to yourself if you had one*—return to her. She has almost every morning to herself. Also the afternoons. Also the nights. She can spend them as she chooses, and where she may have been unclear, once, how to do this, now she's beginning to imagine another way of spending her life, in which she actually gets to consider her own needs, at long last.

86.

The Amazing Adventures of Mineral Man

It's probably no mystery why, when she was nineteen years old, Eleanor had written a book about a ten-year-old girl who travels the world having unlikely adventures, with no parents in sight. Long before she actually became orphaned, at age sixteen, Eleanor had lived her life largely ignored by her parents, Martin and

Vivian—who had always appeared to take more interest in martinis, and each other, than in their only daughter.

After the Bodie stories came her syndicated comic strip, *Family Tree*. During the first days after Toby's accident, when it became impossible to write about a family that resembled hers without telling the story of the brain injury, Eleanor had ended the comic strip. For a while then, she'd supported their family—though just barely at times—designing greeting cards. Then came the children's book that allowed her to stop worrying about where the next mortgage payment was coming from—*The Cork People*—followed by a TV series and a licensing deal for the Make Your Own Cork Person kit. In recent years, by popular demand, Eleanor has created two new stories in the Bodie series, even more popular than the earlier ones.

All told, Eleanor has published twelve books featuring Bodie's adventures—*Bodie Under the Sea, Bodie Visits the Gorillas, Bodie Along the Seine, Bodie Goes to Antarctica.* Eleanor has been writing about Bodie's adventures for so long that sometimes when she visits a bookstore to sign the latest book in the series, the mother of a child who loved the books will mention that when she was a little girl, she'd loved Bodie, too.

But the book Eleanor has been working on for the past several years is a totally different kind of story. Eleanor has told nobody, including her agent and editor, what she's doing this time. This project feels closer to the bone than anything she's created before.

For several years now—off and on—Eleanor has been writing a graphic novel. This time her audience will be teenagers and young adults, not children. The central character of her story is an unlikely superhero named Mineral Man.

Unlike the typical Marvel superheroes or villains, Mineral Man has an unprepossessing body. His shoulders are not broad. Though he appears young—mid-thirties, at most—his abdomen shows no evidence of a six-pack, and his arms lack the kind of muscular definition readers of superhero graphic novels have come to expect. His hairline is receding. In fact, Mineral Man strongly resembles Toby.

Like Toby, he has suffered a brain injury. Like Toby, he walks in a manner that makes it easy for a certain kind of person, of whom there turn out to be many in the world, to make fun of him. One difference between Toby and Mineral Man: Where Toby speaks—slowly, as if he were forming the words one syllable at a time, or carving them out of wood—Mineral Man does not use words to communicate. He acts out what he wants to convey, as if he were playing charades. Sometimes he draws a picture. These pictures—as Eleanor has conceived them—serve as the illustrations for *The Amazing Adventures of Mineral Man.*

In the way that the creators of Superman and Batman and Spider-Man provided followers with their hero's origin story, Eleanor has done the same for Mineral Man. As a boy—back when he goes by the name Jasper—he seems to have been born under a lucky star. He runs faster than all the other children and serves as an unhittable pitcher on his Little League team. He plays the guitar and performs with his best friend, Ernie, in a cool rock band. At his school all the boys admire him; the girls are all in love with him. When Jasper rides his skateboard (performing tricks at a level that inspired invitations for sponsorship and his image on a cereal box) dogs follow him down the street. Birds circle his head. When—single-handedly—he rescues a baby who'd fallen down a well, the mayor of the town presents him with the key to the city.

Among Jasper's many passions, the one that takes precedence over all others—with the exception of his trusty hound, a three-legged dog named King—is rock collecting. In the basement bedroom of the house where Jasper lives he maintains a vast collection of minerals he's collected as a rock hound. Every day before heading out into the world, he selects one of these to place in his pocket—based on its particular properties and the powers he believes that mineral to possess.

When he's twelve years old, Jasper suffers a terrible accident on his skateboard. While performing his most amazing trick yet, he crashes into a tree. He's not wearing a helmet. (There's a lesson here for readers, if they choose to pick up on it.)

Like Bodie, and like Eleanor herself, Jasper appears not to have parents, or if he does, they stay out of the story. So it's Ernie who rushes to the rescue after Jasper's skateboard accident. But Jasper is different now. He no longer knows his name or recognizes anyone.

He can't. When he walks, he does so with a slow, lurching gait not unlike Toby's. The only figure from his old life he recognizes other than Ernie is his dog, King.

Ernie recognizes that Jasper can no longer go to school or play with the team he'd starred on. When Ernie places Jasper's beloved guitar in his hands, he stares at it as if what he's holding were a zucchini or a loaf of bread.

"There's a place we can send your friend where people will take care of him," a doctor tells Ernie. "We all agree that's the best thing." But Ernie shakes his head and packs up Jasper's things and brings him home to live with him and his sister at their old, falling-down house in the woods. He brings along his friend's precious collection of minerals.

That night over a dinner of spaghetti carbonara—always Jasper's favorite food—Ernie suggests that Jasper change his name. "I think you should call yourself Mineral Man," Ernie says.

Jasper—now Mineral Man—nods his head and draws a picture that serves as the prototype for the orange and green suit he'll wear from that day forward in his identity as a new kind of superhero. A hero for anyone who—like Toby—might find himself the object of scorn and derision and bullying in the cruel world of now.

All of this happens in the first five pages of Eleanor's graphic novel. Unlike Toby, Mineral Man never relearns how to speak. But he is able to convey to Ernie what his purpose in life will be, from this day forward.

He will seek out people like himself, experiencing injustice at the hands of those who write off these individuals—the kind of event that seemed more prevalent all the time these days. He will protect and defend them.

Mineral Man wreaks revenge in surprising ways, always making sure that the punishment fits the crime. Among his most despicable adversaries—one Eleanor has added to the story since the election—is a man who goes by the name of Yellow Top. Yellow Top gets his name because his hair is a sickening shade of yellow that Mineral Man's sidekick, Ernie, describes as "the color of first-morning urine." Yellow Top is married to a beautiful but strangely dead-looking woman named Stefania who has sold her soul for the purpose of presiding, with her husband, over his empire of toadlike followers wearing red hats. Their empire is based in the city of Metropolis, in a golden skyscraper called Yellow-Top Towers.

Mineral Man is not the only one who has attempted to rid the world of Yellow Top and his crew. As a person who can't speak and walks with difficulty, Mineral Man appears to pose no threat to Yellow Top, which is how he manages to gain access to Yellow-Top Towers as a lowly janitor. Every time he's told to shred another document outlining the details of Yellow Top's nefarious schemes, Mineral Man—in his janitor's uniform—holds on to it instead, for evidence. His files on Yellow Top eventually fill an entire room in the house Mineral Man shares with Eddie.

Yellow Top has no clue of course. He calls Mineral Man the Idiot and frequently entertains his friends, and the ice queen, Stefania, by doing an impression of Mineral Man's unusual way of walking.

But Mineral Man and his sidekick, Ernie, know they'll get the last laugh.

As was true of her Bodie books, it's not difficult recognizing the origins of Eleanor's Mineral Man story. Over those months when every day's news seemed to deliver a new and disheartening event involving the newly elected president, Eleanor has found it comforting to create a story in which her unlikely disabled hero will ultimately bring him down.

Now that she has time and space—at last—to focus on her work, the story comes easily to Eleanor. On nights she spends in Brookline, Eleanor has few obligations—nobody to pick up and transport from one place to another. If she doesn't feel like cooking dinner, she can heat up soup or have sushi delivered. With few distractions, for the first time in years, she can start work just as the sun comes up. Often it's dark when she finally steps away from her drawing table to get dinner. Other than bowling night with Toby back at the farm and times Ursula drops Orson and Lulu off with her, Eleanor has never known so little in the way of obligations.

Sometimes Eleanor goes to a movie by herself. She buys a tall box of popcorn and puts her feet up on the seat in front of her. Times she's in Brookline, she and Jason, or sometimes Annette, who lives in Arlington, meet up on Saturday mornings at the Arnold Arboretum, taking long walks under the many species of trees and afterward they go out for waffles.

"All this time I thought that when I got to this stage in my life, I'd be cooking big family meals and babysitting grandchildren," Eleanor tells Annette. "It hasn't exactly worked out that way. But it turns out that's okay."

Sometimes late at night she allows herself to think back on how it had felt, walking in the door of some beautiful hotel, knowing that a man she adored was waiting just outside the elevator. She looks back on those days much as she did the days when she floated paper boats in the brook with her children when they were young, Valentine-making marathons with them, Christmas Eve nights with Cam in their old farmhouse, filling the stockings and spreading ashes from the fireplace to look like Santa's footprints—sweet times Eleanor no longer needs to revisit. The coolness and sharp judgments she continues to feel from her daughter have not dissipated. This, more than any other sadness, is the one Eleanor carries with her every day, but she tells herself she's learning to live with it. As much sadness as she'd felt for Toby, when he told her he would probably never get married, for Eleanor at least—Eleanor now, after all the other chapters she's lived—giving up on expectations is not necessarily a bad thing.

She has made her own good life, for once—*good enough,* anyway—instead of working so hard trying to ensure everyone else's.

87.

Every species of flower, in glass

T hough she and Ursula speak occasionally now—usually to exchange information about the grandchildren—Ursula never calls her. Now her name shows up on Eleanor's phone.

"Can you take the kids?" Ursula says now. "There's a problem.

It's Jake." In the background, she can hear the television. Eleanor knows, from her last trip up to Vermont, that Jake keeps it tuned to Fox News 24/7. Ursula drowns it out as much as possible with the music she loves: John Prine and Emmylou Harris and Roseanne Cash, Patty Griffin, Kate & Anna McGarrigle, Eliza Gilkyson, Tracy Chapman, the Be Good Tanyas. For all the topics that seemed to leave Eleanor at odds with her daughter, their taste in music remains aligned.

"Can you turn it down?" Ursula calls out to Jake. "I'm on the phone." The television remains as loud as ever.

"When were you thinking of coming down?" Eleanor asks her.

"Now?"

My daughter's in trouble, Eleanor thinks. Nothing else would have allowed her to make that call. In spite of everything that's happened between them, her chief and only response is concern for Ursula and fear that she's not okay.

Three hours later Ursula shows up in Brookline with Lulu and Orson. Eleanor asks no questions and Ursula volunteers nothing. "We're going through some stuff," she tells Eleanor as she carries the children's things into Eleanor's spare bedroom. Two suitcases. This is more than an overnight. Having finished school the week before, the kids have no compelling reason to be home at the moment. And some good reasons not to be there.

For all the satisfaction she's been getting in recent months over working on her new book, Eleanor is happy to see her grandchildren, but worried about the circumstances that led to their mother bringing them here.

"Jake's gone off the deep end," Ursula tells Eleanor, when they're alone. (Lulu unpacking her things. Orson glued to his tablet.) "I need some time to work some things out."

"I," not "we."

Ursula runs through a list of information Eleanor needs to know. The children have summer camp lined up for July, but not for a few weeks.

"I know you're probably busy," Ursula says.

"The kids and I will be fine," Eleanor tells her.

After Ursula leaves, Eleanor fixes macaroni and cheese, the most comforting meal she knows. Orson scarfs his down and wants seconds. Lulu appears to have no appetite.

"My mom and dad had another fight," Orson says. "My dad got all these cans of beans and batteries and bottles of water at Walmart. He says we might have to live in the basement for a while if the Mexicans come. My dad says they're trying to take over our country and make it so everyone has to talk Spanish."

Lulu shoots her brother a look. Whatever has gone on at their house, she isn't inclined to share it with their grandmother. As she often does, Eleanor recognizes in Lulu the behavior of a child trying hard to maintain her loyalties to two parents at war with each other. Much as her mother did once.

"Your aunt Teresa's family is from Mexico," Eleanor reminds Orson. "They're wonderful people."

"I think he's talking about other Mexican people," Orson says. "The bad ones."

Lulu interrupts him. "We don't believe everything our dad tells us," she says.

"Dad bought a couple of guns," Orson tells Eleanor. "When my mom said she didn't want them in the house he called her a bad name."

"That probably didn't feel good," Eleanor says. *Acknowledge the feeling. Don't ask too many questions. Listen.* Whatever she does, Eleanor knows, it's not for her to weigh in on her daughter's marriage.

"My dad says all these people went to a pizza parlor with some woman that wanted to be president and they made a bunch of little kids take off their clothes."

"Shut up, Orson," Lulu tells him. "That wasn't what Dad said. He just doesn't like Hillary Clinton."

"'Shut up' is a bad word," Orson says. "Mom told us never to say 'shut up.'"

"Dad only says dumb stuff like that when he's drinking beer. He just said that one time."

"More than one time. Lots of times."

"Be quiet."

"What do you say we go do something fun?" Eleanor says.

There's a place Eleanor has always wanted to bring her grandchildren—not Flora yet, she's too young, but Lulu and Orson. It's the Harvard Museum of Natural History in Cambridge. Long ago, when her own children were young, she brought them there, before Toby's accident. He used to love the Hall of Minerals best. Al—though he'd been more interested in the Museum of Science—ended up loving the dinosaur bones. But for Ursula, as for Eleanor, the best part of the museum had been the glass flower collection. She had never forgotten it.

There's nothing like it anywhere else: a collection of hand-blown glass flowers and plants—every species on earth, supposedly, though that was hard to imagine.

The morning after their arrival at her condo, Eleanor announces to the children her plan to visit the museum. Maybe because there are things going on in their lives that they prefer not to think about at the moment, she tells them the story of the glass flowers. More than a person might have supposed, they listen to her.

The idea for the glass flowers originated back in the late 1800s, when a Harvard professor had seen a series of models created by a master glassblower named Leopold Blaschka in his studio near Dresden, Germany, depicting marine invertebrates, created for museums in Europe. This gave him the idea of commissioning Leopold to create models of plant species, equal in detail to those of the marine invertebrates, thereby allowing students whose access to images had previously been confined to drawings and specimens preserved in a flower press to understand what these species would look like in three dimensions. A wealthy Boston family, the Wares, had undertaken footing the bill for Leopold Blaschka's work over the course of what ended up being more than three decades in the glass studio. When Leopold got too old to continue the project—knowing he had not yet documented all the species—he turned the project over to his son Rudolf, who continued to create new models for many years beyond his father's death. More than four thousand models of plant species.

"Think of it this way," Eleanor says to the children as they drive across the bridge to the museum. "It would be like if I'd started writing a book the day your mom was born, and I worked hard every day, but I still wasn't even finished now. That's how long the Blaschkas worked on making the glass flowers we're going to see at the museum today."

Orson has not protested his grandmother's suggestion to visit the museum. At some other moment in his life, he might have offered the opinion "BO-RING." This morning he and Lulu are up for a distraction—grateful, no doubt, that their grandmother is talking about something, anything, other than what has been going on at their house back in Vermont over the last few weeks. The war between their parents.

Glass flowers. Just what the doctor ordered.

At the museum, Eleanor leads the way to the exhibit.

"So, here's how they made the flowers," Eleanor explains. Orson's seven by this point. As a child who, even when very young, cared deeply about his role in the class and aspired to be popular, he had made a vow to give up sucking his thumb when he'd entered first grade. He succeeded, but today his thumb is back in his mouth. Lulu spent the night curled up next to Eleanor in bed.

They approach the first of the rows of glass cases displaying the flowers. Eleanor explains to Orson and Lulu how Rudolf melted glass over a flame, fed by air from a foot-powered bellows. "Can you imagine forming every individual petal and stamen and pistil out of glass? Those tiny little flecks of pollen? Then the Blaschkas had to figure out a way to get them all across the ocean without breaking them."

"Like that bowl Uncle Toby got you that time," Orson says. He's heard the story and seen the pieces of Dale Chihuly glass on the windowsill at the farm.

It doesn't surprise Eleanor that Lulu loves the glass flowers. The surprise is that Orson does. He stands for a long time in front of one replica in particular, the Blue Flag Iris, his breath fogging the glass of the case enclosing it.

"I guess there's something you particularly like about that one, huh, Orson?" Eleanor asks him.

"I was just thinking," he tells her. "What would happen if somebody came here who was really, really mad. If somebody brought a hammer and started smashing everything."

"They make sure everything's safe here," Eleanor tells him.

"It doesn't always work," Orson says. "Sometimes people get so mad they lose it."

Even to a seven-year-old, she could not deny that this was true.

This same week sixty people have been killed at a music festival in Las Vegas where a man opened fire. Orson must have heard about it on television. At the children's school now they participate in drills designed to prepare them for what to do if a gunman enters their classroom. When Eleanor was Orson's age, there was a brief period when people talked about the threat of the Russians dropping bombs. She can remember huddling under her desk in first grade, and a child she knew telling her on the playground that her parents had built a bomb shelter in their basement, stocked with enough cans of Campbell's soup to last six months. At the time Eleanor had worried that her family had no such shelter of their own.

"My dad says Obama isn't even an American," Orson says. "My dad says that football player that won't stand up when they play the national anthem should go to jail."

What to say? They move to the next case of flowers. Bromeliads.

88.

A visit to the planetarium

Orson and Lulu stay all that week in Brookline with Eleanor. After their visit to the glass flowers, she takes them bowling. They go to the movies and swimming at Walden Pond and shopping for camp clothes.

Ursula checks in every night, though her conversations with the children are brief. Eleanor hears only their end.

"Who's taking us to camp?"

"Are you still mad at Dad?"

This is Orson talking. Lulu doesn't venture into dangerous territory. When Ursula calls Lulu just holds on to the phone, listening hard, saying nothing. Orson's the opposite. When his turn comes he spills out his worst fears.

"Are you and Dad getting a divorce?"

"Who are we going to live with?"

"Do we have to pick?"

On their last day before Eleanor takes them back to Vermont (with summer camp ready to begin the next Saturday) Eleanor brings the children to the Museum of Science. They count the rings in a very old tree stump and watch a demonstration of a live owl. At the gift shop, for his special treat, Orson picks out a gyroscope. Lulu wants to spend her treat money on a present for her father—a funny-looking bird with a long neck and a top hat. If you set him down next to a drinking glass and tap his head so his bill goes into the water the bird bobs up and down.

"Just like Dad," Orson calls out, too loud, in the gift shop. "Only if it was my dad there'd be beer in the cup."

The IMAX movie showing that day is *Shackleton's Antarctic Adventure*, and for a moment Eleanor considers whether it's a good idea for her to spend ninety minutes watching a film that shows the place where Guy may be heading at this very moment, ready to embark on a similar quest. But Orson has already spotted the poster with a picture of a ship frozen solid in an iceberg. He wants to see it.

Eleanor knows the planetarium well from all the way back to her own childhood days when her parents used to drop her off at the science museum on Sunday afternoons—before heading out to some bar together, probably.

Back in those days, on her solitary science museum afternoons, Eleanor had loved the feeling of sinking into the special reclining seats, letting the music wash over her as the sound of some deep-voiced narrator laid out the story of how the universe came into being. For Eleanor there had been something weirdly comforting in the knowledge that as vast as the galaxy might be that she inhabited, it was only one of billions. She was not simply a speck, but a speck on a speck on a speck. When a person considered the size of the universe, all those things that seemed so important and so difficult—the vodka on her parents' breath, for instance, when they picked her up at the museum at closing time—really didn't matter in the end.

This was what Eleanor told herself, all those times she waited outside the museum for their car to pick her up after her solitary Sunday afternoons spent studying the exhibits. Eleanor spent more time on her own at the Boston Museum of Science than any other ten-year-old she knew. Sometimes an hour would pass, after closing time, before her parents' car pulled up. She'd learned to bring a book with her for occasions like those, anticipating the wait.

Now here she is back at the planetarium, but as a grandmother, with an anxious eleven-year-old on one side of her and a wriggling seven-year-old on the other—hoping that for the next ninety minutes at least, the two of them might be distracted from the worry that has visibly plagued them over the days since their mother dropped them off with her.

"*In 1914, Ernest Shackleton set out to become the first man to cross the Antarctic continent, every step over unknown territory.*" The voice of the narrator fills the theater. In the seat next to Eleanor, Orson reaches for her hand.

"*They hoped the fates would be kind to them. But the task was beyond their power.*"

A picture comes to Eleanor. It's that slide Guy used to show every time he gave one of his speeches—a picture of himself at age ten. A Cub Scout who dreamed of adventure.

If Guy has made it back to Antarctica now, as she believes he probably has (she has avoided clicking on his website to find out), he's where he has always wanted to be, finally. Eleanor is where she's meant to be also.

Their lives came together for a brief and shining moment is all. They've both moved on. As they needed to.

The next day Eleanor drives Lulu and Orson back to Vermont.

"I appreciate what you did, Mother," Ursula says, meeting them at the door. Eleanor has not expected this, but her daughter offers her a small, stiff hug.

"We had a great time," Eleanor tells her. She hesitates. It's always risky, with Ursula, saying too much. Particularly about anything hard. Meaning, anything real.

"Jake and I just had to work through some things." Ursula's tone makes it plain: *Ask nothing. Stay out of this.*

Eleanor hugs the children goodbye. Orson's already settled in with his tablet. Lulu's upstairs, laying out her new purchases for camp probably. Eleanor heads to the car.

Once she's back home, Eleanor pours herself a glass of wine and opens the door to her studio. The drawings for her Mineral Man book are spread out on the table, her pencils where she'd left them seven days earlier when she got the call from Ursula.

None of what happens in this room or what she does here can fix what's broken—Ursula's anger, Lulu's worries, and those of Orson, or the strange, sad feeling that swept over her that afternoon in the theater, staring up at the giant IMAX images surrounding her of the continent where a man whom she used to love and will probably never see again is.

It's over now. She picks up a colored pencil—cerulean blue—and gets to work.

89.

Something about Flora

As they do every summer, Al and Teresa send Toby a ticket to visit them out west—his seventh trip to Seattle now, an annual tradition. Toby loves everything about his visits to Seattle, but his favorite part—the thing he talks about when Eleanor picks him up at the airport to bring him home—is Flora. She's five years old now. Of all the people in her life, only Toby is patient enough to play Go Fish or Operation with her for a whole afternoon or sit with her on the couch watching Mr. Rogers. When they go to the playground, he always carries her on his shoulders. One time she put every single barrette from her collection in his hair and had him pose for a picture.

"I don't have a favorite person," Toby tells Eleanor now. "But there's just something about Flora. Every time I see her I get this feeling like my heart might explode."

Between visits they talk on the phone. She fills her uncle in on kindergarten and the activities of her hamster. She's been lobbying her parents to get a second hamster, so he won't be lonely. It's no fun being all by yourself in a cage.

"I think you should have a wife," Flora tells Toby on one of their phone conversations.

There had been a time when Toby talked a lot about wanting a girlfriend, falling in love, getting married—a time when he used to play a song recorded by Scarlett Johansson, "Trust Me," from the *Jungle Book* movie, ten times a day. "Everybody's always talking about Adele and Madonna," Toby used to say. "Scarlett's better than any of them."

But something has changed in him. Maybe it happened during that awful stretch of months when he was under investigation for the charges brought by Coco and her boyfriend. Toby seems to have reached a quiet acceptance of the fact that the kind of love he had once hoped to find with a woman will probably never be possible for him. What he'll do instead is be the best uncle ever.

As for Coco and Jesse: they seem to have dropped off the face of the Earth. Nobody—not even Elijah—knows where they've gone, or even if they're together anymore.

"But if you got married I could be the flower girl," Flora says. "Plus, you'd be a really great husband. Also a dad."

"The person I wanted to marry picked someone else," Toby tells Flora. "I was kidding myself that she'd ever be interested in me."

"That girl must be dumb," Flora says. "You're great."

"I guess it depends on what a person's looking for."

"If they were looking for the best person ever," Flora tells him, "they'd choose you."

In the end, Flora does get to be a flower girl. Just not for Toby.

That fall, Elijah and Miriam get married at the farm. It's a small ceremony—just the family, plus their band, and Miriam's mother, who flew in from Abuja. Ursula shows up with the children. No sign of Jake or of Coco.

"I didn't invite her," Elijah says. "I don't even have a phone number for her anymore."

90.

The worst Valentine's Day ever

It's 2018 now—one year into the presidency of Donald Trump, every day of which has felt to Eleanor like an assault. She's established something like a rhythm now: still living on the farm most of the time, but able to make the trip to Brookline at least once a week.

Eleanor qualifies for Medicare now. Also discounts at the movies, if she were ever to go to movies, which she hardly ever does anymore.

All these years later, Eleanor still remembers the young woman who moved in briefly to Walt's old house—his granddaughter, Raine, who had suggested senior citizen discounts as a fringe benefit of her choice to leave town with a sixty-five-year-old from the retirement home where she worked. Eleanor has barely thought of Raine or Spyder in years. She wonders where they are. She tries to picture where the two of them might have landed after they moved out of Walt's old place. Spyder would be eight years old, six months younger than Orson. If they still lived down the road, Toby would have taught him how to milk the goats.

Toby's thirty-seven now; Al, forty-one. Ursula will soon turn forty—a milestone that will go unmarked. (Toby suggested a party, as did Lulu and Orson. Ursula nixed the idea.)

Eleanor wants to call her daughter on her birthday but knows better. Toby calls her—reporting that Ursula's friend Kat and some other friends from the school she runs are taking her out for dinner. This, at least, is good news.

"I'll put Mom on," Toby says to his sister.

"Never mind," Ursula tells him.

Ursula's attitude toward Eleanor appears not to have changed, discernibly, but Eleanor's reaction to it has. Her daughter's choice to keep her at arm's length—further than this, even—no longer eats away at her in the same way it did once. Their estrangement, if that's what it is, is a wound that never leaves her, but it's no longer a bleeding one. "When you can't fix a problem," she reflects, "the best thing you can do is learn to live with it."

Now it's Valentine's Day. Of all the celebrations on the calendar, this one remains Eleanor's favorite. Back when they were young, her children's birthdays had come with the requirement of a party, a special cake, and games, goodie bags, decorations, so much else, none of which prevented the nearly inevitable meltdown by the end of the day of someone—the birthday child, or a guest, or her own self, paying a visit to Crazyland.

Children attached so many hopes and dreams to their birthdays and Christmas that Eleanor always worried about the day not living up to what they imagined. That was the great thing about Valentine's Day. No expectations. All a person had to do to mark the day was what Eleanor loved best. Draw a picture. Write a few words involving love. You dropped your card in the mailbox. Chances were, it made someone happy.

Cam was never the type to buy roses. But one February 14, he'd carved her a rose out of wood. That night in their bed he'd presented it to her. Just when she thought he'd forgotten.

When her children were small, she'd spread out their art supplies over the dining room table on the first of February, and for the next two weeks (a month, possibly, if they started in January, as they begged her to do) the room remained in a state of happy disarray. Glue, sequins, construction paper, markers, rickrack, doilies, old Burpee seed catalogs, scissors, glitter, stickers, googly eyes, more glue. Nobody minded that they had their meals in the kitchen during those weeks, or that the whole house seemed overtaken by their valentine-making. One time, during their annual season of valentine production, Cam had picked up his fork with a piece of chicken on it and announced to them all, "My favorite meal! Roast chicken with red glitter!"

It was late January, the year after Toby's accident—the children five, seven, and eight, Eleanor thirty-two years old, not quite ten years into her marriage to Cam—when he told her he'd fallen in love with Coco and that he didn't want to be married to her anymore. The second piece of news might have seemed obvious enough after he'd delivered the first, but Eleanor might have hung in and tried to repair things between them, only Cam was already out the door.

That Valentine season she'd tried to re-create their tradition. The messy table. The craft supplies. Corny, happy music on the stereo. (Dean Martin, Brenda Lee, early Beatles.) Nobody was into it that year and she made no effort to revive the ritual the next year or any after that ever again. That was the end of their family valentine-making extravaganzas.

Still, in her studio, then and even now, Eleanor makes a valentine for each of her children every year. She sends them via U.S. mail, in thick red envelopes addressed with a gold Sharpie and a heart on the back outlined in glitter glue. She makes valentines for Lulu and Orson and Flora now, too, as she did, for a few years there, for Guy.

This year Eleanor is late with her valentines. She'd planned to get them in the mail the week before but got so wrapped up in her Mineral Man story, she lost track of the days.

Now here it is, February 14. At her work table in Brookline, she's making her cards. They'll arrive late, of course. Still it's important to Eleanor to maintain the tradition.

As she always does when she's drawing, Eleanor keeps the radio on. The station's playing a tribute to a singer who died a couple of days earlier, Vic Damone. This isn't her kind of music normally. She's about to change the station but the song they put on, "On the Street Where You Live," catches her up short.

Eleanor has heard the song before, of course. She's seen *My Fair Lady*. But maybe because this is Valentine's Day, the lyrics get to her in a way they never did before.

She's filling in the shading on a heart. On the radio, Vic Damone's singing about walking down the street of the woman he loves. In the song, he's telling about how he has walked down the street before without paying any particular attention, but now everything feels different. Suddenly lilacs are in bloom, birds sing. His feet don't even touch the pavement.

He's singing about being in love. Eleanor remembers the feeling, though it's like a distant memory now, a song you once loved, whose lyrics you can no longer bring to mind.

A year has passed since the night she and Guy said goodbye to each other in that Los Angeles hotel room. They have not spoken again. Memories come to her, of walking through Harvard Square the day they tried out all those perfumes and riding up the elevator to one of the many hotel rooms where they used to meet. (Here's a strange thing about those rendezvous: for all the nights they met that way, in all the luxury hotels where they made love, Eleanor can't remember what a single one of those hotel rooms looked like.)

Another picture comes to her, from so much farther back: seeing Cam's truck rounding the bend on the long dead-end driveway to their old farmhouse. Running out to meet him, her arms flung open wide, his arms open, too. She was pregnant at the time (with Toby? Ursula maybe?). If you'd told Eleanor then the things that would happen to them all, she might have fallen to her knees then and there. Just as well she had no idea.

Eleanor's cutting out a heart, applying glue to the card she's been working on, in preparation for attaching a row of sequins. This one is Flora's. Suddenly there's no more Vic Damone on the radio.

"We interrupt this broadcast . . ." Familiar words. They never bring good news.

There's been a shooting at a high school in Florida. Just before the final bell releasing students—the hallways decorated with red construction paper hearts no doubt, kids ready to bolt for their lockers—a seventeen-year-old boy walked into the school with a rifle case over his shoulder. He took an AR-15 out of the case and started shooting. Seventeen people are dead. Fourteen of them students.

Did a person, hearing this news, finish making her valentines?

91.

With Dr. Christine Blasey Ford

Half a year goes by, one of the darkest times Eleanor has known. The one thing Eleanor can count on: how swiftly time passes.

It's September. Eleanor's spending the week in Brookline, putting in long days in her studio working on her Mineral Man graphic novel. Toby's making plans to bring four of his goats up to the Verlander farm for the annual insemination trip. In Vermont, she knows, Lulu's got a big spelling bee coming up—the New England regionals, for which she's been preparing all summer. For Orson, it's soccer season. Though nothing has discernibly changed in her relationship with Ursula—who, after that brief moment when she reached out for help, continues to keep her mother at a chilly remove—Eleanor has made plans to drive up to Vermont to see one of Orson's games. It's possible her daughter will barely speak to her. But she'll get to see her grandson and her granddaughter. Now more than ever, Eleanor takes the good where she can.

In the world beyond this one—the one she hears about on the news—back in the summer, Donald Trump announced the nomination, to the Supreme Court, of a man named Brett Kavanaugh—a far-right conservative whose previous opinions indicated opposition to abortion, affirmative action, and same sex marriage. Within days of his nomination a number of women come forward alleging encounters in which Kavanaugh sexually harassed them. One of these, a woman named Dr. Christine Blasey Ford, has agreed to testify under oath to an experience when both she and Brett Kavanaugh were teenagers. She's prepared to testify under oath, before a congressional committee, that the man who is now under consideration for a place on the Supreme Court once attempted to rape her.

It's the day the hearings begin. The Kavanaugh hearings have unsettled Eleanor, more than she might have supposed. Unable to work, she turns on her television. Part of her doesn't want to watch but she has to.

Eyes glued to the screen, she watches Christine Blasey Ford—her voice steady—as she begins to speak. It's clear to Eleanor how hard the experience must be for this woman—not simply testifying as she is about to do, but then submitting to hours of humiliating questions from a row of Republicans on the Senate floor likely to challenge every word she utters and discredit her in any way they can.

Eleanor was almost exactly the same age as Christine Blasey Ford was that night at the party where she alleges the rape occurred, when her friend Patty Hallinan's brother Matt pulled his car over, driving her home from work, unhooked her bra, and stuck his finger inside her underpants. After that first time, it was a daily event that summer.

"And you never told anyone what happened?" one of the Republican senators is asking Dr. Christine Blasey Ford. "In all these years?"

She wants to turn off the television, but she keeps it on all day. On her drawing table, she's got a series of panels laid out featuring the character of Yellow Top sitting at his giant desk in the penthouse of Yellow-Top Towers. But Eleanor can't concentrate. She colors in Yellow Top's hair, using the most garish of the yellow pencils in her box, and red for his tie, that reaches past his belt buckle. On the screen, Dr. Chrstine Blasey Ford is recounting a night from long ago. "I tried to get away, but his weight was heavy," she's saying.

The phone rings. "Are you watching this?" It's her friend Annette. "I can't believe what they're doing to this woman." On the screen, Dr. Christine Blasey Ford is telling about the group of boys who stood watching, as their friend the future Supreme Court nominee pressed her down onto the bed.

"Allegedly," one of the Republican senators points out.

Eleanor thinks about Matt Hallinan. The feeling of that Naugahyde car upholstery against her bare skin, his fingers pinching her nipples, the trip—this came later—to get the illegal abortion. All those bloody sanitary napkins she hid in the dumpster at school, after, when she kept bleeding and couldn't tell anyone.

And why are you only just now telling us this story?

Thinking about her own teenage experience—in the front seat of

Matt Hallinan's car, his hand in her underpants—Eleanor has no difficulty understanding the answer to that one.

92.

The definition of a good mother

]|[n the end, the Senate votes to confirm Brett Kavanaugh as the newest member, for life, on the United States Supreme Court.

It's seven o'clock. Eleanor thinks about fixing something for dinner but has no appetite. As is often the case, times she feels sad about things going on in the world, she just wants to hear the voice of someone she loves. Never Ursula anymore, of course. Sometimes Al. She might call one of the grandchildren. No big discussion. Sometimes it's comforting just hearing Orson tell her how it went at soccer that day.

The one Eleanor calls tonight is Toby. Just back from the barn probably, he will have gotten the girls down for the night. She asks about the goats.

The fire station. Bowling. All the familiar topics.

"What's wrong, Mom?" Though Eleanor has said nothing to her son about how she's spent the last few days, glued to the television, she should know that Toby picks up everything. What he lacks in knowledge of math or history—or the workings of government, including the process of Supreme Court confirmation hearings—he makes up for in a certain kind of simple wisdom about life. Toby can always tell when Eleanor's sad.

"I just wanted to tell you how glad I am you're my son," she tells Toby now. "How proud I am of what a good man you turned out to be."

"You turned out to be a good mother," Toby says.

A good mother. Who even knows what that is?

For nine months, you carry a child in your body. Then you give birth to this person, and they depend on you (for a while anyway) for every single thing in their life, including their survival. What they need: not only food, warmth, safety, diapers, baths, sunshine, fresh air, milk—also comfort, reassurance, protection, encouragement, vigilance, stamina, compassion. Money. Love. You teach them what bread is, and milk, and a ball, a dog, a helicopter, a tree, a car, a lawn mower, a cell phone, a gun. They look to you to tell them about everything, basically. The whole wide world. The meaning of everything. As if you knew.

Every year on their birthday you bake a cake for this person you gave birth to, and at Christmas you fill their stocking, after driving around for hours in terrible traffic probably—a blizzard?—to find the one toy they want more than any other. You teach them letters, numbers, colors . . . the names of vegetables, how to ride a bicycle, how to swim, how to make friends, what sex is. You teach them that someday everybody dies, but in their case (you pray) not for a very long time. You teach them what's the right thing to do. How to treat people. When they get this wrong, you give them another chance. Many.

You take them places. You make sure they get home. You tuck them into bed every night and maybe sometimes they wake up with a bad dream, which means you need to be there once again, to tell them it's all right. Even if it isn't always going to be, you need to say it.

Here is this thing called life, you say. *Now go out into the world and live yours.*

I'll be here, looking out for you. No matter what, I'll be here.

It's an impossible job. How is anybody going to get it right?

You won't, of course. You will definitely screw up, and possibly fail miserably. Your child will suffer disappointments. Some, caused by you. You promised to stay married to her father, but you don't. You told her life was fair, but it isn't. You wanted her to believe people were mostly good. Then someone really bad came along. Or just someone who hurts them badly.

Your child will be angry at you sometimes. You may be angry at her, too, but because you're the parent, you're not supposed to be. One day you may pour a glass of wine over your head or stuff a fancy cake you just finished making into the garbage. You may go crazy now and then. You may get angry at your child's father. You may say things you wish you hadn't.

This child you've raised may forgive you. Or she may not.

On Mother's Day, she may send you a card telling you what a great mother you are. The best ever.

She may send you a text message informing you that as a victim of toxic parenting, she has recognized her profound need for boundaries. She may inform you, in this text message, that this will be her final communication with you. She's severing your relationship. *Don't call. Don't write.* No, she does not want to go into therapy with you.

She may break your heart.

You're a bad mother. You're a good mother. You used to be a good mother but now you aren't anymore. You were a bad mother, but maybe you can make it up to this child whose life you ruined.

You didn't get to be a mother. You did, but you wished you didn't. You wish you could do it over, but you can't.

You were given this person to take care of—egg, sperm, nine months gestation, labor. The easy part. It's all the rest that got you in trouble.

As hard as you tried, your efforts were never enough. None ever can be.

"You turned out to be a good mother," Toby tells Eleanor now.

Well, she's a mother, that's all. That's as much as Eleanor's prepared to say about herself on the subject at this point. About her performance on the job.

I did the best I could, she thinks. But not even that. She could have tried harder. Could have done better. Could have given more. When, in the life of a mother, is that not true?

93.

An old pal returns

It's the week after Thanksgiving. Toby has ridden his bike to the fire station. He returns with big news: There's a U-Haul truck parked in front of the house of their old neighbors, Walt and Edith.

The place has been rented out a few times over the years, but for almost six months it has stood empty.

"Guess who's moving back in?" Toby tells Eleanor. "Raine! And the baby, Spyder. Only he's not a baby anymore."

Spyder was two years old when he and Raine moved away. He must be eight now, Eleanor figures.

"I didn't get to talk to them," Toby tells Eleanor. "They were busy carrying boxes in from the RV." He'd spotted a skateboard and an Xbox. And there was an old guy in a wheelchair wrapped in a blanket out in the yard.

"I guess Spyder won't remember me," Toby says. "But if a person meets you when they're really little, you're always going to be friends."

"You were the only one who could get him to stop crying."

"I remember his little fingers. He liked wrapping them around my thumb. One of his ears was regular but the other one was like an elf's."

The last time they'd seen Raine she was heading west in a Holiday Rambler with a guy she'd met at the old folks' home.

"My little pal is back!" Toby says, as he heads out to the barn to tend the goats. "I always hoped I'd see him again."

94.

Good housekeeping

Eleanor gives it a day before stopping by to welcome Raine and Spyder back to the neighborhood. She bakes them brownies. Toby takes a Wheel of Joy out of the refrigerator in the cheese room to bring to them.

Though it's been six years since Eleanor has seen Raine, she hasn't changed much. She's got one of those asymmetrical hairstyles that's shaved close to the scalp on one side, longer on the other. Purple, mostly. Skinny as ever, she's wearing a tank top—never mind that it's almost December—which reveals an assortment of tattoos. One of a skull, one of a koala bear. On her right forearm, the words "Life is better with a cat."

"We never had a cat," Raine explains. "I was plastered when I picked that one. I thought it said 'car' not 'cat.' But it's probably true, right? Life probably is better with a cat."

"If they made one about goats, I'd get that," Toby tells her.

From where he sits, in front of the television, the old man in the wheelchair lets out a whoop. Someone just won the jackpot on *Wheel of Fortune.*

"Don't mind him," Raine says. "He loves Vanna White. Vanna and the Weather Channel. That's basically how we roll around here."

Over in the corner, Spyder has not looked up from his game.

"Spyder's not exactly Mr. Personality," Raine tells Eleanor. "But he's a good kid."

It turns out the old-timer in the wheelchair isn't Herb after all. "This guy here is Billy," Raine tells them.

"What happened to Herb?"

"We were on our road trip in Herb's RV, the Holiday Rambler. We'd got as far as Mount Rushmore. We were in the gift shop buying postcards when I looked over and what do you know, Herb's on the floor. Heart attack. The excitement was too much for him."

"That must have been hard on you," Eleanor says. "In the middle of a place you didn't know anybody, alone with a young child."

"The problem was, we hadn't gotten around to tying the knot," Raine tells her. "So after Herb died, what did I get? Zippo." She's scrubbing the inside of the stove as she speaks. One thing about Raine: she never sits still.

"Story of my life," Raine says. "All he left me was the Holiday Rambler. You know what it costs to fill the gas tank on that thing?"

After Herb's death, Raine tells them, she and Spyder settled in Modesto, California—living in the Holiday Rambler at an RV park. She got a job at a nursing home, which is where she met Billy. "He had a lot more on the ball then," she tells Eleanor. "Played Scrabble and everything."

Like Herb, he had a pension and veterans' benefits. "You could think I was just after the money," Raine says. "But I'm not a gold digger. I liked the guy. I could tell he wouldn't cheat on me or beat me up."

Eleanor thinks to herself that Raine might have set the bar a little higher. But she just nods.

A few years back, Raine tells Eleanor, she and Billy got married. Things were looking pretty good for a while there. They had some fun.

"He taught me how to play cards. We had this game. Anytime we pulled into a Walmart for the night I'd put Spyder in his lap and push the two of them around the parking lot in his wheelchair, fast. The two of them always got a kick out of that."

Billy was good to her, Raine tells Eleanor. "One time on our road trip, someplace like Indiana, he took me to Forever 21 and told me 'Go buy anything you like. The sky's the limit.' It wasn't even my birthday."

"Nobody ever did anything like that for me before," Raine says. "Definitely not my dad. I probably haven't done that much better with my own kid." She looks over at her son, who has not looked up from the controls of his Xbox since they arrived.

"Not that I haven't tried," she says.

Then two years ago Billy had a stroke. They were living in a condo Billy owned in San Luis Obispo, but it turned out Billy hadn't been keeping up with his payments. The bank took the place back. And Billy just wasn't his old self anymore.

That was when Raine reached out to her father, with whom she hadn't spoken in a few years, to ask about her grandparents' old place in Akersville. Which turned out to be unoccupied at the time.

Not that he was giving the place away. Walt Junior still charges her rent. But Billy's benefits cover that, with enough left over for utilities and pizza money. Now here they are.

Raine pours a bucket of soapy water on the linoleum. She ties a dish towel around each of her feet and steps into the pool of suds. Slowly, she makes her way across the floor, spreading the water as she goes, moving across the floor like a skater, with an odd combination of determination and grace.

"I made up this method for keeping the floor spic-and-span," she says. "If there's one thing I can't stand it's dirty linoleum."

Looking at her as she is now—a skinny young woman with a

skull tattoo on her chest, in a pair of shorts that look like maybe they belong to Billy, held up with a bungee cord—Eleanor considers what it must feel like, being Raine. With the dish towels still tied around her ankles, standing in a pool of soapsuds, she could be in the Ice Capades. Or a mental hospital. One thing's for sure: whatever else goes on here, this house is going to be spotless.

"I'll be honest with you," Raine says. "The first six years of Spyder's life I was getting loaded all the time. Billy and I used to hit the Jack Daniel's in a big way. I guess you could say I was a pretty terrible mother."

A look crosses her face. "Nobody told me how to do it. Raise a kid, I mean. I'm still trying to figure that out."

"Join the club," Eleanor tells her.

These days, Billy mostly just watches TV and studies the bird feeder . . . It doesn't take that much, keeping him happy. And Raine's getting her act together.

"I just know how to take care of old-timers," she says. "They might not be God's gift to women, but you know what you're getting into with them. No surprises."

Eleanor tries to think of something she can say—something affirming. She's drawing a blank.

"You're an author, right?" Raine asks Eleanor. "I think I did a book report on one of those books you wrote, about that orphan that has all these adventures. I could relate! Anytime you want to do one called *Bodie Goes to the Nursing Home,* call me up."

"Interesting idea," Eleanor says. "I'm not sure your average child would be into that."

"Oh well," Raine tells her. "It might appeal to all the losers like me out there."

"You don't seem like a loser to me," Toby says.

"You know my problem?" Raine says. "The day they handed out the rule book of life, I was probably playing hooky."

With Spyder occupying their only chair, there's no place to sit in the kitchen—not counting Billy's wheelchair. Eleanor leans against the counter. Toby helps Raine place dishes in the cupboard. It doesn't take long. She has only three plates.

Someone has changed the television back to the Weather Channel. Billy can still work the remote, evidently.

"Bundle up, folks," says the woman standing in front of the map. "Looks like Mother Nature has some snow flurries heading our way this weekend."

Billy, in his wheelchair, has begun to snore.

"Welcome to my world," Raine tells them.

Eleanor looks over at Spyder. His hair is so long—past his shoulders—that until now she hasn't gotten to see his face. He has beautiful eyes, and long, thick lashes. Eleanor guesses that once Raine enrolls him in school next week, kids will call him a girl.

Raine must have read her mind. "I told him I'd cut his hair but he won't do it."

From his spot at the Xbox, no response.

"I remember the night you were born, buddy," Toby says to Spyder. "I guess that means I'm the oldest friend you've got. We met when you were about one second old."

Spyder looks up from the screen. Maybe it's the concept of having a friend that caught his attention. It's possible Spyder hasn't had too many of those.

"I got sober," Raine tells Eleanor. "I go to AA now. Four and a half months." As she speaks, Raine's unpacking boxes. There's a popcorn popper and a karaoke machine, an empty aquarium, and a pamphlet laying out the Twelve Steps. "I'm up to number two," she says. "But I'll get there."

"Good for you," Eleanor says. She remembers, back when Raine used to come by the farm to drop off Spyder on her way to work, that she sometimes smelled alcohol on her breath. Eleanor and Toby used to worry about that, particularly when she'd take Spyder in the car.

"I want to give my kid a more stable home life," Raine tells Eleanor. "No more RV parks and motels. First thing Monday morning, after we get him enrolled in school and I find myself an AA meeting, I'll look for another nursing home job. As soon as I've saved up the money, I'm taking Spyder to an orthodontist. I never got braces, but you'd better believe my son's going to have them."

Eleanor takes it all in: Billy staring at the television, Spyder with his video game. A Post-it note over the sink: *Get library card!* And another that says *Meditate!*

Raine tries hard. This is what Eleanor notices most about her. They're still unpacking, but she's already got the schedule of AA meetings on the refrigerator, a page from a magazine displaying "Five Essential Exercises for Toning Your Abs," and a recipe for Hawaiian pork chops. You've got to give Raine credit: she's a hard worker. She's managed to take care of her son, in her fashion, not to mention the old man currently slumped in his wheelchair in front of the television screen. She's standing at the stove now, applying steel wool to the knobs.

Raine may not have made the best choices in men, but when a person never had much of a family life, growing up, how was she supposed to know how to create one?

Before they leave, Toby approaches Spyder, still bent over his game.

"Come over to the farm sometime and check out the goats," Toby tells him. "You might like them. They'd probably like you."

Spyder does not look up. From the screen of his Xbox: the sound of missiles and exploding bombs.

"You might not remember," Toby tells him, "but there was one goat you always liked best. Violet. She's an old girl now, but she's still around. She'll be happy to see you."

There was a concept for Spyder. Imagine someone being happy to see him. Even if it was just a goat.

95.

Stronger in the broken places

The blue kintsugi bowl made by June Verlander, that she gave to Toby the day he visited to check out the Verlanders' bucks, sits in a place of honor in the corner cabinet at the farm. Alongside the blue bowl now: the second kintsugi bowl—also made by June, presented to him by Hans Verlander. This one is green, with flecks of deep violet and pale yellow. Now and then Eleanor will observe her son taking one of the bowls down from the shelf and studying it. He runs his finger over the places where June repaired the cracks, the gold lacquer veins that cut through the glaze, a slight iridescence around the lip, the flecks of gold visible, though just barely, along the base of each bowl.

"Stronger in the broken places," Toby says out loud, cupping his hands around one of the two precious bowls. The green one this time. Hans Verlander's words concerning his daughter's pottery— words that apply to his daughter, perhaps, as well as her ceramics— hold a particular significance for Toby.

Since the day of that visit, Toby has never spoken of the young woman who created the bowls, or of his visit to Hans Verlander's farm the day June gave him the first of the two. Unlike the name of Scarlett Johansson—whom Toby used to bring up so often that for a while it seemed as if she were a friend of the family—June's name is never mentioned during these moments when Toby takes one of the bowls down from the shelf.

He makes no effort to seek June out. For two breeding seasons, he and June have not crossed paths. Maybe June made a conscious choice to stay inside the house, times Toby made the trip to the Ver-landers' place. Maybe she was off in her pottery shed, smashing pots or putting them back together. Maybe she was hiding behind a tree, watching.

"Did you see June Verlander?" Eleanor always asks her son. Then one day in early December she shows up at the farm.

Amor is in heat—her tail wagging more vigorously than usual, a thick viscous fluid emanating from her genitals, accompanied by an odd, twitchy behavior. Though the last few times the insemination of Toby's goats has taken place at the Verlanders' farm, this time Hans Verlander drives down to Akersville. He's got one of his bucks in the back of his truck.

Since getting into making pottery, June has had little to do with her father's goat breeding operation. Surprisingly, she accompanies him when they make the drive to Akersville.

"June's always up for a good road trip," Hans explains. "I can play my old sixties music as loud as I want and it doesn't bother her. When I need a hand wrangling a buck, she's ready to step in. That girl knows how to handle goats."

The male goat Toby has selected to breed with Amor is called Euell, named for a man who used to do commercials on TV for health food, back in the day. Euell is not the handsomest of Hans Verlander's goats but on his last visit to the Verlanders', Toby noted Euell's surprising gentleness as well as an interesting habit he had of nuzzling his head against Toby's leg when he stepped into the pen, a certain way he looked up into Toby's eyes. With some male goats, if you got too close to them, they'd spit a big wad of snot at you. When Toby had knelt down next to Euell he had licked his face with his long, beautiful pink tongue.

"That's the buck we're breeding with Amor," Toby said.

Today June has come to help, but with Euell and Amor, no assistance is necessary. Toby has cleared a fenced-in area for the two of them—not what you'd call romantic, but designed for easy access with no distraction from the other girls. Within moments of being released into their private breeding spot, Euell is all over Amor. Young as she is—Toby has not bred Amor before—she knows what to do, as does Euell. Within half an hour he's mounted her five or six times. After each of these interludes, they retreat briefly to their separate corners before getting back to business. This is farm life for you. Humans might conceal their yearnings from each other. With goats, it's all out in the open.

Finally the two goats appear to be finished with each other. Hans announces, drily, "If that doesn't do the job I don't know what will," and throws a rope around Euell's neck, leading him toward a ramp he'd set up, back into the truck.

A little ways off, June has been sitting on a rock, studying something on the ground—a dry milkweed seed pod, it turns out. Toby is probably better equipped than most people to understand how it could be that a person might find herself content, sitting as she has for close to an hour, doing what would appear to most people to be nothing. The temperature's below freezing, with the wind whipping against the barn, but she seems to pay no attention to the cold.

Toby stands there watching. June continues to study the seed pod. Toby studies June. Eleanor stands on the porch, watching them both. Over at the barn, Hans Verlander is almost done packing up, leading his buck into the back of his truck, patting his haunches.

"Looks like those two hit it off just fine," Hans calls out to Eleanor, rubbing his hands together to fight off the chill as he steps into the cab. He's talking about Euell and Amor.

If only it were that simple for humans, Eleanor thinks.

96.

He even loved her stretch marks

Eleanor is ringing up groceries at the food co-op—off in another world, thinking about the work waiting for her back home and the gingerbread house she plans to make for her grandchildren. She has reached a section in her graphic novel where Mineral Man meets a strange, mysterious woman named Alizaron—a name she's taken from one of her drawing pencils. Alizaron Crimson. When she was pregnant with Toby she'd told Cam she thought that would make a great name for a girl. "And if it's a boy?" he said. "Cadmium Orange?"

Unlike the typical romantic heroine in a graphic novel, Alizaron doesn't look like a model or a movie star. Her body does not align with the classic graphic novel style for female characters—tiny waist, large breasts, perfectly curved hips. Alizaron is thin but strong. When she was very young, her family's home caught on fire and half of her face was badly burned. She never conceals her scars.

It's an interesting challenge for Eleanor, drawing a character who doesn't match the mold. She loves it about the hero of her story that he doesn't need or even want a partner like the typical graphic novel heroines. Of the many endearing qualities Mineral Man possesses, this is one: his ability to recognize Alizaron's rare and unconventional beauty.

In Eleanor's graphic novel, Alizaron and Mineral Man fall in love. But as much as they care for each other they will not live happily ever after together. That would be too easy. Something has to keep them apart. This was what occupies Eleanor as she unloads her cart at the checkout—the question: How could it be that two people who love each other might not be able to put their lives together?

Distracted, she sets a container of yogurt on the conveyor belt alongside a bag of pasta, a bunch of broccoli. Coffee. Molasses.

"You don't recognize me, do you?" the cashier says. She looks into the eyes of the woman at the register—fifteen years older than herself, probably, her face deeply lined in ways that speak of more than age.

"I'm Tim's mother," she says.

It takes Eleanor a moment. To her he was always Timmy Pouliot. The first time they met, Eleanor had just made the unlikely choice of buying the farm, with every penny of the proceeds from selling her first book. She was twenty. She'd met Timmy at the waterfall. He was just a kid then, though his voice had already changed. Something about him, even at that young age—eight years younger than Eleanor was—gave Eleanor the impression that this was a person who knew something about trouble, which turned out to be the case.

The day she met him, Timmy Pouliot had admired the drawing she was making. He had mentioned a painter he'd read about in a book who cut off his ear. Vincent van Gogh. He really liked the paintings in that book. He'd never met an artist before, he told her. His father had recently killed himself. He told Eleanor that also.

Sitting on a rock at the edge of the water, she'd offered Timmy Pouliot a sheet of paper and a drawing board. "Give it a try," she said. She handed him a piece of charcoal.

"I don't know how to draw," he told her.

"Just try," she'd said. "The first thing you need to do is just look really hard. Study the shapes in front of you. Then start moving your hand over the paper. What's the worst that could happen?"

For Timmy Pouliot, the worst had happened the day he walked into the family's garage and found his father hanging from one of the rafters with his belt around his neck. After that, all bets were off.

Timmy Pouliot was only thirteen years old the first time he told Eleanor he wanted to be her boyfriend. "I'm too old for you," she told him.

"My birthday's in a couple of weeks," he said.

After that she'd lost track of him. Then one day he turned up on Cam's softball team. Eleanor was married. Alison was two years old. She was pregnant with Ursula. She didn't recognize him at first. Then she saw the tattoo on his biceps with the name of his dead father. He'd carved it into his skin himself, back when he was a kid.

Timmy Pouliot would have been nineteen when he joined the Yellow Jackets. Every season after that he'd show up on his motorcycle with a girl on the back. A different one every softball season.

Women always liked Timmy Pouliot. Knowing him as she came to, Eleanor understood why. Timmy liked women. Not in the way some men would claim to, when what they really meant was that they liked looking at women's bodies, liked having sex, liked feeling important and big in the way some men did when they had a hot woman on the back of their motorcycle. Timmy Pouliot actually *liked* women. He took an interest. He listened. He took good care.

Over the course of those softball years, Timmy Pouliot had shown a surprising interest in Eleanor. Not in a creepy way. Nothing that allowed her to think he was hitting on her. But he offered something that she didn't receive much of in her life as a wife and mother. He asked about her artwork. He said how lucky Cam was to have a woman like Eleanor in his life.

One time at the end-of-softball-season party they held every Labor Day weekend, he told her something she never forgot. "When I think about a dream girl," he said to Eleanor, "I think about you."

At the time, Eleanor had recently given birth to Toby. She still had twenty pounds to lose from her pregnancy and the perm she'd gotten to make herself look better hadn't helped. Hearing him say this, she'd laughed.

"I mean it," he told her. That was another thing about Timmy Pouliot. He meant every single thing he said. He did not lie.

Now his mother stands at the cash register on the other side of the conveyor belt, ringing her up. "You were very special to Timmy," his mother tells her. "Even though he was with that other woman, the day of the crash, you were the love of his life."

Eleanor stands there holding the bunch of broccoli. It's a lot for a person to take in, shopping for groceries. She pictures this woman's son as he was one of the last times they ever spent together—naked, standing on his bed as she lay there, holding his cheap guitar, having just sung her a song he'd written in her honor, which happened to be called "Dream Girl." Summoning the image of him now, a wave of terrible sadness washes over Eleanor.

"You're my dream girl," he sang. *"You make my heart unfurl."*

Could a person's heart unfurl? Timmy Pouliot's had.

"You're my dream girl. You're my true pearl."

Considered objectively, maybe it wasn't a very good song, or Timmy Pouliot much of a singer, but there was no doubting for an instant, as he sang to her, that he meant every word.

"Last month was the anniversary of the accident," his mother says. *Twelve years.* "Tim would be fifty-eight now."

Eleanor used to tell Timmy he was too young for her, though there had been more to it than that. There had been a hundred reasons that Eleanor believed things could never have worked out between herself and Timmy Pouliot: the crummy little apartment where she visited him, Friday nights after dropping her kids off at their father's, with the wall of beer cans and the Farrah Fawcett poster. Pizza boxes on the bed and all over the kitchen counter. The look he'd get in his eyes, after they made love, as if he might cry from loving her so much.

Too much.

For all that stretch of years she visited him, Friday nights, or Sundays, Eleanor had never invited Timmy Pouliot to see her in Brookline. The one time they had gone out to dinner together, in Concord, Timmy insisted on paying. Eleanor ordered the chicken and a glass of pinot noir. He chose a side order of spinach and a glass of water. She knew why.

I could never introduce him to my children, Eleanor had thought at the time. Toby would have had no problem seeing Eleanor with Timmy Pouliot—Toby, who only wanted his mother to be happy. Al would have gotten used to the idea. But Ursula would have hated it that Timmy Pouliot rode a motorcycle, and if she'd known where Timmy lived, she would have hated that, too. Ursula, who wanted so badly to look normal, to be part of a family that resembled other people's families. She liked people with good jobs, who earned money. Timmy always seemed to be down to his last dime.

Bagging her groceries now, handing her money to Timmy Pouliot's mother, Eleanor wonders if she made a mistake. There had to have been other reasons why Eleanor and Timmy couldn't make it work. She just can't think of them anymore. She reaches for her wallet to pay for the groceries.

"I'll tell you why that girl went after my son," his mother says. Speaking of Coco. "Knowing how he always thought you hung the moon. She just wanted to stick it to you."

"She was pretty seriously injured," Eleanor says to her. "She has a metal rod in her leg now. She walks with a cane."

"I can't say I'm shedding any tears over that one," the mother says. "What would I give if all that happened to Timmy was getting his leg messed up?"

Her name is Ruth. Eleanor recognizes her now from the photograph Timmy Pouliot had kept next to his bed. A bed Eleanor knew well.

"I never understood why you two didn't end up together," Ruth tells Eleanor.

Out in the parking lot now, Eleanor loads her groceries in the trunk, still thinking about Timmy Pouliot.

The first thing Timmy Pouliot had done every Friday night when she'd come over to see him was fill the bathtub. He'd bought special soap and bubble bath for her. He lit candles. He tested the water with his wrist before she got in. Then she'd peel off her clothes—self-conscious at first over her stretch marks, but he had kissed them. The stretch marks were a part of her body and they told a story, he said. They were the mark of her motherhood, and he loved that about her.

After she'd lowered herself into the water, Timmy sat on the toilet beside the tub with his beer and listened to her tell him whatever she needed to talk about. Sometimes it was something going on with one of her children. Sometimes work. One night Timmy told Eleanor the story of the day he'd found his father, hanging from a belt in the garage. He was eleven.

She remembers the time he took her out on his motorcycle and they raced over some New Hampshire back road (no helmet for Timmy Pouliot, but he always made Eleanor wear one), and the thought had come to Eleanor, that she never wanted to get off that bike. If they could just keep riding forever.

Timmy Pouliot had not been wearing a helmet on the day of the crash. The only good news was that he had been killed instantly. It was Cam who told her the news, not knowing the name Timmy Pouliot held any particular significance for Eleanor.

Nobody in her life had known about those Friday nights. Not even Jason. It was a secret only the two of them shared, though evidently Ruth Pouliot had known about her son's feelings for Eleanor.

Timmy had done the thing Eleanor never could. He was proud of his love for Eleanor, and wanted to tell people about it. His mother, anyway. While Eleanor never told anyone about Timmy.

Eleanor thinks now that she had probably been in love with Timmy Pouliot, too. But one part of being in love was claiming it, letting the world know, not caring what people thought, because all that should matter, really, was how you felt about that other person. That you'd opened your heart to him.

Timmy had opened his heart to Eleanor. Eleanor had never been able to open her heart fully, back.

An odd thought comes to Eleanor then, as she backs out of the parking lot. She wonders who, among Guy Macdowell's circle of colleagues—board members, the film producers they'd worked with, his lecture agency, fellow explorers, and environmental scientists and activists (and friends? Who were Guy's friends, anyway?)—had ever known about her. She probably knows the answer to that one.

"My son was so proud of you," Ruth Pouliot told Eleanor, when they met at the cash register. "Did you know, he had a copy of every one of your books?"

97.

Man of the family

Toby is worried about Spyder. In the weeks since Raine and Spyder moved back into Walt's old house, Toby has barely seen the two of them. Spyder has not taken him up on his invitation to visit the goats. When Toby passes Walt's old house on his bicycle and waves to the boy—sitting in what Toby now knows to be his preferred spot, in the front seat of the RV with his Xbox, never mind the cold—Spyder doesn't look up. He's set up a target in the back-yard, with an old record album cover he found in Walt's garage, of Donny and Marie Osmond, nailed to a tree. Times Spyder isn't on his Xbox, that's where Toby's likely to spot him. Firing BBs at Donny and Marie. Stopping by the house now, Eleanor hears the sound of bullets pinging against the target.

"My grandfather had this old Colt .45 automatic he kept in the back bedroom," Raine says.

Eleanor remembers. One time a rabid squirrel came onto the farm while Cam was off at a craft fair, and Walt had come down to take care of it for her.

"I'll let Spyder graduate to that one when he's older," Raine tells her. "For now I keep it in my underwear drawer. You never know when it could come in handy."

Once or twice, on their way to town, Toby and Eleanor spot Spyder, with an old backpack over his thin shoulders, waiting for the school bus or trudging home from the bus stop some late afternoon. Even with the weather below freezing as it is now, most mornings, he never wears anything more than his hoodie.

One image of Spyder stands out for Eleanor. It's mid-December, the day after a big storm. She's driving to the post office to mail off some drawings to her publisher.

She doesn't see him right away. The snowdrifts outside the house are too high. What she sees then is just the top of his head. No hat. No gloves. No snow pants—just a pair of falling-down blue jeans. He's shoveling snow.

He does this with a dogged ferocity. He moves along the path like a boy possessed, as if every single thing that hasn't gone well in life—and there have surely been many—lies contained in that snowdrift. The handle of the shovel is taller than Spyder but he never alters his rhythm, cutting the blade into the drifts of white powder, tossing it over his shoulder, digging in again.

It comes to Eleanor, watching him, what the role must be for Spyder, in the odd little household he and his mother and Billy have made together in this place.

Spyder has only recently turned eight, but he's the man of the family.

98.

Where to go to get away from *Wheel of Fortune*

The next day on his way over to the fire station for the annual holiday party, Toby stops by Walt's old house again. He has spotted Spyder sitting in the front seat of the Holiday Rambler with his Xbox. Toby guesses that even with the temperature in the thirties, this may be preferable to sharing a very small space with Billy, with *Wheel of Fortune* and the Weather Channel on 24/7.

"I meant what I said about you coming over to the barn," he tells Spyder. "I could use your help with the goats."

"I don't know anything about farm animals," Spyder tells him.

"Nobody does when they start out. The fun part is learning. For instance, goats are a whole lot smarter than you might expect."

"I never expected goats to be anything, one way or another," Spyder says. "I never thought about goats before."

99.

The birth of Jesus

On Christmas Eve, Toby's goat Gladys shows signs she's close to giving birth. Toby calls Raine. He asks her to put Spyder on.

"If you and your mom aren't busy wrapping presents," he says (an unlikely prospect), "you could come over and see how a baby goat gets born. I could use your help."

He remembers (they all do, with the exception of Spyder) the night Raine had given birth on the bed at Eleanor's house—Toby holding her hand and breathing along with her as she pushed her son out into the world. Once a person's been present for a birth—boy or goat—something happens to them, Toby believes. (And so does Eleanor.) Witnessing that moment brings a person back to the basics.

"There's nothing much going on here," Spyder tells Toby. "My mom found a stack of old VCR tapes Billy had of old holiday specials. She set him up to watch *A Charlie Brown Christmas* and some guy named Perry Como that's wearing an elf hat."

Ten minutes later Spyder shows up at the farm. He has made the walk through the snow, carrying a flashlight. He heads straight to the barn. Toby's there already, of course.

Just before midnight Gladys gives birth to a single kid—all black, except for one white spot around his eye. They name the goat Jesus, pronounced the Spanish way.

They all know that as a buck, Jesus cannot remain on the farm. But from the moment the kid drops—with Spyder holding on to his rear legs—it appears that the boy and the goat share some kind of connection. At first Jesus can't get the hang of nursing from his mother, Gladys, so Spyder takes over with a bottle. For the first week the feedings go on through the night, a challenge made more difficult by the fact that the temperature suddenly dips below zero.

They bring Jesus into the house. Eleanor makes him a bed by the woodstove, using some old flannel shirts of Cam's and a playpen she found in the attic. Spyder stays over to get up in the night with the kid much as Toby used to do with him as a baby. He doesn't want to leave Jesus during the daytime when Christmas vacation ends. Toby takes over the daytime feedings, but the minute school gets out every afternoon, Spyder's back at the farm to help again with the new goat.

"You know, we're going to have to find a home for Jesus when he gets bigger," Toby tells him. He's given the speech before: male goats are aggressive and unruly, not to mention how bad they smell once they come of age.

"Maybe my mom will let me keep him over at our house," Spyder says. This seems unlikely, particularly given Raine's feelings about keeping her linoleum spotless, but Toby leaves it.

"Ralph and I will build him a pen," Toby says. "Jesus will be your goat."

"I never had my own goat before," Spyder says.

100.
Someday this will all be yours

Much as he had when he was a baby, Spyder starts coming over to the farm. Now is different, of course. Back in the old days Toby just held him—all night long, if he was crying, which was often the case. If ever there was a baby who seemed unhappy to have been born, Spyder was it.

Toby has only one rule for Spyder concerning his visits to the barn: no tablet. He'd add "no phone" but Spyder doesn't own one, though he wishes he did. Not that he has anyone to call.

"I'm going to show you how to milk a goat," Toby tells him,

pulling up a stool and setting it alongside Violet, with another stool for Spyder. At first the boy is uncomfortable. "Isn't it like . . . their private parts?" he asks Toby. But the first time he manages to get milk to shoot out of a goat's teat, all that goes away.

"Can I taste it?" he asks Toby.

"Be my guest."

Spyder dips his finger in the bucket and licks it. This is when Toby witnesses a sight none of them has ever beheld. (So surprising he tells Eleanor about it later, at dinner.)

Spyder smiles.

He comes over after school every day now to help Toby in the barn. The truth is, Ralph has things pretty well covered. The guidelines they have to follow for being able to sell their cheese commercially prohibit the participation, in the process, of a boy not yet nine years old milking by hand, rather than using the machines. The goat milk that Spyder collects in his bucket has to be kept separate from the milk they use for Wheel of Joy.

"Take a bottle to your mom and Billy," Toby tells Spyder, when he heads home every afternoon. "It's way better for them than Diet Coke."

The place where Spyder shines—and where he provides true assistance—comes on Saturdays, once the spring comes and the season starts up again for the farmers' market.

When Cam was alive, he used to accompany Toby to the farmers' market on Saturdays to sell his cheese. Toby is hopeless handling money. In the years since Cam's death, the job of taking in payment for cheese sales and keeping track of it all has fallen to Eleanor, or to Ralph, but the commitment to stand at the table with Toby for six hours every Saturday has been difficult to maintain. After Coco and her boyfriend went to the police with their allegations concerning Toby, he'd stopped setting up at the farmers' market for a while. With Spyder assisting, he's ready to come back.

Saturday mornings now, Eleanor or Ralph drop the two of them off with their table and their cheese, along with the money box. Spyder always wears Cam's old Wheel of Joy apron and a cap with the words "Say Cheese" on the front. Never one for saying much, he'll nod to repeat customers and mumble "Good morning." For Spyder, that is a lot.

Young as he is, Spyder turns out to be a natural salesman. He's great at adding up bills and making change. More than this, he runs a surprisingly tight ship at the farmers' market. Toby has a problem of wanting to give away a wheel of cheese anytime he strikes up a conversation with someone, which he does a lot. This habit has significantly cut into his profits. Now, when Toby reaches to give away cheese, Spyder shakes his head. When a potential customer gets overly greedy with the free samples, he points out that the limit is two slices of cheese, two crackers.

Pretty soon customers are greeting him by name. One time a boy from his class stops by the table with his parents.

"You've got like . . . a real job?" he asks Spyder. "Cool."

"Your dad must be so proud of you for helping out," the boy's mother says, looking in Toby's direction. This would be the moment for Spyder to explain that Toby is not his dad. He doesn't correct her.

In between farmers' market days, Spyder shows up at the barn now for milking, and sometimes just to talk. School's been out for a few weeks now. It doesn't seem as though Spyder hangs out with anyone but Toby.

"Who's your best friend?" Toby asks him.

"I don't have one. The kids in my class didn't like me. Nobody asked me to play kickball. They think I'm weird."

"Maybe when things get going again in the fall you can ask them if you can join the game," Toby says. "Kids thought I was weird, too. I just kept trying, is all, and after a while some of them started to like me. The ones that keep being mean probably wouldn't be good friends anyway."

"I don't care," Spyder tells Toby. "They're all idiots anyway. I'd rather hang out with you."

"But it's good to have other friends. Friends your own age. I bet there's someone out there that would like to be your friend."

For Toby, that person had been Elijah. Nine years old when Elijah was born, he'd been the one, of Eleanor's three children, most enthusiastic about the arrival of the new baby. Toby could sit for hours with Elijah, stroking his head and humming to him. Later, it was Elijah who looked out for Toby. If a kid ever called Toby weird, Elijah made him take it back and apologize. The first time he'd started a band, when he was about the age Spyder is now, Elijah had insisted that Toby be part of the group. Out in the studio with Cam, he'd fashioned Toby a hand drum. Never mind if he got the beat right.

"My brother helped me make friends with the other kids," Toby says.

"Yeah, well, I don't have a brother," Spyder tells Toby.

"You've got me."

101.

Try sitting on a rock

Midsummer now. Warm nights. Clear skies filled with stars. It turns out that Spyder has never gone camping. Nights in the Holiday Rambler with his mother and Billy don't count.

"You and me need to spend a night in the woods," Toby tells him. "We'll pitch a tent. Cook up a steak over the fire. Sleep under the stars. That's the life."

"What about wild animals?" Spyder says. Also, he hates bugs.

"If you ask me," Toby tells him, "it's people that make the most trouble. Trust me, you're going to love camping. "

That weekend they hike to a place Toby used to go with his father, Hedgehog Hill. They've got a tent and sleeping bags, the fixings for dinner, and pancake batter for the next morning. Also a little jar of maple syrup. Good syrup is important, Cam always said.

Spyder wants to bring his Xbox.

No.

On the hike up, Spyder says his pack is too heavy. Too many mosquitoes.

He's out of breath.

"That just goes to show we need to do a lot more hiking," Toby says.

"Yeah, right."

"My dad and me hiked this trail a lot when I was a kid," Toby tells him. "Just the two of us, out in nature." He points out a variety of edible mushrooms and another that's poisonous. Lichen moss. Giant granite boulders to climb. A stream running through. Overhead, a hawk. Spyder looks unimpressed.

"I need to teach you the basics about being out in the woods," Toby tells Spyder. "Just like my dad taught me. There's a few things everyone should know, if they're going to spend a lot of time in the woods."

"Who says anything about spending a lot of time in the woods?"

"Number one, always bring water, more than you think you need. Number two, wear the right shoes. Make sure you pick up your trash. Every single piece. Nature's our most valuable treasure. You need to leave your campsite the same as when you got there."

There's more. Not that Spyder appears to be particularly interested.

"If you ever get lost, stay put. That's how they find a person if they're lost. Some people, when they're lost in the woods, they think they should keep walking around. That's a bad idea. Then whoever's looking for you might keep missing you."

"One more thing my dad told me," Toby says. "Bring a plastic garbage bag. In case you're lost, and you get cold in the night. Wrap that thing around you. A person can survive a long time in the woods, with water and a trash bag."

It's late afternoon when they reach the top of Hedgehog Hill—houses, farms, a river, far below. Above them, nothing but sky in all directions.

Spyder has taken out his tablet. "You never told me there wouldn't be any reception up here," he says.

"Try just sitting on a rock for a while," Toby tells him. "See how it feels. Just you and the birds."

They don't speak for a while then. An hour maybe. Toby's setting up the tent. Spyder's already eaten his two granola bars. He's throwing rocks, trying to hit a tree. "This is supposed to be fun?" he says.

Toby builds a fire. "I need you to gather kindling," he tells Spyder. Reluctantly, Spyder does this. Five sticks. One pine cone.

The sun goes down. Toby sets their steaks over the flame. Also two potatoes for baking and a can of root beer for each of them. Just as they finish cooking the meal, the first stars come out. Toby points out the constellations Cam taught him. He knows them all.

"Orion always reminds me of my dad," Toby says. "He had a belt, too."

Spyder hasn't said anything for a while. The two of them are chewing on their steak. Toby hands Spyder a toothpick and a Girl Scout Thin Mint cookie.

Toby looks over at the face of the boy—no longer looking miserable or impatient. Toby's never seen this expression before.

"So what do you think?"

Spyder is lying on the ground now, looking up at the stars. At just that moment, a shooting star streaks across the blackness of the sky.

"It's not so bad after all," he says.

102.

The future CEO of the Wheel of Joy cheese company

For Spyder's birthday that August, Toby buys him a bike—a Cannondale with twenty-one speeds, which is twenty more than the number on Toby's old Schwinn. It's yellow, with RockShox shock absorbers and an odometer.

The two of them go for bike rides sometimes now. One night Spyder accompanies Toby and Eleanor to Moonlight Acres for their weekly bowling night.

"I've been thinking," Toby tells Spyder that night at the lanes. "You've been helping out with the girls for a whole year. I want to start paying you."

"You already bought me a bike. I don't need money."

Eleanor is about to say something, but there's no need to step in. Toby does.

"You've got to think about your future, Spy," Toby tells him. "It helps if you figure out what you really love. Then get a job where you get to do that thing. Like for my mom, it's drawing pictures and telling stories. For me, it's taking care of goats. A person should figure out what they love. If you're doing something you love, you won't mind working hard."

This is a lot for Toby to have said. Eleanor gets the impression he's probably been thinking about saying these things to Spyder for a while.

"So what are your favorite things, buddy?" Toby asks Spyder. "Like . . . what makes you feel good?"

It's Toby's turn to bowl, but he doesn't get up yet. He's looking at Spyder, who's sitting next to him, eating fries.

"I don't know," Spyder tells him. "Video games, I guess. Reese's Pieces. My BB gun."

Toby shakes his head. "I'm not talking about stuff that's fun," he says. "I'm talking about something you love. Something that matters."

Spyder sits there for a moment. One lane over, a girl gets a spare. She's doing a dance. At the far end of the lane, where the police and firefighters play, the machine sets out a new set of pins. Spyder looks up from his fries.

"This will sound dumb," Spyder says, in his usual low mumble. "I always thought I could be a good businessman."

Of all the career paths Eleanor might have envisioned for Raine's son, this one takes her by surprise. Now, as Spyder lays out the details of his future profession, his face becomes uncharacteristically animated.

"I'd be, like, a banker or something. I'd wear a suit and a tie and talk to people that want to get loans at my bank and figure out how they can do it."

"It's hard for some people, getting a loan," Eleanor tells him. "Helping them would provide a valuable service."

"Like my mom," he agrees, uncharacteristically animated. "She tried to get a loan one time to get a car on account of how much gas it takes, driving the Holiday Rambler. At the bank she went to, to fill out the forms, nobody paid any attention to her. They probably didn't think she looked like someone that should get a loan. If I worked at a bank, I'd help people like that. Like, just because a person's got a tattoo or they might not have one of their teeth, that doesn't mean the bank shouldn't give them a loan."

"Then you have to work hard when you start back up at school," Toby tells him. "Especially with math. I don't know how to do stuff with numbers but I know you can."

"I like math," he says.

Eleanor studies the boy's face. It comes to her that until now, she has not taken the time to consider who Spyder might be, other than Raine's silent and probably depressed son, hunched over the Xbox controller. Only he comes over every afternoon now, without fail— pedaling his new yellow bicycle up their driveway, leaning it against the barn, for his after-school visits with the girls, calling out to Toby, "The goat man has arrived!" There's always more to a person if you look harder. As a person who tends to get written off a lot, Toby understands this better than most.

"I bet you'd be great at running a business," Toby tells Spyder now. "As soon as you're old enough, I'm making you a partner in the business. Someday, if you aren't too busy being a banker, you can take over Wheel of Joy Cheese Company. You could make it a bigger operation if you wanted. People always want goat cheese."

"I don't know how to run a company. You should've seen my last report card. I got mostly D's and F's."

"You know what I think?" Toby says. "A long time from now, when I'm an old geezer, you'll be sitting in a giant barn with a hundred goats, running this big cheese operation. In your free time you can push me around in my wheelchair and feed me Klondike bars.

"When you're not driving around in your convertible, that is," Toby adds.

"What convertible?"

"The one you'll buy after you make a million dollars running the world's number one goat cheese business. With custom hubcaps and a beautiful woman in the seat next to you. Your wife."

"I'd push you around," Spyder says. He speaks so softly Eleanor almost doesn't hear.

103.

Clean slate

JHJC ere is something—one of the many things—that Eleanor loves about her younger son. He never writes a person off for being different. No doubt this comes from Toby's experience in his own life, of being seen as stupid, or incapable of understanding anything. If people aren't staring at him for his odd way of walking, more than likely they just act as if he doesn't exist. If they talk to him at all, they speak slowly, and loudly.

They've got him labeled: "Special Needs." Or, as the social worker who evaluated him reported, back when Toby was under investigation for sex crimes he didn't commit, "diminished intellectual and moral capacity."

Eleanor thinks about Raine—a person she has judged and viewed in one dimension only, as a troubled single mother who seems to imagine that her only path to survival lies in marrying an old man with a pension, and if that one dies, finding another. As lost as Raine seems to Eleanor now, she has her story, too, same as Spyder does, and Toby, and herself. Same as they all do.

Eleanor remembers something Raine told her once, long ago, that first summer they met, when she was nine months pregnant, right before Spyder was born. "When everything is going to shit in your life, reach for the Mr. Clean. He'll make you feel better."

"I always wanted to have a cleaning business," Raine tells Eleanor now, when she stops by the house to check on her and finds Raine standing on a ladder in the kitchen, cleaning the cupboard shelves. "People feel better when their house is clean."

She'd have to invest in a really good vacuum cleaner. A Dyson, maybe. And she'd use organic cleaning products. She has another idea for how to get her cleaning company to a whole other level.

"I saw this TV show once," Raine says. "It was about these guys that go into houses after people kill themselves, or get murdered. Places where somebody died and left a giant mess that nobody wants to deal with.

"That's where you get the big money," Raine tells Eleanor. "Crime scene cleanup. I wouldn't have a problem with that. After all these years emptying bedpans, a little blood and guts isn't going to bother me."

She's even come up with a name for her business. "Clean Slate Cleaners."

"Clean slate, get it?" Raine says. "The idea is, even if something really terrible happens, I'll help people get back to having a nice clean slate. Start over again. Spic-and-span."

A change comes over Raine as she describes her plan to Eleanor. For a moment there, she looks happy and excited—two words a person would not think to use, describing Raine. The idea of a clean slate sounds great to her. She could use one herself.

104.

Home

Nearly autumn. How can it be that more than a decade has passed since Eleanor returned to the farm?

For all this time, she's managed to keep her condo in Brookline. She gets back there every week or two now. But the farm has remained Eleanor's base.

When Guy was part of her world, there was always another plane ticket landing in her mailbox, another night in some exotic place to put on her calendar, a getaway to some expensive hotel. Even during those long stretches of time apart from Guy—working at her drawing table, bringing her trash to the dump and the recycling center, or carrying wood in to the stove, helping Toby take off the storm windows in springtime or putting them on again in the fall—she could always transport herself to those other places and imagine herself in the arms of a man who bought her French perfume and met her at expensive hotels. And perhaps, it strikes her now, Guy's elusiveness and the fundamental impossibility of making a future with him had seemed to Eleanor—for a time at least—a good thing about their relationship. As long as there was always one more plane ticket in her future, one more hotel night on the calendar, Eleanor could postpone answering the question: Where do I live, exactly? *Where is my home?*

The odd thing about Guy's exit from her life, she understands now, is how little of substance remains from those few dozen nights they spent together, that weekend in Cambridge, their one dinner in Seattle with Al and Teresa, that one time Guy paid a visit to the farm in the rented Tesla (and left, a few hours later). Guy had shown up in her life like a movie star making a cameo appearance—a shooting star, a migrating hawk. He enthralled and captivated her, but Eleanor was never going to be more to him than a woman he met up with for a night before moving on again.

For Eleanor now, looking back from a distance of a couple of years, it's almost as if she'd dreamed the whole experience.

One part of her times with Guy endures. Those nights she spent with him in all those cities they never got to explore served to open the world for Eleanor. Just because Guy no longer sends her plane tickets or takes her out to dinner, can't she still venture into the world? Did there have to be a man waiting for her in a hotel room to make the trip worth taking?

It suddenly occurs to Eleanor—how is it that she never thought about this before?—that she's spent four decades writing books about an orphan girl named Bodie who travels all over the globe having adventures. Bodie's ten years old. (Over all the years Eleanor's been writing about her, this never changes. Bodie is always ten.)

Eleanor passed her sixty-fifth birthday a while back. What's keeping her?

Not her family anymore. Most weekends these days, Lulu and

Orson are occupied with friends and school activities. They text Eleanor more than a person might expect of kids their ages, but seldom have time for visits as they did for a while, when their mother made her odd, lonely getaways to Concord and dropped them off. Al and Teresa and Flora visit now and then. But never more than twice a year—usually less—and never for more than a handful of days.

There's always Toby, of course—the one who remains, through the comings and goings of all the others, and the deaths of a few, the most constant character in Eleanor's life. But even Toby doesn't need Eleanor in the way he used to. Toby's back to spending time at the fire station now. Ralph's coming over now to work. Spyder shows up every day after school. Toby will always require help—filling out papers, keeping accounts straight, all those tasks Al performs for him, or the ones that Eleanor does—but for the first time she can imagine Toby living on the farm without her.

The funny thing is, she no longer feels the same frustration with staying in this place, or the compulsion to leave.

PART 4

Trouble

105.

What happened to Toby?

That summer two more baby goats were born in the barn. In addition to his herd of eight girls, Toby has held on to Jesus—the lone male goat, now fixed. Spyder's special goat.

Eleanor's been spending three nights a week in Brookline lately. Four sometimes. Toby tells her he's doing fine. But she's been noticing something different about her son. He sounds tired. She tells herself that the strain of the last few years—the charges he faced, his painful exile from the fire station and the bowling alley—have probably caught up with him.

Just before Labor Day, Al and Teresa and Flora come for a visit. They'd rented a house in Martha's Vineyard for the second half of July, but there is no way Flora—now seven years old—would let her parents make the trip east without seeing her uncle.

It's Flora who occupies Eleanor's attention first as she drives up the familiar road to the farm. She spots her older son and his family right away. Flora is down at the pond with Teresa and Al, looking for frogs.

"Abuelita!" Flora calls out to her.

Eleanor is partway down the path to the pond when she spots the figure of a man standing with Flora and her mother. From a distance, she doesn't recognize him—one of Toby's farming friends probably, or one of the volunteer firemen, paying a visit. When Flora runs along the edge of the pond, the unfamiliar man follows her—but slowly, like someone for whom every step requires an effort. Somebody very old.

It's a shock to realize, when Eleanor gets closer, that the person she's been watching at the pond with Flora is Toby. How can it be that she sees him nearly every morning when he heads out to the barn, and again at night when she fixes them dinner, and she is only just now noticing how unwell he appears.

She runs down to the water. First, she picks Flora up and hugs Teresa and Al. Then she turns to Toby.

"What's going on?"

106.

Marrow

At the hospital with Al and Toby the next day, they run tests. The next morning the physician calls. *Come to my office. We need to talk.*

The blood tests indicate that Toby is suffering from a disease called acute myelogenous leukemia. At first the physician who speaks with them appears hesitant to offer the full story. Maybe she doesn't know how much Toby can comprehend or how much Eleanor, who sits with him in the doctor's office, will want him to know.

"You can tell us everything," Eleanor says to the doctor. "Toby deserves to know as much as the rest of us."

The cells in Toby's bone marrow are no longer developing the way they're supposed to, Dr. Fleischman explains. No accounting for why. The result has left Toby's body unable to restore itself.

"You've probably been getting a lot of bruises?" the doctor asks Toby. *Yes.* "And nosebleeds?" He has spoken about none of this to Eleanor, but he nods again. His appetite has disappeared.

"It's cancer?" Eleanor asks. Dr. Fleischman nods. "It's called acute myeloid leukemia."

"My dad had cancer," Toby says. "They gave him a bunch of drugs but he still died. What about me?"

Eleanor watches the doctor's face taking in Toby's question. Dr. Fleischman looks from one of them to the other. Al to Eleanor, then back to Toby.

"We have only one treatment available for a blood cancer of this nature," Dr. Fleischman tells them. "Toby needs a bone marrow transplant. For the transplant to be successful, it should come from an individual whose bone marrow provides a close match to his own."

There were donor banks for this, but by far the best results occurred with a donor who was a close family member. It's good news, she adds, that in addition to his mother, Toby has two full siblings as well as a half sibling. There's a strong chance that among his family members one will emerge whose cellular makeup is compatible to Toby's, presuming that, in the event of a match, they might be willing to become donors.

"There's no question, any of us would do that," Eleanor says. "We'll do anything."

107.

Not the good kind of special

Toby needs to be hospitalized. That first day Dr. Fleischman sees him, she tells them she had no idea how he's managed this long with his white count so low.

Back on the farm, Ralph steps in to take care of the girls. Ursula drives down from Vermont to sit with Toby that first night at the hospital. She sets out pictures of everyone he loves. There's a picture of Cam, and of his goat Bernadette, and of Scarlett, another favorite goat, chomping on one of Eleanor's petunias a few years back. She's brought a picture of his brother and herself, and of Elijah, Eleanor, Lulu and Orson and Flora. Also Teresa, Jake, Raine, and Spyder (she has chosen one taken at the farmers' market in his "Say Cheese" hat).

Looking at the gallery of faces her daughter has assembled for Toby, a thought comes to Eleanor: *This is a family here. A messy one for sure. But they're a family. This wall tells their story. For all their differences and troubles, one thing unites them. Toby.*

Within forty-eight hours they've all taken a blood test to determine who might be the best bone marrow donor. Elijah drives home from Portland, Maine, hoping to be a match. Lulu's thirteen years old now, young to be a donor, but she's adamant. If the most compatible bone marrow proves to be hers, she wants to be her uncle's donor. As fearful as she is of needles, and all other medical procedures, Lulu insists on being tested with the others. Though he's only nine years old, so does Orson.

Next day the news comes back. Not a single member of Toby's family is a match.

"I always knew I was special," Toby says. "I guess this isn't the good kind of special."

They reach out to Cam's brother. He sends back a seven-word response: *Wish I could help. No can do.*

Dr. Fleishman starts checking the bone marrow donor pool. There are thousands of candidates in the registry now. With luck they might find one close enough to serve as Toby's donor.

"What if we can't find one?" Toby asks. It's the question on the minds of all of them, but he alone voices it.

Dr. Fleischman looks at her clipboard—the gesture, Eleanor has come to recognize, chosen by a doctor when she'd rather not look her patient, or her patient's family, in the eye.

"This is our only option," she says.

108.

It's just life

FALL sets in. The days are shorter. Long shadows fall over the field. On the sixth floor at Dana Farber, where Toby lies in a hospital bed now, in a room with warning signs posted on the door, prohibiting all visitors except medical staff, properly suited up, you'd never know what season this was, or even what day. Just a hard one.

This is not the first time Eleanor has witnessed what happens when a person's body betrays them. Over those months with Cam, after they discovered the tumor in his pancreas, when she'd moved back to the farm, it sometimes seemed to her as if she were tending a garden in a drought—and no matter how many buckets of water she hauled in, no matter how long she stood there watering the plants, nothing was enough.

It's happening again, but to their son this time. His skin has changed, also the texture of his hair, his fingernails even. His large, solid frame seems to be shrinking. His lumbering gait, which has been different from that of the average person since his accident, is more of a slow, sad shuffle now. When Toby makes his way to the bathroom—he can still do this, with effort—he does so like a very old man.

Eleanor stays in Brookline to be near the hospital. Al returns to the farm and sets up a desk in a spare bedroom, the same place he'd built the TB-10 long ago so his brother could make music.

Raine calls from Akersville. Ralph has told her the news. "You've got enough on your mind," she tells Eleanor. "But I don't know what to do about Spyder. He doesn't want to talk about anything. He asked if they could test him to be a donor, but I told him it wouldn't work on account of how he and Toby aren't related."

Not by blood anyway.

"They've got thousands of potential donors in the registry," Eleanor says. "I have to believe we'll find someone."

They don't have a lot of time. Every day Toby looks weaker. He has no appetite. He sleeps a lot. For a while there he wanted daily reports on the goats, but he doesn't even ask about them anymore. He's fading.

Al brings flash drives of movies Toby might enjoy. Laurel and Hardy, the Three Stooges. *Happy Gilmore. The Princess Bride*—the all-time family favorite from their childhood.

The movie Toby has liked best is *The Bicycle Thief,* the story of a boy growing up in a very poor home in Italy. When his father's bicycle is stolen, the boy does everything he can to get it back, as the family's life slowly falls into ruin.

Toby can't follow subtitles, but this doesn't seem to matter. He understands everything in the movie—and not only because he's a person who understands better than most the importance of a bicycle. The night Toby and Al watch *The Bicycle Thief* together, Toby weeps in a way he has not done since the death of their father.

"People are always saying 'That's not fair' when something bad happens to them," Toby observes. "I don't get why they say that. What makes them think there's rules for how everything's supposed to go, and if it doesn't work out that way it's somebody's fault? It's just life, that's all. Sometimes things are great. Sometimes they're crummy. It's just life."

He looks out the window to the hospital parking lot, the sea of cars. No fields in sight. No birds other than a few pigeons. If Toby were healthy, he'd be heading down the road to the waterfall to put his fishing line in the water.

"I miss my bicycle," he tells Eleanor. "I miss my goats."

The list goes on. He misses the guys at the fire station, and Ralph. He misses Flora, of course. And Lulu. And Orson. Elijah. He misses his pops. Oh, and does he ever miss Spyder.

He's quiet for a moment. Studying her son's face, Eleanor can almost see a world of losses running through his mind. Everything her son loves about the world slipping away from him.

"I miss my life," he says.

109.

Good cells

The hematology team in Boston calls. They've located a workable donor from the pool. The match isn't anywhere close to ideal, but they're out of options. The bone marrow transplant from the donor pool is scheduled for the following day.

"Too bad they can't put a few of those good cells in my brain," Toby tells Eleanor as they hook him up for the first round of chemotherapy to prepare him for the transplant.

110.

A good place for ashes

The chemotherapy they deliver to destroy all of Toby's own bone marrow leaves him highly vulnerable to infection. They place him in isolation—no visitors or human contact with anyone besides the nursing staff, suited up in layers of protective gear, for three months minimum and possibly longer. The family can come to a window in his room and wave or speak to him through an intercom. Eleanor pulls a chair up to the window and speaks into the intercom. Though he's just inches away from her, a thick pane of glass separates the two of them.

"If I don't make it," Toby tells her, "you know what to do with my ashes. I'm going straight into the waterfall with my pops."

111.

Like Rip van Winkle

The first weeks after Toby's bone marrow transplant, he lies on the bed most of the day, a shadow of himself. Sometime around month two things start to shift. He's doing the exercises Ursula has taught him to keep from getting out of shape. His voice, that was barely audible for a while, is stronger now. He asks about Lulu and Orson and Flora, of course. He worries about how Spyder's doing without him. "I bet that goat, Jesus, is making some trouble," Toby tells Eleanor.

"Ralph had to build him a special pen to keep him separate from the girls," Eleanor says. "Every afternoon, when Spyder comes over to the barn, he visits the girls first. Then he heads over to Jesus's pen. Spyder says we've got to make sure it's not too lonely for him, shut away from the other goats that way."

"I know how he feels," Toby says.

She's there visiting when Dr. Fleischman comes by the room.

"I have to admit we weren't that optimistic about the bone marrow we transplanted being a good enough match," she says. "But it looks like we got Toby into remission. We can send him home in a week."

Toby is like Rip van Winkle, Eleanor thinks. A man who'd just spent months in a hospital isolation unit, returning—in a matter of days—to a whole new world, his very bone marrow transformed. The biggest news in their family concerns him, of course, but Eleanor fills him in on the rest. Teresa and Al have started a nonprofit to assist the children of undocumented immigrants from Mexico separated from their parents at the border. Orson's basketball team has made it to the peewee league finals. Lulu has gotten a part in a play. No good news to share about Ursula. She's just plain sad. Jake's just plain crazy. That's how it seems anyway.

Toby and Eleanor are sitting in his hospital room. Eleanor doesn't have to sit behind the glass anymore, speaking through an intercom. One more week and she gets to bring him home.

"Tell me more about Flora," Toby says to Eleanor. He would never have said this, but as much as he loves every member of his family, Flora is his favorite of all of them. Until he got sick, Toby had been fixing up the old treehouse that he built with Elijah and Cam long ago, to surprise his niece on her next visit. Lulu isn't the treehouse type. Neither is Orson, probably. But when Flora gets to the farm, the two of them are likely to spend hours in the treehouse. Flora likes reading out loud to Toby. He teaches her about minerals.

"There's just something about Flora and me," Toby says to Eleanor. "We're two peas in a pod."

112.

Whatever normal is

Just after New Year's—2020 now—they let Toby go home.

"We'll need to monitor your son closely," Dr. Fleischman tells Eleanor. "He's still vulnerable to infection. But so far, the transplant seems to be taking reasonably well."

Toby has been in the isolation chamber so long his walking is even shakier than usual. But he's put on weight. The color has returned to his skin. In the car on the way home, passing the fire station, he wants to get out and say hello to the guys.

Life is back to normal, maybe. Whatever normal is. He's going home.

113.

The welcome committee

Home.

Even before her car comes to a stop outside the house, Eleanor catches sight of him: a small, skinny figure waiting outside the barn door, in his combat boots and his old gray "Five Finger Death Punch" T-shirt –never mind that it's January, and the temperature's twelve degrees. Even without his "Say Cheese" baseball hat, it's easy to recognize Spyder. Along with Flora, he's Toby's biggest fan.

Spyder stands there now, leaning against the barn door as Toby— his best friend in the world—gets out of the car. His only friend, more than likely. If there's anyone Spyder loves it's Toby. It's just not a feeling Spyder knows how to express—not having found himself on the receiving end of much of it.

When it comes to expressing love, Toby has no such problems. "Man, did I miss you, buddy," Toby calls out to Spyder. He's heading straight for the boy—with that odd, loping gait of his and his arms outstretched.

From back at the car, unloading his things, Eleanor issues a warning. "Don't get too close! Remember what the doctor said." As good as he looks, Toby's still functioning with a compromised immune system. Eleanor has tried to explain this to Toby, but it's not a concept that makes much sense to him. How could it be dangerous, giving someone a hug?

"I've been keeping records on everything that's been going on in the barn," Spyder tells him. "I wrote it all down."

He pulls a folded-up notebook out of his pocket, a page devoted to each goat.

"I want to hear all about it," Toby tells him. Side by side, they head into the barn. Never mind that snow covers the ground. Toby's humming the song Cam used to sing, times he came back to the farm after being away at a craft fair. *Good to touch the green, green grass of home.*

114.

Corona

By the end of February, Toby is almost his old self. But the world is changing. Every night on the news now come reports of the strange and deadly virus that seemed at first to exist only in China, but cases have begun showing up in New York City. L.A. Everywhere.

Some people have started to wear masks. Every day now there's a report of new cases—first in the double digits, then in the thousands.

The president addresses the nation. "We've got this under control," he says.

At the nursing home where she's working again, Raine reports that three of the residents have been taken to the hospital. She worries about Billy—back at the house in his wheelchair, keeping tabs on the weather, as always.

"Billy's in the high-risk category," Raine tells Eleanor. "I don't want to see a bunch of guys in hazmat suits carting him off to some emergency ward to die alone in a room full of people that don't even know his name." She's wearing her mask even inside the house now, on account of being in contact with so many old people at the home.

A woman at the post office comes down with the virus. Then a teacher at Lulu and Orson's school. Then Eleanor's book editor. Then a neighbor of Ursula's, Suzanne, in Vermont. Her case is more serious.

"They took her to the hospital," Lulu tells Eleanor. This is the kind of thing that triggers all of Lulu's worst anxieties. "I saw them take her out in the ambulance. There were all these men wearing masks and gloves. Everyone was scared they'd catch it."

Two days later Lulu reports that Suzanne is on a ventilator. A week later she's dead.

"I'm scared, Grammy," Lulu says. About many things, no doubt. Her mother's making her and her brother wash their hands ten times a day. They wear masks, even in the house. Her father's telling them the whole thing is a conspiracy, meant to make the president look bad in the upcoming election, and anyone who falls for this coronavirus crap is a sucker. He's added a new target to his list of people to rant about: Dr. Anthony Fauci.

The day before, Lulu tells Eleanor, her father put up a sign in their front yard that said, "Fear has no home here." Ten minutes later, her mother took it down. As bad as things seemed between Jake and Ursula before, the pandemic combined with another election in the offing has made it ten times worse.

"I just wish they could be nice to each other," Lulu says. Long ago, Eleanor remembers, Ursula said the same thing about herself and Cam.

115.

No more visits to the fire station

T he world is closing down around them: the bowling alley, the school. Toby can't hang out at the fire station anymore. Out in Seattle, Al and Teresa are running their company virtually now.

For Eleanor, whose work is mostly solitary anyway, the pandemic has had less of an effect than for most people she knows. Mostly she worries about Ursula, and her grandchildren, living in the middle of what's sounding more and more, from Lulu's accounts, like a war zone between their parents. And she worries about Toby, with his compromised immune system. The bone marrow transplant appears to be taking well but the doctors still speak of Toby's status as "in remission," not cured.

The main thing, for him, is being back on the farm—out in the barn again with Spyder and the girls, awaiting the birth of two new goat kids. He's oiled up the chain on his bike. "I never hung around with that many people anyway," Toby says. Just Ralph and Spyder and the guys at the fire station, basically.

His visit out west to see Al and Teresa and Flora will have to be postponed, of course. Nobody's taking any planes. As much as he'd looked forward to seeing his niece, he's okay with this.

"When you love a person, you don't even need to see them," Toby says. "It's just good knowing they're out there someplace."

116.

The death of a friend

Back in February, Elijah and Miriam had flown to Brussels to begin a tour with Dog Blue. Two weeks later the tour was canceled.

"John Prine got the virus somewhere out on the road," Elijah tells Eleanor, when he calls with the news about his tour. "A guy I know who played in a band with him for a while told me he's in the hospital. He's got the virus."

Until now, nobody Eleanor knows personally has caught the virus. The illness of a man whose songs she loves brings the pandemic closer to home. Every morning now she starts her day by googling John Prine's name to see how he's doing. The news is never good.

Then one morning—April now—when she googles his name, his obituary shows up. Reading the words on her screen, a wave of grief hits, deeper than she would have thought possible over the death of a man she never met.

All day she plays his music: "Sam Stone." "In Spite of Ourselves," that she and Cam sang together in the car. Eleanor took the Iris DeMent part, Cam, John Prine's. "Lake Marie."

When Toby comes in from the barn to fix himself lunch, he finds Eleanor playing "Speed of the Sound of Loneliness." She's had the song on repeat for an hour. "I know it's crazy, feeling this sad about a person I never even met," Eleanor says. "But I feel like I just lost a friend."

Was life always this filled with losses? Or did Eleanor just start noticing?

117.

"I can't breathe"

The next week Elijah and Miriam fly home from Europe. "There's no point hanging around here," Elijah tells Eleanor. "Nothing's going on anymore. Nothing good anyway.

"How would it be if the two of us stayed with you and Toby on the farm for a while, till this virus situation calms down?" Elijah asks her.

They make up the bed in Ursula's old room. It's a safe bet Ursula won't be using it.

This is the month—May now—when a posse of police officers in Minneapolis tackles a Black man, George Floyd, outside a convenience store for the offense of paying for a pack of cigarettes with what appears to have been a counterfeit twenty-dollar bill. A bystander has caught the event on her cell phone—a white policeman with his knee on George Floyd's neck as the others hold him down, George Floyd gasping "I can't breathe" before he collapses on the sidewalk.

George Floyd is not the first Black man to die at the hands of police officers for a minor offense or no offense at all. But his murder serves as a tipping point. Within days, Black Lives Matter signs and signs bearing the words "I CAN'T BREATHE" scrawled across them appear everywhere.

As does the backlash from people like Eleanor's own son-in-law, Jake. Now he puts a sign in the yard of the house he shares with Ursula—"God, Guns and Trump." The first thing Ursula does when she gets off work is to take the sign down.

The battle between her and Jake rages on.

With Eleanor it's different but hurts no less. Between Eleanor and her daughter, it's still a cold war. No exchange of angry words. Just silence. Maybe that's the worst.

118.

A bowl suitable for holding ashes

By summertime Toby seems to have regained much of his strength—putting up new fences for the goats, keeping a close eye on the pregnant ones. He asks Eleanor if they could make a drive to the Verlander farm one of these days.

"Now? It's not breeding season."

"I was just thinking about June's pottery," Toby says. "I was wondering if she'd sell me a bowl. I'd like to give one to Flora. She's too little to care about it yet, but someday she will."

They make the drive. Hans Verlander meets them outside the house with his mask on.

"I can't invite you in," he says. "June's sick. It's the virus."

Eleanor says all the usual things. No, Hans tells her, they don't think June needs to go to the hospital. They're monitoring things from home. She's a strong girl. She'll get through this.

A look comes over Toby's face. "I wish I could see her," he says. "Just to say hello."

He can't of course. Even if June Verlander didn't have COVID, she's never been one for socializing.

Eleanor and Toby drive home in silence. As they pull down the long dirt road to the farm, Toby finally speaks.

"You know how we put my pops's ashes in one of his bowls," Toby says. "If the cancer comes back, and I don't make it, I'd like you to put me in the blue bowl June gave me. With the Japanese name."

"You're doing great," Eleanor tells him. "You're not going to die."

"Everybody dies sometime," Toby says. "Just remember about the bowl, okay? The blue one."

Broken and repaired, with gold lacquer filling the cracks. It's not simply a description of June Verlander's bowl. It's a pretty good description of Toby.

119.

No tacos. No Flora.

All the previous fall and early winter, while Toby was in the hospital, Spyder had been making plans for their return to the farmers' market come spring. Over Toby's long absence, he painted a sign with the words "WHEEL OF JOY" in rainbow letters with a picture of a goat under the words. The way Spyder painted the goat it ended up looking more like a dog, but the overall effect was great. Even Raine—never one to offer much to her son in the way of positive reinforcement—commented on what a good job Spyder had done with the lettering.

The week before opening day—the start of summer now—the word reaches them: no farmers' market this season. With their number one source of revenue eliminated, Toby no longer needs additional help in the barn, but there's no way he'll let go of his pal. In the year and a half since Spyder's been working with Toby and the goats, the boy's whole outlook seems to have changed. He's still a loner, but he's not skipping school anymore.

Eleanor and Toby drive to Boston to see Toby's doctor, who reports that his white cell count is looking better. "I'm cautiously optimistic," she tells them. Particularly given these pandemic times, Toby will have to be careful. He's still more vulnerable to infection than the average person.

"That makes sense," Toby said. "I'm not an average person!"

The worst is over, Eleanor tells herself.

One of the girls gives birth in the barn. Though the ewe arrives in the middle of a particularly frigid night, Spyder is there for the event—arriving on foot, in his hoodie as usual—and gets to choose the name for the new kid. Eleanor might have expected him to come up with something crazy and dark, but the name he chooses is Tinkerbelle.

The barn feels like the only place where life goes on as before. No one goes anywhere anymore, and if they do, masks cover their faces. Nobody touches each other. (Touch, the thing Toby loves best: The feel of a baby's cheek. The inside of a goat's ear. Flora's hand in his. A bear hug when he greets Elijah and Miriam, home from Brussels.)

Just touching a person is dangerous now. Touching could kill you.

This is the time of year Toby would normally be setting off on his Seattle trip. No Seattle this year. No fish tacos. No Flora.

120.

The person to call in the case of an emergency

One night—September now—the phone rings around 3:00 A.M. After all those months her son was in the hospital, Eleanor has learned to keep it next to her bed. Even with Toby home again, she hasn't broken the habit.

When she picks up at first all Eleanor hears is static. But the voice is recognizable. Just barely. *Guy.*

More than three years have passed since Eleanor last heard Guy's voice. It comes to her now from the other side of the world, on a line so weak she could be receiving this call from the bottom of the ocean. Last she knew, he was heading to record the Larsen B calving event. Things must be taking a lot longer than he bargained on. More trips back to the United States probably. More fundraising.

"We hit a whiteout today," he tells her. "I thought our plane was going down for sure."

What can she say? No need. He's still talking.

"It's a pretty scary thing, looking out the window of the plane and seeing nothing but white," Guy tells Eleanor. "I thought I was done for. And you know what? At that moment, I thought about you."

Oh.

"This wasn't the first time I've come face-to-face with death," Guy's telling her. "But the first thing I wanted to do when we managed to land the plane, I realized I needed to tell you. Whatever it means, you're the person I'd want to know if anything happened to me."

There was a time when the words he just spoke—"I thought about you"—would have lifted her heart.

Eleanor tries to locate the old feeling. Any feeling. It's gone.

From her solitary bed in Akersville, her son asleep in the room next to hers, Eleanor imagines how it would have been for her if she'd opened the newspaper the next morning to find Guy's obituary. No question, he would have made it into *The New York Times.*

"No known family members," it would have read. In the summing-up of Guy Macdowell's illustrious career, the article would have spoken of his foundation, the heroic work he'd done bringing global attention to the crisis of the melting continent of Antarctica, the story (invariably recounted in the speeches he gave to raise money for his foundation) of the night he met Jacques Cousteau, and that other story well known to all who ever heard him speak, of how—somewhere on that unforgiving continent—his eyes had turned from brown to blue. Had Guy died on the polar icecap, those chronicling the story would no doubt have made much of the irony that it had been melting ice—the very phenomenon he'd been warning the world about—that killed him. You could call Guy a martyr to the disaster of global warming, except it turned out he wasn't dead after all.

"We have to suspend the expedition again," he tells her. "For a while anyway. I'll be flying back to the States."

On the other end of the line, ten thousand miles and a million years away, Eleanor just sits there, holding the phone.

"So," he says to her now. "Where does that leave us? You and me?"

Eleanor says nothing for a moment. "I'm glad you're okay," she tells Guy. "Thank you for letting me know."

"You know that card they put in wallets when you buy a new one?" Guy says to Eleanor now—from his patch of ice somewhere at the southernmost place on the planet. "I'm talking about that card where you're supposed to write 'the person to call in the event of an emergency'? It came to me today, when they were warming me up with the thermal blankets after my near-death experience: I guess that person is you."

The way he says this, it's as if he were conferring an award. He delivers this information with the air of a man for whom it seems like the most wondrous and precious gift, that he has finally recognized her importance in his life. Eleanor gets the feeling he's expecting her to respond with amazement and gratitude. Joy.

He has more to say. He speaks about his findings, measuring sea ice on Larsen B, the alarming disappearance of the krill that a particular species of penguin—the Adélie—depend on for their survival, and the recent addition to the endangered species list of another species of penguin: the emperor, who lay their eggs on sea ice that's melting at ever-increasing rates. He speaks of his board members, the many scientists with whom he continues to consult, his fundraising efforts (going well!), an article about him due to appear in *National Geographic*. He tells Eleanor about the team of men who have joined him on the various legs of his journey so far, and of how—though most are half his age—none of them, other than Guy, has chosen to make the hike in its entirety.

"It's amazing what we're accomplishing here," he tells her. "Your old friend here might just manage to change the world."

"That's really something," Eleanor says. If her voice sounds flat, and less enthusiastic than he might have expected, Guy will probably attribute it to the poor connection.

He has not asked about her or her family—and for a while, in the early days of their relationship, Eleanor had allowed herself to believe that Guy's seeming obliviousness about her family was a kind of gift. With this man—and no other—she could be, for a night anyway, nobody's mother, nobody's ex-wife or grandmother. The two of them had created their own country. Their own continent—a very small one, the size of a luxury hotel suite. There was a time when it had all seemed so beautiful.

It was only later—after his departure from her life—that Eleanor had begun to question the idea that there was anything beautiful about a relationship in which one person in the couple supports the dream of the other, while the other person never gets around to asking the question "What's *your* dream, anyway?"

Here's what Eleanor has learned, since the night he drove away from that Malibu hotel room. For a man to love her, truly love her, there should be space in his heart for the things that occupy space in hers. Guy has a big life, big passions. The idea Eleanor might have something of significance going on, herself, has evidently never occurred to him. This included her work. This included her family.

Family. "I was never very good at that," he'd told her once.

There's silence on the satellite line. Time was, Eleanor hung on Guy's words, but what she registers now is simply this: she wants to go back to sleep.

She might have told Guy about Toby: about the cancer, the transplant, her terrible worry that the bone marrow they'd elected to put in his body—so far from an ideal match—will fail to save her son. In the years since they parted, so much has happened in her life. No doubt the same is true for Guy.

There's no point going into any of that. Who they are now are two people whose paths intersected once—thousands of miles apart in ways that speak to so much more than geography. Why explain any of this to a man who never demonstrated particular interest or concern before?

"I guess that's it then," she tells him.

From all those thousands of miles that separate them, Eleanor feels Guy's reluctance to end the call. She imagines his large leathery hands—the roughest skin she ever touched, the fingers that touched every inch of her body once—gripping the satellite phone. That and a cigar. He isn't saying anything. She wonders briefly if the connection has failed. Then she hears him, very softly.

"Love you, babe," he says.

"I loved you, too," she tells him.

121.

An intact family

After that stretch of days when Ursula left her children with Eleanor in Brookline a few years back—during one of the many moments in Ursula's marriage when life with Jake had come to seem unbearable—Eleanor had believed, briefly, that maybe Ursula was finally going to leave Jake.

Now, almost three years later—though they barely speak—the two of them still live under the same roof. Jake continues drinking too much beer and railing about liberals and immigrants. Lulu remains anxious. Orson plays sports every chance he gets, and when he can't, he retreats to the world of his tablet. Nothing has changed.

As had been true for years, Ursula tells her mother almost nothing, but Eleanor has learned from Al that Jake recently joined a group called the Order of the Patriots, whose mission, as much as Al chose to learn about it, is "to return America to the real Americans." According to Al, who researched the group online, Jake's group talks a lot about "the welfare state" and, as always, the importance of building the wall separating the United States and Mexico.

Emboldened by the man in the White House now, Jake and his cohort meet on Sunday afternoons in a field somewhere over the Vermont border, in New Hampshire, where they go through militia training led by a former U.S. Marine. Everyone has at least one gun, usually more.

"I don't understand how Ursula can tolerate this," Eleanor says, when Al tells her about Jake's activities.

"You know Ursula," Al says. "Stiff upper lip. Put on a happy face. Never mind that one of them is living in the bedroom and one is living in the basement and the only time they talk to each other is to figure out who's picking the kids up from soccer. Just keep that family intact."

Not for the first time, Eleanor considers the phrase "an intact family." Whatever it is, it's probably not what Jake and Ursula have going on in Vermont.

122.

Flags on trucks, more pinot noir than usual

No doubt her son-in-law's anger is fueled by the president and the upcoming election. As the months pass, heading to November, it feels as if Eleanor's neighbors are at war with one another.

When Eleanor drives along New Hampshire back roads now, almost every house she passes has a sign in the yard screaming out not simply the name of a candidate, but a message, almost like an assault. By fall the battle lines seem drawn in blood.

In Boston to watch one of the debates with Jason and Hank, Eleanor sits in the living room drinking pinot noir and eating more cheese and crackers than normal, she's so nervous. It makes no sense, but she connects Toby's illness—the threat of the cancer returning—to Donald Trump. If he loses she'll take this as a good omen for Toby. If he wins . . . she doesn't want to think about it.

In her own family there's unity on this topic, with one painful exception. Up in Vermont—where his father continues to live in the basement, Orson reports—Jake now spends his days driving around with two large flags on his truck billowing in the wind as he blasts "The Star-Spangled Banner" or standing along the side of the road—outside an abortion clinic one time, and another time, a housing project serving Guatemalan and Honduran refugees— holding a sign that says "America Is for Americans." The school where Jake once worked as a soccer coach has recently hired, as their new athletic director, a Mexican American man named Edgar Cruz. Jake sees this as clear evidence that his country has been taken over by foreigners stealing jobs from taxpayers like himself. He's been unemployed long enough that he has gotten very good at playing video games.

It's election night. Four years earlier, confident of good news, Eleanor threw a party to mark the event. This time she's made no plans—no fancy appetizers, no chocolate cake, no champagne.

Tonight, the news is good for Eleanor and her friends. But as relieved as she feels at the defeat of Donald Trump, she can't celebrate as she might have expected. Eleanor's heard enough of Jake's attitudes about politics now to recognize he and his Order of the Patriots friends, and all those others out there who share their beliefs, won't take the defeat of their candidate without a fight. Driving home from her friend Jason's house that night, she gets a call from Lulu. It must be midnight, but her granddaughter is up. She's calling from her bedroom, with the door closed tight, and she's whispering.

"Things are pretty weird here," she tells Eleanor. "My dad says the election was a fake, and Donald Trump is still the president. He's driving around with a loudspeaker on his truck telling everyone there's going to be a revolution."

123.

"Be there, will be wild."

The man who will remain president for two more months—Eleanor tries not to speak his name—is sending out tweets saying the election was rigged. They've stolen all these ballots, bussed in unregistered voters—people from other countries, probably, not real Americans. He's not leaving the White House.

Every morning now—she can't stop herself—Eleanor checks to see what he has tweeted to his followers over the past few hours. The man stays up all night from the looks of things.

"We're going to take back our country!" he writes. "Never give up." "Fight like hell."

Then this: "Big protest in D.C. on January 6th. Be there, will be wild."

Reading his words, Eleanor fears for her country. She fears for her daughter.

This is a moment when Eleanor longs to call Ursula. "Come to the farm," she'd say. "Bring the children. I'll roast a chicken. We'll play Clue."

She knows better now. There's that card on her refrigerator to remind her if she forgets. *Respect boundaries.*

Be patient. Don't push. Let your adult child come to you.

The one who calls Eleanor is Lulu. She's fourteen now—still a worrier, who tries hard to keep her father from looking bad in the eyes of her mother and grandmother, same as Ursula used to do, with Eleanor, when her parents went to war with each other. Lulu has given up trying to conceal what's going on in her family now.

"My dad's gone crazy," Lulu tells Eleanor. "We don't know what to do anymore." Right now her dad's in the basement with his friends, watching Sean Hannity and yelling at the television set. Also, they're drunk.

After she gets off the phone with her granddaughter, Eleanor sends Ursula a text.

"If you think Jake might do something to hurt you and the children, you need to get out of there," she writes.

"I don't need your help," Ursula texts back. "Jake would never let anything happen to the kids and me." No further discussion.

The next day comes a text from Orson.

"My dad's truck is gone. We think he went to Washington. He took his guns."

It's the sixth of January, 2021.

Then comes a text from Ursula. "I need to bring the kids someplace safe. Can I drop them off with you?"

124.

Why is that man wearing animal horns?

Eleanor tries to keep the television off, but Orson wants to know what's happening. On the screen: a few hundred men are climbing the wall of the Capitol building. They're wearing camouflage gear and work overalls, gas masks, flannel shirts, T-shirts with pictures of Donald Trump, bulletproof vests. One of them appears to be dressed as George Washington, except that he's painted his face red.

They're waving sticks and flags, baseball bats. A mob is screaming about hanging the vice president.

"Why is that man wearing animal horns on his head? And no shirt. I bet it's cold out," Orson says. Eleven years old, he's trying hard to make sense of what he's witnessing on CNN. Most of all, Eleanor knows, he's worried about his father. What they see bears no resemblance to what they say at his school about the way government is supposed to work in the United States of America.

When the cameras cut to the police officers loading protesters into a van—still screaming about how the election got stolen—Lulu leaves the living room.

"I'm going to do my homework," she tells Eleanor. She won't be going to school in the morning, probably, given that they're staying at the farm. But Lulu is the kind of person who believes in doing your homework no matter what. More than that, Eleanor knows she doesn't want to risk seeing her father.

The next afternoon, Ursula returns to pick up the children. From the looks of her, she may not have slept. Eleanor knows better than to remark on this.

"Thank you for taking Orson and Lulu," Ursula says. As always, her tone when she speaks with her mother is wary, her mouth tight, as if saying the words might cost her something.

Eleanor learns the rest from Al, later.

"Jake got arrested, but they let him go sometime around eight thirty," Al tells her. "He's taking a bus back to Burlington, where he left the truck. His friend's still locked up. I guess the guy hit one of the policemen over the head with a hockey stick."

"Jake used to be the kindest person I knew. I can't imagine him being part of a violent mob."

"Something happened to Jake," Al says. "Maybe something happened to our country."

For as long as she can remember—since before Jake and Ursula got married, even, and that was over twenty years ago—Ursula has said she'd never get a divorce. The way she'd delivered this announcement to Eleanor, it has always come across as an accusation. *You failed to keep our family together. I'll do better. Just watch.* But it's been a while now since Ursula delivered one of her speeches about the selfishness of parents who divorce.

"I think Ursula's finally hit the wall with Jake," Al tells his mother.

125.

Feetfirst

onald Trump announces that he's not leaving the White House. Ursula's not talking to her mother, but Al reports that up in Vermont, Jake says the same thing about the home he and Ursula have shared with their children all these years.

"They'll have to carry me out feetfirst," Jake has told Ursula. But in the end, he moves out of their house.

Jake gets an apartment in Bellows Falls. What little information Eleanor has concerning this comes from her grandchildren, who will be allowed to see their father every other weekend now, so long as he manages to refrain from drinking, which doesn't happen. Much in the same way that, long ago, Eleanor's children offered few reports, if any, after their parents' divorce, on how things went when they spent time at their father's house, now Lulu says almost nothing to Ursula about Jake. "My mom's already super mad at my dad," Lulu tells her grandmother. "If she knew what was going on there it would get worse."

Jake has joined a men's rights group now, evidently. He's still drinking a lot. "We mostly watch TV when we go to our dad's," Orson tells Eleanor. But not the shows he'd like. Their father keeps the television tuned to a news channel. Sometimes they go over to the apartment of another single dad, Bryce, whose two-year-old twins stay with him on Saturdays. "We're supposed to play with Bryce's kids," Orson says. "But they wear diapers."

Sometimes, late at night, Ursula has reported to Al, Jake calls her up crying. When she doesn't want to talk to him—which is always, now—he keeps calling back, over and over. One time it went on like that for an hour. When she finally picked up—just to get him to stop, finally—all she heard on the line was a recording of George Jones singing "He Stopped Loving Her Today"—a song about a man so faithful to the woman who left him that he kept loving her for years after she'd abandoned him. The song ends with a verse about what finally got him to stop loving this woman. He'd died.

"That's Jake for you," Al says to Eleanor. "Loyal to the end to two people: my sister and Donald Trump."

Not necessarily in that order, at least. One thing about Jake that none of them would deny: He loves Ursula.

A few days later Jake shows up close to midnight at Ursula's house—the house he and Ursula used to share. He's drunk. When Ursula won't open the door, he begins to bang on it so loudly he wakes the children.

"You've stolen my family," he says to her. Orson and Lulu stand at the top of the stairs, hearing everything.

"Dad . . . Dad . . . Dad," Lulu says to him. "Please don't." She could be Ursula, thirty years ago. Pleading with her parents to get along. With no more hope of achieving her goal than her mother had, long ago.

126.

Cutting out hearts

It's February break at Orson and Lulu's school but Ursula has to work. She drives the children to the farm again to spend their vacation week.

Ursula has filed for divorce. Given Jake's drinking and erratic behavior, the court has awarded Ursula temporary custody of their children. It's a good moment to get Lulu and Orson out of the house.

In the careful manner she always adopts with her daughter, Eleanor asks Ursula how things are going with Jake. She has heard that many of the January 6 rioters have been charged with crimes. Because he didn't physically attack anyone that day, Jake has gotten off with only a suspended sentence for his participation.

"Everything's fine, okay?" Ursula tells Eleanor. "Do you need to know every single detail of my life?"

After she leaves, Eleanor decides to introduce Lulu and Orson to their old family tradition of making valentines.

"Back when your mother and Uncle Al and Uncle Toby were little, we used to lay out all our art supplies on the table and make valentines together," Ursula tells her grandchildren. "What do you say we take out the glitter and get to work?"

They spend the afternoon cutting out paper hearts and decorating them using old magazines, buttons, and scraps of lace. She had expected Orson to protest but he doesn't. All afternoon, he doesn't take out his tablet even one time.

After, they all go skating on the pond. Eleanor fixes a pot of hot chocolate and a big bowl of popcorn. When Toby comes in from the barn, they play a few rounds of Parcheesi by the woodstove. Nobody brings up cancer, or the riot at the Capitol, weekends in Bellows Falls, or the fact that Lulu and Orson can only see their father now when a social worker is present.

"It's nice and peaceful here," Lulu says. "I wish we never had to go home."

"I don't get why my mom's mad at you," Orson tells Eleanor.

"Just because people don't always get along doesn't mean they don't love each other," Eleanor says. She wants to believe this.

127.

A foil-wrapped baked potato

There's a word Eleanor has tried to avoid, in speaking of her relationship with Ursula. "Estrangement." She prefers to think of herself and her daughter as simply "taking a break." They're working on their relationship. (But are they? How?)

They're going through a phase.

When she looks back now, Eleanor realizes that this phase started more than twenty years ago. First came Ursula's silent hostility, moving on to her barbed remarks and, for a while, total silence between them.

At the moment they're maintaining the appearance of reconnection minus much semblance, if any, of affection or warmth. A Mother's Day card might arrive from Ursula, with a handwritten message inside: "Hope you have a good day. XO." On her birthday: another card, with a single sentence in Ursula's hand, under the Hallmark message. Ursula's addition reads, "Many happy returns of the day."

On rare occasions, Ursula might display nostalgia, at least, for days when things had been good between them—almost as if, for a moment there, she forgot she was angry at her mother, or simply dropped her guard. One time, a few years back, a text message popped up on Eleanor's phone with a picture of Lulu and Orson rolling out pie dough and a sentence: "Probably not as flaky as yours." The day Ursula sent that, Eleanor felt close to euphoric. Maybe it was the beginning of better days to come. Only it wasn't.

The last time Ursula displayed one of her brief, hope-inspiring bursts of what appeared to be interest in connecting with Eleanor was a couple of years back. Out of the blue, Ursula had called her.

"I was trying to remember that book you used to read to us, where the mother bakes a potato for the girl to put in her pocket to keep her hands warm walking to school in winter. I wanted to read it to Lulu."

"*Understood Betsy,*" Eleanor told her.

"You baked me a potato one time," Ursula said. "For my walk to the bus."

Eleanor remembers now how happy she felt that day Ursula asked her about the book. Of all the things she'd done over the years, as a mother, it was a potato she'd baked, wrapped in foil, and stuck into Ursula's pocket, that had seemed—for a moment anyway—to soften her heart.

Times like these, it seems to Eleanor that maybe Ursula wants Eleanor to be part of her life again, as opposed to simply tolerating her. Times like these, Eleanor has allowed herself to hope things are getting better between the two of them. Eleanor may even imagine a trip they could take together—a weekend with the children to Maine, a night, just the two of them, in Brookline. They'd go shopping, or to the ballet, maybe. Like mothers and daughters she sees in cafés sometimes, sharing a glass of wine or out for a walk together—something as simple as that.

They never seem to last, these moments when Ursula reaches out to her. It's like a wave washing up on the sand when the tide comes in. The water touches your feet, comes all the way up to your beach towel. Then recedes. In the end, she's gone again.

Or Ursula is there, but not really. No sooner does she extend her hand to her mother than she withdraws it. She resumes her old way of dealing with Eleanor: occasional exchanges of superficial information—about Orson's soccer team, Lulu's violin recital—as if she were a receptionist, or someone's personal assistant. Anyone but Eleanor's daughter.

Sometimes this is the hardest, Eleanor thinks—when your adult child goes through the motions. Not as a way of bringing the two of you together. More as a way of keeping you at arm's length.

The moments of greatest distance seem always to come at those times when a daughter needs her mother most. Times when things are hardest—this one, for instance—Ursula drops off the face of the earth.

Eleanor asks herself: After all this time, what has happened to all that love she had for Ursula? How long can you keep loving a person whose actions keep hurting you? Does a person's heart freeze over eventually, like a pond in winter?

Hers never does. Not for her child, anyway.

"I have no control over how Ursula chooses to see me," Eleanor tells Al. "Ursula will always be my daughter. I will always love her. If she lets me back into her life, that will be a great day. If she never does, I'll keep loving her anyway."

128.

Good at love

For over four years now, Eleanor's been working on the manuscript for her graphic novel, *The Amazing Adventures of Mineral Man*. It's almost finished now. All that remains are the last few chapters, but for the first time in her many years as a writer, Eleanor has no idea how to end the story. Over breakfast with the children that week, she brings up the problem with her story.

"I need Mineral Man to perform his most heroic deed ever," she tells Orson. "But it can't be like something a regular superhero would do. Mineral Man is not the type who bounds up tall buildings or climbs out onto the wings of planes in midair to capture bad guys."

"Maybe Mineral Man can deactivate a bomb that's about to blow up New York City," Orson suggests. Eleanor shakes her head.

"How about he comes up with a vaccine?" Lulu suggests.

"He should do something that involves his greatest superpower," Eleanor says. "The thing that sets him apart from all the other superheroes."

"What's Mineral Man's superpower?" Orson asks her.

Strangely, Eleanor has never asked herself this question, but the answer comes to her easily.

"It has to do with love," Eleanor tells her grandson. "Mineral Man is really good at love." Like someone else they all know.

129.

A boy, a girl, five dogs, and a llama

Since her breakup with Guy, Eleanor has made a point of not following news concerning the final leg of his quest. Then it turns out they're airing a segment about him on television during Orson and Lulu's vacation week visit with Eleanor. Remembering how much Orson had loved the IMAX movie about Ernest Shackleton the three of them had watched together a few years back, she tunes in to the broadcast.

In the segment, the reporter explains that Guy Macdowell's back in the United States at the moment, recuperating, following a life-threatening accident on the ice sheet. He'll be back to complete his historic quest as soon as he's able. Meanwhile, he's embarked on a fundraising tour.

Eleanor is in the kitchen with Orson and Lulu when the program comes on.

"That's the person that used to be your boyfriend, right?" Orson says. It's always Orson who raises the potentially awkward topics, Lulu who avoids them.

"He's my friend," Eleanor says. Leave it at that.

"Why didn't you get married?" Orson asks her.

"Even when two people love each other it doesn't always work out," Eleanor tells him.

"Like my dad and my mom," Orson says. "They love each other, too. It just didn't work out. Maybe you loved my mom's dad, too, back when my mom was a kid. Maybe that just didn't work out, either. Lots of things just don't work out, right?"

This isn't the message Eleanor would have chosen for her grandson to take away from the conversation, but she can't argue the point. Maybe the real wonder is not that things don't always work out between two people who love each other, but how amazing and wonderful it is that they ever do. Eleanor thinks of Elijah and Miriam—young and in love. Jason and his partner, Hank. Al and Teresa. She thinks of Toby's hero, Jimmy Carter, and his wife, Rosalynn. The Obamas.

"It's great when someone finds a partner they love and they make a family together," Eleanor tells Orson. "You may do that someday. I'd say the odds are good."

What she knows now, that she didn't before, is that a family may take many forms. A family might include children, it might not. It might, like Eleanor's, include the child of an ex-husband's second wife, or a ten-year-old loner who rides his bike over to the house every afternoon, even in the month of February, to sit with you while you milk the goats.

"You don't necessarily need to have a partner, either," Eleanor says. "Look at your uncle Toby. Look at me. A person can be happy without being in love or getting married."

Orson looks dubious. Lulu agrees. "I'm never getting married," she says.

"I'm definitely getting married," Orson offers. "My wife is going to be beautiful. We'll have two kids, a boy and a girl, and five dogs, and a llama. Also a boat."

"Sounds like a perfect plan," Eleanor says.

"Good luck with that," says Lulu.

The children return to Vermont, sending Eleanor occasional texts. From Ursula, no communication. Eleanor learns from Al that Jake is no longer contesting the divorce or filing for custody.

130.

"When does it get to be your turn?"

It's Eleanor and Toby's bowling night. Outside, in the parking lot, one of the men from the Akersville fire and police squad, Cam's old teammate Quince, calls out a greeting to Eleanor.

"So when are we going out for a drink?" he says. "I'm still waiting."

"Maybe one of these days," Eleanor tells him. "I've got my hands full at the moment with my family."

Quince starts to head into the bowling alley. Then he stops, turns around. He has a kind face. Eleanor always remembered that about him, even from way back in softball days. "When does it get to be your turn, Eleanor?" he asks her. "Nobody's going to drop dead if you take a night off."

Eleanor just laughs.

As the two of them take their places at their lane, Eleanor watches her son lacing up his shoes—remembering how many months it took Cam to teach him that skill, how Toby struggled, and how proud he was the first time he managed to tie a knot by himself. The picture comes to Eleanor of her son and his father, making a high five. It was hard to say which of them looked happier.

Ever since Toby's release from the hospital—a full year ago now—the family has celebrated the return of Toby's health, but she's noticed a change in him recently. His shoulders seem slumped, and the way he carries the bag containing his ball—Al's birthday present right after he got out of isolation—suggests that even a fourteen-pound ball feels heavy to him. Normally Toby would bowl for two hours at least, but twenty minutes into their game, he tells Eleanor he'd like to go home.

"I guess I just didn't have it in me tonight," Toby says, heading to bed.

"I think we should go see Dr. Fleischman," Eleanor tells him. No argument.

131.

A bad season for cork people

The cancer is back. The bone marrow transplant Toby's doctors had never set much store by has suddenly and dramatically failed. All those good cells they'd pumped into Toby's body are being overtaken again by the ones that kill a person.

It's March now—a time Eleanor has always associated with springtime coming, garden planting on the horizon, sailing cork people with her children. For Eleanor, March always signaled new beginnings. More even than January did.

Nothing about the season feels good this time, and not just because the trees are bare of leaves, the remnants of snowdrifts receding from the edges of the road, a bitter wind whipping over the field. Down at the waterfall, Eleanor guesses, the brook will be racing from the runoff as it always does at this time of year, but for the first time since she can remember, Eleanor doesn't walk down to the bridge and the brook to take in the sight. The days aren't quite as short as they were in midwinter, but a more profound darkness has settled over Eleanor and her family now. Toby's white cell count is dropping daily. This time the doctors have nothing further to offer.

We did all we could, they say.

When Eleanor asked about a second bone marrow transplant, Dr. Fleischman shook her head. "The one we tried was a poor match, but that one was the best we had," she told them.

"No point putting Toby through another transplant with a donor specimen that's even farther from what we need." Even if they found a reasonable match, Toby was probably too weak now to receive it.

They give him hemoglobin, which seems, briefly, to restore some of Toby's energy, but the doctors remain clear. All they can hope for now is a temporary reprieve, nothing more, the doctor tells them. He may get a few good weeks from the treatment. Not more than that.

The ground under Eleanor's feet gives way.

132.

John Lennon only got to be 40

April. The snow has disappeared. Crocuses push through the no-longer-frozen ground. Down the road from the farm, the water races over the rocks again. Some things, at least, never change.

Elijah interrupts his tour with the band to come back to the farm. He wants to spend as much time as he can with Toby. "If you want to see him while he's still got strength," the doctors advise, "now is probably the time."

The brothers are eating breakfast with their feet up on the porch railing—a rare early spring day warm enough to sit outside this way. Out in the field, Bernadette stands on a boulder chewing a crab-apple. Under the eaves, a robin—the first of the season—swoops in and out, carrying twigs. Same as always, every year at this time, she's building her nest.

"I guess I'm going to die, huh?" Toby says to Elijah. The two of them are finishing their cereal before heading to another doctor's appointment.

"I want to play you something," Elijah says. It's John Prine's *The Tree of Forgiveness*—the last record he made. Elijah has the whole album on his cell phone.

Now he plays Toby a song from the album called "Summer's End."

At this particular moment—the two brothers eating cereal together as they have all their lives, with the first day of summer still months away—it seems as if John Prine is talking just to the two of them. The song is about endings—all the things that don't last forever though you wished they did. He lists some favorites: swimsuits on the line . . . stars . . . valentines.

Elijah knows all the words to the song. Across from him, Toby hums along and bangs out the beat as if he were a drummer in the band.

Elijah's voice cracks when he gets to a line *"Summer's end came faster than we wanted."* He starts to cry.

Nobody talks about this but they both understand how unlikely it is that Toby will experience another summer. Back in December, Toby celebrated his fortieth birthday. Odds are slim he'll make it to forty-one.

Now Toby takes his brother's hand. He hardly ever sings but now he does, throwing his head back like a dog howling at the moon. As if the one in need of comfort is Elijah, not himself.

"Come on home, come on home, no you don't have to be alone."

"It's going to be okay," Toby says.

Elijah spends a full week back on the farm with his brother. They play Parcheesi and go bowling—only one frame because Toby doesn't have much energy these days. The two of them cook up one of Toby's wild dinners—pasta with anchovies and hot peppers and walnuts and goat cheese. Elijah teaches Toby to play a C and D7 chord on the ukulele. Toby gives Elijah two of his favorite mineral specimens from his collection—obsidian for Elijah and rhodochrosite for Miriam. The two of them hike into the woods—this, too, is hard for Toby now—to check out the old treehouse they built together with Cam one summer long ago, where they used to hang out together playing Ninja Turtles. Toby was always Donatello. Elijah, Michelangelo.

It's a good week. Toby's energy is failing, but he rallies for Elijah, he rallies, and when he can't do much, Elijah takes out his guitar and plays for Toby. Sometimes they just sit by the woodstove together. No need to say much. They know where they stand.

Every afternoon they fix a pot of hot chocolate and play *The Tree of Forgiveness* album on Elijah's iPhone. Elijah never says this, but Eleanor understands what he's doing: he's imprinting a memory here for later. Every time he listens to this one, his brother will be with him. Even when he's not anymore.

They're on the porch again with the sun going down. It's chilly enough they've got their winter jackets on, their feet on the railing.

"Play that song again," Toby tells him. "The one where John Prine talks about going to heaven. I love that part where he says when he gets there he's going to kiss the pretty girl on the tilt-a-whirl."

He's talking about a song called "When I Get to Heaven," where John Prine sings about all the things he's going to do when he gets to heaven. Including the kissing part. Elijah pushes *Play*.

"You know something?" Toby tells his brother. "I never kissed a girl before."

"I'm sorry about that." Elijah is not the type to pretend things are great when they're not.

"It's okay if I die," Toby tells Elijah. "I've had a lot of great times. I love my family. I know my family loves me. Everything's been pretty great."

Here's the moment Elijah might tell Toby to think positive. He might still beat the cancer. There might be some great medical breakthrough.

He says none of this. There's never a point, lying to Toby. He always knows what's real.

"Look at John Lennon," Toby says now. "He didn't get to be that old, but I bet he had a really great time while he was alive. Playing with the Beatles and everything. Making up all those songs."

The two of them sit there awhile as John Prine sings to them from Elijah's phone. It's almost as if he's calling them up, having a conversation—just the three of them.

"There's only one thing that makes me a little sad about what's happening to me," Toby tells his little brother. (No matter what, Elijah will always be this to Toby. His little brother.) He waits for the song to finish to tell his brother what he says now.

"I wish I got to have sex one time. I wish I knew what it was like."

"I get it," Elijah tells Toby. "We're going to take care of that."

133.

The tilt-a-whirl

Toby is familiar with two airports. The one in Boston, where Eleanor has brought him every summer for ten years now for his annual visit with Al and Teresa and Flora, and Seattle, where they pick him up from his flight. Now it's him and Elijah on the plane. A different kind of trip. Different destination.

Toby's surprised, when he and Elijah land in Las Vegas, to see slot machines lining the walls, with flashing lights and spinning rainbow wheels and people sitting in front of them, dropping coins in the slots and yanking on levers.

"Is that supposed to be fun?" Toby asks Elijah.

"Some people think so. They're hoping to hit the jackpot."

"How does that happen?"

"Every once in a while a whole lot of coins pour out of the machine."

"Like milking a goat," Toby says. "But not really."

Elijah has rented a car. Under other circumstances, he would have gone for an economy model, but he's reserved a BMW Z4 Roadster. Red would have been the obvious choice, but Elijah says black is cooler.

According to Google Maps, the drive will take a little over seven hours. They could have cut their travel time down considerably by flying into Sacramento instead, but in Elijah's opinion, the trip across the desert is part of the experience. They'll listen to Sirius radio and stop wherever they want for any kind of food they choose, though Elijah has also brought along a selection of beef jerky. Four different varieties.

For long stretches theirs is the only car on the road, which makes it possible for Elijah to crank the BMW up to a hundred.

"If you want to give it a try behind the wheel, you can do that here," he tells Toby. "We aren't going to crash into anyone out here, that's for sure. Just take it a little slower."

Except for at the station house, times he'd take a child into the cab of the truck and pretend they were going off to fight a fire, Toby has never sat in the driver's seat before. He draws a long, deep breath before turning the key in the ignition. "I'm going to pretend I'm Tom Cruise," he tells Elijah.

"Tom Cruise on a slow day," Elijah suggests. "Tom Cruise, picking his kid up from school on a dirt road in Akersville, how about that?"

The desert stretches before them as far as the eye can see. Perfectly flat. Not a house or gas station or another vehicle in sight. At the wheel, Toby sits up very straight. He's whistling "Zip-a-Dee-Doo-Dah."

The BMW continues along the highway. At eighteen miles an hour, this may be the slowest anybody ever drove on this particular stretch of highway.

"You could go a little faster if you wanted, Tobes," Elijah tells him.

"We're not in a rush, right?" Toby says. "I was just thinking I wish this trip lasted forever."

At one point a roadside stand appears, with a sign out front: "Fresh Jerky."

"That seems like a contradiction in terms," Elijah observes. In all their years together, he has never spoken to his brother any differently from how he speaks to other people. The thing is, Toby always understands.

"That's a good one," he says.

At one point, Toby tells Elijah he needs to pee.

"Be my guest." Toby pulls over alongside a cactus.

"It's a great feeling, peeing on the desert," he says, zipping up his pants. "You could make a design in the dirt. Or your initials if you had enough pee."

It's almost dark when they reach the Palomino Ranch. The place looks like a normal hotel—an unremarkable building surrounded by a metal gate and beyond that, sagebrush and cactus, not much else. Elijah has wondered if business might be slow as a result of the pandemic, but the parking lot is full. Trucks, mostly. Not many minivans and SUVs. Though it's late April now, Christmas lights still hang out front, and a giant wreath no different from what a person might expect to see outside a Holiday Inn. In the lobby, the decorations suggest a Valentine's Day theme.

"I guess you could say it's always Valentine's Day, in a place like this," Toby says. "Seeing as how this place is about love."

Elijah has explained things to Toby. "Not that I've ever been someplace like this myself," he adds.

Toby's studying everything. The chairs, the paintings on the walls, a bowl of mints. Most of all, the people here. Mostly men. All ages. Nobody who looks like him, or like Elijah, for that matter.

"I thought you had a lot of experience," Toby says. "With sex."

"Not this kind."

The woman at the reception desk is dressed differently from normal receptionists. She has on a tight golden dress, cut very low, and when she walks over to the concierge desk to get them what she refers to as the menu of services, they can see she's wearing extremely high heels.

"Those shoes probably aren't very comfortable," Toby says. This is definitely not the kind of footwear women favor in Akersville. Or even Manchester.

"Are you two businessmen?" she asks them. "Out for a fun getaway?"

"This is my brother," Toby says. His voice, whenever he speaks the word, is full of pride. "He's showing me the ropes."

"You two will probably want to settle in first." The receptionist hands Elijah a pair of keys. She tells them to call her Tanya. "Take a shower, then come on down to have a drink at the saloon. The girls will be waiting for you."

Elijah has reserved the Cowboy Suite, one of the lower-priced accommodations. The most important part isn't what goes on in this room. Still, Toby checks everything out: the velvet chair, the place you put two quarters in a machine to make the bed vibrate. The large flat-screen TV, with a remote.

"I don't get it," he says. "Why would a person come here and watch TV?"

In the car earlier that day, Elijah had explained to him how it worked at the ranch. "There's going to be a lot of different women. You get to meet them and decide which one you'd like to spend time with. Then she'll take you to her room. You get to be with her for an hour."

Elijah figures that this is probably a long enough session for Toby's first time. He's brought enough cash that if his brother wants, he can have another round the next morning. They don't have to drive back to the airport until noon.

Elijah fills Toby in on a few last details. He reviews the part about condoms, though Toby knows about those. "Sometimes, when a guy gets excited, things might happen faster than he wants," Elijah tells him. "You might want to slow it down if you can. To make the experience more exciting. You might try thinking about something else."

"Why would I think about anything else when I'm in bed with a woman that doesn't have any clothes on?"

"Just to . . . I don't know . . . keep the experience going a little longer."

"I want to get to know her first," Toby says. "I'll ask about her family and her hobbies. I'll tell her about me if she's interested."

Over the sound system, the Weeknd is singing "Save Your Tears." He's gotten to the part about breaking his girlfriend's heart. Running away.

"I'd never do that," Toby tells Elijah. "Run away. I'd stay forever if she wanted me to."

"Not too likely, buddy," Elijah says. "I didn't bring enough cash for that."

"I just hope I don't do the wrong thing," Toby says.

"Don't worry about any of this. The woman you're with will be an expert. She'll know what to do."

One thing, though. Elijah needs to explain this part to Toby. Knowing his brother as he does. His brother's heart. That thing Toby said earlier, about this place being all about love.

"What the woman is going to do with you is her job," Elijah explains. Like the waitress at the diner they'd stopped at for their hash browns and eggs that morning. Or Ralph, cleaning out the goat pen. "It's not that she doesn't like you, but she isn't someone to fall in love with. She might have a boyfriend at home. She might even have kids."

"I'll ask her."

"If I were you, I'd leave that aspect of the conversation out."

Toby chooses a woman named Edie. "I knew the second I spotted her, that was the girl for me," he tells Elijah. "The kind you'd kiss on a tilt-a-whirl."

Of all of them, Edie may be the least attractive, measured by the usual standards anyway. She's a little chubby, and short, even in five-inch heels, which she walks on unsteadily. Her breasts are smaller than those of all the others, which Elijah guesses must mean that they're real.

Here's how it works at the ranch: First you sat in the saloon for a while, until you decided which of the women you wanted to go upstairs with—"the girls," they were called, but Toby only applies this term to his goats. Once you made your selection, you approached whatever chair or barstool she was sitting on and introduced yourself.

Elijah asks if Toby would like him to come over to meet Edie with him, just for the introduction part. "I think I can handle it by myself," Toby says. "I'll just explain to her that I never did this before. It will probably be a good idea if I let her know about my brain injury, too. So she won't think I'm just dumb."

"She wouldn't think that," Elijah says. "But you could tell her you're not that experienced. She'll take it from there."

"I wonder if Edie has any pets," Toby says.

Elijah waits for his brother in the bar. Exactly one hour after Toby goes off with Edie, he returns. From the looks of him the experience has gone well.

Over the time Elijah has spent waiting for Toby, he's seen a number of other men return to the bar from their sessions upstairs. They were all on their own—their first stop after, the bar. Whoever the woman might be that they spent the hour with, she certainly didn't go out for a drink with them after.

Edie accompanied Toby back to the saloon. The two of them walk over to the table where Elijah is drinking a beer.

"Now you can tell I wasn't kidding when I told you my little brother is handsome," Toby says to Edie. "Not only that. You should hear him play the guitar."

He has told her about Dog Blue and Miriam and her mbira, and his mineral collection and his kintsugi bowls, and Lulu and Orson and Flora and the goats.

"If you're ever in New Hampshire you should come by our farm," he says.

Elijah studies Edie's face as his brother speaks. He might be wrong, but it seems to him that she has tears in her eyes. Maybe Toby has also told her he's dying. Not as a sympathy ploy. Just because he is.

"You take care of yourself, buddy," Edie says as she gets up to go. Before she returns to her barstool she kisses him on the cheek.

Back in the Cowboy Suite, Elijah asks Toby how it went.

"Edie explained everything. At first I thought I was just going to explode, like there was g-force or something going on inside, but then I did this thing you told me, where I thought about Mrs. Mortenson, and that helped hold it in."

Mrs. Mortenson was a reading teacher Toby had worked with when he attended the special school who wore a bad wig and looked at her watch a lot during their sessions and made him read the same book over and over. *Hop on Pop.* Even after he'd memorized it, so there was no point.

"But you did it, right?" Elijah asks him. "You and Edie had sex?"

"Of course. It was great."

"You could do it again. I brought enough money for another session tomorrow." Three thousand dollars, all told. His budget for the trip, including the car. When he'd explained to Miriam that he wanted to take Toby on this trip, she understood. The recording equipment they were saving up for could wait.

Toby shook his head. "That's a nice offer, Lije," he says "But if it's okay with you, I'd just as soon head out in the morning. I wanted to know what it was like making love to a woman and now I do. I see why people like doing it so much."

Plus, he's tired. He's held up well all day but in the elevator going back to the Cowboy Room he'd leaned on the wall with his eyes closed. For a few hours there, the two of them had almost forgotten this part of the story. The cancer part.

The next morning they drop the keys off at the front desk, where a different woman from the one before is checking in a couple of men dressed in business suits. Today's receptionist wears a green dress, low cut. High heels. When she sees Toby, she gives him a look.

"Edie's a lot prettier than her," Toby says. "Also nicer."

The two of them head out to the parking lot. Toby sits in the passenger seat this time. Elijah reaches over to turn on the Sirius radio.

"If it's okay with you, maybe we can hold off on the music. I want to think for a while. Take it all in." This was a big experience, Toby tells Elijah.

"I get it."

"It's not like she was going to be my girlfriend," Toby says, as they head out onto the highway again, back across the desert. "A girlfriend would have been the best. But life isn't perfect. I already knew that."

134.

An unexpected gift

few days after Toby and Elijah return from Nevada, Al calls. "There's something we need to talk about," he tells Eleanor.

"Teresa and I are flying back east this weekend. We want to have a family meeting."

As always, Flora accompanies them. Flora, Toby's favorite person. Eleanor prepares the dinner they all loved best growing up, spaghetti carbonara. They go out to the barn to see two baby goats born earlier that week. Orson performs a magic trick he's been working on. Making a quarter show up in a person's ear.

They gather in the living room. Ursula has driven over from Vermont, with Lulu and Orson. Elijah and Miriam are here.

Eleanor looks across the room, taking it all in. *Hold on to this moment.* Here sit her three adult children, lined up on the couch just as they had been thirty-five years earlier, the night Eleanor and Cam sat them down to tell them that they weren't going to be married anymore. They had looked so hopeful that night, imagining that the news their parents were about to deliver might involve some wonderful family adventure. A new brother or sister on the way, maybe.

"Your father and I . . . have come to a decision."

"We'll always be your parents. Everything that matters is going to stay exactly the same."

"The important thing is, we love you so much."

Blah, blah, blah, blah, blah.

Now here they are again, all together at the farm, even the three grandchildren. Elijah sits in the middle—the only one of the adult children, besides Teresa and Miriam, of course, who wasn't present that other night long ago, because he wasn't born yet, and never would have been if Cam and Eleanor had stayed together—if his mother, Coco, hadn't come on the scene. Now Elijah's right arm drapes around Toby's shoulders. He rubs Toby's neck. How will they ever get along without him?

At the other end of the couch, Al stands up. He clears his throat and looks at Teresa. She nods. "Estaras bien," she says. "Es tu familia."

"Okay," Al says. He takes a long breath. Whatever it is he's about to tell them, he's having a hard time getting the words out. "So here's the story.

"Teresa and I need to tell you all something. We talked about this a long time." He's taken a set of file cards from his pocket. He studies one, then puts them all away.

"It hasn't been easy making the decision to share this. We know we shouldn't have kept this from you all this time. We hope you'll be able to appreciate our reasons."

"You two aren't getting a divorce, are you?" Lulu asks. When they said "family meeting" she got worried. As usual.

Of course not, Teresa tells her.

"We just love Toby so much," Al continues. "And of course we had to think about Flora."

His voice breaks, saying her name. Teresa stands next to him. She's holding his hand now. Al covers his eyes. When was the last time Eleanor saw him cry? So long ago she can't remember. She gets up now to put her arms around him. Whatever is going on—and she has no idea what it is, no idea in particular why Al would bring up his daughter at this moment—all she knows is that she needs to comfort her son. Whatever age a person's child may be, that never changes.

"Toby knows all of this, by the way. Toby has known from the beginning."

Toby nods. "It's okay, Al," he says. "You don't have to do this."

"But we do." This is Teresa.

Al collects himself. He's sounding, once again, like the Al they know. Firm, steady.

"You all know how much Teresa and I wanted a baby," Al tells them. "We kept trying to convince an agency to let us adopt."

They all remember. The idea that anyone would have ever questioned Al's ability to be a father makes no sense. It never did.

"So we started in on the IVF," Al says. "Meaning, our doctor would harvest some of Teresa's eggs and use a sperm donor to create a fetus. Our child."

Gathered around him now, the family's still trying to understand what this is about.

"Meanwhile," Al continues, "Teresa's family kept talking about how much it meant to them that our baby would have a Mexican heritage, that their grandchild would share their blood. I knew I'd love any child we had, but I can't pretend that I didn't feel a certain regret knowing my genes weren't going to be part of the equation."

He pauses. They are all looking at him.

"Then we thought about Toby."

The room has already been quiet, but when Al says this, something changes. No room has ever felt quieter than this one. It takes a moment, but they're beginning to understand.

"So we bought Toby a plane ticket. We wanted to ask him in person. To be our sperm donor."

The room had been quiet already. Never more so than now.

For the first time since they all sat down together, Toby speaks. "Nobody made me do anything," he says. "We talked a lot. We went to a counselor together, right, Teresa? The counselor wanted to talk to me alone, without Al and Teresa in the room. She wanted to make sure I understood."

Nobody says anything. They wait. Each of them is taking in the news in their own way. Elijah looks interested and curious. Ursula's stunned. Eleanor can't explain this yet, but a feeling of happiness is coming over her, unlike any she's known.

"You all get it," Toby says. "They probably thought I wasn't smart enough to understand what was going on. But I did. I know how reproduction works. It's my brain that got messed up. Not my sperm."

He delivers this observation as easily as he might have when discussing a case of pinkeye or vitamin B_1 deficiency in one of his goats.

"Before you judge us, I want you to understand, we worked really hard to make sure Toby was okay with this," Al tells them.

"Okay? So much better than okay! I got to do something good for my brother and Teresa." Toby's beaming now.

"We worked with a very progressive physician on Vashon Island to procure the specimen," Teresa says.

"The insemination took on the first try."

Nine months later, Flora.

They are all still taking this in when it comes to them why it is that Al and Teresa have chosen this moment to reveal the news. Only now does it come to them what this could mean for Toby. There is, in fact, one more potential bone marrow donor who has yet to be tested—a close blood relative. Close as any of them. She's nine years old.

135.

The same ears. Among other things.

)H(er parents had a long talk with Flora before they made the trip east. They told her everything, including the part about the IVF, and that, biologically, Toby was her parent, not her uncle. Flora took this information in with no evidence of shock or surprise.

"I think I figured that out already," she said. "Nobody told me, but I just got this feeling. Plus, we have the exact same ears."

Like her cousin Lulu, Flora is adamant that her age (though she's six years younger than Lulu) should not rule her out as a bone marrow donor for her uncle.

"It might not be a match," Al reminds them all.

"I know my bone marrow is going to match with Uncle Toby," Flora says. "We're two peas in a pod."

As it turns out, she's right.

A guardian is appointed to assess Flora's competency in making the decision to be a donor at such a young age. "Under normal circumstances, a nine-year-old would be ruled out as an acceptable donor on the grounds that she could not be considered of an age to make the decision on her own," the guardian had written to the hospital ethics committee. What had convinced the committee to allow this was a letter written by Flora herself, explaining her reasons for wanting to become a bone marrow donor. She wrote about the close connection she'd had with Toby for as long as she could remember.

"I love my parents a ton," she wrote. "They're my mom and dad! But Toby is my magic person. If I was in a house and it caught on fire, he'd run in to rescue me. He wouldn't worry about getting hurt. That's how I feel about giving him my bone marrow cells. It makes me happy I get to do that."

Eleanor and Toby drive down to Boston again. Eleanor knows

how many obstacles remain for Toby, how much could still go wrong. For starters, he's weaker this time than he was the first time he underwent a bone marrow transplant. The cancer has advanced. Sometimes, too, Dr. Fleischman has explained to them, even with everything going for them—including a donor like Flora, viewed as a near-perfect match—a person's body may reject the new bone marrow.

Toby could still die. But all Eleanor focuses on, heading over the bridge into the city, is the prospect that thanks to Flora's utterly unexpected gift, her son has a shot at staying alive. For Toby, there's another piece to the story, she knows. Her son is a man who's been delivering baby goats for almost twenty years now. Baby goats, and one human baby—Spyder. But he has never gotten to be a parent, and though he will never question Al's role in Flora's life—nor will Flora—he has been granted this rare opportunity, to know that somewhere on the earth (Whidbey Island, Washington) there's a child whose blood carries his DNA. He always knew this, in fact, but until now, he had to carry the secret. Now he gets to share it.

."Did you ever wonder why Flora hums so much?" he says to Eleanor. "And the part about how much she likes Klondike bars?" Not to mention her interest in rocks and goats, of course.

It made all the sense in the world.

The doctors need to irradiate his existing bone marrow before he can receive Flora's healthy bone marrow. Meanwhile he'll be highly vulnerable to infection and in need of total isolation—for the second time. As much as Toby hates being away from home, he doesn't question this. "I'll be out of here in time to bring the girls up to Verlander's place," he tells his mother. And all the other things he loves: corn season, the annual firefighters' bowling tournament, afternoons in the barn with Spyder, Lulu's fall spelling bee.

For Flora, the procedure of donation is simpler than what Toby has to go through, though not without pain. For the five days leading up to the extraction of her bone marrow, Flora receives a daily injection of something called granulocyte-stimulating factor—G-CSF—to encourage white blood cell growth. On the day of the actual donation, a nurse places a needle in each of her arms.

As her parents have explained to Flora, one of these needles removes blood from her body and sends it to a machine to circulate it and collect stem cells. The second needle returns the blood to her body.

They perform the procedure two days in a row. Teresa stays with Flora at the hospital. In the morning, Al and Eleanor relieve her. Later that day, Flora's stem cells are pumped into Toby's body.

That night, before leaving the hospital, Al wheels her past Toby's room. She can't go in, but they wave.

One of Flora's arms is a little sore but otherwise she's fine. "I'm going to write a report for school, all about bone marrow transplants," she tells Eleanor, before they head to the airport to fly home.

Within a week, Toby looks like a different person. Eleanor can't enter his room yet and won't be able to do so for a few months, but as they did before, the two of them wave through the glass.

"Everyone's doing a great job here taking care of me," Toby says. Back home, Ralph and Spyder are coming over twice a day to look after the goats. The thought comes to Eleanor—though fleetingly—that for once, none of what's going on depends on her. Maybe she doesn't have to try so hard all the time. Life goes on, is all.

136.

How to give a homeless person a sandwich

Eleanor's in Concord, shopping for art supplies to bring Toby at the hospital, when a homeless woman camped out on the sidewalk in front of the bagel store catches her attention. It takes a moment to realize. It's Coco.

The weather's warm—lilac time—but Coco's bundled up in what appear to be several layers of sweaters and a pair of white leather boots. They used to be white, anyway. She has spread what looks to be a doormat out on the sidewalk with a cardboard sign that says, "No amount too small." There's a cane on the ground next to her and an old pizza box for donations.

Eleanor hasn't laid eyes on Coco since that day she showed up in their driveway at the farm demanding money for her fabricated allegations concerning Toby. She should hate Coco for that. But Coco is also Elijah's mother. Eleanor has known Coco since she was eight years old.

What would it cost her to put a couple of bills in Coco's box? Only to do so would involve some kind of interaction between the two of them. She doesn't have it in her.

Eleanor steps into the bagel store. "Tuna salad sandwich on a sesame seed bagel," she tells the kid behind the counter. After all these years she remembers this. That Coco loved tuna fish.

"I need to ask a favor," she says. "When you get a minute, would you mind bringing the sandwich to the woman on the sidewalk out front? Wait till I'm gone, okay?"

After she pays for the sandwich, she heads down the street to pick up a set of oil pastels for Toby and—because he misses the stars so much, in the hospital—a card showing the constellations. But Eleanor can't get the sight of Coco out of her head—her sunken face, those glazed, expressionless eyes.

This is what comes to her then. Coco, the onetime cartwheel queen of the softball field, the woman who appeared to break up her family, has fallen just about as low as a person can go. Can't Eleanor even place a sandwich in her hands? Now of all times—her son's health restored, thanks to something close to a miracle—shouldn't she extend some small fraction of generosity to a person sorely in need of it?

Crazily, a question comes to Eleanor—the same one Toby asks himself, on occasion: *What would Jimmy Carter do?*

It's almost her turn to pay, but she sets down the purchases she was about to make and walks out of the store. The bagel place is a block and a half away. She's running now.

"Did you bring that woman the sandwich yet?" she asks the boy at the counter. Catching her breath.

"It's still there," he says, pointing to a bag. "I'll bring it out to her as soon as we're through the lunchtime rush."

"No need," Eleanor tells him. "I'll give it to her myself."

She could not have imagined doing this thirty years ago, the first time she drove up to the house she used to live in with Cam, after moving out, and saw, hanging on their old clothesline, a row of bikini panties clearly belonging to Coco. Or that other day—a more recent one—when Coco appeared in that same driveway with the demand that Eleanor cough up five thousand dollars or see her son accused of sexually violating a seven-year-old. That day, Eleanor could sooner have slapped Coco across the face than offer her a tuna fish sandwich on a sesame bagel.

Here's what Eleanor knows that she didn't before—a gift that comes only with age. Whatever injury Coco has inflicted, no angry recriminations Eleanor might deliver to the sad figure on the sidewalk outside the bagel shop will erase any of that. Eleanor might just as well hold tight to a red-hot poker as carry around her anger over injuries incurred in a whole other lifetime from the one she inhabits now. The only person who gets burned will be herself.

When you can't look a person in the eye, you are telling them they don't exist. Eleanor knows this better than most, as the mother of Toby.

She thinks about how it has been for her son all these years, living as he has, surrounded by so many people who fail to acknowledge his humanity. People who act as if he's invisible.

What's the difference, really, between the people who look away when her son passes, and herself, willing to pay for a sandwich for a woman at the bottom of her luck, but not to put that sandwich in her hands herself?

At first, when she gets back out on the sidewalk after picking up the sandwich, it appears Coco has left. She's not sitting on the patch of sidewalk she'd been crouched on before, with her cane and her sign and those once-white leather boots.

Oh God, Eleanor thinks. *I missed my chance.*

Then Eleanor spots her. Coco has moved over to the other side of the bagel store. Maybe the sun was in her eyes. Maybe she just wanted a minor change of scene.

She approaches the small, crumpled figure on the sidewalk. She bends low to reach Coco at eye level. She extends her hand, holding the sandwich.

"I thought you might be hungry." She's about to say more—offer a memory, maybe, of how the two of them used to make tuna fish sandwiches together for the children on softball nights before heading to the field to watch Cam play. It was Coco who suggested they put chopped-up hard-boiled eggs in the tuna fish. And toast the bread. *You always loved tuna fish sandwiches*, Eleanor might say now.

Their eyes meet.

On Coco's face, no flash of recognition. Not even the slightest indication that they knew each other once. She accepts the sandwich. Nothing more. She's already tearing off the paper as Eleanor turns to go.

One moment stands out for Eleanor, from that summer she and Cam took Coco to Maine with them: They had rented a house in Ogunquit—a big splurge for Cam and Eleanor. They'd invited her to come along to help with the children. She was probably no more than thirteen years old then—a child herself. That was probably one reason why Al and Ursula and Toby all adored Coco as they did. She still actually enjoyed playing Red Rover and tag. Though it was also on the Ogunquit trip that she'd gotten her period for the first time, and Eleanor had taught her how to use a tampon.

Cam and Eleanor were in a good place in their marriage that summer—the last time that was true for the two of them, maybe. They had made love every night over the week they spent in Maine. Not only in the night. In the early hours of their last morning at that beach house, they made love again, when they thought nobody in the house was awake.

After, Eleanor had stepped out of the bedroom to take a shower, with nothing on but one of Cam's T-shirts. Her hair would have been a mess. To Coco, young as she was—and already crazy about Cam, no doubt—it must have been obvious what Eleanor and Cam had been doing.

Eleanor remembers now how the girl had appeared to her at that moment—how small and thin Coco looked, sitting by herself in the kitchen eating a bowl of cornflakes and flipping through a J.Crew catalog—a lonely only child. She probably heard Eleanor's and Cam's voices through their closed bedroom door.

Thirteen years old, Coco was in that excruciating place being both child and woman. She was both and neither, stuck in the middle, with a wild crush on Eleanor's handsome husband, who'd just made love to Eleanor. Of course she wanted Eleanor to disappear off the face of the earth. Of course she wanted to marry Cam and have babies of her own with him. Of course it was all going to fall apart.

She couldn't have said this that winter, five years later, when Cam told her he'd fallen in love with Coco, but she knows this now: Coco was never going to remain with Cam forever. Cam was a fantasy for Coco, dreamed up when she was not yet in her teens. Coco was a fantasy for Cam, too. In the eyes of his wife, he was a failure. With Coco, Cam got to be a hero again.

137.

Home. Again.

It's almost Christmas when Toby returns to the farm. This is the second time he's been released from the hospital following a long period of isolation from a bone marrow transplant. But this time feels different. Where, after the first transplant, the doctors spoke cautiously of "remission" and said "there's still a long road ahead," this time the hematologist is close to unequivocal in her assessment of Toby's status.

"We'll want to follow up in six months," she says, "but Toby's out of the woods."

The first thing he does when they get back to the farm is check on the goats. Spyder's already there in the barn to greet him. He's put up a "Welcome Home Toby" sign in cardboard letters and tied a ribbon around every one of the girls' necks.

From where she stands at the kitchen window, looking out to the barn, Eleanor offers a silent prayer.

138.

Opposite ends of the bench,
and the Hoʻoponopono prayer

January 2022.

Toby's weak, and he has to be careful of infection still, but back in the barn now, working alongside Spyder. In years past, they've had Jesus fixed, so he won't smell so bad. "We can't give him up," Toby tells Eleanor. "He's Spyder's first goat."

A full year has passed now since Jake headed off to the capital to protest the election. He's living in a one-bedroom apartment in Bellows Falls. Ursula and the children have stayed in their house. Her divorce from Jake is almost final now. He has contested nothing.

The relationship between Ursula and Eleanor remains as it has been for a long time now—Ursula keeping a chilly distance from her mother, as always. She still drops the children off at the farm for a night on the way to one of her weekend getaways to stay with her friend Kat in Concord, but Eleanor's given up inviting her daughter in for a cup of tea when she comes, or asking if she'd like to stay for dinner when she returns to pick the children up. Eleanor's glad to know that her daughter is getting a little time without the responsibilities of children and home—something that she, at Ursula's age, had never allowed herself. Most of all, she's grateful for the times she gets to see her grandchildren.

All through those hard, cold days—over a thousand of them—when Ursula wasn't speaking to her, after the birth of Lulu, Eleanor had prayed that some big event might take place, Jason would have called it their come-to-Jesus moment, when the two of them, mother and daughter, would sit down and work things out. One of them would cry. Maybe they both would. Ursula would need to tell Eleanor some hard things about how it had been for her in their family, and Eleanor would resist the impulse to defend herself or offer her side of the story. She'd just listen. The experience would probably hurt, but she would learn some things. When it was over, they'd put their arms around each other as they used to when Ursula was young.

They'd say *Thank you. I'm sorry. I forgive you. I love you*—the Ho'oponopono prayer she keeps tacked to the wall over her drawing table. Things would be better then. They would always remember that day.

After that everything would be different. Like before.

For a long time, this had been Eleanor's dream. As time passed, it seemed less likely that the scene she envisioned would ever take place. The big moment when the two of them talked it all out, screamed it out, cried it out, has never happened. Though that three-year stretch of radio-silence ended, what took its place has been an ongoing state of perpetual uneasiness in which Eleanor walks on eggshells when in the presence of her daughter, always aware that at any moment she could once again be shut out of Ursula's life, and that of her grandchildren.

Eleanor has let go of her expectations of the night at the ballet with her daughter, the trip they might make—just the two of them—to Paris, or just Boston, or shopping at Marshalls, sharing a dressing room, laughing. On her better days, she chooses instead to accept the distance that will very likely always exist between her only daughter and herself, much as she has accepted Toby's brain injury, and found a way to appreciate—even celebrate—what remains. With Ursula, it's been harder to let go of the old dream she had for the two of them. But what choice does she have?

Who knows what the future may bring? Ursula will grow older. At some point, she may experience with Lulu or Orson some form of what Eleanor has discovered as her own children have grown older and made their own lives: that even a person who tries her best raising her children will probably disappoint them in a variety of ways—some inconsequential, some vast and painful. One day Ursula's children may tell their mother they need boundaries. They may recommend she go into therapy. Work on herself. One of them may even speak the words, to Ursula, that Ursula spoke to Eleanor once. *Don't come back. Don't ever come back.*

Eleanor prays no child of hers will ever know the grief of hearing the words "I don't want you in my life." But if that happens, she hopes they can discover, as she has, that it is possible to survive even a loss as terrible as that one. The sadness Eleanor feels, that her daughter has chosen to distance herself as she has, never goes away. But she has discovered how to carry on, too. There is a way even the hardest experience may offer lessons. Painful though they may be.

When a child estranges herself from you (there's that word Eleanor tries not to employ when speaking of her situation, but it applies) you can allow it to crush you. Or you rebuild your world—smaller maybe, less ambitious, imperfect, with space for sorrow, but also occasional joy. Maybe you see your child only once a year. Maybe never. Maybe she doesn't want you to see your grandchildren. She may rewrite the history of her childhood, casting you as the source of her greatest trauma. She gets to have her story. But nobody can take away yours—that you loved her, you tried your best. The door remains open.

Now Ursula and Jake sit on opposite ends of the bench at Orson's games and Lulu's recitals—same as Eleanor and Cam used to do, back when Al and Ursula and Toby were young, performing the same sad ritual of transferring them from one parent's house to the apartment of the other and back again. Eleanor takes no joy at seeing her daughter in the place she inhabited once, the place she swore she'd never go. But loss is a great teacher. So is failure. Maybe, having finally acknowledged her need to leave her marriage, Ursula may one day be less quick to judge her mother over the end of hers.

A thought comes to Eleanor: For so long—most of her life, in fact—she's been waiting for the next big thing to happen. Waiting for a baby to be born, a child to begin school, another child after that. A third. She kept waiting for her husband to start making money, and when it became clear that wasn't happening, she waited for news that she'd sold a book, then waited again for the check to arrive, and an idea to come, for the book that came next. She waited for summer, and for her tomatoes to ripen, for Toby to master *Hop on Pop,* for Al to stop being depressed, for a man to show up in her life—and once he did, for another night with him in another hotel room, and for the charges to be dropped against her younger son, a grandchild to visit, a daughter to forgive her, a bone marrow donor to come up as a match.

Eleanor has waited in doctors' offices for results of a blood test, a biopsy, a scan. She's waited for a new president to be elected, as if everything would be okay once that happened.

And a new president did get elected. And there are still angry, dangerous people out in the world—her former son-in-law among them.

For as long as Eleanor can remember, no matter what was going on in her life at a particular moment and however hard it might be, she has always been ready to believe that some other, better time lies ahead if she just waits for it.

Eleanor no longer waits for much or allows herself to pin her hopes to some magical turn of events in the future. It isn't that her life holds everything she has hoped it might. The gulf between herself and Ursula remains, for Eleanor, her greatest source of regret. What she aspires to now is acceptance.

There have been times over some of those years when despair overtook her. She's past all that. It's been months since Eleanor has heard from Ursula, but she carries on. What else can a person do?

Let life be good enough is what she asks for these days. *Good enough* is more attainable.

This is my life, she tells herself. In the balance, she considers it a good one.

139.

Home free

Six months after his release from the hospital, Toby and Eleanor drive to Boston to check in with his doctors. At the end of his day of testing, Dr. Fleischman delivers the news: Toby's cancer free. "Go live your life," she tells him. "We won't be seeing you here again."

140.
Not the type to end up on the cover of *Time* magazine

Eleanor's editor, Rita, calls with a question. "Whatever happened to that graphic novel you were working on?"

She doesn't add but could: "Haven't you been working on that book for—like—five years maybe? Six?"

Eleanor's been working on her graphic novel, *Mineral Man,* for almost seven years, actually—the longest she's worked on any project, ever, other than the biggest project of her life, which was raising her family.

"The book is basically finished except for the last chapter," Eleanor tells Rita. She's written nine or ten different endings. None ever feels right.

"I keep trying to figure out what Mineral Man does at the end," she says. "He can't just keep taking minerals out of his pocket and fixing people's problems. There needs to be something big. Something of meaning."

"Have him find a cure for every crazy virus that keeps popping up, just when we think they're over," Rita says. "Not just another vaccine. Something to wipe all viruses off the face of the earth." She moves on to another fantasy, involving eradicating terrible Supreme Court justices, homophobia, sexism, racism. Getting rid of toxic U.S. senators and congressmen, convincing everyone to give up their cars and start riding on public transportation to reduce their carbon footprint. The list goes on and on.

"Saving the world is not Mineral Man's style," Eleanor tells her editor. "He's not the type to end up on the cover of *Time* magazine as Person of the Year or win a Nobel Peace Prize. I just want to find one really good, simple thing he can do that makes the world a better place."

141.

Target shooting with Donny and Marie

A woman Eleanor has known since they were both raising young children greets Eleanor at the supermarket as the two of them stand over the produce. "Toby bouncing back?" she asks. "Life back to normal yet?"

Normal life. Eleanor no longer knows what that might be. Or if the concept exists.

"I'm not complaining," she says.

Eleanor sees less of Raine these days, now that she's working full time at the nursing home, but Spyder rides his bike to the farm every afternoon as soon as school gets out to help out with the goats. Through the woods, she sometimes hears the sound of gunshots coming from the direction of Walt's old house, times he takes out his grandfather's old Colt .45 automatic for target shooting practice. Toby has convinced Spyder to take down the Donny and Marie album cover he'd been using for a target before.

"It's not that I'm some big fan or anything," Toby tells Spyder. "It just doesn't seem like a great idea, shooting at a picture of a couple of kids that way. What do you say we paint you a nice red circle to aim at instead?"

Elijah and Miriam cut a record and go out on tour again, no longer as an opening act. On one of his visits to the farm, Elijah comes upon Al's invention from long ago, the TB-10 that he made for Toby back when he was a teenager, hoping to interest Toby in making music again. Somewhere along the line Al must have brought the device back to the farm.

Elijah charges it up. The sounds that come out of it are like nothing he and Miriam have ever heard. He calls Al in Seattle.

"This thing is amazing," he says. "Do you think I could borrow it? We could use this in our shows."

In addition to guitar, mandolin, bass, and mbira, Dog Blue now features Elijah on the TB-10. Wherever the band plays, people want to know where they can get one.

"It's a one of a kind," Elijah tells them.

142.

If you're happy and you know it

Ralph, the man who has worked with Toby in the barn all these years running the cheese operation, decides to retire, but his son Pete—somewhat less knowledgeable on the subject of goat farming and cheese-making, but ready to learn—steps in for his father.

With Pete on duty, and Spyder—and Toby back to health—it's not difficult for Eleanor to get away to Brookline to see her friends Jason and Hank and Annette. Though her friends regularly urge her to try online dating, Eleanor's not interested.

"It took me a long time, getting to the place where I could finally live my life as I choose and meet my own needs for a change," she tells them. "I'm not in any hurry to accommodate anybody else now."

Eleanor goes back and forth regularly now, between Boston and the farm. She attends a toy fair in Chicago for the unveiling of the Make Your Own Cork Person kit. Eleanor still wishes they could have packaged it with real corks instead of plastic. But maybe, she thinks, the toy will inspire children to get off their tablets and phones and get out into nature.

She returns to France, where translations of her Bodie books as well as *The Cork People* have become popular with young readers. Her favorite part of the trip are her visits to schools, where children are amused by her imperfect French, particularly when she brings out her box of craft supplies and teaches them how to make their own cork people. Here is one of the many great things about France: they have plenty of corks. None of them plastic.

In a kindergarten classroom in Nantes, she teaches an entire classroom to sing a song she sang with her own children long ago, in that other lifetime, "If You're Happy and You Know It." A journalist who's been following Eleanor around for the day, doing a story about her for *L'Express*, captures the moment on his phone—Eleanor, surrounded by five-year-olds, calling out the words to the children in English. *If you're happy and you know it, clap your hands* . . . They all clap along.

A thought comes to her, in the middle of the song. She *is* happy. Possibly the happiest she's ever been.

143.

Catching the light

TWO years have passed since the last time Toby was able to make the trip out west to see Al and Teresa and Flora. Now he does. Flora's eleven years old now.

"You know, we never really celebrated the big 4-0," Al tells his brother. "So Teresa and I decided to celebrate 43."

They take him on a road trip into the Cascade mountains—to a rodeo, and the Timberline Lodge, and Snoqualmie Falls. On their last day, Toby and Flora pan for gold together in the Cle Elum river. They bring home a jar of gold flakes for Flora to keep on her windowsill.

Home again, Toby pays a visit to the Verlander farm. As always, Eleanor does the driving. Toby brings a glass container that used to hold Dijon mustard, containing the gold flakes he found, panning with his niece. He wants to give these to June Verlander. As usual, June's not around, so he presents the flakes to her father.

"I bet June can do something beautiful with these," he says, handing over the mustard jar filled with the flakes of gold. Just like the pieces of his broken Dale Chihuly bowl, they catch the light.

On the drive home, Eleanor asks her son a question. "You really like June, don't you?" she says. "I'm just mentioning this because I wouldn't want you to get disappointed if she doesn't reciprocate. June's a lovely young woman, but she lives in her own world."

"I like June's world," Toby says. "I could go there with her."

144.

Too pure for this world

It's midsummer now. Eleanor's in her studio, with the radio on as usual, working on her Mineral Man book—when she learns the news. Sinead O'Connor has died. They're not saying she took her life, but Eleanor guesses that in one manner or another the singer, who had struggled for years and recently lost a son to suicide, must have died of a broken heart.

Eleanor sets down her pencil and clicks on YouTube, and for the next hour she just sits there listening to Sinead's pure, haunting voice. She studies the singer's face on the screen—sorrow never absent from her eyes. Sinead had been beautiful once. But even in her youth, at the height of her beauty, Eleanor can see something else. Even then it was there, the sense that here was a woman too pure, or maybe just too fragile for this world.

How is it some people survive tragedy and others do not? Maybe Eleanor was simply born with some kind of resilience that Sinead, strong as she was, had been unable to summon. And who could blame her?

The death of a child was the worst, of course. Eleanor has stared down that dark hole more than once, herself, but never descended into it. For all the losses she's survived, that's one she escaped. Eleanor can't pretend to know where she might be now, if things had gone otherwise. She thinks about all the nights when listening to Sinead O'Connor had offered comfort, the endless loop she used to play of "This Is to Mother You." Everyone needed somebody to mother them sometimes. Including mothers.

145.

Mom

A few months have passed since Eleanor has heard from Ursula—and even then, it's been only the most cursory kind of communication—something to do with Lulu's college trip, her hope that the two of them might use the Brookline condo for a night or two to check out schools in Boston. Eleanor's not even sure if this is good news or bad, but she's come to accept the idea that maybe her daughter is simply never going to be a meaningful part of her life again. The distance Ursula chooses to maintain between herself and Eleanor no longer feels like an open wound. More like an old injury, deep in her bones, that flares up sometimes on rainy days. Mostly manageable now.

It's sometime in August, with summer winding down, when she gets the call. It's Ursula.

Her voice is thin and shaky at the other end of the line, barely recognizable. "I need your help, Mom. Can you come get the kids?"

Mom. How long has it been since Ursula called her that?

Just when Eleanor gave up looking for her daughter, here she is.

146.

Shampoo and conditioner can make you cry

U rsula has come down with COVID. She's spent the last two weeks in bed. Jake's been helping out with the kids, and her friend Kat has come up a couple of times from Concord, but it's not enough. Everything's falling apart.

"I just can't take care of anything anymore," Ursula tells Eleanor. "I hit the wall."

Twenty minutes later, Eleanor's in the car headed to Vermont to pick up her grandchildren.

Since she was very small, a central concern of Ursula's life has been trying to make sure that everything remains under control. For Eleanor, the days of her own young parenthood had contained what felt to her like a happy kind of chaos, but maybe it had felt too unpredictable for Ursula. Maybe she'd needed more structure and order than Eleanor and Cam had provided.

Ursula has always been the most fastidious of Eleanor's children and the most highly organized—she used to keep a chart on the kitchen wall awarding stars to Orson and Lulu for every household chore, and two different color-coded calendars identifying their extracurricular activities, playdates, doctors' appointments, and homework assignments. Ursula alphabetizes her spices. She used to creep into Orson's room when he was asleep to sort his Legos by color.

Now, as she enters the house Ursula shares with Lulu and Orson, Eleanor finds the sink piled with dishes and a variety of empty cereal boxes and what appear to be several days' worth of cereal bowls, unwashed. One of her grandchildren has done a load of laundry, but neglected to throw it in the dryer, which has filled the house with a moldy smell. They've run out of toilet paper so someone—also one of the kids maybe—has set a box of Kleenex on the floor next to the toilet. A stack of unopened mail spills across the kitchen counter. Nobody has changed the kitty litter in a very long time.

In the living room, Ursula lies stretched out on the couch wearing a pair of sweatpants and one of Jake's old basketball shirts.

She lifts herself partway off the pillows. "Thanks for coming," she tells Eleanor. "The kids have been trying to keep on top of things, but it's gotten to be too much."

"Your grandma's here," Eleanor calls upstairs to the children. "I brought sandwiches."

It turns out that Ursula's illness has been going on for a while. Ursula has something called Long COVID.

Until it got this bad, Ursula didn't tell anyone what was going on. Just climbing up a flight of stairs is hard for her. Her brain feels foggy, she tells Eleanor. She doesn't trust herself to drive. School's on vacation for all of them, but classes start again in a couple of weeks. She has no idea how to take care of anything anymore.

Jake has offered to take Orson and Lulu. Ursula had been uneasy about trusting him to drive them, but he's been sober for six months now, attending meetings regularly. "Dad's doing a lot better," Lulu told her mother. "It's going to be okay. But we don't want to go back with him to Bellows Falls."

Seeing Eleanor at the foot of the steps now, Lulu and Orson look relieved.

"I'm taking you to the farm," she says. "Your mom, too. Pack your things." Ursula doesn't argue.

The plan is for the three of them to stay with Eleanor for a week, until Ursula gets her strength back. Lulu and Orson will be happy on the farm. Neither of them is a particular fan of goats, but they love their uncle Toby. Mostly they're just grateful that things seem under control again. At Eleanor's house there's dinner on the table every night. Orson's found a pickup basketball game down at the rec center. Lulu's doing virtual SAT prep and practicing her violin.

Ursula sleeps most of the day. But in her waking hours she seems like a different person. She doesn't say much. But the wary look Eleanor has come to expect from her daughter—the sense Ursula has been conveying to her mother for years now, that she's being judged, and found guilty of something without understanding what it is—has vanished.

One afternoon a few days into her time back on the farm, Ursula gets up and makes her way to the kitchen. Her skin is pale. Her hair's matted.

"Maybe I can wash your hair," Eleanor says.

She brings a chair into the bathroom and lays out hair products and towels. Slowly, with Eleanor's help, Ursula sits with her back to the sink. Eleanor wraps one of the towels around Ursula's shoulders and neck and lowers her head very gently over the sink. Slowly, taking care not to let the water spill onto Ursula's nightgown, she pours it over her daughter's hair and applies the shampoo. She takes her time massaging Ursula's scalp before rinsing, then applies the conditioner, working the hair product through the ends, separating the tangles from all the days Ursula's been in bed. As she works the conditioner through the tangles, she realizes her daughter has started to cry. Tears stream down her face.

"Am I hurting you?"

Ursula shakes her head. "I just don't know why you're so good to me," she says.

"I'm your mother."

She wraps the second towel around her daughter's head. She helps her back to bed.

"I need to ask you something," Ursula says. "I need to ask you to take care of my children."

147.

Boundaries

Nobody really knows the story with Long COVID. But it's clear to them both by now that Ursula won't be going to work or taking care of her family any time soon. The doctor has said it might be six months before she gets her strength back. She's taken a leave of absence from work.

"School's starting in a little over a week," Ursula says. Her voice is so soft, Eleanor strains to hear her. "Jake's offered to take the kids at his place but they don't want to go there. I was wondering how you'd feel about having Orson and Lulu stay on and enroll in school here. They could probably finish up the year in Vermont, if you could just get them through the fall semester."

If Eleanor were willing, Ursula would return to Vermont to re-cuperate on her own, without the responsibilities of caring for her children. She needs to build up her strength. Her friends can help her do that. Even Jake will help. Since getting sober, he's abandoned his allegiance to the conspiracy theories he'd subscribed to once.

"If I could just rest for a few weeks," Ursula says. "Without wor-rying about the kids. I can get back on my feet."

Lulu will be starting her junior year. Orson's going into eighth grade. It's not easy changing schools, but there's been so much uncertainty in their lives for so long now—with their father's rages and the drinking, their parents' divorce, now Ursula's illness—that the prospect of staying with their grandmother is a welcome one.

The old Eleanor would not have needed a moment's thought before agreeing to what Ursula's suggesting here. Eleanor as she's been all these years would have stepped in without a second thought. Fourteen years ago, hearing that the man who left her for their babysitter was dying of cancer, she had barely hesitated before suggesting that she move back to the farm and take care of him.

But Eleanor has changed. The years since her return to the farm revealed to her a life beyond motherhood and caretaking. A long time has passed since her love affair with Guy ended. But she took a valuable lesson from it. Whatever else Guy failed to provide over that handful of years they'd spent in something that may never actually have qualified as a relationship, it was her time with Guy that revealed to Eleanor an aspect of herself she had never before known—who she might be, separate from her children's mother, her ex-husband's wife.

Now here comes Ursula, home again. Her daughter, reaching out to her.

Only Eleanor's a different person now.

In part, no doubt, it was Ursula's turning away from her that forced Eleanor to change as she has. All those years Ursula invoked her need for boundaries to protect herself from her mother encroaching on her personal territory. For the first time in her life, Eleanor has constructed them as well. She's given herself away so many times over the years. Before she says yes to Ursula's request, she has to consider a question she never would have considered before: *What about me?*

Her daughter stands in the doorway. This is a moment Eleanor has dreamed of. *Ursula, home again.* Ursula, asking for her help.

"I need to think about this," Eleanor tells her. "It's a lot to take on."

"That's fair enough," Ursula tells her.

"Let's talk in the morning."

That night, alone in the room that feels, finally, like her own—Eleanor considers Ursula's request.

She's over seventy now—an age that would once have seemed to Eleanor impossibly old. The surprise is that she's still the same person she was at sixteen and twenty-three and forty-five. People look at her differently now. But the girl she used to be is still there. She never went anywhere. For the first few years after her hair started to go gray she colored it. Not anymore. It took her a while, but Eleanor has finally reclaimed her life—the freedom to take a tap dance class even if she's not very good at tap dancing or fix herself a bowl of popcorn for dinner if she wants, or drive to Boston to have dinner with Jason and Hank, or stay in bed on a Sunday morning watching four episodes in a row of *The Crown*.

Most of all, in the face of her losses Eleanor has discovered a source of joy she never fully appreciated until now. It's her work. She was always so busy trying to provide what her children needed (and her husband, and her lover)—always ready to drop everything, if any of them needed her—that she didn't get around to looking at what she might deserve, for herself. She had failed recognize how much it had meant to her, getting to write books as she has done all these years, and illustrate them, and send them out to the world of readers who cared about the characters she created. She thinks about all those children who send her letters telling her how much her ten-year-old orphan hero Bodie means to them—the ones who send pictures of the cork people they've made (by hand, not from a kit), the women lined up at bookstores with their children, suggesting ideas for Bodie's next adventure, the kindergarteners who made a circle around her at their school as she taught them her song. *If you're happy and you know it.*

This, too, mattered. This was precious.

It had been going on for years, and years before then, this habit of giving pieces of herself away—since before Al's transition and Cam's illness and Guy's comings and goings (goings, mostly) and Coco's accusations, and Toby's cancer, and Ursula's quiet rage, and her grandchildren's worries over their parents' divorce. Eleanor has suffered every one of their problems and taken them on as her own. It's what mothers do. (And sometimes, it's what mothers get blamed for doing.) Only in the last few years—as each of them has found their way without her—has Eleanor allowed herself, finally, to make her own good life.

She loves starting her mornings alone at her drawing table with her coffee and her colored pencils. Even when the work doesn't come easily, she has learned to treasure the time she gets to spend there, making up stories and illustrating them, dreaming. She's not preparing meals or driving people places (nobody but Toby, and mostly he rides his bicycle now). She's not filling prescriptions for painkillers or getting on planes to accommodate a man's lecture schedule. She has finally taken back her life.

Right now, she's deeply immersed in the manuscript of her graphic novel, *Mineral Man*—possibly the most challenging project of her career. She's having trouble with this book. But it has been a good kind of trouble, the kind she has grown to love. She puts in long days at her drawing table, but she doesn't mind it. There's nothing like that moment when you finally figure out where the story should go and you make it happen.

Now Eleanor lies in her bed, turning over in her mind the proposal Ursula made to her tonight, that her grandchildren move in with her for the first half of the school year. She knows she'll say yes, but she doesn't want to offer herself up to her family as readily as she used to.

She hears a knock. It's Ursula. Her daughter doesn't make it out of bed much at the moment, but she's standing in the doorway, barefoot in her nightgown.

"I did have this one other idea," Ursula says. "An alternative to you taking the children on your own. Something that might make the whole thing more workable."

Eleanor sits up on the bed. Ursula—the new Ursula, the old Ursula, back again, but different, too—sits down next to her.

"I could move in here, too," she says. "I could stay with you and Toby and the kids. I'm not saying I'd be much help with the driving or the cooking, but at least I'd be around, and maybe I could keep track of the kids' homework or help make the lunches."

What she has to say next is probably not easy for her. "It might be a good thing for you and me, too, Mom," Ursula says. "It's been a long time since we've really connected with each other. I'd like to try."

"I never stopped loving you," Eleanor says.

As the two of them sit there together on the bed, a memory comes to Eleanor of a person who hardly ever crosses her mind anymore. Her own mother, dead for more than fifty years.

It's an old story, and one she thought she was done with a long time ago—how her parents had gone off (without her, as they generally preferred) on a ski weekend to Vermont while Eleanor was in boarding school. Her junior year.

No doubt they'd been drinking. They usually had been. Her father had failed to navigate a turn and crashed head-on into a truck.

As the only child of two people who had never shown particular interest in being parents, Eleanor had found herself, at age sixteen, alone in the world. But the truth was, long before she was orphaned, Eleanor had lived like an orphan.

It's no accident that Eleanor has spent her career writing a series of children's books about a girl without parents. She was such a girl herself. No doubt it was this that shaped Eleanor's fierce commitment—no, her obsession—with being, for her children, the kind of parent who placed their needs above her own.

Her children's father could be selfish, neglectful, inattentive. All of this was true. But in the end, he was doing the very thing for which Eleanor had lost the capacity, if she ever had it in the first place: the capacity for recognizing one's own needs, separate from those of one's children. No doubt the fact that Cam allowed himself to have a good time—simple as that—was partly responsible for his enduring good nature. It had been his greatest failure and his saving grace that Cam had been a man who could do something Eleanor never allowed herself: fall asleep in a hammock.

Somewhere in the story of how two people fall in love and decide to make a family, a person had to find a balance. Ursula had absorbed, early on, the lesson that it was the job of a loving mother to take care of the people she loved, even at the expense of her own needs. She had failed to provide her daughter with the model of a woman who took care of her own self.

Ursula was seven the day Toby almost drowned. Who might each of them have become, if that day had gone differently? Though it had been Toby who bore the most obvious and unmistakable legacy of his near-drowning, each of them had suffered it in their own way and been transformed by the experience. Cam, the casual, too often oblivious parent, became the most attentive father, devoting his days to his son's care and rehabilitation. Alison, the girl who never wanted to be their daughter in the first place, stepped into the role of the lost son. Eleanor, who had adored and desired her husband, even when they were too exhausted to do much about it, had become overtaken by bitterness and blame to the point where she could barely touch him.

As for Ursula: She had tried to make the family whole again by the sheer power of her fierce devotion, not simply to each of them individually, but to their family above all else, as so much more than the sum of its parts. When none of her efforts to make them whole again had worked, she let go of her old role as the family cheerleader. For the first time in her life then, Ursula was angry. She's been angry for a few decades now.

Now here she sits, beside her mother on the bed. She's still so weak she leans against Eleanor's shoulder. Or maybe she just does this because it's been so long since she leaned against her mother's shoulder. She melts into Eleanor's arms. For once, Eleanor sees no bitterness in her daughter's eyes. It's easy, then, for her to speak the words.

"I want to help you. I'd love to have you move back to the farm."
It doesn't feel like a sacrifice, saying this. It feels like a gift.

148.

The best thing

The next day Kat drives over from Concord. She brings Ursula back to Vermont just long enough to pack her things. It's dinnertime when they make it back to the farm. Toby and Lulu have made the meal. Orson's set the table on the porch. Eleanor's in the garden, picking tomatoes for the salad.

Ursula steps out of the car. Kat's got her suitcase and a box full of papers and files from her job that she hopes she'll be strong enough to work on soon. She's the thinnest Eleanor can remember. Eleanor takes Ursula's arm—as she did with Cam, and more recently with Toby—and helps her into the house.

"I guess the truth is, this is what I really wanted to happen," Ursula says. She starts to cry but stops herself. "Kat's been great, but I just needed my mom."

"We all need that sometimes," Eleanor tells her. Imperfect as our mothers may be, we need them.

149.

Fun with Jell-O

Orson enrolls in middle school, Lulu in high school one town over. Ursula's so weak at this point that the job of getting their transcripts from their old school falls to Eleanor. But it's not so much. Her grandchildren help. So does Ursula when she can.

It turns out that Orson likes to cook. On the kitchen shelf he's found a couple of old cookbooks Eleanor picked up at a yard sale once, mostly because she'd thought they were funny—one of them *Betty Crocker's Party Book*, the other called *Fun with Jell-O*.

Every night Orson studies the recipes, choosing what he'll make for them the next day. More often than not he bases his selections on the color photographs in the cookbook—pigs in a blanket, mashed potatoes sculpted into snowmen—and lays out his creations on a cheerful checked tablecloth or an oilcloth place mat depicting a bowl of fruit. One night he makes Shrimp Salad Delight—rolled up bread with a filling so pink there has to be food coloring involved. Another time he prepares Ham and Bananas Hollandaise, arranged over a bed of iceberg lettuce and grapes. Lulu creates a game she calls "Name Your Poison," nominating the worst meal of every week.

Jell-O features prominently in Orson's dinner selections for the family. Eleanor and Ursula and Lulu never have the heart to suggest that Orson tone them down, and Toby actually loves the food Orson serves them. Every dinner is an event. He lights candles, puts on a record from the stack of his grandfather's old vinyl albums. Sometimes he puts on one of Toby's vests or a bow tie to serve the meal.

The truth is that even with the odd meals, and the children's worry about their father, and Ursula's continued frailty—and the sudden need to stock the refrigerator with large quantities of food that seem to disappear almost as fast as Eleanor brings it home—they're happy. For Lulu and Orson it's a relief to be released from the battleground of their parents' marriage. For Toby, it's always wonderful to have his family around. For Eleanor, the reward is simple, and huge. She has her family around her. She can still do her work. She has her daughter back.

150.

Becoming an entity

Toby and Spyder are in the barn, finishing up with the milking and checking on the progress of the most recent batch of cheese that Pete has set in the cooler. As he often does at the end of their afternoon's work, Toby brings out a couple of Klondike bars from the house for the two of them. They sit on their twin stools—a forty-two-year-old man and a thirteen-year-old boy who have known each other since the day the younger of the two was born, an unlikely pair of friends. This is the moment in the afternoon Toby likes to check in with Spyder to hear how things are going in his life.

"How's it going at school?" he says, knowing that Spyder has just started eighth grade. "Any particular girl you like?"

"Maybe." Spyder's rubbing the place on Amor's head where she always likes to be scratched. Just under her left ear. "She probably hates me."

"Why do you think that?"

"They all do."

"You've got a lot to offer, man," Toby tells him. For starters: How many eighth graders have an actual job, with a paycheck, and responsibilities for handling cash the way Spyder does at the farmers' market? All those other kids get driven around everyplace by their mothers. Look at Spyder, getting around on his own on the Cannondale. Even in winter.

"Yeah, well. You do that, too."

"But you're great at things I can't do," Toby says. Just the other week, one of the milking machines got jammed. Who was the one that figured out what the problem was? Who spent a whole night sitting with Tinkerbelle, when she was giving birth to her twins, and they were breech? How about that sign Spyder painted for their Wheel of Joy table, with the smiling goat head?

"Not to mention you're a really good person," Toby says. "You help out your mom. I've seen you with Billy, pushing him around in his wheelchair. Lots of kids wouldn't take the time."

"At school I'm like . . . a nonentity," Spyder says. The word showed up on a vocab list his teacher handed out in English recently. Definition: *A person who does not exist.* That's him.

"We need to get to work on this," Toby tells him. "We need to turn you into an entity."

Toby has not forgotten Spyder's aspiration to become a businessman. He reminds Spyder periodically of his plan to hand Wheel of Joy over to him when he gets old enough. He'll be the youngest CEO in Akersville, probably.

And the thing is, he's great in math.

"I got a B minus in algebra on my report card," Spyder tells Toby.

"I bet you didn't study for your test. I'm guessing you gave up before you gave it a chance."

"Maybe."

"Here's the deal," Toby says. "You bring that math grade up to a B plus and keep it there for the rest of eighth grade and I'm getting you something really great for a reward."

Toby hasn't come up with what that might be yet. But he's thinking. If he were somebody else, some other kind of person, this would be the moment when he'd hold out to Spyder the promise of a new Xbox, a trip to the water park, paintball. Two tickets to see the show of some rap artist at Boston Garden. (Toby doesn't know the names of any of these. Burl Ives, he knows. John Prine. The audiobook of Jimmy Carter's story about growing up in Georgia, *An Hour Before Daylight: Memories of a Rural Boyhood*, recorded by President Carter himself. Every song Scarlett Johansson ever recorded. None of them a hit.)

This becomes their project: Getting Spyder's algebra grade up to a B+. Making it so he won't be a nonentity anymore. Getting girls to take an interest in him. All a person needs is one. The part about Spyder becoming an entity. That most of all. Nobody should ever feel invisible.

They get to work. "I can't help you with the math part," Toby says. "I'm no good at numbers." He asks Eleanor to buy a book that could help Spyder bring up his grade. His mother orders *Basic Mathematics for Grade 8 Algebra and Geometry: Graphs of Basic Power and Rational Functions*. Toby sets up a table in the barn where Spyder can do the workbook problems. Spyder works through these so fast Toby asks Eleanor to order a second book. The Grade 10 edition.

One afternoon when Spyder pedals up to the barn on his bike, he's got an envelope in his hand. His first semester report card. Algebra 1: A-.

151.

Choosing a Swiss Army knife

So, Spyder earns his reward.

"I bet you never had a Swiss Army knife," Toby says to Spyder.

Toby was nine when his dad gave him his. *The Rambler*. Scissors, bottle opener, nail file, three different blades. After all these years, he keeps it in his pocket at all times.

Toby's not one to go online. But he has sent away for the catalog. Now he and Spyder sit together on their side-by-side milking stools, checking out all the models of Swiss Army knives. *Ranger. 79M, The Soldier, Hunter Pro.*

They spend most of the afternoon comparing models of knives, discussing the features of each and which seem most useful for someone like Spyder.

"How about this?" Toby says. He reads off the list of tools included in a model called the Skipper."Screwdriver, can opener, marlin spike, shackle opener, wire stripper, screwdriver, combination pliers."

"This one even comes with a toothpick," Toby says. "Those come in handy more than you think."

"It costs a hundred and three dollars," Spyder tells him.

"You're going to have this knife for the rest of your life," Toby tells him. "When you look at it that way, the Skipper's a bargain." Not to mention it comes with a lifetime guarantee.

"I don't even know what a marlin spike is for," Spyder says. "Or a reamer."

"We'll find out," Toby tells him.

152.

How to be a super-brainiac

According to Spyder, all the girls at his school hate him. Toby's not buying it. But he also wants to point out to Spyder that if a girl doesn't like him, she's probably not the one for him anyway.

"I was in love with Scarlett Johansson once," he says. "It was hard, giving up on her. But in the end I did."

There is actually someone he likes, Spyder tells Toby. *Veronica.* She's in his algebra class. She's on the Mathalon team.

"There you go," Toby tells him. "We need to get you on this team."

"It doesn't work like that," Spyder says. "There's only so many places. You have to try out. The Mathalon kids are the super-brainiacs."

The tryouts are coming up in just a few weeks.

"We'd better get to work," Toby tells him.

Spyder asks his algebra teacher, Ms. Alvarez, about the Mathalon team. He reports to Toby that Ms. Alvarez had rolled her eyes when she heard he was thinking of trying out. But she gave him a sheaf of examples of the kinds of problems that might come up at the tryouts.

Every day now, when he comes over to the farm after school— after he finishes his chores with the goats—Spyder gets to work on his algebra review, going over his workbook and tackling the sample problems in his packet. Toby's job is keeping his eye on the timer.

Spyder stays till past dinnertime sometimes, working on problems. He doesn't even play video games anymore or spend time on target practice the way he used to. He's that focused on *Basic Grade 8 Algebra*. When he finishes that workbook, Toby gets Eleanor to order the follow-up, Volume 2.

More than this, he's focused on the Mathalon tryouts now.

"I don't want to get my hopes up or anything," Spyder tells Toby, "but I think I've got a shot at getting on the team."

Afternoons in the barn, Toby looks over at him sometimes, bent over the desk. "You know that feeling where you feel so proud of a person your heart could burst?" he tells Eleanor. "That's how I get, seeing Spyder work on his math."

Eleanor does know that feeling. She has it now, for this son of hers. So much love it hurts.

153.

Not a talkative guest

One day that fall, a month or two after Ursula and the children move in, June Verlander drives down to the farm by herself.

This is not a goat-breeding trip. Without a word—she speaks no words—she makes this plain to them. She wants to see Toby. She's brought him another kintsugi bowl.

Toby brings June a glass of lemonade. When a person wants to talk with June, they need to position themselves so their lips are clearly visible. Toby understands this better than most. He asks if she'd like to see his mineral collection.

Toby wants to show June every specimen, one by one. Many visitors over the years—including Al and Teresa, Miriam, and even Elijah—have probably wished the mineral tour could be less exhaustive. But Toby has so much to say about each piece in his collection, the tour can take a few hours.

June takes things in slowly, as Toby does. June understands what it means to pay attention. To take your time. She may be deaf, but June knows how to listen.

More than two hours pass before Toby has shown June every one of the minerals in his collection. By this time it's dark out. Eleanor's making dinner. (Eleanor, not Orson this time. This is probably good news.) Before she has a chance to invite June to stay for dinner, the two of them have passed out the side door of the house leading to the field. The last rays of sunlight are gone. It's dark now. Toby's holding her hand.

They walk down the hill together in the direction of the old pear tree and stop in an open place in the field. Eleanor watches as Toby turns on his flashlight. For a moment she has no idea what her son is doing. From where she stands at the kitchen window she watches her younger son reach into his pocket. What he takes out must be a mineral from his collection. Eleanor knows well which one.

A moment later, a single shaft of light seems to rise in front of the two of them—faintly blue and glowing, pointing skyward, like something in a religious movie depicting the moment when God speaks.

It's Toby's selenite crystal that he and Cam had picked out one year at the Gilsum Rock Swap. When you shine a light into one end it travels through the crystal, creating a mysterious glow, like the sword a superhero might wield in an ultimate confrontation with the forces of evil. Or a beam of pure love.

Toby leans in close to June. Her long braids and the darkness around them conceal their faces, but Eleanor knows. They're on the tilt-a-whirl.

154.

She brings her suitcase

June visits many times after this. The farm where she has lived with her father all her life is too far for Toby to go on his bicycle, but June is an excellent driver. After that first visit she made, on her own, her truck starts showing up more and more in the driveway at the farm. After a while, it stays there.

More kintsugi bowls appear at the farmhouse. Then it's June herself who arrives with a single suitcase. And stays.

155.

It doesn't have to be Valentine's Day to fall in love

After all that time when it was just Eleanor and Toby alone together in the house Cam had built, the farmhouse feels very full now, but mostly this is a good thing. Eleanor likes to see the row of differently sized shoes lined up alongside the front door again, the way it used to be when her own three children were young. On weekends Kat drives over from Concord to help out. Her visits make it possible for Eleanor to go back to Brookline for a few nights to have time for herself. She keeps her work schedule, mostly. She's managing to do something she never accomplished before: finding a balance.

The animated movie now titled *Zoe at the Pole* is released—an event that inspires no particular response from Eleanor, one way or another. The film disappears from theaters within two weeks of its release. It appears to have come and gone without having created a discernible wave of elevated concern over the crises of global warming and climate change. From the studio's point of view, probably, the larger disappointment had to do with its poor numbers at the box office.

On the farm, the big news is that four of Toby's goats are pregnant. Due in the spring. And Toby and June are in love.

156.

The ninth step

Out of the blue, Jake shows up at Eleanor's door. The last time she's seen him was in a blurry newspaper photograph—barely recognizable in full beard and bandanna, easily forty pounds heavier than the man she remembered standing in front of the justice of the peace over twenty years before with tears in his eyes promising to love, cherish, and protect Ursula for the rest of their days. Along with more than two dozen other members of the Order of the Patriots, he'd been charged with engaging in unlawful acts of violence and desecration of a federal building associated with his participation in the January 6 riots at the Capitol.

Jake was lucky. Unlike many of his fellow members of the Order of the Patriots, he'd wielded no weapons at the Capitol building. In the extensive news footage documenting the insurrection, no images were found of Jake attacking anybody.

Three years have passed since his arrest. He got off with a suspended sentence and the requirement of paying twenty thousand dollars in restitution for damages incurred by himself and others, including vandalizing a congressman's desk.

"We were invited by the president," Jake told a reporter at the time. When his day came in court, Donald Trump had nothing to say on behalf of the men who had seen themselves as valiantly defending their commander in chief. Jake has noted this.

"We got taken," he says. "We were loyal to a man who showed no loyalty to us." For Jake, Eleanor knows, loyalty is everything.

Jake is religious about attending AA meetings—virtually, when he can't show up in person. It turns out that his love of coaching is greater than his affiliation with the Order of the Patriots. Some-where along the line, he tells Ursula—on one of the weekend hand-offs of the children once he'd been allowed to take them overnight again—it came to him that kids of Somali refugees had just as much right to know the joy of dribbling a ball down the court or going for a foul shot as his son or his daughter.

The last time he came to pick up the kids at the farm to spend a night with them, Jake told Ursula, he realized he'd been a fool. It's too late to save his marriage. But he's doing well with his children now. He's sober now, and he has a job at Home Depot. He's still broke, or close to it, driving a truck that seems unlikely to pass inspection next time around, but he sends money to Ursula every month and shows up to parent-teacher conferences clean-shaven and respect-ful. You could call him a broken man or simply a humbler one.

Orson and Lulu are at school, when their father comes by the farm—a fact for which Eleanor feels grateful—Jake explains, he has deliberately shown up when they won't be around. Though there is never a time he wouldn't wish to see the woman he was married to once, and will probably never stop loving, the person he has come to see is Eleanor.

Ursula's asleep upstairs. (Ursula still sleeps a lot. This is part of what Long COVID has done to her. She's exhausted most of the time.)

"I wouldn't blame you if you hate me," Jake tells Eleanor. "I put your daughter through hell. The kids, too. I had a wife I loved more than anything and the greatest family a man could ask for. I threw it away. Call me an asshole and I won't argue. But I needed to come here and tell you I'm sorry."

He's still standing on Eleanor's doorstep. She has not invited him in. The red hat that had remained a part of Jake's uniform for over three years is gone, revealing for the first time that Jake is losing his hair. He's trimmed down considerably, probably due in part to giving up beer, though getting back out on the basketball court has probably also helped. He looks older and sadder, but his eyes are clear again. Eleanor can see in his face, as she had been unable to do for a while, the teenage boy he'd been when he came round long ago to take Ursula out to dinner at Friendly's, and the night he sat in the kitchen with Eleanor, wearing a white shirt tucked into slightly too-short dress pants, to tell her that he hoped to marry her daughter. "I came here to announce my intentions," he'd said.

Jake has no family of his own to speak of. Father dead. Mother, drinking, then gone. One brother on the streets someplace. Opioid addiction.

"I know my background might not look that great," he had told Eleanor that night long ago when he and Ursula sat in her kitchen in Brookline and told her they wanted to get married. "But I promise I'll do everything I can to be a good husband to Ursula. She's the best thing that ever happened to me."

"I'm not the type to judge a person by where he came from. Just who they are," Eleanor had told him.

Jake and Ursula waited seven years to have a baby, during which time Jake had worked three jobs to put Ursula through college, then grad school. The day Lulu was born, when he'd called to tell Eleanor the news, he kept saying the same thing over and over. *I'm a dad. I'm a dad. Can you believe it, I'm a dad?*

It was two days after that when Eleanor went to Vermont to meet the baby. That was the visit in which she told Ursula the story she'd been holding on to all those years about her father and Coco.

Eleanor had been cradling Lulu in her arms when she spoke the words. All these years later she can still see Jake crossing the room and taking his daughter from her arms. It had been Ursula who told her to get out of their house, go away, never come back, *You will never know your granddaughter.* It was Jake who escorted Eleanor to the door. Whatever Ursula said in those days, that was enough for Jake. Whatever Ursula said was always the most important thing to Jake. For a brief period there, he'd lost sight of his north star, and followed Donald Trump instead.

Look where that got me, he says. "I told you. I was an idiot. At least I can admit it.

"I know you and my wife had your problems," he tells Eleanor. "I hope it's better between you two now."

Eleanor studies the face of her son-in-law, the father of her grand-children. If she'd never met Jake, she could believe every one of those men who climbed the walls of the Capitol that day was an irredeemably terrible person. The fact that she stands here now, looking in the eye a man with whom she has disagreed about nearly everything in recent years, requires Eleanor to consider that there's humanity to be found, even in the most unlikely places.

"I didn't understand how complicated it is having kids," he says. "When they're babies all you have to do is hold them and feed them and love them. Change their diapers. Nobody tells you that's the easy part."

Eleanor just listens. There's no need to say anything.

"In AA they have this step," he says. "The ninth. Making amends. In the eighth step you make a list of everyone you hurt while you were drinking. In the ninth step you go to them and do what you can to make it right."

Eleanor knows about this. When she was young and her parents were still alive—the cupboard at their house full of vodka and mar-aschino cherries—she got a copy of the Twelve Steps and studied them in secret, in her room. She used to imagine what it would be like if the two of them signed up for AA together, and all of a sudden she'd get to have parents. The regular kind.

"When I came to pick up the kids last week I noticed your gutters looked pretty clogged up," Jake says to Eleanor now. "I brought a ladder. I figured I could clean them out for you."

"That sounds great," she tells him.

Jake works on the gutters all morning. Eleanor returns to her desk. She hopes Ursula doesn't wake up to see him there but know-ing how much she sleeps at this point it seems unlikely she will.

When he's done, he knocks on the door again.

"I just wanted to say I'm glad Toby's okay," he tells Eleanor. "He was always a good brother-in-law. I would have given him my bone marrow, too, if we were a match. Only mine was probably still full of booze at the time.

"My wife loves you a lot, you know," Jake says.

My wife. He still thinks of Ursula that way no doubt. Knowing Jake, he always will, probably.

Eleanor wishes him luck. He drives away.

157.

Hunting season

The wife of one of Cam's teammates on his old softball team, the Yellow Jackets, calls with the news.

Somewhere in a vast section of woods in northern New Hampshire, a homeless woman who had been living for some time off the grid in an abandoned sugar shack appears to have set out to look for mushrooms after some heavy rains. Authorities figured this out later from the contents of the basket she'd been carrying at the time. Mushrooms.

Mistaken for a deer, the woman was shot in the heart by a seventy-three-year-old hunter who, discovering what he'd done, then put a bullet through his own heart as well. The homeless woman's name was Coco.

Elijah was in Amsterdam again with Miriam, on tour with his band, when Eleanor called with the news. From three thousand miles away he wept over the phone.

"I always thought maybe someday things would be better between my mom and me," he said to Eleanor. "Now that can never happen."

Eleanor remembers a similar feeling when her own mother had died young. As will be true for Elijah, Eleanor has had to make peace with her mother in the years after losing her. "Sometimes you're lucky enough to work things out with a person while they're still alive," Eleanor tells him. That happened for her, with Cam. "Sometimes you have to do it on your own. I hope you can, eventually."

For all the damage Coco did, all three of Eleanor's children take the news of her death with shock and sorrow. They had loved her once. They remember who she was before everything went wrong.

Toby, being Toby, has even forgiven her for the bogus charges of child abuse. He is a person incapable of holding on to bitterness. It's a good lesson for the rest of them.

Like others they have known, and even loved, Coco lost her way. That's how Toby sees it. Now, hearing of her death in the woods, he weeps. So do all of them, then.

158.

A night out, a melting ice sheet, a six-figure book deal, a pregnancy

The weather turns bitterly cold. Eleanor's just dropped Orson off at the school bus. Home again, she pours herself a cup of coffee and opens *The New York Times* online. A story catches her eye. ANTARCTIC EXPLORER NARROWLY AVOIDS DEATH. A few hundred feet from the destination he'd set for himself more than thirty years earlier, at a latitude referred to as ninety degrees south—Eleanor could never understand why it wasn't zero—Guy Macdowell stepped onto a piece of melting ice sheet that gave way, plunging him into a deep crevasse. Incredibly, he survived, having lost another finger to frostbite but expected to make a full recovery. The news story went on to say that Guy had been airlifted to Argentina and from there to the United States where, the article reported, he would be embarking on writing a memoir. His agent reports that he has evidently signed a "high-six-figure" book deal.

The article goes on. The first thing Guy Macdowell had done, upon returning to New York City, was marry the prominent socialite who had served as the chairperson of his foundation's board for more than twenty years. They would be making their home in Ojai, California, and Martha's Vineyard.

Eleanor is relieved to discover she feels no pang of loss, taking in the news. Only a momentary shiver that has nothing to do with the temperature in the room.

What matters: Ursula's health is improving. She can spend a few hours a day working at her desk now, conferring with faculty at her school. She attends a concert of the school orchestra in which Lulu is playing first violin. She and Eleanor go out to dinner in Brattleboro one night—just the two of them, Eleanor's old dream.

"A night off from Orson's cooking!" Ursula says to her mother, as the two of them study the entrees. "There's not one thing on this menu that doesn't look good."

Driving home from the restaurant, with Ursula in the passenger seat, Eleanor counts her blessings. For once, nobody in her family is struggling with a big problem. Orson and Lulu are happy in their new school. They're staying on in Akersville with their mother and grandmother—also their uncle—into the final semester of the school year. Ursula's back to working every day, virtually, for the school in Vermont where she's been serving as assistant principal. Sometimes on weekends she drives to Concord, as she has done over the years before she got COVID, the many years of painful distance between Ursula and Eleanor. Sometimes Jake drives down to pick up the children.

One Sunday afternoon Elijah and Miriam call from Amsterdam to let everyone know Miriam's pregnant. Al and Teresa and Flora have bought a Boston terrier. Eleanor has not yet finished her graphic novel, *Mineral Man,* but she's close. She's still stuck on the final chapter. Her French editor has already announced he'll publish the new book the following fall. Once again, she'll be heading to Paris.

159.

What everybody deserves

Eleanor's carrying in wood. Ursula's waiting for her by the stove.

"I was hoping we could talk, Mom," she says.

Things between them are good these days—a fact for which Eleanor registers daily gratitude. It's also true that once an adult child has cut you off as Ursula did, the worry never fully disappears that it won't happen again. Sometimes, even now—on a walk to the falls with her daughter or watching her at work on her laptop, discussing some aspect of the curriculum with a member of her school's faculty, clearing the dishes away after dinner—a wave of fear passes over Eleanor.

What if all this is a dream, and tomorrow Ursula disappears? The worry never leaves her. Maybe this is the moment it all falls apart again.

Ursula pours herself a cup of coffee. When she takes off her knitted cap, Eleanor realizes something she has not fully taken in before, even though they've been living together for a few months now. Ursula's hair is more gray than brown. Her face is lined. She's not old, in Eleanor's eyes at least, but she's no longer young.

They sit in the kitchen next to the warm stove. Eleanor's first thought: What has she done to offend her daughter this time? Maybe something she said to Orson or Lulu had bothered Ursula. But when Ursula begins to speak, there's no trace of the old reproachfulness and judgment.

"I've never said much to you about what I do in Concord," Ursula says.

Ursula never said much to Eleanor about anything.

"I want to tell you something important. It's about Kat. We're in love. We've loved each other for years. That's why she left her job at my school. I was trying to get over it and put it away and make things work with Jake. But I never got over my feelings for Kat.

"Jake probably knew. I think that's what made him go off the rails."

Sometimes the best thing a person can do is simply listen. Now is one such time.

"Kat and I are meant to be together," Ursula says. "I want to tell Lulu and Orson, too. It may be a bit of a shock, but I think they'll be fine."

"I figured that out a long time ago," Eleanor tells her. "I just hoped you'd tell me when you were ready.

"You deserve to be loved. The way you want to be loved. Everybody deserves that."

160.

A bad day

Toby's waiting in the barn for Spyder, the afternoon of the Mathalon team tryouts. Three o'clock passes. Four. Five thirty.

It's after six o'clock when Spyder shows up. Not on his bike this time. He has walked over. The minute Toby catches sight of the boy, he knows things didn't go well.

"The minute I walked in to take the test," Spyder says, "Ms. Alvarez made this face like she just found a turd in her soup.

"'This room is reserved for Mathalon tryouts,' she says. Like I must be looking for shop class or something. I told her I came to try out. A couple of the kids started laughing. Not Veronica, but the others."

Toby sits on his old milking stool, taking it in. He's never seen Spyder like this before. The boy paces back and forth across the floor of the goat barn, talking so fast he barely stops for breath.

"They had us all sitting at desks in the cafeteria with a giant buzzer in front and Ms. Alvarez walking up and down through the room looking at our papers. These problems kept flashing up on the screen. Just when I got to the middle of one problem, they zapped it off the screen and put up a different one."

That's how it had gone all afternoon, Spyder tells Toby. Over and over. All these equations up on the screen, disappearing before Spyder could get his thoughts together.

"Everyone else looked so busy, scribbling numbers on their notepads like they knew what to do," he tells Toby.

Partway through, when Spyder realized how hopeless it was, he had gotten up from his seat and walked out. No point waiting to hear the results.

"Veronica was sitting at the front of the room the whole time," he says. "She's already on the team, so she didn't have to try out. She was just there to help Ms. Alvarez tally the results."

On his way out, Veronica had spoken to him. "She was nice, like always," Spyder says. "She told me I should try next year."

He's never going back.

"Kids like me don't get on Mathalon," Spyder says. "I don't know why I ever thought I belonged there."

When he left the school, he'd gone to the bike rack, like always, to pick up the yellow Cannondale. Only it wasn't there. That's when he remembered he'd been so wired up for the tryouts he'd forgotten his lock that morning.

"That sounds hard," Toby says. "I can see why you feel bad."

"I'm a moron," Spyder says. He's finally stopped pacing. He sits on a milking stool, shaking his head. His whole body is trembling.

"You aren't a moron," Toby says. "People call me a dope, too. That just shows how stupid they are.

"Let's go say hello to Jesus," Toby tells him. "He's been missing you."

This is the place he belongs, Spyder tells Toby. The barn. Forget school. Forget having a girlfriend, or any friends. Forget having a bicycle, even. He's got Toby. That's enough. That's everything. Toby, his one true friend in life.

161.

Luck of the draw

It's the last day of school before winter break. Lulu and Orson will be heading to Bellows Falls to spend the week with their father. Finally beginning to feel more like her old self, Ursula chooses to drive Lulu to school that morning so the two of them can spend a little time together. Orson can always take the bus, but for the same reason that Ursula drives Lulu, Eleanor drives Orson this morning. It's increasingly rare, getting time alone with any of her grandchildren. Before she knows it, they'll be gone. Not just back to

Vermont, when school gets out. Off to their lives. She'll savor this moment with her grandson while she has it.

Eleanor pulls her car up in front of the school to let Orson out. She watches him take the steps, two at a time, calling out greetings to his many friends, all of whom look happy to see him. Wherever he goes, Orson finds friends. He's a boy who walks on the sunny side of the street. This has been true all his life.

Eleanor's just about to pull away from the curb when she spots Spyder, on foot, crossing the parking lot, wearing his perpetual uniform, hoodie and baggy jeans. As he makes his way into the school, he keeps his eyes on the ground. Nobody speaks to him. He speaks to no one.

Give or take a few months, the two boys, Spyder and Orson, are the same age—thirteen going on fourteen. Neither one has been spared hard times. (For Orson, these include his father's drinking, and rage, then the divorce. For Spyder, just about everything.) How has it happened that their lives have unfolded so differently?

Eleanor could say it was all about a person's family. Their parents, their home life, the luck of being good-looking, or athletic, having money, or simply being born with a positive outlook, as Eleanor believes to be true of Orson.

But some of it is pure luck, Eleanor thinks: Which cork people make it down the brook, and beyond, even. Which get lost in the weeds.

Look at Coco. Timmy Pouliot. Raine. Look at her old friend Darla, murdered by her husband three days after she finally made her escape from a decade of abuse. And Cam's softball teammate, Harry Botts, dead of AIDS at age thirty-seven, and the six-year-old daughter of another teammate, lost to cancer. Her own parents, killed on the highway on their way home from a weekend ski trip.

Look at Cam.

Some cork people float. Some sink. Sometimes a flimsy boat makes it over the rocks. Sometimes a sturdy one sinks.

Some of it has to do with the choices you make. But some of it's luck, too. Good luck or bad. Luck of the draw. *Life.*

162.

The death of Billy

Just when they think winter might be winding down, a storm covers the ground again and the temperature drops to single-digit numbers. Driving past the place she will always think of as Walt's old house, Eleanor notices a wheelchair, upended, lying on the ground, half buried. It's none of her business, she tells herself, but because she sees Raine in the yard she pulls over.

"You were wondering about the chair, huh?" Raine's got a snow shovel in her hand, working her way down the path, clearing the snow.

"Billy's?"

"It was the darnedest thing," Raine tells her. "I brought Billy his tray the other morning, same as usual. Hard-boiled egg and a bowl of Lucky Charms. I knew the second I laid eyes on him he was a goner."

"I'm so sorry," Eleanor tells her.

"I was going to give him a shave," Raine says. "He always loved it when I did that."

This is a surprising aspect of Raine, Eleanor thinks to herself. You can think she's a tough little operator, and you might not be wrong. But she actually cared about Billy. Maybe she even loved him, in her way.

"The thing is, I was counting on Billy's social security," Raine says. "Come to find out, when I bring in the death certificate to get the paperwork going on the benefits, he never got around to signing the marriage license. So now I end up with zip. Not to mention the funeral home wants three thousand dollars."

Eleanor follows her into the house. The kitchen floor is lined with trash bags—Billy's worldly possessions, probably. Otherwise, the place is spotless as usual.

Raine stands there, surveying the scene. Except for the tattoos, she could be sixteen years old. "I don't know what to do," she says.

Eleanor puts her arms around the girl. *Girl.* That's how Eleanor sees her at this moment. A young, scared, motherless girl, with a thirteen-year-old son and a mortuary bill to pay. When she wraps her arms around Raine, she realizes something: Here is a person who doesn't know how to be hugged. Her small, thin body stiffens, like a rescue dog you bring home, that—when you try to pet it—slinks away.

"Funny thing is, I guess I cared about the guy," Raine says. "Not in a sex way or anything. Billy was just like . . . I don't know . . . this safe person that wasn't ever going to mess with me. That put him in a class by himself."

"You probably made him very happy."

"I did. Not that he said a lot about it, but I could tell. For someone like me, that everybody thought was a screwup my whole life, it felt good knowing there was this one person that actually believed I was pretty great."

Eleanor would like to refute Raine's assessment of herself as a lifelong screwup. But Eleanor has to admit that she herself is one of those people who has looked at Raine that way.

Standing in the middle of Raine's kitchen now—the linoleum sparkling as usual, her schedule of AA meetings posted on the refrigerator as always, along with an assortment of store coupons and what must be a reminder to Spyder, *LEAVE STINKY SNEAKERS OUTSIDE*—it seems to Eleanor as if she's seeing Raine in a new light. From the day they met, Eleanor has viewed her as lost, neglectful, foolish, irresponsible. Maybe she's all of those things. It's the part that does a woman in—the label, *a bad mother.*

Why was it, Eleanor thinks, that women should judge themselves this way, and see themselves judged: That how they raise their children should serve as the ultimate measure of their worth in the world?

Raine does the best she could, probably. Maybe it isn't enough. If anyone knows how that can happen, it's Eleanor.

Raine may be lost all right. But she's a hard worker. No matter what's going on in her life—car not running, cramps so bad she's practically doubled over, racoon infestation in the attic, her son sitting outside on a rock, not talking—Raine puts in her forty hours a week at her minimum-wage job over at the nursing home and still makes it to her AA meeting every day.

She's earned her sobriety coin. She's saving up to get braces for Spyder, and a good vacuum cleaner. In her way, she's taking care of her son the best she knows. To Raine, marrying a senior citizen with a dependable social security check coming in every first of the month—and then another one—must have seemed like the only way to accomplish that. You could call her a scam artist. Or an entrepreneur.

It turns out her father, Walt Junior, stopped by the house today, she tells Eleanor. Not exactly a condolence call. Raine's rent was a week late. He came to remind her she had to pay up.

"There's just no way I can meet the rent payments on my own without Billy's check coming in anymore," she says.

"I could lend you a little money," Eleanor offers.

Raine shakes her head. "I don't take handouts."

She's throwing more of Billy's possessions into another trash bag now. Jigsaw puzzles. Slippers. Boxes of Depends.

"Maybe you can go down to the Social Security office and talk to someone," Eleanor suggests, as she's leaving.

"Why bother? It's hopeless."

"No harm trying," Eleanor tells her. "I know what it's like dealing with the bureaucracy over there. All that paperwork. Toby's been receiving SSI payments since he turned eighteen," she says. There were so many forms to fill out at first. The good news was, once you took care of all that, the money came in like clockwork.

"Toby gets SSI?"

A person has to have a disability to qualify, Eleanor explains. It's probably not something anyone would aspire to. She's out the door.

Eleanor's getting in her car when Raine calls out to her.

"Thanks for stopping by," she says. "I've never been the type that had friends."

"Good luck," Eleanor tells her.

"I still can't believe it," Raine says, as Eleanor reaches for her keys. "Toby gets SSI. Who would've guessed, a young guy like him. I thought only old guys collected social security."

On her drive back to the farm, an image comes to Eleanor, of Raine's kitchen as it was this morning. The bags of clothes. The mop and bucket. The tray where Raine used to serve Billy his meals when he watched *Wheel of Fortune*. The razor and shaving cream, still set out.

But it's none of those things Eleanor's thinking about. It's what she'd spotted on the counter by the sink. A bottle of Jack Daniel's. Open.

163.

Cimonnan rolls

That night Raine calls. It's past nine thirty. Eleanor's just heading to bed. Toby and June are up to the final scene in *Old Yeller*, the part of the movie that always makes him cry. June's never seen the movie before. Now she's crying, too.

"I know it's late," Raine says. "But I was wondering if Toby could come by for a minute. I think there's a bat in my bedroom. I'm kind of freaked out."

"Can't Spyder help you?"

"He went out someplace."

"It's kind of late. Maybe this can wait till morning," Eleanor says. She'd like to believe Raine is just tired, but the way she's talking tonight—a certain fuzziness to her speech, and how she has to try three times to get the word "cinnamon" right, when she tells Eleanor she's just baked rolls—it sounds as though she's drinking.

"Are you okay?" Eleanor asks her. "Maybe you should call your sponsor?"

"I'm not used to being alone in the house. It would mean a lot if Toby could come by. Just to check things out."

"It's okay, Mom," Toby tells Eleanor, when she tells him about Raine's request. "I'll walk over and make sure everything's okay."

He heads out into the night. Eleanor goes to bed.

164.

A thing for red-headed men

Morning now. Eleanor's in her studio, trying to work. Not that she's having much luck. She's still thinking about the call from Raine the night before. Eleanor wants to believe Raine was just tired. Who wouldn't have been, at that point?

The radio's on. They're talking about a blizzard somewhere out west—unprecedented snowfall in Northern California, flooding in the south. A possible typhoon reaching landfall in Asia. Whatever else may or may not be true about Guy Macdowell, he got this part right anyway. The planet is changing. The world her grandchildren will inhabit, forty years from now, may be barely recognizable.

Toby appears in the door. He stands there for a moment. She can see him summoning his thoughts. For Toby, these come slowly.

Eleanor sets down her colored pencil. She turns off the radio.

"I need to tell you something, Mom," he says. "It's about last night."

Toby had been reluctant to go over to Raine's house that night. June wanted him to stay home. But this was his friend's mom. Toby was not a person to say no. So he headed out in the night and walked over to their house.

Now comes Toby's story.

Raine was standing in the doorway when he got there, waiting for him. She was barefoot, wearing some kind of bathrobe and crying. Toby stepped into the house—trying to keep his eyes away from her body on account of she didn't seem to have anything else on under the robe.

She looked upset. (*Drunk* is not something Toby knows about, much. Eleanor wonders, now, if Toby has ever seen a drunk person, apart from Jake. Probably not.)

"I need to talk to you," Raine said.

It was past ten o'clock. Before walking over, he'd put the goats down to sleep—including Jesus—but one of them, Bernadette, had been struggling with an infection in her teat. Toby needed to get home to her. Whatever it was Spyder's mom needed him to do, he hoped it wouldn't take long.

"Come on in."

How could he say no to Raine, standing in the darkness, crying and begging him to sit down and talk with her? She asked him, did he like Jack Daniel's? Baileys Irish Cream? She had a bottle of that, too, that they gave her at the home, after one of the residents died. Back before she got sober.

She laughed, sort of. *I guess I blew that one, huh?*

"I thought you needed help with something," Toby said.

"I do. My life."

"I can only stay a few minutes," he said. "One of my girls is having trouble."

"So is this girl," she told him.

There was a plate of cupcakes on the counter. The Duncan Hines box was plainly visible, along with a package of pink frosting.

"I made dessert," she told him. On the counter, the Baileys Irish Cream. He knew this drink. Jake used to bring a bottle over at Christmas, though the only one who ever drank it was himself.

Toby was confused. A minute ago Raine had acted like this was an emergency, but now it seemed like she just wanted to shoot the breeze. Maybe this was one of those times where his brain wasn't smart enough. All he knew was, he should get home. Back to the barn, where things always made sense. Back to June.

"Where's Spyder?" he asked Raine.

"Out someplace. You know kids. Always getting into one thing or another."

Maybe some kids were that way. Spyder never had been. If he was out anywhere, it was generally the goat barn.

"Did anyone ever tell you what great hair you have?" Raine said. The way she talked was different from normal. The words came out super slow, like how it is when you've got some toy like Talking Mr. T and the battery's running down so the words come out funny. The way she walked, when she got up to bring him a cupcake, was also different. Like a person who was spinning around and around and then they stopped all of a sudden but their head was still going in circles.

"I don't want to hurt your feelings," Toby told her. "I can't stay here long. My mom said there was a bat someplace?"

"The thing is, I'm lonely," Raine said. "My husband died."

"I'm sorry about that," Toby told her. "I never got to know Billy, but he was probably a nice guy. I was never married to anybody but I bet it's hard if you're married to someone and then they die."

His dad died. He knows the feeling of missing someone a whole lot. But what could you say about a person who'd been sitting in a chair for the last three years, staring at the birdfeeder or an old album cover of the Osmonds mounted on a tree?

Raine reached across the table. She touched his hand. "The thing is," she told him. "Even before Billy passed away, he wasn't . . . how do I put this? . . . performing his husbandly duties."

Now Toby was confused. Maybe Raine wanted him to carry in firewood for her or light the woodstove or something. The only other thing he could think of was she might need him to change one of her tires. If so, he'd ask Ralph to stop by in the morning to help her. Toby was good with goats and bicycles. Cars, not so much.

"I'm talking about sex," she said, still speaking in that same unusual way, like she had marbles in her mouth. Or how it is when you go to the dentist and they give you a shot and your lip gets numb.

Raine had a glass in her hand. She was drinking from it. "Billy was old. Certain body functions just weren't working anymore. I think you know what I mean."

Toby did. These were body functions that worked fine for him, actually. Better all the time, since June moved in. Whatever else had been difficult for Toby over the years, his penis worked great. In fact, this had sometimes been a problem for him. When he used to think about Scarlett Johansson, for instance. Now he's in love with a real person who loves him back. His favorite times in the world are nights he gets to climb into his bed next to June.

"People probably tell you all the time how handsome you are," Raine said.

Actually, they didn't.

She told him she'd always had a thing for red-headed men. Ed Sheeran drove her crazy. Maybe she knew that song of his, "Perfect"?

This was the moment she reached for her phone and pressed the *Play* button. She must have had the song cued up. Now she was singing along with Ed Sheeran, as much as she remembered of the words. *"Barefoot on the grass . . ."*

She was struggling for the words—effects of the Baileys Irish Cream, most likely.

"La di da da . . ." Raine sang. *"Listening to our favorite song."*

"What do you know?" she said. "I'm listening to my favorite song right now!" She laid her leg across the table. Barefoot. Pink nail polish.

Raine sang the song's last lines with Ed Sheeran. Not totally on key, but close enough.

"I bet you think about me sometimes," she told Toby. This was when she reached her hand across the table. She touched his cheek. Then the inside of his thigh.

She pulled him up from the table. It wasn't just that Toby couldn't dance very well. He didn't want to dance. Not here. Not with Raine.

"A drink will loosen you up," she said, holding out the bottle of Baileys Irish Cream. The song had ended. She pressed *Play* again. Now it was starting all over again. She was singing along with the part where Ed Sheeran was telling some woman she should just dive right in. Follow his lead.

Then Raine was pouring more Baileys Irish Cream. Then she was pressing herself against Toby's body. She took his arm, that was hanging by his side, and draped it around her shoulders. She smashed her mouth against his lips and pressed against them. She stuck her tongue in his mouth.

This was when the door opened. Now came the worst thing that ever happened in Toby's life besides his dad dying. Worse than falling in the pond. Spyder walked into the house.

He stood there for five seconds maybe. Taking it all in. Then he walked out.

"I ran after him, Mom," Toby tells Eleanor. The minute he saw Spyder walk out the door, into the night, Toby ran after him.

"I looked everywhere," he says. All that night Toby had searched for Spyder. In the woods, the field behind the house, the road, the pond, the woods again. No sign.

They're in Eleanor's studio now, her colored pencils laid out as usual. Eleanor won't be touching them today. Toby paces the floor.

"You didn't do anything wrong," Eleanor tells her son. "Raine should never have done what she did."

"Raine's not a bad person," Toby says. "She just went to a bad place last night. It's like she got lost for a while."

"That used to happen to me sometimes," Eleanor tells Toby. She'd never gotten drunk as Raine had. Never gone after a man like that. But she'd lost her way sometimes. She even had a name for it. *Crazyland.*

"That's what it was," Toby says. "Raine got scared and she drank too much and she went to Crazyland. And then Spyder saw Raine in Crazyland and he went to Crazyland, too. And now Spyder's gone, but I'm not going to Crazyland. I just need to find Spyder."

Eleanor puts her arms around her son. What more could a mother do?

165.

Jesus. Gone.

There's more. With the sun up now, Toby figures it will be easier to resume his search for Spyder. First he just has to take care of the goats. June will help him.

When he comes back from the barn, Eleanor knows something is terribly wrong. Not just the thing she already knew about but something else.

"Jesus is gone," Toby says. "Last night before I went over to Spyder and Raine's house I put him in his pen. He's not there."

Toby spends all morning looking for the two of them. The boy and the goat.

Sometime that morning Raine calls.

"Is Spyder over there?" she asks Eleanor. "He didn't come home last night. He didn't show up at school today."

No.

"Could you give him a message when he shows up? To call his mom?"

Only he doesn't show up. Toby spends all afternoon looking for Spyder, as well as Jesus. No sign of either one.

Late that afternoon, Raine calls back. "Listen, I'm going to be honest with you," she tells Eleanor. "Something happened over at my place last night. My son probably got the wrong idea. I think he's upset. He's probably mad at me."

"I'll let you know if we see him," Eleanor tells her.

Darkness falls. It's very cold out. No Spyder. No Jesus.

Sometime around nine thirty, Raine calls again. That slurring sound Eleanor heard in her voice the night before is gone now. She sounds like herself again. Herself, scared to death.

"The truth is I got drunk last night," she tells Eleanor. "The truth is I did something stupid. My son probably hates me. He's probably mad at Toby, too."

Spyder, mad at Toby. His one safe person.

166.

The one time Toby ever gets mad

The next morning Toby's out again looking for Spyder and Jesus. It gets to be three o'clock—the time Spyder always shows up, rain or shine, regardless of the season. Four o'clock passes. Five. Six. Seven. No Spyder. No Jesus.

It's even colder now. This is no night for a goat to be out of the barn. Or a boy.

"I'll go with you," Eleanor tells Toby. June makes the same offer.

"Stay at the house," he tells them. "This is my problem, okay?"

It's nine o'clock at night. Toby comes in the house just long enough to scarf down a peanut butter sandwich. He's putting on his boots again now. No parka. It's as if Toby believes that if his best friend and his goat are going to be out there on a winter night he should be that cold, too. There's a new moon out.

"Check your old treehouse," Eleanor says. The place he built with Cam the summer after the accident, where—later—he and Elijah used to hang out together.

"I already looked." The snow would help him track Spyder, only it warmed up today. Just enough that the ground is mostly bare again. No footprints visible.

He checked the waterfall, he tells Eleanor. And below the waterfall. The woods go on forever there.

When Eleanor suggests, a second time, that she can help him, Toby raises his voice in a way she's never known her son to do in his whole life, probably.

Stay away from me, he tells her. *Just keep out of it.*

"I messed up, okay?" he says. "Everything's my fault."

A memory comes to Eleanor. A time long past. A different man—same red hair—sitting in this same chair, speaking the same words to her that her son speaks now. It was her husband, after they came home from the hospital, after the doctors told them their son's brain would never be the same.

Why is it she could never forgive Cam? With her son—with every one of her children—forgiveness comes easily.

167.

"Why hast thou forsaken me?"

Ten o'clock. The second night now. The temperature's dropped again and the wind whips across the field, but the cold is not a factor for Toby at this point. They all know Spyder never wears a winter jacket or even gloves. In all the time Toby's known him, he's never seen the boy with a hat on. Just that old hoodie of his. The baggy jeans, too short now, since his most recent growth spurt. Raine's not a great one for taking her son clothes shopping.

After Toby heads back out to search again, Eleanor stands at the window. She's looking out across the field. With the leaves off the trees, she can follow the glow of Toby's flashlight until it disappears behind a hill. Then it's just the moonlight she sees, making a gash across what's left of the snow, not enough of it left that footprints remain visible.

All night long, from the window, Eleanor follows the little beam that is her son's flashlight. It comes in and out of view as he makes his way through the moonlit woods.

The sun is just coming up over the trees when Eleanor spots Toby again, emerging from a stand of pine trees at the farthest end of the field, headed toward the house at last. He's carrying something in his arms. At first it looks like a piece of wood he's picked up.

When he gets closer the form becomes clear. It's the body of a goat—Eleanor knows which one, of course. Toby must have wrapped Jesus in his jacket, but the goat's legs dangle down as her son makes his way slowly across the snowy field toward the house.

Eleanor puts a pot of water on the stove. Nothing will be enough to warm him now.

Inside the kitchen, Toby lays the body of Jesus on a blanket Eleanor has found—Ursula's once, now relegated to the rag pile. June is there now. Also Ursula.

Before Toby wraps him completely, the four of them take a moment to study the dead goat—stiff and hard now, a single drop of frozen blood visible on his snout, his large brown eyes fixed and vacant. He looks almost human, and heartbroken, or maybe imploring. *Oh Lord, why hast thou forsaken me?*

"Do you think another animal got him?" Ursula asks. "Or did he just freeze to death?"

Toby says nothing. He wraps the blanket around Jesus with the slow, tender care of a person swaddling a newborn. He just sits there by the woodstove holding the dead goat.

"It was Spyder that killed Jesus," he says. His voice is a whisper. Just the act of speaking these words about a boy he unquestionably loves appears physically painful to Toby. "I knew it the minute I found him. I knew it before."

Eleanor hadn't seen this but Toby had. The goat's throat had been slit.

"I don't understand," Eleanor says. Spyder had loved the goat as much as he loved any living being with the exception of Toby himself.

"He was mad at me. He was mad at everything. He just got so mad he went crazy.

"I hope Spyder has water with him," Toby says to Eleanor. "And a trash bag, like I told him when we went camping, to keep him warm."

168.

Find that boy

As reluctant as she is to involve authority figures in her life, on the second day Raine calls the police. There are men out looking for Spyder now, along with a group of volunteer firemen. Toby joins them on the search. Eleanor has come along this time.

"We're going to find that boy, Eleanor," one of the men, Quince, tells her, when she approaches a group of them getting out of their squad car, fanning out into the woods—familiar faces from years of Tuesday-night bowling.

Quince has served on the Akersville force since before Toby was born. He's the captain now. In recent years, he's asked her out for dinner a number of times, but she hasn't taken him up on his invitation, and it appears he's finally given up.

"Kids," he says. "We keep on loving them but damned if they don't make it tough doing that, sometimes."

169.

How to bury a goat in winter

It's not easy burying a goat in the middle of winter. There's been enough of a thaw over the last couple of days to melt most of the snow, but the ground's still frozen solid.

Toby has chosen a place by their old pear tree—the place where every other beloved animal in the family has been laid to rest over the years, along with the placenta of each of Cam and Eleanor's children. Now he takes a mattock to the patch of frozen ground that will be Jesus's grave and starts to swing it. Over and over, he does this. It takes him many hours—first breaking the ground, then digging the hole. This is the one time, over the three days since that night Spyder walked in on Raine kissing him, that Toby has stepped away from the search for his friend.

It's hard for Toby to understand the next part, but he does actually: How a boy who loved a goat as much as Spyder loved Jesus could do the thing Spyder did, which was to take him out in the woods that night, with a Swiss Army knife in his pocket. Toby sees it as clearly as he can see his own hand. Spyder, snapping out the sharpest blade and laying it against the delicate pink neck of his beloved goat.

170.

A small hooded figure

Three days have passed now with no sign of Spyder. It's a little after nine o'clock on a Tuesday morning. Day Four. Still in her pajamas, with a cup of coffee beside her, Eleanor's at her work table, staring at the drawings she made the week before, the storyboard for her *Mineral Man* novel, still lacking its final chapter.

Her mind is on her son. And on the boy who ran away, believing that his one and only friend in the world had let him down.

As he has been from that moment to this one, Toby's out in the woods searching for Spyder. At this point others have joined the search of course—local police officers from three towns. Volunteers. Nobody's spotted the boy.

Eleanor's grateful that it's school vacation week. Orson and Lulu have been up in Bellows Falls with their father. It's good they haven't been around to witness Toby's despair over the disappearance of his friend, the death of Jesus, and all the rest of it.

Eleanor looks out the window again—for the one hundredth time probably—then studies her most recent drawing, sharpens her pencil, turns on Spotify.

Ursula appears in the doorway. The mother of one of Lulu's friends who's an EMT just called to report something she picked up from the scanner. Nothing's confirmed, but a suspicious person was sighted inside the school carrying something that might have been a gun.

"What school? Where?" *Texas, Colorado, Michigan, Minnesota, Idaho, Maine. It could be anywhere.*

"Akersville," Ursula says. "The junior high."

There are no kids in school this week. That's the one good thing. A janitor spotted a small, hooded figure moving through the empty halls early that morning. Possibly nothing more than criminal trespass.

As of now no shots have been fired. There might not even be a gun involved. The authorities aren't calling this a school shooting yet, but three police officers—the entire Akersville force—are on their way. They haven't identified the person at the school. But Eleanor knows who it is.

Toby—the only person Eleanor knows who doesn't carry a cell phone—is somewhere in the woods with a couple of his fellow volunteer firemen. No way to reach him. Eleanor grabs her car keys.

She reaches the school first, before the police arrive. No cars in the parking lot except the one that probably belongs to the janitor.

Eleanor doesn't need to think what to do and nobody's there to stop her. She runs into the building.

171.

The trophy case

After this everything happens fast. Making her way down the corridor toward the principal's office, with her heart beating hard, Eleanor hears a popping noise, loud enough to make a person want to cover her ears. A single shot. This time it's not a BB gun. Eleanor ducks into a classroom, crouching behind the door.

From behind the partly open glass door, Eleanor can see the shooter now. In his hands, his grandfather's pistol, the Colt .45. Was he always this skinny?

The boy stands in front of a glass case—the place where they display the trophies of students and teams who've achieved honors over the years at Akersville Junior High—a case where, Eleanor knows, no trophy will feature Spyder's name. On the front of the case, in large cardboard letters, they've spelled out the words "We love our Meerkats!"—the school mascot. Inside: row after row of trophies and medals. *Basketball, baseball, soccer, field hockey, cheerleading* . . .

Spyder points the gun at the trophy case. He opens fire. The door of the trophy case breaks into a thousand pieces. On the floor around him fragments of glass explode in every direction.

Eleanor hears men's voices now. Three police officers in their heavy boots come running, guns at the ready. Their boots make a pounding noise as they approach. Eleanor remains hidden behind the door. Nobody knows she's there. She feels the beating of her heart. The men round the corner, Quince in the lead.

From the classroom where Eleanor has hidden herself it's not possible to see Spyder's face but she can picture it—that ferocious intensity she'd witnessed that day she watched him shovel his way through snowdrifts taller than he was. She remembers the look on his face, the day he came to the house to tell Toby he didn't get chosen for the Mathalon team.

He's still pointing the gun at the trophy case.

"Put the gun down, son," Quince calls out to Spyder. He's got his weapon pointed at the boy. "We're not going to hurt you. Nobody's been shot here. Let's keep it that way."

Spyder fires another round, shattering another door of the trophy case. *Wrestling. Lacrosse. Debate. Mathalon.*

Eleanor wants to say something to him. But what? The night he was born, she wrapped him in a kitchen towel. This same boy killed a goat he loved. What else might he do?

"Put the gun down," Quince says. The other two have fanned out on either side of him, a few feet away from where Spyder stands with the gun in front of what's left of the trophy case. They've got their guns trained on Spyder, too.

"You don't want to do this, son." The police chief's voice is firm but not unkind. One of the men has gotten on his radio now. He must be calling for assistance.

"Lay your weapon down peacefully and everything can still be okay. Nobody wants to see you get hurt."

"You think that matters?" Spyder looks at the pistol. It's as if he has no idea how it ended up in his hand. Like this whole thing is some kind of terrible amusement park ride that he got on by mistake. "You think I give a shit what happens now?"

Things can get better, Eleanor wants to tell him. She wants to believe this could still be true, but the boy is one shot away from throwing everything away.

For the first time since they entered the school, Spyder turns to look at the three men surrounding him. Until now, his back has been turned, but they can see his eyes now, a look of indescribable hopelessness—the eyes of a person without a friend in the world.

Eleanor stands there behind the partly opened classroom door. She must be breathing, but it feels as if she can't.

Pop. Pop. Pop. Spyder fires another round into the door of the trophy case—the last one remaining that hasn't been shattered already.

"Put your gun down now." Quince again. He has to raise his voice now, over the sound of the shots. The weapons of the other men are locked and loaded. Pointed at Spyder.

For a moment it looks as if the boy might set down the gun. He even starts to.

A look comes over Spyder then. He turns away from the trophy case. He's no longer pointing the gun at the glass. He's pointing it at his own head.

"Don't do anything crazy. We're here to help." The officers lower their guns partway, just below shoulder level. Nobody breathes.

From where Eleanor sits crouched behind the classroom door, she wants to call out to him. What do you say to a boy with a gun in his hand, his finger on the trigger?

Eleanor can see it all on Spyder's face. The story of his life for the last thirteen and a half years.

It's as if every awful, unfair, mean, hard, lonely, terrifying, humiliating, heartbreaking thing that ever happened to him flashes before his eyes—starting with the moment of his birth. Urine-soaked diapers his seventeen-year-old mother never got around to changing, whiskey in his formula to make him sleep, all those hours in the Swyngomatic—*wind it up, wind it up again, and again and again after that*—while his mother went off in a room with a person who liked to twist his ear, times he cried. His father, she told him. But not really.

And more. His mother's old-man boyfriends in their wheelchairs. Jack Daniel's under the sink. On the counter. In her flask.

He sees it all—the kids at school calling him Feeb (the exact same name they'd called Toby once), the girl he sat down next to on the bus who changed her seat. The math teacher, Ms. Alvarez.

The pictures keep coming to him in triple-fast time, like a TikTok video on fast-forward, including a few good parts. Nearly every one of which has to do with Toby. That day Toby sat down next to him on the rock and said, "Mind if I join you?" That first time he taught Spyder how to get milk to squirt out of a goat's teat. Camping out with Toby, cooking trout over the fire. The gift of the yellow Cannondale. The birth, on Christmas night, of the black goat, Jesus. Making change at the farmers' market, wearing his "Say Cheese" hat. Toby telling him *one day this will be yours.*

It wasn't the part about getting to have his own cheese company that mattered to Spyder. It was Toby calling him his pal.

Then comes the worst part in the TikTok of Spyder's life. Walking into their house that night and seeing her standing there—his mother in a bathrobe with no clothes on underneath. His mother kissing his one and only friend in the world.

After that all the rest turns into a horrible joke. He'd been conned, was the truth. He only thought he had a friend. He thought because Toby was different that he was the one good person. Then it turned out Toby was exactly like everyone else, only worse, because with the others at least you knew all along they were assholes.

This is when Eleanor hears another pair of feet moving down the hallway. Even before she sees him, Eleanor recognizes the sound of his footsteps—the rhythm of that odd, loping gait.

For once in his life—the first time since the day he fell in the pond—Toby runs. Now he comes into view at the far end of the corridor—her red-headed boy, his body hurtling toward them. If you didn't know, you could think he was drunk but he's just propelling himself down the hall the only way he knows. In spite of everything going on, Spyder must have caught sight of his friend—the person he thought was his friend until three days ago. He doesn't move. He doesn't speak. He turns his head in Toby's direction.

Eleanor's son, in the line of fire.

"I'm here, buddy," Toby calls out to him. He has almost caught up with them now. Still lumbering as fast as he's able. "Don't be afraid."

Spyder looks at Toby. "Go away." His hand still holds the pistol. His finger remains on the trigger. Whatever comes next, Eleanor doesn't want to see it. She closes her eyes.

Quince speaks to Toby now. He knows Toby, knows his story. He knows Toby doesn't belong here. *"Stop right there."*

Toby obeys the command. Stops in his tracks.

Spyder's still standing in front of what's left of the trophy case— the gun pressed against his temple.

Toby again: "Hold on, buddy. You're going to be okay."

Quince, to his men: "This guy won't hurt anyone. Just get him out of here."

Until this moment, none of them has noticed Eleanor. This is when she steps out into the hallway from behind the classroom door—a woman in pajamas, placing herself in the middle of an active shooting scene. Her voice is steady. She faces the men. Forty years ago—when they were all in their twenties—she brought a casserole to the captain, Quince, when his wife died of non-Hodgkin's lymphoma. That day she'd sat on the couch with him as he wept, their infant daughter in his arms. Now there's a loaded gun in his hand.

"Please, Quince," she says. "Let my son talk to the boy." In another five seconds, one of the men will take Eleanor away, too. There's no time to waste.

"Toby's Spyder's best friend," she says. "Give him a chance to help."

Time stops. Or seems to.

The officer must have seen something on Spyder's face when Toby appeared. Some small flicker of hope maybe—the boy, taking in Toby's words. In another lifetime this would be the moment when Eleanor would run to her son, protect him any way she could, with her own body if necessary. Now she just stands there. Her time for taking care of everything is past. It's for Toby to do that now. To try, anyway.

She stands there with her hands outstretched. *Please.*

Now something wonderful happens. Quince nods in her direction. "Step back, Eleanor. I need you out of the line of fire."

"I'm giving you three minutes," he says to Toby.

Eleanor can breathe now, but just barely.

"I'm sorry I let you down," Toby tells Spyder. "I get why you were mad. I know how it looked. But nothing happened with your mother. You got that part wrong."

Eleanor's eyes remain fixed on the two of them, standing in a pool of shattered glass—Spyder still holding the gun to his head. Toby—calm and steady, reaching out his large, barn-worn hand.

"What happened with Jesus. You went crazy for a while there. I know you loved that goat."

"He was my favorite." Spyder's voice is barely audible.

"I dug a hole for him under the pear tree. Good spot."

For a surprisingly long time—thirty seconds maybe—the two of them say nothing. A few feet back the three police officers stand at the ready.

"I screwed everything up," Spyder tells Toby. "At school everybody thinks I'm the biggest loser in the history of the world."

"Probably not," Toby says. "Just a regular loser like the rest of us."

"I actually thought I was good at math," he says. "I'm an idiot."

"You don't need to be on a math team. You're on my team. The important thing isn't winning prizes at school. It's what you do in the world."

"Yeah, well, I screwed up pretty good in the world, too."

From under their feet, Eleanor can hear the crunching sound of their boots on broken glass. Static from one of the officers' radios. Down the hall, the sound of more men running. More boots. Reinforcements. Time's running out.

"This trophy case cost a lot of money," Spyder says.

"It's just money."

"They'll probably send me to jail."

"Not forever. And after, you'll help run our company. I'll be in the barn, you'll run the business."

Spyder just listens. The gun at his head.

"I bet you'll fall in love someday," Toby says to him. "When you have kids, I'll be like the uncle."

"Girls hate me."

"You wait.

"There's so many good things about life," Toby says. "The waterfall. The Gilsum Rock Swap. Cassiopeia. Maple syrup. Goat cheese. John Prine."

Toby does an odd thing now. He isn't singing—just humming—but Eleanor knows the words. *Come on home.*

Eleanor studies Spyder's face. This could be her grandson. He isn't even shaving yet.

She looks over in the direction of the police officers. For now anyway, they're staying put. At this particular moment, a person could think Toby's an angel, touched down at Akersville Junior High. They might not be wrong.

"I don't get why you kissed my mom," Spyder says, no longer sounding angry. Just heartbroken. "I get why you'd want to kiss somebody, but not my mom."

"Your mom was having a hard time that night," Toby tells Spyder. "She got off the track for a few minutes. Just like you told me about what happened with Jesus. She won't do that again."

"I made a campsite in the woods," Spyder tells Toby. "Just like you showed me. I wrapped myself in a garbage bag to keep warm. Like you said."

"We've had some great times," Toby says. "We'll have more."

For all this time the gun has remained pressed against Spyder's temple. "I have no life," he tells Toby.

"You have me."

Where Toby has placed himself, he's close enough that he could touch Spyder's shoulder, but he doesn't. He reaches out his two hands, palms up, like a street beggar, or a farmer standing in the middle of his cornfield taking in the first drops of rainfall after a long drought. He says no more. Just stands there.

Briefly, Spyder turns his gaze down the long corridor. In another thirty seconds there will be many more men here. The sound of them, running—someone's radio, someone calling out commands—is getting louder. In another thirty seconds, a small army of police officers will have reached them.

Spyder takes it all in: the three police officers, still in ready position, the pool of broken glass at his feet, the posters lining the cinder-block walls—reminders about an upcoming dance, student council elections, tryouts for the spring play. He turns his eyes to Toby, in his bib overalls, his large, rough hands outstretched. Toby hasn't spoken another word. His hands convey everything.

From where she stands, just behind the head man, Quince, Eleanor has a clear view of the boy who faces her son—his too-short pants with their too-big waist, held up by nothing more than his hipbones, that oddly folded-over ear that Toby used to say made him look like an elf, his long hair falling in front of his face, the fingers of his hand clutching tight to the pistol. It would take Spyder no more than a split second to direct the gun to Toby's chest and fire, point-blank, if he wanted to. The two of them are that close. No need to take aim. From this distance, the target could be the red Dickies tag across Toby's chest. The target could be Toby's heart. His big, big heart.

Toby, in his bib overalls and barn jacket, makes no move. He hasn't taken his eyes off the boy. His hands embrace air.

How long do the two of them stand there? Eleanor can feel the beating of her heart.

She studies Spyder's face.

His mother has been saving up for braces. His mess of a mother, trying to do the right thing. If she only knew what it was.

"I'm your pal," Toby says, "I'm still your pal. I'm always your pal."

This is when Spyder lowers the gun and hands it to Quince.

"I'm going to have to ask you to put your hands out, son." As he snaps the cuffs on Spyder, Spyder's eyes meet Toby's. Toby nods. Quince is leading Spyder away now, but the two of them keep their eyes locked on each other all the way down the long corridor. Into the sunlight.

172.

Her life, in some alternative universe

T he thought comes to Eleanor. All this time she had it wrong. All those years she spent grieving the loss of her son's brain cells. All those years when it seemed something inside him had been broken and that nothing could ever be all right again.

What she sees now is the beautiful part. There is a reason some people are broken. If nobody ever broke, if everything always turned out the way you wanted, if the sun always shone and the rain never fell, if there was only spring and no winter, only music and no silence, only love without loneliness, where would beauty come from, or amazement? If nobody ever died, how could they know the preciousness of every day they got to be alive in the world?

All this time Eleanor could never stop mourning what had been lost, grieving what she no longer had. She made her children's sorrows her own. That may have been the thing that was hardest for Ursula: her mother's sadness, that she couldn't fix. She, who tried so hard to fix everything.

Eleanor understands now what it is she failed to recognize over all those years. With her gaze perpetually focused on what was gone, she had failed to recognize not simply what remained but what lay ahead—a rocky and winding path she and her family might never have discovered if not for all the times they'd gone off course.

For one brief moment—no more than this—Eleanor allows herself to picture the beautiful, perfect, brilliant, red-headed, rock-loving, violin-playing boy she'd raised, those first four and a half years. If things had turned out differently. Who might he have become?

Somebody extraordinary no doubt—a boy, and then a man, who could run as gracefully as a deer, and express opinions about big ideas, solve equations and read difficult books, and maybe write some, and win prizes at school, and earn a degree at some great university, perhaps. He might have had an important job, made lots of money. He would have been able to drive a car. Travel. Play on a softball team. Who knows, he might actually have won the heart of a movie star.

He would have become a wonderful man. Beloved in their family. Beloved by many. Good at so many things. Instead, here is this odd, red-headed man Eleanor has raised who is good at very little. *Just good.*

Here they are now, all these years later, walking out into the day, Eleanor and this boy of hers—the sky a more brilliant shade of blue than any pencil in Eleanor's box, sunlight reflecting on what's left of the snow. It's almost spring, the time of year when the brook starts running fast over the rocks at the waterfall. It's the season for the cork people again.

Ursula comes running toward her mother now, with her arms open wide. Also June. Even Raine. They're all crying, all talking at once. *It's okay, it's okay, it's okay,* Eleanor tells them. Over and over, the words. She's not just talking about what happened today. She means everything. "It's going to be okay," Eleanor says.

None of them would be here now, if her web-toed boy hadn't run down to the pond that day with his pockets full of stones, in search of just one more. They wouldn't be here now, if her husband, so long dead, had kept his eye on this boy of theirs.

He will win no prizes. He will never see Paris. Give him a ten-dollar bill for a wheel of cheese that costs $6.50 and he can't make change. He will spend his life milking goats, pouring milk into bottles, placing wheels of cheese in the cooler and taking them out again. Riding his bike to the bowling alley every Tuesday night. Loving a woman—June, for whom he would throw himself on the tracks in front of a moving train, if that's what it took to protect her.

You could call Toby a nonentity. This beautiful, damaged, perfect boy—now a beautiful, damaged, perfect man.

Maybe, that morning long ago at the pond, he'd spotted a stone lying just below the surface of the water. Maybe a tiny fleck of mica lay embedded in the granite, catching the light at just that moment in just the right way, and he'd reached down to pick it up. Maybe there'd been a frog swimming past. Eleanor will never know.

Imagine all they would have been spared if her son hadn't run down to the pond that day.

A world of trouble. An ocean of tears. Her heart, broken in a million pieces and put back together.

How could she ever have missed this?

Epilogue

Many things will happen later. They always do. There will be times that make you wonder if it's worth taking one more breath and others so beautiful they take your breath away. Great love. Great loss. Goats and dogs, songs and stories. Poetry, tomatoes, the Mark Morris Dance Group, ceramic bowls, colored pencils, bicycles, soccer games, magic tricks, peanut M&M's. Three-point shots, fortune cookies, Beethoven's Piano Sonata No. 31. Herkimer diamonds, spaghetti carbonara. Guitars, violins, bongos, mbiras. Good fortune and bad luck. Addiction and recovery. Twelve steps and StairMasters. A crime, a punishment, a crushing defeat, a miraculous victory. Terrible choices and brilliant decisions. Kindness and cruelty. Large-hearted behavior and small. A breast cancer diagnosis. A message from God. A car accident, a lottery win, a wildfire out of control, a spring rain, a blizzard, a moment of utter despair, a stroke of inspiration. A death. A love affair. A baby. Many of those.

If you live long enough, everything happens. The good and the terrible. And it may be the case—it probably is—that a person's glorious triumphs seldom serve as the best teachers of what it means to be human. The lessons are all in the failures.

Failure keeps you humble. Failure opens your heart to all those other people out there who also fall short. It makes a person try to do better.

If she pays attention. If she doesn't give up.

Miriam and Elijah will have a baby, Fiona. They take her on the road with them when they perform with Dog Blue. Kat and Ursula will marry. Jake won't. The girls' basketball team he coaches will make it to the Vermont championships. He will never get over Ursula. He will never stop loving her.

Lulu will not get accepted to the college of her choice. She will go to Barcelona instead, with her violin, and become a street busker and learn to speak Catalan. Orson will win a soccer scholarship but break his leg in a penalty kick during the first game of his season and switch his major from physical education to English literature and discover a love of the villanelle. Whoever would have guessed?

June and Toby will decide not to have children. For them, goats are enough. June's kintsugi pottery will be exhibited in museums in numerous American cities and beyond. With the significant proceeds from her sales of ceramics, the suggestion will be made to June that she might wish to undergo cochlear implant surgery that would allow her, for the first time in her life, to hear music, birds. Also the sound of her husband, humming John Prine tunes and the strange, haunting melodies he makes up. She considers this only briefly but opts to remain in her mysterious silent world.

Toby will learn sign language. Often, now, when Eleanor sits at her drawing table, looking out the window to the field behind the barn, she will see the two of them—Toby and June—moving their hands in animated conversation only the two of them understand.

Al and Teresa will sell their software company and buy a farm in Hancock, New Hampshire, where they will raise blueberries organically. Also Christmas trees. At some point, Al will take out his old TB-10 invention and, after adapting it with more sophisticated software, he will sell the patent for a great deal of money—most of which he and Teresa will give away.

Because the shooting initiated by Spyder occurred during school vacation when no students or faculty were present, the resulting damage involved only school property, and the fact that he didn't direct the weapon at anyone but himself, Spyder is spared a prison sentence. He will spend a little over a year in a juvenile mental health facility, after which time he'll return to Akersville and earn his GED. As predicted by Toby, he will ultimately take the helm of the Wheel of Joy cheese company—a line of work in which his math skills, as well as his surprising talent for salesmanship, prove highly advantageous. At the farmers' market one Saturday, he will reconnect with Veronica, the girl who was kind to him in junior high when nobody else at their school was. The two of them will raise three children who call Toby their uncle. Every summer they go camping together in the White Mountains of New Hampshire, leaving their cell phones back home.

When she's fourteen years old Spyder and Veronica's oldest daughter, Jade, will join a cult and run away to California to live with the fifty-eight-year-old cult leader, a native of Long Island who calls himself Sun Shanti Shanti. Spyder will drive his truck across the country and bring his daughter home. He understands better than most people how, at certain moments in the life of a very young person, their whole future may hang in the balance, and one person, on a single day, offering a few words at the right moment, might save that young person's life.

Raine will trade in the Holiday Rambler for a Sprinter van and a Dyson vacuum cleaner. She'll clean the house of anybody who hires her—and many do—but her particular niche, as she'd always dreamed, will involve going into crime scenes and areas where particularly bloody events have occurred, leaving them spotless. As planned, she'll call her company Clean Slate. She always said she'd use only safe, biodegradable cleaning products, but doesn't. Forced into early retirement due to lung damage from the use of harsh chemicals, she'll collect SSI and move into a guest house behind Spyder and his family, who will take care of her for the rest of her days.

Flora and Toby will maintain their unique connection as two peas in a pod—a bond intensified, if such a thing were possible, when—at the age of twenty-seven—a rare infection she picks up on an ayahuasca trip to Peru puts Flora into acute renal failure that leaves her in need of a kidney transplant. Toby—not surprisingly, a perfect match—will donate one of his kidneys to her. Like the bone marrow transplant Flora provided to Toby, years earlier, the operation proves 100 percent successful.

Having finally figured out the last chapter of her graphic novel—in which the hero, Mineral Man, talks a thirteen-year-old boy out of killing himself—Eleanor publishes what proves to be the most successful book of her long career. When she returns to Akersville from her twenty-one-city book tour (some of which takes place in France), Quince will take her out for coffee, and later dinner. They go bowling every Tuesday and get a two-person kayak. Though they keep their separate houses, they share a garden with so many tomatoes that every August they can enough to last them until the next year's crop and still give bushels away.

They do not marry. They do love each other.

How things end up, at the end of Eleanor's long, hard, complicated, interesting life, bears little resemblance to anything she'd imagined, once. There's no prize at the end, unless you call it a victory, getting to be alive another day and another after that, which she does.

Eleanor has a good man at her side—not all the time, but enough of it. She has her children, and their children, and most of them get along. It's not everything. Nobody gets everything. It's more than enough.

Every day, she's grateful.

Author's Note

THE MUSIC IN THIS NOVEL

Maybe because music occupies such a significant place in my own life, it's important that when I bring a character to life on the page, I consider the music he or she listens to and loves. Sometimes these are songs I love, too. Sometimes not; they're songs that mean something to a character in the story with vastly different musical tastes from my own.

Because I also write about life in America—generally the America that is the United States—it has always been important to me that the stories I tell unfold against a backdrop of the sounds of American culture—sometimes just a line or a musical phrase coming from the radio and television, or through our headphones and earbuds and Bluetooth speakers. They drift into the story so randomly we may barely recognize it's happening—when we turn on our car and the radio comes on, or we step into an elevator or a supermarket to the Muzak version of a Beatles song or pass a beach bar playing an endless loop of Bob Marley or ride a bike past a house with the window open and music playing inside. A kid whizzes by on a skateboard with a speaker attached to his backpack, blasting rap. Suddenly he's part of the story.

Now and then a particular song will strike me as capturing the mood of a moment in time, and the world of a particular character or group of characters. (This was particularly striking in my novel *After Her*—set in the year 1979, when the song "My Sharona" seemed to be everywhere. For my novel *To Die For*, the song that seemed to exemplify the mood was Tom Petty's "American Girl.")

Way back in the nineties, I went so far as to create an actual soundtrack CD to accompany my novel *Where Love Goes*. At the time, people didn't know what to make of that idea. Now, thanks to Spotify, I've been able to make a playlist featuring the tracks my characters listen to and talk about in the novel, for any reader who may want to check them out for herself. You can find this playlist on Spotify under the title "Eleanor's Playlist (How the Light Gets In)." The songs contained here speak to a wide range of musical styles. What they add up to is the soundtrack of this novel, and of Eleanor's world.

Here, now, comes a rundown on some of the music mentioned in *How the Light Gets In*:

Israel Kamakawiwoʻole's recording of "Somewhere Over the Rainbow" is the song played at the crematorium where the body of Eleanor's former husband, Cam, is transformed to ash. I remember how, the first time I heard this recording on the radio, I had to pull my car over along the side of the road. Eleanor does the same. Like Eleanor, I experienced the bitter irony of hearing that beloved recording played at the facility where the body of my late husband was cremated. I could never listen to the song again in the same way.

"The Riddle Song" is a classic English folk song I used to sing to my children. Eleanor did the same with hers.

Warren Zevon's album *The Wind*—recorded as he was dying of lung cancer—features a couple of songs that can tear your heart out, in which a dying man (Zevon himself) speaks to a woman he loves. The songs mentioned in these pages are "Please Stay" and "Keep Me in Your Heart." Warren Zevon also recorded a painfully beautiful rendition of Dylan's "Knockin' On Heaven's Door" for this album. This rendition moves me even more powerfully than Dylan's own.

"Simple Gifts" is a Shaker hymn Eleanor and her family sing, holding hands, before sharing a meal. In my opinion, families don't sing together enough. Mine always did.

I wanted to honor the folk/Americana singers and songwriters Eleanor and Cam listened to. These are favorites of mine too: Greg Brown, Townes Van Zandt, Iris DeMent, Alison Krauss, Richard Shindell, Tracy Chapman, Emmylou Harris, Buddy Miller, Gillian Welch ("Orphan Girl" could be Eleanor's theme song), Patty Griffin, Eliza Gilkyson, Joni Mitchell, John Gorka, to name a few, and David

Mallett—a folk singer from Maine I first heard in 1978 and follow still.

"The Garden Song," also by David Mallett, sometimes finds its way onto the program at children's school concerts—as it does in this novel, performed by Ursula's daughter, Lulu, complete with gardening hand gestures. A modern classic.

When Jake is trying to convey to Ursula—after she's left him—the depth of his devotion to her, he has no words. So he calls her up and—over the telephone—he plays her George Jones's "He Stopped Loving Her Today," about a man (like himself) who stays in love with a woman until the day he dies.

A very different kind of music Jake plays—when he gets caught up in extreme right politics and his belief in Donald Trump—is exemplified by Kid Rock, blasted out the windows of his truck, with the American flag flying. I may not be a Kid Rock fan myself, but that's not the point. What matters: Jake is one.

When I thought about what music Raine would be playing the night she gets drunk and tries to seduce Toby, the song that came immediately to mind was Ed Sheeran's "Perfect." What Ed Sheeran describes in this song (a huge hit) is a twenty-nine-year-old's picture of perfect love. The reference to the man and woman "listening to our favorite songs" is an image of two people who may not have words, themselves, to convey their emotions, so they share song lyrics instead.

A very different kind of character from Raine—Guy Macdowell—chooses obscure, offbeat world music to play in his rented Ferrari and on nights with Eleanor in four-star hotels. I picture Guy playing John Coltrane, Maria Callas, a recording of a Tunisian singer named Dhafer Youssef. Guy's tastes run as far from Ed Sheeran or George Jones as you can get. For a romantic interlude of his own with Eleanor, he puts on Miles Davis, "My Funny Valentine."

More songs on the radio waft through the background of my story—sometimes playing, sometimes only imagined: Peter Gabriel singing "Red Rain." Vic Damone singing "On the Street Where You Live." The Weeknd, "Save Your Tears." Eminem, "Love the Way You Lie." The Everly Brothers, Hank Williams. Johnny Cash. (This may be the only novel I've published in which no Dolly Parton songs appear. But I have no doubt that Eleanor loves her music, as I do.)

Sometimes, the place a singer occupies in a listener's life goes beyond the music he or she made. There are singers whose music, and voices, and words, have moved me so powerfully that I care about them, not only as artists but as human beings. Three such singers appear in these pages. All three of them died over the years I follow in this story. Their deaths mattered, as much as their music does.

The first is Leonard Cohen, who died the day before the election of Donald Trump. A line from his song "Anthem" became the title for this novel and its epigraph.

Sinead O'Connor died just as I was finishing the final revisions of this novel—an event I chose to incorporate into the story because Eleanor loved her music—the haunting purity of her voice, and the depth of feeling she brought to every song she performed: Check out Sinead O'Connor's recordings of traditional Irish music if you want to crack your heart open. Or the one Eleanor plays on endless loop at one particularly hard time in her life, "This Is to Mother You."

Finally, there's one singer/songwriter whose music—more than that of any other—keeps turning up, over many years in the life of Eleanor's family, as it has in my own. I'm speaking of John Prine, whose music I have loved since his first album came out in 1971, the year I graduated from high school. Over the more than fifty years that followed, his songs have never ceased to hold meaning for me.

I got to hear John Prine perform live many times. The songs I mention in these pages include "Fish and Whistle," "Glory of True Love," "Sam Stone," "In Spite of Ourselves," "When I Get to Heaven," "Summer's End," "Speed of the Sound of Loneliness," and what is probably my favorite Prine song—a strange and dark one called "Lake Marie." A phrase from that song, quoted here, functions as a kind of refrain for Cam and Eleanor as they contemplate the breakdown of their relationship: *We found ourselves in Canada, trying to save our marriage and perhaps catch a few fish.*

I call that a perfect line.

When Eleanor—learning of John Prine's death—reflects that she feels as though she's lost a friend, her sentiments were borrowed from my own at the time. Sometimes a singer becomes something more in our lives than the creator of songs. He's a character in our lives.

For me, this was true of John Prine. I never met him, but in these pages, I honor his musical legacy of humor, wisdom, passion, and tenderness. He lives on in song.

Acknowledgments

Writing a novel whose story spans fifty years in the lives of a dozen characters, set against the backdrop of the United States of America between the seventies and the year 2024, requires a daunting amount of memory and attention to detail.

Among the areas about which I had to educate myself this time around, I'll mention a few of the more challenging: the role of Antarctica in the study of climate change; raising and caring for goats; the events of January 6, 2021; police practices employed by law enforcement officers during a school shooting incident. In my attempt to portray these vastly different worlds believably, I sought the advice of a range of friends and experts.

I am indebted to Katie Pindell, of Sage Hill Goat Farm in Stowe, Vermont, for educating me on raising goats and painstakingly explaining goat labor, goat breeding, and goat behavior—and making me fall in love with goats.

Laura Tenenbaum—former senior science editor of NASA's Global Climate Change division and a writer, speaker, and educator committed to raising awareness of issues around climate change—advised me on all matters related to the quest of my fictional character Guy Macdowell in Antarctica.

For material in this story concerning parental estrangement from an adult child, I was fortunate to speak at length with Dr. Joshua Coleman, and am grateful for his seminal text, *Rules of Estrangement*, quoted in these pages. Equally valuable were the experiences shared with me of women with whom I have worked over my many years, teaching the art and craft of memoir, who bravely entrusted me with their own painful stories of parental estrangement.

To present, as accurately as possible, how a potential school shooting like the one described in my novel might play out, I relied on the expertise and counsel of two retired law enforcement officers—my friend of over twenty-five years, Detective Daley, formerly of the Chicago police, homicide division, and Detective Elwood, twenty-six-year veteran of the Ridgewood, New Jersey, Police Department, trained in tactical police responses. Both Luke and Patrick devoted huge care to advising me on how a responsible team of officers would approach a school shooting event like the one described here.

My longtime editor at William Morrow, Jennifer Brehl, has worked with me for fifteen years. I will be forever grateful for her support and belief in me as a writer of fiction and the countless ways she has made every novel we worked on together a far stronger piece of work than the one I first submitted to her. My thanks go, as well, to the team at William Morrow, most particularly to Nate Lanman.

This time around, I was guided by a terrific editor, Celia Johnson, whose deeply perceptive and painstaking work made this a far stronger novel than the one that first landed on her desk. Any writer who works with Celia may call herself lucky.

My good friend, the writer Meredith Hall, was an early reader who—in addition to pointing out countless small areas of concern—raised essential questions concerning an aspect of my story—ones that ultimately led to crucial changes. For a writer with consuming work to do, of her own, to concern herself as Meredith did with another writer's story is a rare act of creative generosity. I am forever in her debt.

Spending one's life writing—as I have done for over half a century now—is a lonely enterprise. My agent, Laurie Fox, remains a steadfast voice of support, encouragement, and guidance on the other end of the phone, as well as ceaseless good humor and kindness. So, too, is my entertainment agent, Judi Farkas. Huge gratitude and affection to them both.

It is unusual for a foreign editor to occupy a place of central importance in the life of a writer, but for me this is true of Philippe Rey, publisher of my work in France. Philippe has followed the story of Eleanor and her family from its earliest days, and weighed in on the lives of my characters with tenderness, enthusiasm, and passion, in ways that go far beyond what a writer might expect of an editor publishing her work in another language, on the other side of the Atlantic Ocean.

I am indebted to MacDowell for the residency—in the depths of a New Hampshire winter—that gave me the space and quiet and support I needed to complete the revisions on this novel. I know of no better place to work.

Fiona Prine made it possible for me to include the lyrics from the music of her late husband, John Prine. I want to encourage all who love the music of John Prine and mourn his loss, as I do, to check out the Hello In There Foundation and see all the good work that continues to be carried out in John Prine's name, supported by his music and those who love it.

Thanks, also, to Crystal Zevon, for our conversations concerning the work of Warren Zevon.

My love and gratitude always to Jordan Moffet for his unstinting good humor and support over the many months in which I virtually disappeared to complete this story.

Judith Swankoski provides the most brilliant social media assistance a writer could dream of, as well as wise counsel and valued friendship.

My treasured assistant, Jenny Rein, takes care of the thousand things that would keep me from doing my work, if she weren't there taking care of them with patience, foresight, good sense, and good humor. If the day ever comes when Jenny can no longer work with me, I'll have no choice but to retire.

My publisher and I considered countless ideas for the cover of this novel. In the end, I found the perfect image hanging on the wall of my home in New Hampshire—a painting of my bedroom there made by my friend of more than forty years, the artist Daniel Thibeault.

Finally, I want to say a few words about the man to whom this novel is dedicated. I first met Graf Mouen when we were seventeen years old, in our final year of high school at Philipps Exeter Academy. For over fifty years, Graf has remained not simply the most treasured friend, but a source of unceasing inspiration, enlightenment, and what I can only call essential life force.

Every page of this novel reflects examples of the care with which Graf reads and considers my work and makes it better. This time around he provided invaluable guidance concerning a subject about which I knew virtually nothing—technology in the nineties. The invention I describe here—a device that makes it possible for a non-musician to create music, created by my fictional character, Al, for his brother, Toby—is one Graf himself created in his teens.

Graf and I spent hours on the phone, talking through the final scene of this novel—with Spyder and the gun. Graf approached the task as the talented—no, I'll say brilliant—theatrical director he is, blocking out every character's every move with me, as if we were shooting a film. And in fact, I see myself doing precisely that. Only the film I make plays in my reader's mind. I hope it kept you on the edge of your chair, and if it did, much credit for that goes to the man to whom I dedicate this novel.

Whether we are talking about Rachmaninov or Sondheim, love or politics or theater or religion—whether we're sharing a breakfast that goes on for hours in a New York City diner or swimming across a New Hampshire lake, Graf never fails to expand my world and inspire my best work. For over fifty years, Graf has served as the collaborator, agitator, questioner, and truest of friends, the closest to a brother I will ever know.